# A Noble Murder

*A Novel in the Fragmented Series*

Paul E Smith

First paperback edition December 2024


pesmithwrites@gmail.com



Cover design by Paul E Smith

ISBN 978-1-0683059-0-0 (paperback)

ISBN 978-1-0683059-1-7 (ebook)

Published by Beholder's Basement Books
www.beholdersbasement.co.uk/books

# DEDICATION

To Frances for her continued love and support, her proofreading skills and her knowledge of grammar, which is much better than mine!

To Amy, for her endless encouragement, enthusiasm and constant pestering to make me write this book.

To Mark, for his positive feedback, plot suggestions and sterling detective work in trying to uncover the killer.

Thank you all!

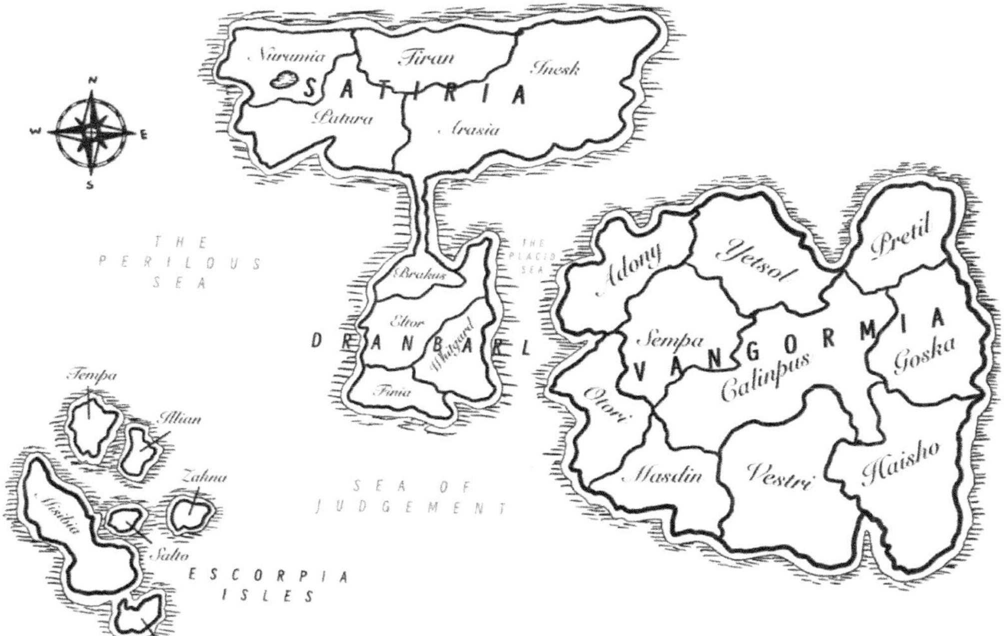


# WORLD OF MINDORIUS

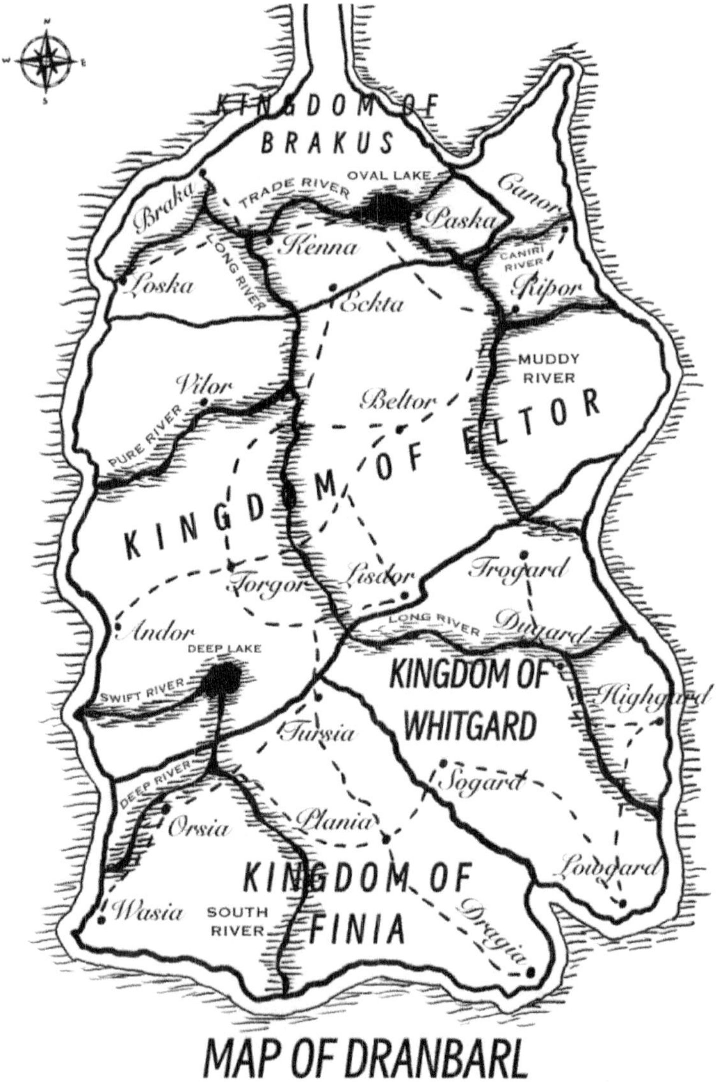


MAP OF DRANBARL

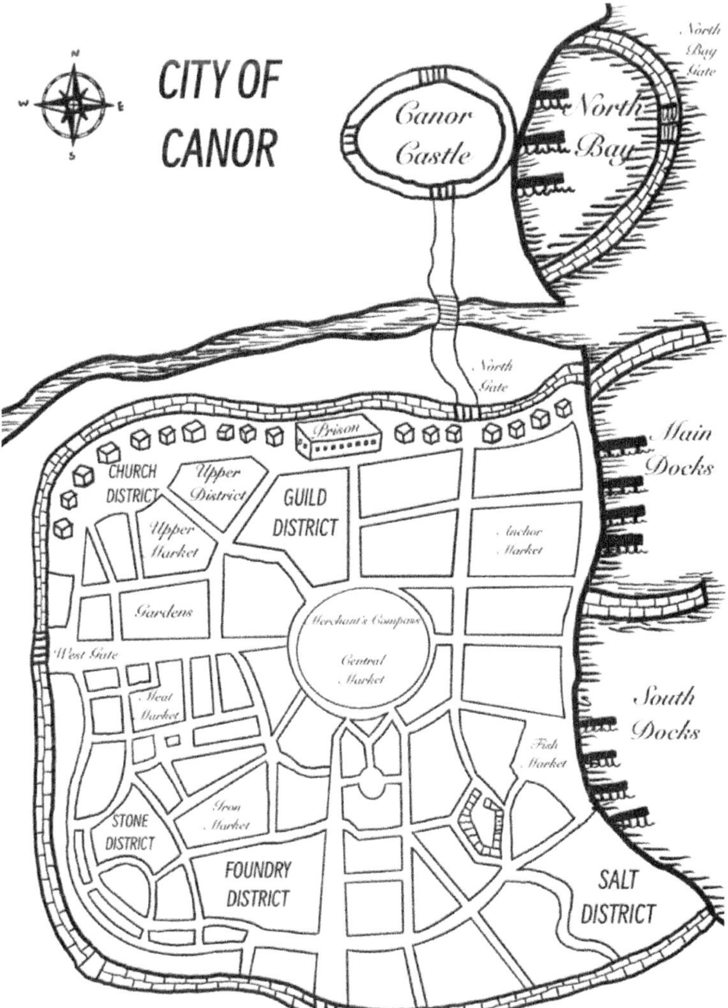
N
W
E
S
CITY OF CANOR
Canor Castle
North Bay Gate
North Bay
North Gate
Main Docks
Prison
CHURCH DISTRICT
Upper District
GUILD DISTRICT
Upper Market
Anchor Market
Gardens
Merchant's Compass
West Gate
Central Market
Meat Market
South Docks
Fish Market
Iron Market
STONE DISTRICT
FOUNDRY DISTRICT
SALT DISTRICT
South Gate

# CHAPTER 1

# AN ENDING

"He's dead."

"No shit! I was hoping for a bit more than that."

"He's very dead!" Teelan said sardonically.

"Very funny. I thought you were supposed to be good at this. Don't they call you The Necromancer?"

Teelan tilted his head sideways so that his long white hair fell over one eye and stared at the big man next to him. "Do they? Whatever for?" he asked.

"I heard it was because you could speak to the dead," the older man said, running his hand over the dark stubble on his chin.

"Ha, what nonsense," Teelan laughed. "Nobody can actually speak to the dead. Not even the grim High Priests of Necomthia claim to be able to do that."

"So, what is it you actually do, then?" asked the other man, putting his hands on hips.

"I do not speak to the dead, but it is more the case that they speak to me," said Teelan, dismissing the uneducated buffoon next to him and looking down again at the body sprawled in the undergrowth at his feet. The young man was naked and his skin was a very unhealthy-looking shade of yellow. That, along with having no eyes, several fingers and toes missing and being able to see his rib bones and internal organs all drew him nicely back to his original conclusion.

"And how do you do that exactly?" asked his companion, shrugging his broad shoulders, which set off a faint metallic jingling noise from his chain mail shirt.

"Through patience, knowledge, training and, well, too many things to go into right now to someone like you," Teelan said, exasperated. Honestly, where do they get these grunts from to come and drag him out of the city and then question his abilities?

"Anyway, do I look like a necromancer to you?" Teelan asked, spreading his arms out wide and letting his loose white robe dangle from his skinny arms.

"No, you look like a lanky, baby-faced streak of piss who would blow over in a strong breeze and get sunburnt just glancing out the window."

"Rude!" Teelan replied. "In my line of work I don't get to be outside much, as I tend to find that dead bodies and scorching sun are not a great combination. Not if you want to keep the contents of your stomach on the inside anyway. Also, people tend not to want to see me doing my job in the middle of the street on their dearly departed loved ones."

"Alright, shall we get on with this? Can you tell me how he died?" asked the warrior, bringing Teelan's attention back to the body on the ground before them.

They both looked down at the figure that was lying on his back, half hidden under loose leaves and low scrub, nestled in a dip between the surrounding trees. He had a face that was probably once lean and handsome, before the crows had got to it, and his short blond hair was now matted with twigs and leaves. His tall, slender frame suggested that he had been fit and athletic. However, his gaping chest told a different story now and was a mess of congealed blood and half eaten innards. His empty eye sockets gazed up into the sky as though he could still see the grey clouds that were gathering over the slightly swaying canopy.

"I imagine that great big hole in his chest had something to do with it," Teelan said sarcastically.

"Are you always this facetious?"

"Ooh, the muscle-bound oaf knows a big word," Teelan replied, making an O of his mouth in a display of mock amazement.

"I'll take that as a yes," said the older man in a deadpan voice.

"Why are you so interested in this poor young man's death, anyway?" Teelan asked, suddenly finding his natural curiosity piqued and deciding to indulge him to find out the reason they were both out here.

"Because if I am right this is the baron's eldest son Ridozir, so he is anything but poor, and the baron has hired me to find out what happened to him. If we return to him and just say 'he's dead,'" said the man, mimicking Teelan's voice, "and nothing further, we may find ourselves in a similar situation shortly afterwards."

"Oh my," said Teelan. A cold tingle ran from his head down his spine and seemed to settle in the pit of his stomach, where it met a churning geyser of hot acid and bile and then tried to proceed back up through his throat. His face went even whiter than its normally pale complexion as the blood drained from it. "Baron Sutter's eldest son. Next in line to the throne. Mad Baron Sutter. Sutter the Cutter." The words kept spilling out of his mouth in a nonsensical fashion as he tried to comprehend the danger he was now in when the baron was told about this.

"Well, I wouldn't call him that to his face, but yes. Baron Sutter will be distraught by this news. And instead of consoling himself with drink and women, like any normal man would, he tends to find that carving pieces of flesh from those bearing bad news is more to his liking."

"But I am his official coroner and highly respected. I have served him faithfully and loyally for the last year," Teelan said, now on the verge of panic. "He can't do anything to me, can he?"

"All of that means shit all to a man like Sutter. He will cut you into a hundred strips and feed you to his dogs if he thinks you've done him wrong or failed him. So do you have any more insights to offer on this 'poor' young man's demise now, necromancer?" asked the man, gesticulating to the body on the ground.

"My name is Teelan, as you well know." He replied stiffly, trying to master his fear and regain some authority. "Very well, let's get on with this, shall we?"

Teelan knelt down and started inspecting the body. He placed his hand on the wide hole in the young man's chest and then pushed it inside. "Something has opened this hole in his chest and either killed him outright or caused him to bleed to death. Scavengers have obviously been at him though so it's difficult to tell how much of the damage was caused initially," he called up. "Hmm. It feels like some of the ribs are damaged as well."

"What could cause such damage, do you think?" asked the other man peering down at him.

"I suspect that someone hit him with one of those ridiculously oversized weapons your kind like to swing around." Teelan said, removing his bloody hand from the body and waving it in the rough direction of the longsword strapped to the other man's back. "A sword or axe could have done this, but I won't be able to tell for sure until we have got him back to my place and I can get a closer look."

"Anything else you can tell me? Like who did it?" asked the big man casually.

"Ha, very funny. I am good but nobody is that good!" Teelan went back to inspecting the body, running his hands gently over it and peering into his open chest. "Help me turn him over, will you?" he asked.

The warrior knelt down slowly, then bent forward to help Teelan grab hold of the body. The long sword he carried on his back stuck out over his shoulder and the iron pommel was just inches from Teelan's face.

"Careful with that thing," snapped Teelan. "Honestly, men and their overcompensating."

They gently rolled the body over onto its side, releasing a powerful stench of rotting flesh and vegetation. Teelan ran his hands along the man's back and then inspected the grass and brush underneath the body. "Ok, put him back down now."

They rolled the man onto his back again and both stood. Teelan noticed that the older man rose more slowly, and it involved a lot of creaking and scraping of metal and the groaning of joints.

The crows that had been watching them from the high branches of the trees cawed and flapped their wings, clearly impatient to get back to their meal. Teelan looked around the small clearing, squinting as the morning sun flashed through the leafy branches. Not a bad place to end up in I suppose.

"Well?" asked the older man.

"Well." said Teelan, wiping his hands on a cloth he produced from a pocket of his robe. "The cause of his death was stab wounds to the chest, approximately five days ago. The fact that he didn't resist or try to defend himself suggests either that someone caught him unaware, or that he knew his killer. It is likely that the deed was done elsewhere, and he was kept indoors for a few days in a cold and dirty place, and then recently dumped him here in a lamentably poor attempt to hide the body. It's clear that he was not held captive or tortured, so we can eliminate the possibility of a 'ransom gone wrong' attempt. Oh, and he had issues with his father." Teelan turned to look smugly at the other man who stood there open-mouthed.

"Horseshit! You can't possibly tell all that about him," said the warrior. "You are making it up."

Teelan let out a dramatic sigh. Why was he always forced to explain himself to people of much lower intelligence than himself? "His body has lost its stiffness, and his skin has taken on that lovely shade of yellow. His stomach and face are bloated and there is a sizable cluster of maggots inside him, all of which indicates death occurred around five days ago. There are no other wounds on his body apart from those made by animals. If he had been in a proper fight he would have wounds on his knuckles or cuts on his hands and arms.

The ground underneath him is dry and not stained and the local wildlife has only just begun feasting on him, so he hasn't been here for more than a few hours. There are no marks on his wrists or ankles, which there would be if he had been restrained, and there are no puncture or burn wounds that would suggest torture. Finally, the absence of bruises or signs of malnutrition before death suggests that no one starved or beat him. Satisfied?"

"Shit. You are good. That was incredible." the warrior said, scrubbing a hand over his stubble. "Wait. How do you know he had issues with his father?"

"He was a young man with a father in a powerful position. Of course they had issues." Teelan remarked, as if it was obvious. "Now, if you have finished questioning my proficiency, you need to pick him up and put him on my cart. I need to take him back to my workshop and do some further investigating."

"Why do I have to carry him?" complained the man.

"Because 'I might get blown over in a strong breeze', remember." Teelan said, mimicking the man's voice.

"Fine, but you could at least ask nicely and call me by my name at least."

"Apologies, your kind all look the same to me," Teelan replied. "What was your name again?"

"My name is Drevin," said the warrior, bending to pick up the body. "As you well know."

"Well Drevin, pretty please, could you pick up the bloody body and deposit it on my cart. And on the way back into the city, you might like to explain to me exactly how you knew where to find him."

# CHAPTER 2

# ABOUT FOUR DAYS AGO

Drevin sat in his usual corner seat, staring at the pitted wooden table in front of him. The almost empty bowl of oats just had a smear of crushed brown pieces clinging to the bottom. It seemed to be an apt summary of his life, all the fresh, best bits gone and just the old, unwanted remains left.

He had had little work for a while now and was running low on both coin and motivation. Maybe it was time to move on, try another city, head south to Finia or Whitgard or maybe even be really brave and cross the ocean to Vangormia. No, he knew he would never be that brave. He supposed he could go back to the docks and get a day's work as a labourer again, but his shoulders and lower back were still protesting at him from the work he did there last week.

Drevin scanned the sparsely populated inn. His table in the corner gave him a good view of the whole room, including the dozen or so dark tables with a motley assortment of mismatched benches or chairs around them, the long, greasy looking bar against the wall to his left and of course the door, directly in front of him. There were only a few other occupants in at this time of the morning; a couple of apron-clad labourers sneaking in a quick ale before work; three petty merchants who looked about as down on their luck as he was and an old man with his head on a table who could well have been there all night, judging from the distinctive sounds of snoring coming from him. Verlida was behind the bar as usual, trying futilely to scrub the permanent stains off the bar. Her long brown, wispy hair was plastered to one half of her sweaty face and her meaty arm was pumping for all it was worth.

Maybe he could just do nothing today except drink the weak ale they served here until he could no longer tell how watered down it was. Or he could go back upstairs to his room and the dubious comfort of his bed. He had paid for the month already and he didn't exactly have anything pressing to do. Drevin was just reaching for another swig of his ale when suddenly the front door burst open and a man dashed inside.

"Hear me, hear me!" the man cried in a well-practised tone of voice. He was wearing a crisp blue tabard, yellow stockings and a bright red puffy hat. He looked like he had got dressed in the dark. "Master Ridozir Sutter, son of our gracious Lord Suttor, Baron of Canor, is missing, afeared to have run into misfortune. Our most generous lord is offering a reward of twenty silver rounds to anyone who can provide information as to his son's whereabouts. Any interested parties should report to the castle by second bell to register their intent." With that, he turned smartly on his heel and dashed back through the door, no doubt to repeat the message around the rest of the docks.

Drevin pulled his arm back from reaching for his wooden mug. Well, there goes my bad intentions of having a restful day.

****

The inner courtyard of the castle was full of people and noise. Drevin stayed near the back wall and scanned the crowd, who were watching the steps in front of the great wooden doors, waiting for the announcement to come. He noticed a vast array of people, from salty dock workers to the usual low-life thieves and mugger types who were always looking for an easy way to make some coin. He spotted that some of the local nobles were there with their bodyguards, and he suspected they had come to either gloat inconspicuously or commiserate openly, depending on their current relationship with the baron. Drevin chuckled as he saw they looked very discomfited at having to be in such close proximity to the common rabble.

He also recognised one or two other mercenaries there who stood with a calm confidence and an array of weaponry. One he vaguely knew from previous encounters, a bulky man wearing a full-length, weathered brown leather coat. He had small pieces of metal shaped into tiny swords tied into his long black hair, which was gathered in a ponytail. That, along with his tanned skin, identified him as an Irian from the northern continent. As if sensing Drevin's attention he turned his head to stare over at him and gave a slight nod of his head, from one professional to another. Drevin returned the nod.

The second bell had rung a while ago and the mood in the crowd was getting more tense and impatient. They should have known better by now. As if the rulers of the city actually cared about needing to be on time for anything, particularly if that anything was to do with the general public.

Just before the atmosphere worsened, however, the gigantic doors creaked open, and a procession of people walked out. Instantly, the atmosphere changed, and everyone started pointing and talking excitedly to each other as they identified the individuals above them.

Drevin eyed the group now spread out at the top of the stairs. Right in the middle stood the baron, Lord Sutter, his long black and grey hair hiding half of his thin face which appeared to be sinking into itself. His rich indigo blue robes hung from his spindly frame, looking almost black apart from where the gold trim occasionally caught the sunlight. Standing next to him was a shorter, much stockier man whose rosy cheeks and full black beard were at complete odds with the baron and Drevin wondered again at how two, so very different men, could be brothers. Serzin stood close to his brother, almost shielding him from the crowd below. Alongside him stood a shorter lady with long black hair in a tight-fitting black gown, clutching the hand of a young boy who looked out with wide eyes from his round face. Drevin had never met them but knew that they must be Serzin's wife, Myelandra and eldest son Weslin.

In front of the baron, on the step below, stood a boy that Drevin assumed must be Greffin, his youngest son. His navy robe was not as rich as his father's and the sleeves were ink stained. He squinted out into the crowd, nervously twisting his hands together and looked like he would have preferred to be anywhere else but here. To his right stood a young lady with long golden blonde hair which fell to her waist. She stood tall and proud looking over the crowd and anyone watching could tell that she was Mistress Islia, the baron's only daughter. Small sparkling stones dotted her slim white dress, catching every weak ray of light and reflecting it into the courtyard.

Next to her stood her maid and two men in fine tunics of checked blue and green with the symbol of the rugged coastline of Brakus on their left breast and the jumping fish of the Barony of Paska on their right. Drevin wondered why men of Brakus were here and quickly avoided making eye contact with them.

Once the general hubbub of the crowd subsided a little, Serzin raised his arms for quiet and the crowd went still. "Greetings people of Canor," he began in a deep voice that projected right around the courtyard, "it is heartening to know that so many of our citizens are concerned about the whereabouts of our lord's eldest son. As you have heard, Master Ridozir is missing. He left the castle yesterday morning and nobody has seen him since. This is of great concern to us and, of course, to his father," he said, indicating the baron.

"Now, we know that Ridozir occasionally went into the city incognito, but he always returned by nightfall. So, we fear that something may have happened to him. He may have gone hunting in the woods to the south and had an accident whilst there or run afoul of brigands. Or he might have gone down to the docks to sit and watch the ships coming in and out, as he often liked to do, and run into trouble. The guards who were with him when he left returned late yesterday, saying that Master Ridozir had told them to leave him alone for a while and they had done so. Only when they went to meet him at their usual place, he never showed up and they couldn't find him anywhere. Needless to say, the guards in question are being interrogated thoroughly. So, we are asking you, our people, to help us find Ridozir. Anyone with any information as to his whereabouts or anyone who will go in search of him please speak to the steward." he continued, sweeping his arm out to point out a skinny man sitting behind a plain wooden table stacked with parchments in the corner of the courtyard.

"There will be a reward of twenty silver rounds as well as the gratitude of the baron for anyone who leads us to him. We thank you all for your assistance in this matter." With that, he turned back to the door, which was promptly opened by the guards standing there, and ushered everyone back inside.

All at once, the crowd started talking again and people rushed over to form a long queue in front of the harassed-looking steward. *Well, that's going to stir up a right shit storm!* Drevin slowly walked over to join the back of the queue.

****

The courtyard was almost empty by the time Drevin got his notice paper with his name on it stamped by the steward. Many of those in front of him in the line had talked excitedly about searching the forest or heading down to the docks to look for the missing son. Drevin was in no hurry to rush anywhere. He had tried talking to the steward to get some more information on Ridozir, but the man was frenzied with issuing the notices and quickly brushed him off. He had now disappeared back into the castle with an armful of unused parchments, leaving his table standing there, ink-stained and bereft.

Drevin glanced around at the few remaining people. Some had just come to hear the news and hadn't actually signed up to help. They were talking in small groups, many looking quite pleased at this development, and Drevin wondered what they stood to gain from Ridozir's disappearance.

Others were members of the castle's staff, some servants going round picking up anything dropped by the crowd, whilst the rest were sweeping the dust out the main gates or leaning on their brooms to chat to their fellow workers for five minutes whilst no one was watching them. Drevin took a slow walk over to the nearest group of servants, who had decided it was time for a break. "Good morning, at least I think it still is morning, isn't it?" he called, looking up into the grey clouds that were making a mockery of the sun today.

"Aye, it is just about still morning," replied a woman with a dress as grey as the clouds and hair to match, "At least I haven't heard third bell yet, although my stomach says that it must be fast approaching. So, you one of those fools who be going to look for the master are ye?" she asked, looking Drevin up and down as though he was a rat found in her kitchen.

"Guilty as charged," he replied with a little mock bow.

"Well, don't look too hard on our account," she muttered, eyeing her fellows.

Drevin put on his best consoling expression, "Oh and why is that good lady?"

She looked at him as if he was mocking her, "Right nasty piece of work he is. Only ever paid any attention to two types of people. The pretty young uns he took off to his bedchamber, whether they were willing or not. And the old and slow he used to clout round the head and kick out of his way if they weren't quick enough to get out of sight."

"Sounds like a real charmer. Any idea who would most want to do him harm or get him out of the way?"

"Ha, that would be a long list, my burly friend," she cackled. "I don't think anyone liked the young prick. Even his father used to argue with him all the time, when he bothered to speak to him, that was. The only one who actually wanted to spend time with him was Mistress Islia. Mind you, they are two of a kind. We all knew to scurry off to our hidey holes when those two were together. She is the only one who seems genuinely upset by his absence."

Drevin fished into his belt pouch for a small copper bit and handed it to the servant. "My thanks, lady. May the Allmother watch over you."

"Ha, it is more likely Necomthia who has her eye on me, what with me being closer to the grave than the cradle. Good day to you and I hope your search goes badly. No offence." With that, she straightened up from her broom and resumed her methodical sweeping of the courtyard as her fellows did the same. Drevin paused for a moment and watched as they went about their work.

For the next couple of hours, he engaged in conversations with various servants and workers of the castle who were coming and going on with their daily business. Among the gossip he heard, most of it being irrelevant or only intriguing to its speakers, there was some recurring information about the baron's son that caught his attention. He seemed to be generally feared by the staff and most of them tried to avoid him at all costs.

He was known to be vain, petty, cruel, wasteful, selfish and a complete womaniser. So pretty standard fare for an heir-presumptive baron then.

Drevin was about to leave the castle when he heard a loud snorting noise and spotted a young stable hand wrestling with a huge stallion. The horse's black coat was glistening with beads of sweat as it strained at its leash, which the young lad was desperately trying to hold on to with one hand, whilst a brush dangled limply from his other hand.

Drevin quickly made his way over and grabbed hold of the leash, adding his strength to that of the boy's, to pull the horse back under control. The horse soon realised that he was no match for the two of them and settled back down with a loud huff. Drevin swiftly tied it to the stable's strong wooden rail and turned to the boy. "Always tie the horse up first before trying to brush it down lad," he said kindly, eyeing the now relieved looking stable hand.

"Thank you, sir," the boy stammered. "I got carried away and forgot to make sure that Master Ridozir's horse was well cared for," the boy admitted. "I didn't think he would object to being groomed."

"Horses have their own moods and tempers, just like us humans," he replied, gently stroking the beautiful black mane. "You just have to learn how to read them before shoving a brush in their face. Wait, did you say that this is Ridozir's horse? Does that mean, then, that you are his groom?"

The boy glanced around nervously before turning back to the big man, "Yes sir I am," he replied, "Although I only have been for a month now and I don't think that I am up to the job, but nobody else was keen to volunteer after what happened to his last groom."

Do I want to know? It is not likely to be a pleasant story and it is probably not going to help me find him. But the kid looks fit to burst to tell the tale and knowledge is knowledge. With a big sigh, Drevin asked the inevitable question, "What happened to his previous groom then?"

"Well," the lad replied excitedly, "Apparently the last groom was late feeding his horse so when Ridozir found out he got a big nosebag and filled it up with oats then tied it to the boy's neck and shoved his face in it. He made him eat the oats and if the boy stopped, he rammed his head further into the bag to force him to eat. Well, the boy kept choking and others warned the master that he should stop, but he just kept pushing that lad's head in. Then he choked and coughed so badly he couldn't stop until he collapsed on the floor, shaking. Someone pulled the bag off his head, but the boy's face was all purple and swollen and he stopped breathing, then died."

"Damn. That is terrible," Drevin exclaimed, genuinely shocked again at the lack of humanity of those in power. "Can you tell me anything else about Ridozir? What he liked to do? Where he liked to go? What might have happened to him?"

The young groom suddenly looked fearful again. "No sir, I can't tell you anything about the master. Didn't you just hear what I told you about what he does to people who upset him? If I told you anything about him and he found it, I would be a gonna."

"But I am looking for the master, so if you told me something that helped me to find him, his father would be very grateful to you and might look kindly on finding you a less precarious job in the castle. I would be happy to tell him how helpful you have been. Or if you fancied a change, I know people in the city who could use a smart kid who knows his way around a stable. I'm sure I could put in a word for you with them if you like. The pay might be less, but at least you would have much more of a chance of staying alive to be able to spend it, eh?"

The boy still looked uncertain, but a glimmer of hope shone in his eyes now. "Ok then, but you mustn't let the master know I told you. Sometimes he goes into the city in disguise with just a couple of guards so that he looks just like a rich merchant. He often visits the Central Market in the Merchant's Compass, and I have heard the guards who return with him say that he buys some fancy jewellery there but doesn't return with it. He then often goes to the South Docks and tells his guards to leave him for an hour, then meets up with them in the fish market afterwards. Rumour has it he meets with a, ah lady friend for a while in the Salt District. The guards searched for hours down there when he didn't return, but they couldn't find any sign of him."

Drevin stroked his chin thoughtfully, "Thank you lad, that is very helpful." He reached into his now lighter pouch and produced a couple of copper bits, which he handed to the delighted groom. "Keep safe, lad, and think about my offer. No doubt I will be back. By the way, my name is Drevin."

"Thank you, Drevin sir. I'm Ostin. And I will think about what you said." With that, he turned back to the black horse and started gingerly brushing his coat down with long, slow strokes.

Drevin turned away and made his way to the main gate leading back to the city. Looks like I'm paying a visit to the South Docks. His stomach suddenly rumbled loudly. Although maybe I'll stop for something to eat first.

***

Drevin stood and looked across the way at the dilapidated barn that was just about still standing, although from the angle it was leaning at, it probably wouldn't be for much longer. He had spent the last few hours searching the South Docks and fish market for any hints of where Ridozir might have gone after ditching his guards and this barn was his last, uninspiring looking hope. He had heard just about every rumour and wild story about the baron's son as there could be. Everything from him running off to become a priest of The Union or joining the Cult of the Outcast, to him eloping with a kitchen maid, or being killed in a hunt by a monstrous wild boar that is said to roam the southern forests. However, some of the more realistic tales had led him from the docks, via various brothels and low rent taverns, to the very southern edge of the city and to the Salt District. This part of the city nestled up tight to the dark, weathered grey stones of the tall city wall that loomed above it, casting a perpetual shadow over the modest buildings.

He had heard a rumour that, despite looking completely deserted, there had been some activity within this decrepit barn of late. Apparently, a local fisherman's wife had been walking past yesterday on her way to the market and had seen a horse and black cart pull up and two men get out and enter the barn. She had thought it strange as nobody had owned it since the old man who had died last year, but she was in a hurry to get to the market so hadn't hung around. As she had walked on further, though, she saw the cart driving away again, heading along the southern road towards the west of the city.

So, Drevin had taken up a position a short distance away and watched the place for the last hour or so. Now his legs were stiff from standing around and his back was seizing up from the lack of movement. So far, he had seen and heard nothing. The sky was darkening from more than just the persistent grey clouds now as evening descended. It was now or never. He started striding unsteadily across the road towards the long barn.

The wooden doors were closed tight, although it looked like a gust of wind could do for them at any moment. Drevin pulled open the right-hand door, which squeaked alarmingly like it had a nest of mice hidden inside it. Inside, darkness shrouded the large open area, with only faint shafts of light pushing through the gaps in the wooden walls from the last of the day's sun. His feet rustled through the straw and rushes on the floor as he entered, carefully scanning the shadowy corners for any signs of inhabitants. A ladder to the left led up to a hayloft, and there were a couple of rickety wooden partitions at the back that could have been used to stable horses. Drevin saw an old glass lamp hanging from the ladder and quickly took it down and used his flint to light the last of the oil in it. The feeble light did little to banish the shadows, but at least let him see where he was putting his feet. He looked up ruefully at the steep, cracked ladder. Why are there always steps involved? He sighed and climbed up.

Once at the top, he could see the narrow hayloft that ran along this side of the barn. Straw littered the floor along with some old torn hessian sacks, empty wooden crates and rusty buckets. He crept along the side railing overlooking the ground below, scanning the floor of the loft. At the end of the wall, he noticed a cosy-looking pile of hay that appeared to have been arranged as a makeshift bed. Someone had flattened down and shaped the hay into a large rectangular fashion, with piles of hay on either side. He crouched down and brushed the hay with his fingers. A heavy weight, probably someone lying down here, had definitely crushed it. He sifted some of the hay through his fingers and felt the wooden boards beneath it. His hand touched something hard and cold underneath. He grabbed it and lifted it up to the lamp for a closer look. A fine metal chain with a silver cat figurine with amber eyes attached to it dangled in the light. Someone was definitely here. Someone with expensive tastes and who must have left in a hurry to forget something like this. It must be worth at least ten silver rounds. Drevin put the necklace in his belt pouch and headed back down the ladder.

The ground floor of the barn appeared empty. In the stable area, the straw was soft and damp and stank of mould. Obviously, it had been out of use for some time. The rest of the barn was largely empty with just some old broken equipment and tack lying around. Drevin's feet crunched through the straw in the centre of the barn as he made his way back to the main doors.

Suddenly, he stopped and looked down. He crouched and picked up some of the straw and brought it to his nose. It smelt fresh and was still firm between his fingers. Why would someone put down fresh straw in an unused barn, and only in one place? He knelt and began sweeping the fresh straw away with his arms to uncover the knotted wooden floorboards beneath. Once he had cleared a large area, he grabbed the lamp and put it in the centre of the space. Then he saw it. A large, irregular dark stain, almost the size of a man, covered the old timbers. It was hard to tell in the lamplight, but it looked a dark reddish colour to him, and he would bet his life that it was blood.

What were the chances that this was just some poor old nag's blood? Not much knowing my luck. Drevin stood up and left the barn just as the sun finally gave up on its futile mission to bring light to the day. Time to contemplate all that I have found out today and I find that I often do my best contemplating with an ale in my hand.

***

Drevin pushed his plate of half-eaten fish stew away and leaned back wearily in his chair. The stew wasn't that bad, cod cooked in a watery gravy with potatoes and carrots, and a hint of some eastern spice, but he was just fed up with eating fish. But I suppose that is what you get for renting a room in a dockside tavern. However, it wasn't just the lack of variety in his diet that was responsible for his loss of appetite. He felt frustrated. After finding promising leads yesterday, he had thought today he might discover more information or even locate the missing baron in waiting. However, he had found nothing.

He was pretty sure that something bad had gone down in that barn and that it was likely that Ridozir was involved. If that blood on the floor had been his, then he was in a very bad way or dead by now. He was sure he was on the right track but had come to a dead end.

That morning, he had retraced his steps to the old barn again, which was miraculously still standing and looking as unappealing as ever. Then he had followed the road until he came to the Great South Road. Deciding that if someone had a heavily bleeding noble with them they were unlikely to risk either going past the guards of the Southern Gate and out of the city or to the bustling Merchants Compass, he had carried on west towards the Foundry District.

However, it turns out that finding a horse and cart commonly used by merchants and labourers in a city full of merchants and labourers is, well, about as difficult as it sounds. The Foundry District was its usual smoke filled, clanging, hot, sweaty, industrious self. It was like walking into hell, if hell was full of smoky devils that kept asking you to part with your money for some new blade or sharp tools. Drevin had tried asking around if anyone had noticed a suspicious-looking horse and cart going past around second bell two days ago, but he soon realised how ridiculous he sounded as everyone just looked at him as if he was mad. They kept asking him if he couldn't see how busy they always were, what with their hammering, moulding and keeping their fires hot and so on.

So, he had quickly left there and kept heading west. He told himself it was because he didn't think any criminals on the run would hide out there, but mainly it was because he wanted to escape the noise and gritty, smoke-filled air.

After that he had gone into the Stone District, so named for the small mining community that lived there and worked in the northern hills to mine for iron ore. Now, however, the district was more well known for its astounding poverty and lawlessness. This was a much more promising area to hide from the city guards and the townsfolk searching for the missing son, and Drevin's optimism had risen.

But it had turned out to be a fruitless and frustrating search. Nobody would talk to him. Most people put their heads down when they saw him and hurried on their way. Those he had managed to stop looked like they either wanted to run away, stick him with a knife, or quite possibly both. He guessed he shouldn't be surprised. When you lived in a place like that, you soon learn to keep yourself to yourself and to keep your mouth shut. Those who told tales on their neighbours tended to disappear shortly afterwards, along with their families.

After wasting a few hours there, he had become desperate enough to go back to the castle to ask to talk to the guards who had been accompanying Ridozir when he had gone missing. The horrified look on the gate guard's face when he asked told him all he needed to know. He eventually said that the baron was 'speaking to them personally' and that they were in no fit state to talk to anyone else. In other words, 'Baron Cutter' had been let loose on them, undoubtedly letting his dagger do his talking. Drevin shivered at the thought of what those poor bastards were going through.

And so dejected and defeated, Drevin had returned to the inn and his uninspiring stew. He would need to rethink his plan if he wanted to find out anything new tomorrow. Maybe he could go back and see if he could find the fisherman's wife again. Get a better description of the men and the cart. Or maybe he could talk to some of his acquaintances in the guard as they might have heard something new. Yeah, and maybe the snotty kid will just turn up at my inn, caked in blood and asking me to take him back to his father for a fat reward.

Drevin looked around the bustling tavern at the dockworkers and merchants who were sitting at their respective tables drinking, chatting, laughing and eating. At least his bad mood hadn't affected the rest of the patrons tonight, but staying here would not cheer him up either. He stood up and waved to Verlida as she walked past, precariously balancing a tray of frothing ales in one hand and a plate of stew in the other.

"Night Verlida," he called out to her, heading up to his room at the back of the inn.

"Night Drevin," she called back over her shoulder. "See you in the morning."

Let's just hope that by then I have got some idea of what to do next.

# CHAPTER 3

# TWO LIKELY LADS

The sun woke Drevin up early the next morning, which was unusual. Not just for the fact that the sun was actually out and shining brightly, but also because he could normally sleep through anything. But he had endured a restless night's sleep.

His dreams had been filled with images of a young man appearing in various scenes; sprawled in a bed with a naked girl on either side of him; lying face up in the placid waters of the dock and sitting in his seat in the inn. However, in each vision, the man always had blood covering him and a sword sticking out from his chest, although he appeared alive and healthy apart from that. Every time he looked at Drevin he asked him the same question over and over, "Why haven't you found me yet?"

So it was that Drevin found himself sitting in the bar on his own. The clanging noises and muttered curses coming from the kitchen indicated that breakfast was not ready yet and that nobody ought to dare ask for it!

Drevin sighed. He still had no brilliant plan to find the baron's son and didn't want to face trudging around the city again, asking questions to random people who couldn't care less. Still, he also wasn't going to find him by just sitting here. As his mother had always said, 'the work won't do itself.' So, he creaked to his feet and headed out the door.

A few hours later he found himself in yet another dingy tavern in the Stone District, drinking yet another piss weak beer. He had changed his tactics today and decided to hit all the inns and taverns in the area to talk to the owners and patrons. His theory being that gossip was more easily spread after a few drinks and that people were creatures of habit and often returned to the same establishments. If anything out of the ordinary had happened in the area someone would have noticed it. He also knew that people were more likely to talk to a stranger if they bought them a drink or three.

So, after supplying a plentiful amount of alcohol to various people of dubious natures in many disreputable inns, Drevin had heard more gossip in a few hours than a whole town full of new mothers could have spread in a year. Most of it was the usual boasting of inadequate men, often concerning their supposed prowess with the ladies. Or it was the bitterness of old men who could find fault with everything and everyone in the city. When he had steered the conversation in the right direction however, he heard some tales of the area and its inhabitants.

Apparently, the mining folk who still proudly lived here were in constant conflict with the gangs who rampaged, almost unchecked, through the district. There were several criminal outfits led by the usual bully types who had given themselves ridiculous sounding nicknames like Stonejaw, Rockfist, and Pebbledasher. He wasn't sure whether that last one was serious or just that its owner didn't know its alternate meaning.

He also heard stories of the common struggles of the people living in the area and how the baron did little to nothing to help them. Occasionally, a guard patrol would come through the area, but more often than not they stayed well clear, and the people were left to fend for themselves. There was certainly no love lost for the rulers of Canor here and the disappearance of one of the nobility was only a cause for mild celebration.

When questioned about events in the last few days, everyone said that things were pretty much the same as always. Apart from perhaps the gangs being more active than usual, due to the scant attention of the law being firmly directed elsewhere in the ongoing search. However, a few of the long-term drinkers did talk about a couple of the local low-life's who seemed to be rich in coin of late. Drevin's interest was definitely piqued, so he came to this tavern where they were known to be regulars.

Drevin drained his mug and pushed a few copper bits across the rough, wooden slab that served as a bar to the bald, broad man on the other side. "Same again, barkeep and have one yourself," he said in his most conversational tone.

"Aye, don't mind if I do," the man replied gruffly, swiping up the coins with practised ease and making them disappear somewhere in his stained apron. He opened the tap on the keg behind him and filled two wooden mugs, passing one back to Drevin.

Drevin looked around. The bar was quiet for this time of the afternoon, with just a few regular patrons at the tables drinking and eating and talking in low voices. "How's business?"

"Not great," the barman was wiping up the wet patches on the bar with a cloth that looked dirtier and wetter than the stains. "People ain't got the coin to spend these days, except those who get it any way they can, and I don't like having their sort in here."

"Really," replied Drevin, raising an eyebrow, "I heard you had some regular guys in here who fit that description perfectly and who had come into plenty of coin to throw around."

"Not anymore I don't. If you're talking about who I think you're talking about, that is." Drevin just sat quietly waiting for the man to continue. And he did. "Kicked those two pieces of dung out two nights ago, and they ain't been back since."

Drevin took a hefty swig of his ale. Nope, it still didn't taste any better. "What did they do?"

"What they always do, no good. Filthy scum tried robbing the purses off my customers, even though they both already had full pouches. People like that just can't help themselves I guess."

"They sound like real nice guys. What else can you tell me about them?" Drevin asked, leaning forward on the bar.

"Brothers they are, I think. Work for a gang leader called The Hammer. They go by the names of Picket and Sticket."

Drevin couldn't help but chuckle, "You're shitting me! Really."

"Really. Well, those were the names they earned, see, on account of what they do, and they seem right proud of them too. You see one of them lifts your purse while the other one…"

"Let me guess. Sticks a blade in you?" Drevin said wearily.

"You got it," said the barkeeper, smiling grimly. "I wouldn't normally squeal on anyone round here but, thing is, those two are real nasty and they prey on the weakest and most vulnerable."

"Don't all criminals?"

"Sure, sure, to an extent. But most do it purely for the money or the power. These turds do it because they enjoy terrorising and hurting people. They will often beat or stick someone even when there is no need, and their victim doesn't put up a fight."

"Hmm, I would just love to meet these delightful fellows. Can you tell me where I might find them?"

The barkeep looked at Drevin curiously, the wet rag limp and dripping in his hand. "Apparently they now go to a shithole tavern called The Slagheap, down Gravel Alley."

"My thanks to you," Drevin said, standing up and turning towards the door.

"Hey mister," the man called out to him and Drevin turned back, "If those two just happened to disappear I don't think anyone would shed a tear over them."

"Thanks," Drevin called back, "I'll keep that in mind." With that, he headed out the door.

***

The Slagheap seemed to be living up to its name in that it resembled a grey heap of some unnamed waste material, roughly piled up into the vague resemblance of a building. The interior didn't look much better than the outside, with rough looking barrels serving as tables, with even rougher looking customers sitting around them.

The bar was actually a long row of large kegs with precarious looking three-legged stools in front of them. A large woman stood behind the barrels frowning out over the motley assortment of customers from behind a prodigious fringe of blonde hair. Drevin approached the makeshift bar, "Evening miss, pint of ale please and have one for yourself." He said, sliding over a couple of his fast dwindling supply of coins.

She scooped up the coins without a word and retrieved two dirty looking clay mugs from a large trough. She filled them from a barrel behind the bar, placing one in front of Drevin and taking a large swig out of the second.

"Thanks," said Drevin, hefting his mug, "I have heard that there may be a couple of your regulars in tonight that go by the names of Picket and Sticket. If you happen to see them I would appreciate it if you would let me know." The woman raised one of her bushy eyebrows at that but otherwise remained silent, then stalked off to the far end of the bar where more patrons were waiting. Drevin took her surly silence as confirmation and moved to take a seat along the back wall of the tavern, with a good view of the door and the bar.

He had stopped at a local market earlier and picked up a meat pie and cheese tart from a street cart, which he had eaten on his way here. The pie had been mostly pastry with some dry, unspecified meat inside and the cheese in the tart tasted slightly off. Now his stomach gurgled loudly, whether from hunger or complaint at his choice of foods he couldn't be sure.

For the next hour or so Drevin watched the people in the tavern and concluded that this tavern really was a shitheap of the lowest order. According to the locals he had talked to, this place was built for the miners, as a spot to eat and rest after a hard day's work. However, a local merchant bought it after the last descendants of the first miners died some years ago and pretty much ran it into the ground. When he ran out of coin he sold it dirt cheap to a loan shark to pay off his debts. Since then, it had been passed around the hands of many criminals and assorted lowlife, eventually ending up in the sorry state that it was in now.

There were a few greybeards in one corner that looked to be old miners from their dirty ash blackened faces and stooped postures. However, most of the groups of people around the tables looked to be in the criminal crews from their scars, scruffy clothing and assortment of sharp weaponry on show. Many had crude symbols denoting their gang affiliation scratched or crudely painted on their jerkins or cloaks. Drevin spotted symbols that looked like fists, daggers and quite a few hammers, so he was hopeful that he was in the right place.

Eventually, he spotted two short, wiry men with long cloaks and greasy hair who looked like the epitome of scum. They talked together excitedly and were very animated. They approached the bar and ordered some drinks, which the bar lady got them with her usual lack of enthusiasm. As she put their drinks in front of them, she looked over to Drevin and gave him the faintest of nods, then went back to glaring at everyone.

Drevin casually approached the bar and the two men, thinking that it was time to get to the bottom of this.

"Good evening gentlemen," Drevin called over to them. "Can I get you another drink?"

The two men looked up at him from their excited chatter and smiled. They were not pleasant smiles to start with and taking into account their lack of teeth, this made them positively repulsive.

"Who are you?" asked the one on the right just as the one on the left said, "Yes, you can." Drevin signalled the reluctant bartender over again.

"My name is Drevin," he said expectantly, waiting for them to respond.

"Good for you," said the one on the right, then snorted with laughter as if it was the funniest thing he had heard.

"Picket," said the one on the left looking at the other man, "And this funny git is my brother Sticket." Drevin could see the similarities in the two men. Both had the same slim physiques, bent noses and weak chins. Picket seemed the more amenable of the two as Sticket just continued to drink and stare at him. Both were twitchy and speaking too quickly, and Drevin noticed that they both had red smears on their gums and around their lips. Great, they are Mushheads and on Reds. It is going to be hard to get any sense out of them tonight.

Devin tried a simple approach, "So did you two hear about the baron's son being missing? Apparently, they have asked everyone to be on the lookout for him or any news of him and have even offered a reward."

"We don't know anything about that," said Picket quickly, his high-pitched voice whining.

"Nothing to do with us," said Sticket. "Why would we care what happens to some snot nose noble?"

"I guess you wouldn't know, but I heard that a couple of your gang recently came into some coin. I just wondered if you knew how they got it and if it was related."

Picket tried to focus his attention on Drevin and sat straighter on his rickety stool. "We just did a big job for the boss, is all. That's why we got us some coin. Ain't that right Stick?"

"Yeah, a right big job it was," said Sticket, leaning forward on his stool and peering into Drevin's face, trying to be intimidating. His hand had strayed under his cloak. "A nice removal job. And we got a juicy bonus too."

"Yeah, real plump and juicy."

"Really?" asked Drevin nonplussed, "I didn't take you two for removal men. It must have been something important that you had to get rid of?"

"What's it to do with you?"

"Why are you asking?"

"It's none of your business?"

"You tell him Stick."

"I don't think we should talk to you anymore."

"Yeah, get lost arsehole. Before we 'remove' you."

The two men were talking over each other in their haste and getting very agitated, now standing up and pressing themselves up close to Drevin. Clearly the mushrooms were having an effect on them, along with the line of Drevin's questioning. Drevin suspected they knew more than they were telling him, but they were attracting attention now and Sticket had a hand on the short sword at his belt.

Other hard-faced men were looking over and more than one had a hand under the table, no doubt close to a weapon. Not wanting to start a brawl with so many men eager for violence in a place full of sharp objects, Drevin raised his hands and stood slowly. “Easy fellows, I didn’t mean anything by it. Just trying to make conversation is all. I’ll leave you to enjoy your own company,” he said, backing away to his previous seat against the wall.

“Yeah, piss off prick,” sneered Sticket then he snorted another laugh as he realised what he had said.

Drevin nursed his ale and caught the attention of a young girl wearing an apron who looked like she had just arrived for the evening shift. He asked her for some bread and fruit to see if that would settle his stomach and resolved to keep an eye on the two men at the bar. A little while later he was picking at the remains of his slightly crusty, stale bread when a group of four men entered, talking loudly.

“Another wasted day,” said a round, red-faced man plonking himself into the nearest chair.

“Yeah, maybe we should knock it on the head now,” complained a younger, skinny man scraping a chair out from the table and sitting next to him.

“I for one am tired of getting leaves in my hair and thorns up my arse from traipsing around that damned forest,” said an older man with more grey than brown in his long hair, gingerly sitting down.

“We’re not giving up yet lads,” called a man with a pointed face and a sharp nose in a long green cloak, “think of the reward we’ll get when we find the brat. I know I am and what I intend to spend mine on.”

"Aye, I could feed my family for a month with my share of that money," the first man said

"Sod that Mordi," said the young man. "My family can eat shit, far as I'm concerned. That money is for me to spend on booze and women."

"Well, ain't you the charitable one Fost. Still, it would be nice to have it, whatever we do with it," said the older man. "But that is only if we find him."

"Don't worry lads, I have got this covered," said, green cloak, still standing and looking around the tavern. "Alright, listen up everyone," he called out, brandishing a sheet of parchment which he had whisked out from under his cloak. "Me and my friends here are on the baron's business, looking for his missing son. If anyone has any information as to where his lordling is you must tell us immediately or face the baron's wrath. We have his signed agreement that grants us the authority to act on his behalf in this matter. Therefore, you must treat us with the respect you would show to one of his family."

The mood in the tavern changed instantly. Everyone was now staring at the man with a range of expressions, from incredulity to simmering rage. Angry muttering arose all around the room and the recalcitrant bartender had made herself scarce. Shit. That was a dumb move.

"I'll show you how we treat the noble kind in here, son!" shouted a brawny fellow making an obscene gesture with his scarred arms, prompting some nasty chuckling.

"No one comes in here and orders us around!" shouted another equally mean looking man half rising from his seat.

"Jez, sit down for Luciana's sake," called Mordi, tugging on his cloak and pulling him down into the last vacant chair with a thump. "Are you trying to get us done in?"

The one apparently called Jez settled himself somewhat huffily in his chair and the room gradually returned to its sullen atmosphere of before, although several people still cast angry glances at the table of newcomers.

"Well, that went well," said the older man sarcastically.

"Shut up Wylad," snapped Jez, "At least I am trying to do something to find him and not just complaining all the time, like some people."

"Come off it, Jez," Wylad replied. "We have been looking for days and found no sign of the damned boy yet. I'm sure that between us and the other groups, we have covered every inch of that prickly, bloody forest now."

"Alright, I know. We will move our search into the city now, starting in this district." said Jez, looking around the room meaningfully.

Wylad leaned in and muttered something to him. Then they continued their conversation at a quieter volume, which was absorbed by the noise of the rest of the room.

Drevin shook his head at the foolishness of the men. They had the bearing of desperate men, out of work and down on their luck, looking for any way to get coin. He also took hope that his first instincts were right and if the boy was to be found, it would be in the city.

He glanced back over to the bar to see what Picket and Sticket were doing and noticed them talking quietly to themselves and casting glances over at the group of newcomers. Then they stood up and slid out of the side door of the tavern, heading outside.

Drevin quickly finished his drink and followed them out the door. The chill evening air was a welcome respite from the musky tavern, despite the lingering scent of dust in the breeze. Drevin caught sight of the two men turning into a street on the left and headed in that direction, trying to look like he was out for an evening stroll.

He spotted them hustling down the street, huddled together, faintly illuminated by the lights from the close-packed houses, then turning into a narrower alleyway. He tailed them as they continued on. As they moved into a more squalid, less populated area he often had to rely on just the faint moonlight to light his way as the surrounding buildings became squatter and darker, until they soon came to a row of warehouses sitting flush against the outer wall of the city. They headed towards one and Picket produced a key to unlock the heavy padlock on the doors, then they disappeared into the dark interior.

Drevin stopped at the end of the alleyway, making sure that he remained in the darkness, untouched by the few lamps lit high on the city walls. He studied the warehouse from his position.

It was a dumpy, ugly building that lurked under the stone wall like a fat toad crouching under a huge rock. The light from above cast an orange glow on it, making it look slightly demonic. There were lots of heavy scratches on its wooden walls and old paint was flaking off it in several places. The clay tiles on the rounded roof looked uneven and he could see some substantial gaps in them. However, the wooden shutters at the windows were thick and tightly closed and the doors looked heavy and newer than the rest of the building.

Drevin watched and pondered his next move. He could try to get inside and confront them, but he couldn't be sure that they were on their own in there. Also, he had doubts about his ability to pry open those doors. He could go to the guard with his suspicions about them being involved with Ridozir's disappearance, but he had no evidence yet and they were unlikely to come all the way down here just on his say so. Or he could just bide his time and see if they came out again, but he hated waiting around and it was getter colder by the minute. Eventually, he made a decision and crept closer to the warehouse to see if he could see or hear anything that might tell him what they were up to in there.

He made it to the side of the building unnoticed and pressed himself up to the rough walls, running his hand over them, looking for any gaps. A sudden stabbing pain in his finger almost caused him to curse out loud as a splinter of wood wedged itself under a fingernail, but he just about contained himself. Shit, shit, shit, he raged inside, pulling the painful splinter out. Sucking his injured digit, he then noticed that where his hand had been, there was a small hole in the wall between two badly fitted planks and he could see light flickering inside.

He slowly lowered his eye to the gap and tried to peer through whilst straining his ears for any sound coming from within. Much of the interior that he could see was in darkness, with a weak source of light coming from somewhere off to the right. He could make out vague bulky shapes and silhouettes, but they were smothered by darkness, so could be almost anything. Then he heard snatches of voices off to the right.

".......our chance." That sounded like Picket's voice.

"Not sure..........risky." The voice was faint, but Drevin thought it sounded like Sticket.

"Can't ......here. Looking .....................close."

"........yet. ..........move..............later."

They were definitely planning something and knowing their type it wasn't something good. Drevin was in two minds now whether to go in or to wait and watch when he heard a familiar raised voice coming from down the street.

"Answer my questions, you old fart," shouted Jez. Drevin looked that way and saw the group from the Slagheap now accosting an older man. They had gathered around him outside a row of houses further along the south wall. The lights from the wall above cast a faint glow down on them, creating a pool of light in which they stood.

"Yeah, tell us what you heard," cried the youth Fost, waving a heavy wooden stick in his face.

"I, I, I don't know anything about the baron's son. I swear it on Erebornia's beard." stammered the old man with his hands raised in a placating manner.

"Well, we heard that you did some work up at the castle a few days ago and know some people there. Tell us what they know," said Mordi, his bulk shaking, whether from anger or the cold, Drevin couldn't tell.

"What is going on out here?" called a woman coming out of the house just in front of the group. Her hair glowed silver from the light coming out of her windows and she looked to be around the same age as the man being questioned.

"Nothing dear, go back inside," said the old man quickly.

"This your missus, is it?" sneered Jez, grabbing hold of her arms and forcing them behind her back. She screamed at him to let her go and the man also started shouting at Jez to leave her alone.

Drevin cursed. Dammit! Why is it that whenever you get a group of men and add alcohol to them they turn into complete macho arseholes? Drevin hurried over to them to stop the situation from escalating.

"Alright fellows," Drevin called cheerfully when he reached them.

The four men all turned, startled at his appearance and the old man looked relieved, although Jez still held onto his wife.

"Piss off," said Jez. "This is none of your business. We are on the baron's official business."

"So I heard," said Drevin amiably, "But this is not how you get information. Leave these poor people alone and go home."

"You don't tell me what to do, old man. Get him lads!"

Fost rushed at Drevin first, swinging his stick like it was a sword, albeit a very short sword wielded by someone with the skill of a five-year-old. Drevin simply rolled his shoulders and sidestepped, shoving him to the ground as he hurtled past. Mordi then lowered his head and ran at him like an enraged bull. Drevin had no time to get out of the way so took the impact and rolled backwards with Mordi on top, then used his momentum to throw him straight off, sending him into the just rising Fost, both of them hitting the ground hard.

Wylad had been hanging back, but at a look from Jez closed in warily on Drevin, both arms extended. He reached out and grabbed Drevin's left wrist with his right hand, then grabbed his elbow with his other hand and tried to twist Drevin's arm behind his back. Drevin's arm rotated slightly, but he locked it in place as his strength was greater than the other man's.

Drevin then grabbed Wylad's wrist with his trapped arm and with his other hand, he grabbed Wylad's other arm. With a quick twist of his hips, he swung the lighter man around and straight into the path of the again onrushing Fost, who was bringing his stick down. There was a crack of splintering wood as the stick connected with the back of the unsuspecting Wylad's head and his eyes rolled up into his sockets. He stood for a second longer then he collapsed soundlessly to the floor.

Fost's wide eyes were unbelieving as they darted between his broken stick, the man on the ground and Drevin. Before he could react, Drevin launched a right fist into his stomach, doubling him over, then brought his knee up into his weak chin, sending him down to land on top of his comrade.

Drevin risked a quick glance around. Mordi was back on his feet, several yards away, red faced and panting and Jez was still holding onto the old woman.

Then Drevin heard iron wheels grating on the road and a rattling noise coming from ahead. A horse and cart was approaching, with two men sitting on the front board. Everyone stopped and froze for a moment, watching the cart. It came towards them but steered wide of the group, showing no sign of wanting to intervene. Drevin went to call out to them to ask them to send the guard when he realised he recognised the two men driving. Picket and Sticket! Shit! Drevin took a step towards the cart as it rolled slowly past, but then he heard Jez shout, "Get him, Mordi!"

Just as he turned back around, a tremendous weight crashed into him and sent him sprawling to the ground, banging his head against the hard mud.

Pain blossomed in his head and his eyes lost focus for a second before he realised what had happened. Mordi was on top of him.

He caught one last glimpse of the cart disappearing along the south road before Mordi's fist connected with his jaw and his full attention was returned to the matter at hand.

# CHAPTER 4

# DREVIN'S DISCOVERY

Pain awoke Drevin the next morning. His head pulsed in waves of throbbing misery and his face was aching and stiff. He felt like his head had been crushed under an anvil and then caked in soft mud, which had set hard. Which wasn't actually that far off from the truth.

He had managed to eventually incapacitate the big lunk Mordi with a combination of his fists, knees and a sturdy brick wall. Then the coward Jez had thrown the woman to the ground and fled, leaving Drevin to stagger back to his room at the inn and collapse onto his bed.

He had slept like the dead for several hours before the aches and pains of his body had demanded his attention. Now he had washed the blood and mud off him, got dressed in cleanish clothes and had a couple of strong drinks, he felt almost alive again. His knuckles were still sore and scraped and he had avoided looking at any reflective surfaces, so he could only imagine what bruises were currently colouring his face.

Dammit! Those two idiot lowlifes were his only lead, and those self-serving, overeager, money-grabbing bastards had ruined his best chance to catch them in the act. He was convinced that Picket and Sticket played a part in Ridozir's disappearance.

The evidence of blood in the stable, the description of the two men and a black cart being spotted outside the stable, them unexpectedly coming into money for performing a 'removal' job and their general reputation as unethical scumbags all pointed squarely to them. He was sure that they took that cart out last night to either pick up or transport the missing son somewhere.

Why had they left the bar just after that group had come in complaining that they had searched the entire forest for the boy and found nothing? Maybe they thought to take him into the forest, believing it clear now.

One thing he did know for sure was that he wasn't going to find out anything for sure by sitting here, contemplating if his bruised jaw was up to eating breakfast. Deciding it wasn't, Drevin stood with a groan and made for the front door.

He returned to the scene of last night's altercation in the Stone District on the South Road. The road was quiet, with just a few labourers heading out to start work early. He smiled grimly as he noticed the patches of blood on the ground and the wall from last night until he remembered that some of that blood was his own.

He made his way slowly along the road in the direction the cart had gone, the sun bright in the autumn sky, sending rays of pain into his aching skull. Soon he came to a crossroads where the road joined the Great Southern Road that turned right towards the South Gate and left towards the Central Market. Thinking they may have headed into the forest, Drevin turned right.

The wooden gates were tall, broad and wide open when he arrived. Two pairs of guards stood on this side of the gates monitoring traffic out of the city, whilst another two pairs stood outside the city doing likewise with traffic entering. There was a trickle of people coming in, mostly farmers and locals from the surrounding villages bringing in their produce to sell or looking to buy from one of the many markets.

Drevin approached the nearest pair of guards, one an older man with short grey hair and beard and the other a young lad, barely out of his teens, looking awkward in his heavy mail and holding his spear lopsided. They both wore the dark blue tabards with the white compass of Canor on the left breast.

"Morning, fellas," he called, trying to sound cheerful despite the constant pain he was in. "How goes things?"

"All quiet this morning, just how's I like it," replied the older guard, glancing over at him. "Are you going out of the city?" he enquired.

"Maybe," Drevin said, "But first I wondered if I could ask you some questions if you don't mind."

"I suppose it will help pass the time until our shift finishes, hey Pols," he said, nodding to his young comrade. "As long as you don't interrupt our duties that should be fine."

"Thank you. Been on all night then, have you?" asked Drevin.

"Yes, unfortunately for us, we pulled the night shift again. Supposed to be training up young Pols here, but so far all he's learnt is how to stand still for hours on end and pretend he's not bored stupid."

Pols then looked over at Drevin and gave an almighty yawn that lasted for several seconds.

"And he's not even learnt to do that well." chuckled the older man.

"So, no excitement overnight then? I was hoping you could tell me if a cart with two riders had come through the gates in the very early hours of the morning, whilst it was still dark."

"Oh aye, we had a cart come up. Can't say it was exciting though. Not unless you call a cart full of rotten vegetables exciting," said the guard.

"Is that what they were carrying?"

"Yes, so they said. Not that I took a close look, mind. Smelt like the dead gone rotten in the back of that cart, even with the heavy tarpaulin over it. Said they had to dump it in the forest before their master found out they had let it go bad, or they would be in for it."

"And you let them out?"

"Aye, that we did, didn't we Pols. Likely if we turned them away they would have just dumped it in an alley or the harbour. Couldn't have that smell polluting up the city any more than it is already," said the veteran.

"Did you notice anything else about the men or the cart?" Drevin pressed.

"Can't say as I did. Like I said, I didn't get too close to it."

"It was black." Pols spoke up in a surprisingly deep voice. "I saw it in the light from the torches."

"Interesting," said Drevin. "Anything else you can tell me about it, Pols?"

"The wheels of it appeared to have dust on them, not fresh dust but dust that had been ground into the rims, suggesting that it was used often in the Stone District. Also, the two men were shifty looking, and one kept a hand under his cloak, like it was on a blade."

"Bah, you think everyone who comes and goes through these gates is shifty Pols," said the greybeard. "What about that visiting priest of the Union who you thought was an escaped convict in disguise."

"Yeah, well, he looked really suspicious. He had a long object strapped to his back under his grey robes that looked like a longsword." Pols objected.

"But it wasn't, was it Pols? It was a wooden pole with a metal symbol of Erebornia's face attached at the top. A weathervane, I think he called it. A present for the church of the Storm God. And you stopped him and made him strip his robe off to show it to you," chuckled the older man.

"Yeah well," said Pols, now blushing, "You can't be too careful. Isn't that what you are always saying?"

"I wouldn't have minded, but the poor fellow was about seventy years old," the older man was laughing now.

"Well, we all make mistakes, lad," Drevin said, with a nod to the young guard. "Good observation skills last night, Pols. Thanks for the information." He turned back to his mentor. "It looks like the young lad has learnt something after all. My thanks to you both. It looks like I will be heading out." With that, he turned towards the gates and left the city.

***

Drevin walked down the straight, mud packed road that led southwest towards the city of Ripor, some two days away. The road angled away from the coast and just ahead, he could see the beginnings of the forest off both sides of the road.

The sun was now beating down on him, causing him to work up a sweat as he continued walking, adding more discomfort to his still protesting body. As he reached the forest, which stopped about twenty paces away from the sides of the road as if to respect its space, he paused for a breather.

I'm getting too old to be walking around everywhere. Maybe it's time I got my own horse. That would mean having enough coin to buy a horse though, something that was a rare commodity lately.

Pushing aside his thoughts, he carried on down the road, scanning both sides of the forest for any telltale signs of a recent disturbance. After a short while, his attention was drawn not by anything he saw but by what he heard. Ahead and off to the right, a short distance into the forest, a flock of black-winged birds were circling. That was never a good sign.

As he proceeded a little further, he eventually noticed an area to the right where the grass was flattened, and the short bushes were bent over. He followed this trail, noticing the squashed plants and undergrowth heading deeper in, towards the circling crows.

He soon reached a small opening between the trees and saw a loose pile of leaves and branches that were heaped into an untidy and unnatural mound. Squatting down with an alarming crack of his knees, he swept away some leaves to reveal a face staring back at him. A very pale, eyeless face. The face of a dead man. Quite likely the face of the dead noble, Ridozir, the baron's son.

Shit! Drevin stood wearily and sighed. He turned and headed back to the road and then back to the city. He was not looking forward to what came next.

***

Once back in the city Drevin made straight for the coroner's building in the Upper District. By law all deaths had to be reported to the coroner, especially those that were suspicious or unnatural, and this death was definitely suspicious. Also, Drevin didn't fancy carrying the body all the way back to the city and the coroner had their own horse and cart. The other reason for going there and not straight to the castle was because Drevin was keen to put off that meeting for as long as possible. He told himself it wasn't because he was afraid of the baron, but in truth he was, as was every sane man in the city.

So, he soon found himself outside the large, stone built, low building that served as the coroner's place of business. It didn't look very impressive. In fact, it looked like a huge white stone tomb. The pale clay tiles of the roof were only interrupted in the centre by a round dome with small windows set into two sides of it, giving it the appearance of an eyeball with two black eyeholes. Apart from the large, double wooden doors, there was no relief in the anaemic looking building.

Drevin approached and pushed open one of the heavy doors, which surprisingly swung open soundlessly. The interior was dim but lit by flickering candles in holders around the room. Off to his right there was a dividing wooden slatted wall and the distinctive smell of horseshit. Against the wall in front of the stable was a cart with large wheels and a driving seat big enough for two people. Off to his left was another wooden wall, this one sturdier looking, with a couple of doors visible along it. This wall stopped short of the far wall, leaving a patch of blackness in the corner.

In front of him was a wooden table which served as a counter and had numerous sheets of paper, an inkwell and quill, a candle and a small clay bowl on it. Behind the counter against the far wall was a large bookcase filled with all manner of objects, such as clay jugs, small glass bottles, odd shaped ceramic ware, metal tools and several items that Drevin couldn't even begin to tell what they were. There were even a few books on the shelves too. However, the most important thing seemed to be missing. The coroner. The room was uninhabited. Drevin had heard rumours about this man and was unsurprised to find him absent.

He walked over to the snuffling noises he could hear coming from the stable and saw a large brown stallion in there. His mane was long and scruffy, dirty brown and his bushy tail swished lazily behind him. His eyes settled on Drevin but looked slightly hollow and there were patches of grey hairs around his muzzle. That, along with his dull coat hairs, told Drevin that this animal was obviously past his best.

"Hello fella." Drevin said, slowly reaching his hand out to stroke the horse's nose. "What is your name, then?"

The horse, unsurprisingly, didn't answer him, except to give a little snort and a small shake of his head. "Well, I'd best go find your master, then we will have some work for you to do."

Drevin left the stable and headed to the other side of the building. He knocked on both doors and then, when there was no response, he tried the handles but both rooms were locked. Thinking that it was probably bad luck to try breaking into a room in a place for the dead he moved on.

At the end of the wall, he noticed in the darkness a steep set of stairs leading downwards with a single lamp flickering at the bottom of them. Stairs again! Why are there always stairs? Carefully and slowly, he made his way down.

At the bottom was another wooden wall that faced him, creating a narrow, dim corridor off to the right. Suddenly he shivered and noticed how cold it was down here, compared to the upstairs. The skin on his arms had pimpled with the sudden drop in temperature. He followed the corridor a short distance before it opened to his left into a large room brightly lit by many lamps.

Off to either side of the room closest to him were two old wooden tables filled with more pots and bowls. Shelves filled both sides of the room, displaying an array of paraphernalia and curious objects. Directly in front of him stood two large, rectangular stone slabs and a wooden wall at the far end of the room contained more doors.

On one slab lay an old man with grey hair and greyer skin, clearly quite dead, with his chest gaping open and his insides plain to see. Standing over this body stood a young man with pure white long hair, wearing a long white robe. He tilted his head to look at Drevin as he entered and spoke in a quiet but caustic voice. “Who are you, and what are you doing down here?”

“My name is Drevin Borlea,” he replied, “And I’m looking for the coroner. That wouldn’t happen to be you by any chance, would it?”

"No," replied the man sarcastically, "I just happen to like playing with dead bodies for the fun of it. What do you think?"

"Well, that is good news because I have got a prime body for you to play with."

# CHAPTER 5

# BREAKING BAD NEWS

Teelan paced in the corridor outside the ornate wooden door that led to the baron's personal chambers. Drevin sat in one of the stone alcoves, trying to look casual, fiddling with the small silver ring on his little finger. Teelan felt anything but casual. His stomach was churning so fast he thought he might vomit. His head was spinning, and he felt faint and although he knew that these were all just symptoms of his nerves he still couldn't stop feeling this way.

Earlier they had reported to the castle after retrieving the body from the forest and depositing it in Teelan's mortuary. When they had asked to see the baron, the slow-witted gate guards had thought that they were joking, then they had eventually noticed their anxious faces and fetched the steward out to see them.

The steward, when he arrived, was a long man with a completely hairless head and nervous eyes. He wore a deep rich blue robe which looked far too large for him, and he was delicately nibbling on a pastry. He introduced himself as Esklin Wilburton and took them into a small private room and insisted that they tell him their news, as he didn't want to disturb the baron unless it was absolutely necessary.

Once Drevin had told him of their discovery, Wilburton's face had turned several shades paler, and his incessant twitching had increased exponentially. After much more fretting and hand wringing, he finally sent for the guard captain and when he arrived, Wilburton scuttled off. Teelan was glad to see the back of him. The steward's heightened anxiety was infectious, and he was already nervous enough.

The captain turned out to be an unremarkable-looking man in his middle years. His homely features and short brown hair made him indistinguishable from hundreds of other men. The only thing noteworthy about him were two identical scars on his face, one on either cheek that ran from just under his eyes and stopped just short of his lips. They were thin white lines on his otherwise tanned face that indicated that they were old scars. He went by the name of Korac Nilstan, and he was as equally shocked by the news as Esklin was, although he was much more stoical about it. He duly followed Drevin and Teelan back to the mortuary and confirmed that it was indeed the body of Ridozir, the baron's eldest son.

All three of them then returned to the castle and Korac found the steward, who slipped off to gather the baron and his family in their chambers and told Drevin and Teelan to wait here. And wait they had. For over an hour now they had waited, getting more apprehensive, or in Drevin's case more irritable, by the minute.

"Dammit, how much longer will they keep us waiting?" complained Drevin for about the fifth time.

"Oh, I don't know. Let me just consult my '*how much time does it take to gather a noble family that you are about to break bad news to*' hourglass and I'll let you know," replied Teelan sarcastically, his uneasiness making him extra snappy.

"I only asked."

"No, you only asked yet again!"

Drevin opened his gormless mouth to respond when suddenly the door swung open silently and Wilburton appeared. He looked terrible with fat beads of sweat on his bald pate and his twitchy hands working overtime.

"Please do come in, gentlemen," he gestured to them, then stepped aside to allow them to enter.

Teelan let Drevin go first. He was incredibly reluctant to be here and the last thing he wanted was to be in the spotlight. Drevin had found the body. Let him do the talking. That, at least, was something he was good at.

The door shut behind them and Wilburton stepped in front of them to announce them.

"My lords and ladies, please let me introduce you to Drevin Borlea of ……?" he looked questioningly at Drevin. Drevin just stared back at him without saying a word. Esklin quickly looked away and coughed then continued. "Of unknown origin. A mercenary and friend to the barony of Canor. And this is Teelan Esposito of Sempa from the continent of Vangormia, chief coroner of Canor." he said, gesturing to the two men with a practised flourish of his arm, then he scuttled out of the way giving them a clear view of the room.

Teelan looked around at the compact but well-appointed room. Dark wooden panelling covered the walls, with bookshelves dominating the left-hand wall. A small open stone fireplace was in the middle of the back wall, with an ostentatious painting of a grand ship in a storm above it. The room was well lit by numerous highly decorated silver wall sconces and a low hanging chandelier in the centre of the room, finished in brass and moulded into the shape of a compass. Underfoot was a thick weave carpet of vermillion, patterned with a dark blue geometric design that disappeared under the heavy wooden chairs and thickly padded leather cushions that were spread around the room. The rich furnishings spoke of a prosperous reign and Teelan briefly considered the idea of asking for a rise in his pay, then remembered why they were here and quickly dismissed it.

In front of them, three heavy wooden chairs were arrayed and all were filled. To the right sat Serzin Sutter, the baron's brother, his rotund frame filling his chair completely. Behind him, in a too tight black dress, stood his wife Myelandra, displaying a more than appropriate amount of her ample flesh. Islia, the baron's daughter, occupied the chair on the left, in a beautiful golden dress which matched her long shining hair. Behind her stood two young noblemen in slightly faded chequered tunics with a symbol of a fish jumping out of water on their left breast.

The centre chair, of course, contained the baron himself, Zandir Sutter. He sat in the largest chair, which looked like it was swallowing up his slight frame, with his long grey hair pushed to either side of his equally grey, hollow face. Teelan had only really met him once before when he was appointed to his role, and that was only briefly as he greeted him with a handshake and provided him with his contract papers. However, he still remembered the grip of his bony hand and his grey eyes boring into him. Teelan tried not to meet those same eyes now and quickly looked elsewhere.

On a large cushion in front of Islia sat a teenage boy with a chubby face and short, black hair. Teelan recognised him as Greffin, the baron's youngest son. He was reading a heavy tome of history and was so engrossed by it he hadn't noticed their arrival. On another cushion in front of Serzin sat a young boy around ten years old with a round, vacant looking face. He was holding some wooden toy soldiers, but instead of playing with them he just sat and stared at them.

Standing at the rear of the room on either side of the fireplace was the nervous steward, Wilburton and a grim-looking Korac, along with two other guardsmen. That completed the not-so-happy tableau and made the small room feel positively claustrophobic, especially as everyone's eyes were on the pair of them.

"Well," grated the baron, his voice sounding brittle and hard. "I understand you have some important news as to the whereabouts of my son. Please tell me you have found him."

Teelan glanced at Drevin and prayed internally that he would answer that! After a few seconds of absolute silence and much to his relief, Drevin cleared his throat.

"My lords and ladies," replied Drevin in a very courtly voice that Teelan would never have suspected he was capable of using. "We have come to inform you that we have indeed found Master Ridozir. However, it is with great regret that we must inform you that he has unfortunately passed from this world."

A sharp intake of breath and gasps filled the room at this announcement. Islia let out a great sob which she tried to hold in but failed. Then she rose from her chair and fled from the room via a door along the back wall. Her two noble friends glanced anxiously at each other, then followed quickly behind her.

Teelan kept his head lowered and scanned the faces in the room. Serzin slumped in his chair, concern etched on his face. His wife reached down to place a hand on his arm, her long black curls falling over her face. Greffin glanced up briefly from his book, frowned at them, then continued reading. The young boy just continued staring into space, his toys forgotten in his hand. Wilburton and Nilston, though they both knew this information, still looked shaken, with Wilburton particularly distraught.

When Teelan finally looked at the baron, he saw his face shift quickly through a series of emotions, as first disbelief, then shock, sadness and anger manifested themselves in his features. Unfortunately for them, his face decided to stop its emotional tour and settled on the last one, anger.

"How did he die?" Zandir asked, his voice barely above a whisper but containing a menacing tone all the same. His right hand was stroking the bone white hilt of the vicious looking, serrated black dagger at his belt.

"We are not sure yet, my lord," replied Drevin, "But we suspect foul play. We are terribly sorry for your loss."

"You there!" called the baron in a much sharper voice, turning his gaze to Teelan. "You are supposed to be my coroner, are you not? But you can't tell me how he died? Isn't that the whole point of your job? Don't just stand there like an anaemic-looking willow tree. Answer me!"

"S, S, sorry my lord," stammered Teelan, raising his head and pushing his long white hair away from his face. "I have only just received the b…I mean, your son and I haven't had the time to carry out my investigations yet. I can tell you he didn't die of natural causes, my lord."

"Well, I gathered that much, seeing as he was a fit young man who hadn't turned eighteen yet," Zandir replied caustically. "You should stop wasting time and go find out what happened to my son and who did this to him. After all that is what I am paying you for, isn't it?"

"Yes, my lord." Teelan's head dipped again. He was sure that everyone could see him trembling, but he could not stop himself.

"And you, mercenary," the baron turned his attention back to Drevin, much to Teelan's relief. "You will help him and bring me whoever is responsible for this tragedy. Now both of you get out and leave us in peace to grieve and don't return until you know the perpetrator's identity."

Drevin stared at the baron in surprise, whether from the announcement that he had to assist Teelan or their brusque dismissal Teelan wasn't sure.

As the steward stepped forward to usher them out of the room, Drevin again cleared his throat and spoke.

"My lord, my apologies for bringing up an indelicate subject at this time, but there was mention of a reward for finding your son. And I have found him, although I appreciate it was not in the manner that you would have wished. However, if you desire me to continue the investigation I will need coin for supplies, sustenance and for loosening people's tongues. I have already spent almost all the last of my coin in tracking down your son."

No, no, no! For Luciana's sake Drevin, why did you have to bring that up now, Teelan cursed, invoking the name of the supposed Goddess of luck in his panic. Are you insane? You are going to get us killed or tortured, or more likely both!

"A reward. A reward!" shouted Zandir, leaning forward on his padded chair, his hands clutching the arms tightly. "You fail to find my son for four days, then casually walk in here and announce that he is dead and expect to be rewarded for it? You are pushing your luck, mercenary. Your only reward will be to walk out of this room in one piece. And even that is currently not guaranteed." A hostile silence settled between the two men who remained glaring at each other.

Teelan could see Drevin's fists clenching and unclenching at his sides and was now grateful that he had been obliged to surrender his weapons at the gatehouse. Otherwise, he could foresee Drevin pulling a blade and that would not end well for anybody, himself included! Please keep your mouth shut, he implored Drevin silently. He glanced back at the baron, noticing his smouldering grey eyes fixed on Drevin with eagerness, as if he desired the very opposite of Teelan. Teelan's heart was pounding so hard he thought that everyone in the room must be able to hear it and he felt rather faint. Amazingly, for the second time that morning, Drevin did what Teelan had silently prayed for and stayed quiet.

Zandir leaned back in his chair, still angry but also looking worn out by the confrontation. "Now get out of here and find out what happened to my son before I change my mind and send you both to join the guards who failed to protect him." His hand was now gripping his dagger, his knuckles as white as the hilt.

"Yes, my lord." Drevin replied in a surly tone with the barest nod of his head, his eyes still locked on the baron's. Then, after a few more seconds, he spun on his heel and marched to the door, opening it before the startled steward could react and left the room. Teelan was momentarily shocked and frankly astonished that they were still alive and being allowed to leave. Not wanting to push his luck, he hastily bowed deeply to the baron, then turned and quickly stepped out of the door.

As the door closed behind him, Teelan noticed Drevin was already halfway down the long corridor, stalking away. Teelan scurried after him, eventually catching up with him as he turned into a wider corridor in the main section of the castle.

"Damn, self-important, stuck up, ignorant, shit for brains nobles." Drevin was muttering to himself as he went.

"Well, that went swimmingly," said Teelan sarcastically. Relief and anxiety were fighting a raging battle in his stomach. Currently, relief was on top, but he could feel anxiety regathering its forces for a resurgent push that would soon overwhelm it.

"It's not fair Teelan and it's not right." Drevin continued fuming, ignoring Teelan's comment as if he hadn't spoken. "A baron should keep his word. He promised a reward for finding his son. There were no conditions attached to what state he should be in or how long it took to find him. I spent most of my coin tracking down that brat and for what, nothing. It's not my fault that he was too stupid to not get himself killed."

"Well, your sense of justice may well do you credit Drevin, but your sense of self-preservation is sorely lacking. The next time you want to challenge a baron in his castle, surrounded by his family and armed guards, please do so when I am not in the presence of your company." Teelan snapped, his own anger now rising at Drevin's lack of regard for his safety.

Drevin just glared at him and continued walking, but he stopped muttering for now for which Teelan was grateful. They soon made their way back to the gatehouse and had to wait again as a baby-faced guard went off to look for where they had put Drevin's weapons. Needless to say, that this delay didn't help to improve Drevin's mood, and his mutterings and cursing resumed.

Eventually, the guard returned, burdened with an armful of sharp weapons that Drevin snatched off him ungraciously. Honestly, he was not sure why Drevin needed so many weapons, but he was pretty sure that neither of them was in the right mood for him to ask. Drevin was just finishing strapping his short sword to his belt when a flustered-looking Wilburton dashed up to them.

"Borlea," he called out, waving his arm at Drevin. "Please wait a moment." Teelan noticed he had managed to pick up a round of bread from somewhere and was leaving a trail of crumbs in his wake. A small black cat was following him, weaving in and out of his legs and threatening to trip him up at any moment, occasionally stopping to munch at the crumbs.

"I have a message for you from Lord Serzin." he announced, slightly out of breath, wafting a sheet of parchment in the hand that didn't contain the diminishing bread. "He says to give his thanks to you for your work in finding Ridozir and he would like to apologise for his brother's bad manners. The baron has had temperamental moods ever since the death of his wife and the news of his son's death brought that back to him.

He wishes you to have the reward money now and to inform you that you are not required to continue the investigation if you don't wish to. However, if you decide not to investigate, it may be best if the baron never hears of you again, which may mean that leaving the city would be the best option for all concerned." With that, he untied a heavy leather pouch from his belt, which jangled as he handed it over to Drevin.

"Well, I'll be," exclaimed Drevin with a big smile on his face, his previous foul mood instantly forgotten. "It looks like there are some nobles with decency and honesty after all. Thank you Esklin and tell Serzin the same. Oh, and tell him I will do my best to find out what happened to Ridozir. After all, I don't like to leave a job half done."

"Very good, sir," said the steward. He nodded to Teelan. "Master Esposito." Then he backed away as if to race off to his next task and tangled with the black cat at his feet. "Damn it, Snatcher, you are always underfoot!" he cursed at the cat as he staggered away, the cat still dogging his footsteps.

"Well, I would say that went swimmingly," parroted Drevin with a smug look on his face.

Teelan was still mad at him and felt like hitting him right then. With a scathing look and a deep breath, he composed himself and walked out of the wide-open doors into the bright courtyard.

# CHAPTER 6

# DEFINITELY NOT FRIENDS

Teelan was still sulking by the time they got back to his mortuary. Drevin had tried chatting away to him on their way back, but he had remained mostly silent and sullen. He had even spent some of his shiny, new found wealth on buying them some warm fruit tarts from an enterprising street seller outside the castle walls, but Teelan just ate his without comment. For his part, Drevin ironically felt much lighter for having a heavy purse at his belt. His head still pulsed from last night's altercation, but he was pretty happy with how things were turning out, so it was easier to ignore.

"Well, here we are again then," Drevin said, gesturing expansively at the still too white building. "Back at the Dead Shed."

Teelan gave him a sharp look and looked like he was about to say something, but then thought better of it and just unlocked the door and went inside.

Drevin sighed and headed inside after him. As Teelan was being uncooperative, he headed over to the stall to see the large, sad-looking horse. "How are you today my boy, eh?" he asked, stroking his fuzzy nose. "Hey Teelan, what's your horse called?" he asked.

Teelan glanced over wearily from his desk. "It doesn't have a name. It's a horse," he replied flatly.

"Well, he should still have a name. What do you call him when you talk to him?"

"I don't call it anything because I don't talk to it, because it's a horse. Horses can't understand human speech and they can't engage in discourse. So, I don't talk to it in much the same way as I don't talk to a chair."

"He's not a chair though, is he?" Drevin replied, incredulous at his lack of affinity with animals. "He's a living creature and deserves a name. And they can understand us, at least to some extent. They can tell what moods we're in."

Teelan just looked at him like he was mad.

"Don't worry, boy, I will give you a name if he won't." Drevin whispered to the horse. "How about 'Hinch', no, maybe 'Herbe', no I've got it 'Harri', that's what I'll call you."

"Really?" Teelan had approached the stable and looked at Drevin with one raised pale eyebrow. "Harri the horse! Goodness, sometimes you are such a child, Drevin." Drevin just smiled at him innocently.

"Don't listen to him Harri." Drevin said, turning back to the horse and picking up a mouldy carrot from its trough, rubbing his nose with his other hand. "He's just jealous because he didn't think of it first. Hey, you need to buy Harri here some better quality food," he said to Teelan, waving the offending carrot at him. "This is going rotten and Harri deserves better than this."

"Well, since you like him so much and as you have now got the money you so desperately wanted, you can buy him some food." Teelan snapped. "Now if you two are quite finished can we actually get on with the proper task at hand of discovering what happened to the baron's son, before we find ourselves succumbing to the same fate?"

"Fine," said Drevin, dropping the unpleasant carrot back in the trough. Harri looked at it with gloomy eyes, then looked away again. "Lead the way, Master Esposito." he said with a flourishing gesture.

Drevin followed him down the steep steps leading to the basement where they had laid out Ridozir on one of the stone slabs. He shivered again at the chill in the air and watched Teelan collect an array of metal implements, bowls, jars and vials and place them at the edge of the slab next to the body.

"What's all that for?" asked Drevin waving his hand towards the equipment.

"Tools of the trade. I hope you are not squeamish, as it is about to get very messy in here." Teelan added as he pulled on a heavy red leather apron.

"If it's a messy job why do you wear white robes then? Is it so that you look more like a priest?" Drevin asked, perusing the shelves of medical objects and books of anatomy.

"Well, that's insulting." Teelan replied, looking up from the body.

"Why, there's nothing wrong with being a priest, is there?"

"Not if you believe in that sort of thing."

"And I take it you don't?"

“No, I do not.”

“Even though you work with the dead? Surely you must believe in Necomthia, goddess of death? Don’t you have to say prayers to her when people bring you their departed?”

“Not if I can help it. And if they insist, then I say the words, but it doesn’t mean I have to believe them.” Teelan was prodding about in Ridozir’s stomach with a long metal pair of tweezers, removing fat white maggots and depositing them in a bowl. Drevin looked away again, his stomach churning.

“Oh, I forgot you Vangormians worship your own god, don’t you? What’s his name again, Saponus?”

“It is Sapious, and I don’t worship him either.”

“Huh, I thought all Vangormians believed in him.”

“Well, that is a rather sweeping generalisation and a narrow-minded view that a rather large percentage of the population should think and act in the same way.”

“Isn’t that partly what religion is?” Drevin said, shrugging.

“A fair point, but not everyone in Vangormia believes the same way.”

“What do you believe, then?” Drevin asked. He was curious to know more about this strange young man.

“I believe Sapious was a man like any other. A great man, to be sure. He was a powerful Mind who used his abilities for the benefit of our country, but he lived and died as a man, same as everyone else.”

“Don’t they say that he lived for over two hundred years and then, when he died, he ascended to godhood some four hundred years ago?”

“So they say.” Teelan replied in a flat tone of voice.

"But you don't believe that?"

"I wasn't there, so I couldn't possibly comment."

"So you have no faith at all. Wow. Must be hard to live like that," Drevin said, looking at him and shaking his head slowly.

"I manage." Teelan answered, meeting Drevin's gaze. "I take it you believe in your five gods of the Union?"

"Yes."

"Of course you do." Teelan said, returning to his disgusting task of picking maggots out of the chest wound.

"What is that supposed to mean?" Drevin asked, crossing his arms.

"Nothing."

"If you don't believe in any gods, what do you believe in, then?"

Teelan put down his tweezers and straightened up, sighing at Drevin. "I believe in education, knowledge and learning. I believe in what I can see, touch and feel and that there are infinite possibilities that we are all ignorant and unaware of. I believe people are capable of amazing achievements and grand discoveries; or total decimation and annihilation, sometimes concurrently, with most of our energies unfortunately leaning towards the latter. I also believe that you are irritating me even more than usual today, so please let me get on with my work."

"So, how did you learn about all this stuff in the first place?" Drevin asked, ignoring Teelan's mood, finding himself intrigued by the young man.

"I trained at the academy in Sarpus in Vangormia, if you must know."

"What's Vangormia like?"

"Big."

"I was hoping for a bit more than that," Drevin huffed.

"It's very big," Teelan replied, smirking. "Oh fine," he said, seeing the reproachful look on Drevin's face. "It is a vast continent ruled by an emperor and split up into ten provinces. The western provinces are well-populated, cultured and civilised and are the mecca for knowledge and learning, whilst the eastern ones are more rural and tribal. It is a hot but bountiful land, producing large amounts of fruits, rice and spices. Maybe you should go there, see what it's like for yourself."

"I'm not sure I would fit in. Besides, there's a whole lot of water between here and there." Drevin said with a slight shiver. The thought of all that water underneath him making goosebumps prickle on his arms.

"What, you are not afraid of a bit of water, are you Drevin?" Teelan mocked. "I mean, it doesn't surprise me given the foul odours you emit, but I thought that was just down to a lack of personal hygiene."

"Very funny." Drevin replied, not in the least bit amused. "Let's just say I prefer to keep my feet on something that doesn't keep moving underneath me. Anyway, this academy you went to. They teach you how to read the dead by doing... whatever it is you are doing to that body?" Drevin wafted a hand towards Teelan who had picked up a sharp knife and was slicing a line down through the remaining flesh of the chest.

"Not exactly." Teelan replied, using two thin metal poles with large semi-circle shaped paddles at the ends to pull apart the flesh from the cut he had made.

"Well, what did they teach you then?" Drevin asked, feeling nauseous at what Teelan was doing, but also strangely fascinated and unable to look away.

"They taught me to mind my own business, which seems to be something that was severely lacking in your education." Teelan snapped, focusing on the gory red ribs and innards that he had now exposed.

"I was only trying to get to know you," said Drevin defensively, twisting the little silver ring on his left finger.

"Well, don't. We are not friends, buddies, pals, or chums. We are being forced to work together when really I would much rather prefer to work alone in peace and solitude. I do not need to tell you my life story. You may have noticed that I haven't pried into your life and your business, so please do me the same courtesy." Teelan barked. His hands were now inside the body and were red up to the wrists with blood and gore, but he seemed completely oblivious to the mess.

"You could ask me about my life if you wanted to." Drevin replied. "I am happy to tell you anything about myself."

"Really?" sneered Teelan. "Okay, well why don't you tell me about that ring you wear on your little finger with the amber stone in it. It is clearly a woman's ring but not on your wedding finger and you haven't mentioned a wife. And you play with it a lot."

Drevin cursed as he noticed he was still spinning the ring around. Shit. Damn kid, why did he have to ask about that? "That's personal," he replied, flushing slightly.

"Hah, you see Drevin, everybody has their secrets and their 'personal' details that they don't want to share. Now please go away and let me get on with my work."

Drevin stared at Teelan and suddenly the wall behind him wavered, the three doors blurring into one, then back again. Oh hell. He looked at the hard packed mud floor. It appeared to be swirling underneath his boots, and he felt like he was standing on the deck of a ship in a storm. Swaying, he leaned against one of the stone slabs as casually as he could, trying not to let his dizziness show. He was having one of his head spins again. He just hoped Teelan hadn't noticed. But of course, he had.

"What is wrong with you?" Teelan asked, squinting at him with his head tilted sideways. "Have you been drinking? Or is it the sight of a little blood that is making you swoon?"

"I'm fine." Drevin lied, unwilling to let his weakness show. Gods, he needed to lie down. "I have seen worse than this in my time and no doubt will see worse yet. And as for drink, no I haven't been drinking yet, but that sounds like a fine idea. I will leave you to do your…thing. I'll come back later this evening, see if you found out anything." Teelan had already gone back to inspecting the body and didn't respond or even look up from his work.

Drevin turned carefully and staggered back up the stairs, keeping both hands on the walls. It was going to be a long walk back to his inn.

****

It was dark by the time Drevin returned to the mortuary. An old man with a stooped back was further down the street, using a long wooden pole with burning rushes at the top of it to light the street lamps. Hmm, you can tell when you are in the richer areas of a city, Drevin reflected bitterly. You don't get lamplighters or even street torches in the poor quarters.

However, he didn't let this spoil his good mood. He had eventually made it back to his inn, with only a few more scrapes and cuts from where he had stumbled into walls or misjudged doorways. Once there, he had headed straight for his room and had a brief doze, not a nap, as naps were for old people.

When he awoke, his dizziness had subsided, and his head had decided a dull throbbing pain was enough punishment for now. After stashing most of his coin in his room he had then eaten a surprisingly tasty stew of pheasant and vegetables, which even had some spices in it, and he had mopped it up with some thick dark bread. Some apples and pears baked in honey and a few tankards of a rich, dark ale followed soon after. Feeling pleasantly sated and able to walk in a fairly straight line again, he felt ready to face the world.

He had wandered from his dockside inn to the Central Compass and the Great Market where traders were hawking all manner of goods bought in by ship, cart or hand. He had stopped at a moneylender's house to change some of his silver rounds into copper bits. It didn't do to be wandering around with too much silver after all. He had eventually received the full exchange of ten copper bits for a silver round; despite some of the shadier lenders trying to convince him that the copper mines were running low and therefore bits were worth more, so they could only offer six bits per silver.

He hated those places. They smelled of desperation. Desperate lenders trying to convince people to borrow money they couldn't afford to repay, especially with the extortionate interest. All hoping they had something else of value they could take or could force them into servitude. And desperate borrowers who didn't know better or who had no other options.

He had then perused the market stalls for a while, looking out for any interesting items. There were sellers there from Iria with wooden coins clattering in their hair and dark-skinned Vangormians from across the sea selling exotic fruits and spices. Even though it was heading towards fourth bell, it was still full of people doing some late shopping before heading home for the night. The shouts and cries of the traders overlapped each other, each merchant claiming to have the 'best of this' or the 'freshest of that'. Drevin picked up a few minor items; an almost sharp razor, a whetstone, a small leather pouch and some fresh fruit.

He also found several merchants selling jewellery and, remembering the cat necklace he had found in the barn, he located a trader who sold similar items. However, when he showed the weaselly old man behind the stall the necklace and asked who he may have sold it to, he just shrugged and said he couldn't remember. He then tried to sell Drevin an ornate silver brooch, 'for his lady friend', that would have looked out of place on an ostentatious queen. Eventually, he left the market and headed back to the mortuary. He wanted to see if Teelan had found out anything from the body and hoped that his mood had improved.

****

Drevin entered the mortuary, which was unlocked and dimly lit. He headed over to see Harri, who snorted at him with either reproach or recognition, pulled out some fresh carrots and apples from his bag and deposited them in his trough. "There you go, Harri, some treats for you." Harri bent his head, snatched up an apple and chomped a sizeable chunk off it. Drevin smiled happily and patted his nose. "Better go find your temperamental master," he said.

Drevin headed back down to the basement, careful on the steps in the near blackness. As he entered the much brighter basement, he spotted Teelan standing over one of the stone slabs, looking down at a body. However, it was not the body of Ridozir. It was a rather plump body of a young man with short, sandy hair. Teelan was still wearing his, now even redder, apron and his hands were still bloody. He was holding a long metal implement that looked like an oversized spoon and was digging around in the fat man's open chest.

"You really need to get a secretary or something," Drevin called over, "or to lock your doors. Anyone could wander in here."

"It looks like anyone just has," Teelan said, glancing up at him.

"Seriously, you should have someone to let people know where you are and what you are doing. And to save them coming down here in the dark and almost breaking their necks."

"That sounds like a terrible idea. Why would I want people to know where I am and what I am doing?"

"Never mind." sighed Drevin. Gods, the boy was totally odd. "What are you doing and who is this fellow? Why aren't you working on Ridozir? Do you know what happened to him yet?"

"Goodness me, what a lot of questions." said Teelan, dropping his tool into a metal bowl with a clang. "First of all, what I am doing is my day job. You know, being a coroner. Which, if you don't know, means that when someone in this city perishes in unnatural circumstances, I am called to determine what happened to them. Usually, it is a most mundane reason, such as hunting accidents, common illnesses or 'alcohol related misadventures', but sometimes it can be more interesting."

"Alcohol related misadventures?" Drevin asked, one eyebrow raised.

"Yes. You would be surprised at how many people get drunk and simply fall over or off something, cracking their heads open, or those who walk straight into rivers or canals."

Drevin shuddered at the thought of falling into a deep body of water and drowning. "So how did this young man die then?" he asked quickly to take his mind off that image.

"From tying up his bootlaces, according to the friends who were with him." Teelan replied, watching him from the corner of his eye.

"Bullshit! He can't have died from doing that."

"That is exactly what his father said, although more eloquently, of course. And why he has asked me to investigate his death. He suspects that one of his friends killed him and the others are all covering it up."

"That makes more sense," said Drevin. "So have you found out how he really died?"

"Yes," Teelan replied, smirking again. "He died from tying up his bootlaces."

"No shit! You are having me on." Drevin said.

"Okay, that is only partially true. You see, he was playing a game with his friends where he had to stand upright and let one of his friends untie one of his bootlaces. Then he had to bend down and quickly tie it up before they could untie the other boot. If he failed to do it before they untied the other boot, he had to stand up and then repeat the process with the other boot and so on."

"Sounds like a thrilling game," said Drevin laconically.

"Well, it is a way to pass the time for the privileged children of rich merchants who don't have to work. Anyway, apparently our rotund friend here wasn't very good at this game and had been playing it for several minutes, getting redder and redder in the face until he eventually just collapsed to the street. You see that mild exercise, possibly the first of his young life, combined with his terrible diet of rich food meant that his heart could not take the strain and gave up. The tubes in his heart were so clogged with fat they couldn't pump blood back in fast enough. Simply put, he was too fat to live."

"Damn. That is harsh. I hope you are not going to tell his parents that." Drevin said, half jokingly.

"Whyever not?" It was Teelan's turn to raise an eyebrow. "His father is a renowned baker and if he hadn't overindulged his son by letting him eat half of his stock he may still be alive. Surely it would be of benefit to let him know this so that he can become a better parent, then at least his other children might survive for longer."

"My god Teelan, have you got no empathy at all?" Drevin exclaimed. "The man has just lost a son. How do you think he would feel if you told him that? Can't you at least soften the blow?"

"I get paid to find out the truth, not to show empathy! Anyway, how would I do that if I even wanted to?" asked Teelan scathingly. "Lie to him, tell him his son was in perfect health and just happened to fall down dead?"

"No, but couldn't you just say, I don't know, something like he had a condition or problem with his heart, and nobody could have done anything about it?"

"That would be lying, and I don't lie."

"It wouldn't be lying as such. He did have a problem with his heart. You just said so. You just wouldn't have to tell him why he had this problem. It is called protecting someone's feelings, Teelan." Drevin implored, shocked at his lack of compassion.

"I am not in the business of protecting people's feelings. Anyway, let us go back to one of your earlier questions before we got onto the distasteful topic of emotions. The reason I am not working on Ridozir is that I have completed my investigations now and drawn several conclusions." Teelan shot back.

"Such as?" Drevin asked, following Teelan over to the other slab where Ridozir still lay and trying not to look inside him.

"He was stabbed multiple times with a short thin blade, not very expertly either, as none of them found the heart. There are puncture wounds in his stomach, liver and lungs though, so he would have bled to death within minutes."

"How do you know what type of blade was used? Surely any blade can cause wounds to those organs?"

"Because some of the stab wounds to the lungs damaged the rib bones. Let me show you," he said, picking up a yellow curved bone with bits of congealed blood still sticking to it.

"Is that what I think it is?" Drevin asked uncertainly.

"Well, I don't know what you think it is as I can't read minds, even simple ones, but this is one of his rib bones."

Drevin whistled softly. "I hope you are going to be putting him all back together again before the baron sees him."

Teelan ignored him. "Hand me your sword."

"Do I have to?" Drevin asked, looking distastefully at the bone. Teelan just stared at him with his hand extended.

"Fine," he said, drawing the short sword from his belt.

"No, not that one. The ludicrously big one."

Drevin shrugged and drew the long sword from its scabbard on his back, handing it to Teelan reluctantly. He had to suppress a smile when Teelan almost dropped it immediately, misjudging the weight of the weapon.

"That is not amusing." Teelan said. Apparently, Drevin hadn't totally stopped that smile.

"Look at the groove on the bone here," he said, thrusting the bone towards Drevin's face. After recoiling a bit, Drevin looked closely and noticed a shallow V-shaped groove in the bone.

"Do you see the groove?" asked Teelan impatiently.

"Yeah."

"That is where the blade went through the body and sliced off a piece of the bone. Now if we put your blade on that groove," he said, placing the blade of Drevin's longsword over the notch in the bone, "we can see that this blade is thicker than the groove and if this blade even only went halfway in the body, the cut in the bone would be deeper." Drevin could see what he meant as clearly the blade was thicker than the narrow slice in the bone and much wider than the depth of the cut.

"Now, take this back and hand me your slightly more appropriately sized sword." Teelan said, passing the heavy blade back to him.

Drevin did as he was told and Teelan repeated the process again. "This blade is much thinner and not as wide, so is a much better match to the groove in the rib," Teelan said, demonstrating how this blade almost sat nicely in the slot, being just a fraction too thick. "This is almost a perfect match, but still just too thick. So, the blade that made these cuts was probably of a poorer quality than yours. You see?"

"I see," said Drevin, impressed despite himself.

"Additionally, I found iron flakes in the bones and wounds, indicating that the blade was made of iron, not steel. And the attacker was most likely shorter than Ridozir."

"Impossible!" snorted Drevin. "There is no way you can tell how tall his attacker was."

"Actually, there is," Teelan said, a satisfied look on his face. "Look at the rib bone again. Look closely at the groove in it. You can see it starts off deeper at the front, then gets shallower the further in it goes. This means the blade went in at an upward angle, which usually indicates a shorter attacker using an upwards thrust trying to find a killing stroke." Teelan demonstrated by thrusting the short blade up at an angle as if facing a tall enemy. "If the assailant was the same height as the victim the blade would have gone in straight and made a groove of even depth all the way along."

“Bloody hells! Now I realise why people call you the Necromancer. You really can make the dead speak, can’t you?” Drevin said, astonished by the skill and knowledge of the precocious young man.

Teelan gave him a smile which, for once looked genuine. “I try.” He said with false modesty.

“Wait, could two people could have attacked him?” Drevin said, remembering the two scumbags he had encountered in the bar. They were definitely short, both in stature and in common decency.

“Well, I suppose so, if both of them were of similar heights and used similar weapons.”

Drevin recalled that Picket and Sticket were about the same height and although he hadn’t seen both of their weapons, he assumed they would be similar, as they seemed to copy each other in most things.

“I haven’t finished yet,” Teelan continued, drawing Drevin out of his reverie. “He had ground in rock dust and ash in his back, so I would say he had been laying in it for a while.”

“Hmm, that actually makes sense.” Drevin said, thinking back to the warehouse in the Stone District where he suspected the body had been kept.

“But the pièce de résistance is this,” Teelan said excitedly, bending over a clay bowl with a small pair of tweezers in his hand. Drevin noticed how young and enthusiastic, almost childlike Teelan was when he was showing off his work. He turned to Drevin, holding the tweezers steady in one hand right in front of his eyes. Drevin squinted toward what he was holding and eventually spotted a long strand of hair pinched in the tweezers.

"A hair." Drevin replied. "That is what you are so excited about?"

Teelan looked momentarily crestfallen before he became animated again. "Yes, a hair. But this hair tells us two very important things. First of all, it tells us that someone with long hair was with him when he died or afterwards."

"How do you know that? That hair could have got onto him at any time."

"Because of where I found the hair. I pulled it out of his chest, Drevin, which means that someone was with him after he got stabbed."

"Okay, that is interesting. And what is the second thing that hair tells us?" Drevin asked, feeling his excitement rising to match Teelan's.

"Look at the colour of the hair." Teelan said, turning it slowly towards the candlelight. "Golden blonde. Now, who do we know who has long golden blonde hair and who has a connection to Ridozir?"

"Islia." breathed Drevin. "Hang on, look at this". He rummaged around in one of his belt pouches and pulled out the fine, silver cat necklace and showed it to Teelan. "I found this in the barn where I believe Ridozir was killed."

"And?" Teelan said, sounding annoyed that Drevin was going off on a tangent.

"And did you notice what Islia was wearing earlier?"

"Not really. I was too busy being terrified. A yellow dress, wasn't it?"

"Yes, a yellow dress. With a silver brooch in the shape of a cat pinned to it."

"Well," Teelan said, his voice showing interest in Drevin's reasoning. "I think you may need to have a conversation with Mistress Islia."

"We will," said Drevin, emphasising the word 'we.' "But not tonight. We will go back to the castle in the morning and see what she has to say about this."

"Hang on a minute," Teelan said. "Does that mean that she was with him in the barn? But that is his sister! Eeoow." His face scrunched up into a perfect display of disgust.

"Let's not make any judgements until we have spoken to her, shall we?" Drevin said wearily. He had heard of such things happening, of course, and sadly it was not even one of the most unusual things he had ever heard. "I'm off to bed and you should get some rest, too. It's been a long day. I will come by in the morning and we will go to the castle together."

"Yes dad." replied Teelan mockingly.

Drevin just gave him a look and headed wearily for the stairs.

# CHAPTER 7

# REVELATIONS

Teelan had almost finished preparing the body of the baron's son for his funeral when Drevin appeared in his basement. He had slept fitfully last night and had risen early to start his work. He had put all Ridozir's organs back in his body and replaced the rib he had removed. Then he had inserted a selection of fragrant herbs, mint, rosemary and sage, into his open chest to help prevent further decay and to combat the rotting odour.

Finally, he had sewn up all his wounds and used a roll of linen treated with wax and honey to wrap around his legs and abdomen. Now Ridozir was whole again and with his eyes closed looked almost peaceful, as if asleep, which he supposed he technically was.

"Are you ready to head to the castle?" Drevin asked, making his way over to him.

"Just a moment." Teelan replied, removing the last of the bowls and tools from the slab on which Ridozir lay.

"Wheew, you have patched him up nicely," said Drevin, admiring the tight, neat, yellow stitching that ran down the boy's chest.

Teelan waited for a crude or mocking comment to follow and felt an unexpected feeling of pleasure when it didn't.

"Thank you. Can you help me with the wrapping and then getting him dressed so he is presentable before he goes to meet his father for the last time?" He said, waving his arm at a bundle of rich clothes piled up on one of the wooden benches.

"Sure," said Drevin, again surprising Teelan with his sincerity. Together they finished wrapping his chest in the honey smelling linen, then wrestled the stiff body into the clothes, a fine white ruffled shirt, black trousers, a deep blue tunic and a long navy blue velvet cloak. Drevin tied up the black boots as Teelan brushed Ridozir's hair. They had carried out the task in a respectful silence which Teelan had once thought that Drevin was incapable of.

"Can you help me carry him into the storage room please?" he asked the big man, nodding his head towards a door against the far wall. Drevin nodded. Teelan opened the door then returned and grabbed hold of Ridozir's legs whilst Drevin took hold of his shoulders. They lifted him off the slab and carried him into the next room.

"Bloody hell, it's freezing in here." Drevin said as they entered the rectangular room. He noticed Drevin looking at the long, stone recesses in the walls on either side set at different heights, then his gaze settled on the old stone fireplace behind him. "Is that a great big block of ice?" he asked.

Teelan shifted his gaze towards the massive chunk of ice that sat ironically in the fireplace, performing the exact opposite task of its intended purpose. "Yes, it is," he said. "I need to keep this place as cold as possible to stop the bodies from decomposing any further and to stop them from smelling too bad."

"Well, you have succeeded on the first part anyway." Drevin said, wrinkling his nose. "How do you stand the stench?"

"Apparently I have a very poor sense of smell," Teelan said, shrugging. That was what he had always been told anyway and he assumed it was true, but he had no way of telling what a normal sense of smell was. "Over here," he said, gesturing to an empty alcove off to the right. They shuffled over and gently laid Ridozir in the six-foot gash in the wall. "This is where I store the bodies before they get collected for burial. The priests from the castle will be down later today to retrieve him."

"How on earth do you get those enormous ice blocks down those narrow stairs?" Drevin asked, moving over to look at it.

"I don't." Teelan said nonchalantly. "That's what big, beefy men like you are for. I just order them and let someone else worry about the delivery."

Teelan watched Drevin bend down to look at the floor of the fireplace. "There's a gutter on the floor here."

Teelan stepped over to him. "Yes, I got them to dig out some channels in the floor to drain the melted ice water away. It goes through all three rooms and then disperses under the grounds of the park outside."

"That's damn clever," said Drevin. Teelan was not sure what to say to that, so he remained silent. Drevin was obviously still in a good mood, and it was disconcerting him.

"Shall we go?" said Teelan.

"Lead the way." Drevin replied.

***

A short while later, they were standing in a luxurious room; the walls covered in fine silks of pinks and yellows, and an overabundance of soft furnishings. Teelan recognised the quality of the furniture and the decorations as befitting a noble. That, along with the small army of servants and maids that hovered inconspicuously around the edges of the room confirmed that this was indeed a room used by someone of authority.

The steward Wilburton, who escorted them here, was surprised that they wanted to speak to Mistress Islia, but he hadn't objected. He had been his usual flustered and sweaty self, his unwanted feline companion still following him around.

"Teelan." Drevin said quietly, "Look at the paintings." Teelan glanced over at him and almost laughed out loud at how out of place he looked here. His dishevelled hair and rumpled, stained brown jerkin over a mail shirt made him look like a vagabond knight down on his luck and come to beg a favour. The fading, yellowing bruises on his rough, square face only served to complete that picture. Teelan looked away before his humour showed on his face and located the pictures in question.

There were many paintings of various sizes in the spacious room, but he knew straight away which ones Drevin was referring to. Several of the paintings depicted cats of black, white and brown in artful poses, some lying on their sides playfully, whilst others gazed unnervingly straight out of the painting.

"I see them," said Teelan, equally quietly.

Just then a door at the far side of the room opened and in breezed Islia, only daughter of Baron Sutter.

"Gentlemen," she said, arranging herself delicately on a large stuffed couch. She was wearing a simple, yet elegant robe of pale blue with a golden trim at the sleeves and neckline. Her hair was braided into a long tail, and she wore a silver necklace, shaped like a dolphin with small sapphires for eyes, on her pale white skin. Behind her came the two young men in chequered blue and green tabards, following her like lost lambs, stopping behind her chair. Teelan noticed Drevin trying to hide a frown on seeing them.

"Please be seated," she said, gesturing to the many padded chairs, stools, cushions, and sofas that littered the room. Teelan perched himself on the edge of a small chair whilst Drevin slumped into a large, cushion laden chair. "These gentlemen are Evrin and Larin from the Barony of Paska in the Kingdom of Brakus." she continued, indicating the men behind her chair with a casual wave of her arm. "Now what can I do for you gentleman?"

"Mistress Islia," began Drevin with a slight bow, again surprising Teelan with his courteous manner. "Thank you for agreeing to speak to us. I am afraid, however that the matter we wish to speak to you about concerns your late brother Ridozir."

Teelan saw Islia stiffen in her seat, although admirably she managed to keep her face as still as marble.

"What is it you wish to ask?" she said tightly.

"When was the last time you saw Ridozir?" Drevin asked gently.

"The morning he disappeared," she replied too quickly. "I saw him leave the castle with those incompetent guards, and I never saw him again."

“I see,” said Drevin. “It is just that I found the barn where he was attacked, and we found some evidence that he was with a woman when he died. A woman with golden hair.” Drevin paused and for a moment a tense silence settled. Teelan noticed Evrin and Larin quickly glance at each other before looking at Islia.

“Well, what of it? It is no secret that Ridozir liked to sneak off and have his way with whoever was his flavour of the month. That hair probably belongs to some pretty fisher girl or a prostitute.” Her eyes flashed angrily like blue spears of lightning, and Teelan was glad that they were not directed at him.

“Maybe,” said Drevin, “but I also found this.” He casually pulled out the cat necklace from his pouch. It hung between his fingers, the amber eyes glowing from the reflected candlelight.

This time her face did move. Her lips trembled, she blinked rapidly and when she opened her eyes fully, moisture was gathering at their corners.

“Everyone leave, now!” she barked, waving her arm in the vague direction of the servants behind her. They all quickly scampered out of one of the many doors. “You two as well,” she said, noticing that the two men from Paska were still standing there. They left more reluctantly, casting backward glances as they headed out of the same door.

“That is mine,” she snapped. “Hand it over.”

Drevin leaned forwards with his arm extended and she reached out and snatched it from him. She gazed at it longingly for several uncomfortable seconds. Teelan watched as a single tear fell from each eye, leaving a trail through her powdered cheeks.

"This was the last thing that Ridozir brought for me," she breathed. Teelan squirmed in his seat and even Drevin looked slightly uncomfortable. She then stood and walked over to a small round table on which stood several bottles of coloured drinks and a variety of shaped glasses. She plucked up a bottle of pink wine and poured herself a large glass full, then returned to her chair, sitting with less grace this time, and taking a gulp of the wine. Teelan felt slightly offended that she didn't offer them a drink.

When she looked back at them, her eyes were dry and cunning. "You know that there are guards right outside my door. I could scream and accuse you of assaulting me, and they would throw you into the dungeons. It would be my word against yours and no-one would believe you," she said, looking at Drevin with disdain.

"Yes, you could do that," said Drevin amiably, relaxing back into his over-padded chair. However, Teelan could see his eyes flicking around the room, no doubt calculating potential escape routes. Teelan held his breath, his nerves heightened. Not again, Drevin. Don't put me through this again!

"Fine." Islia said after a moment's pause. "What does it matter now, anyway? Yes, I was with Ridozir in that barn."

Teelan let out his pent up breath in a big puff then coughed to cover it up, holding his hand in front of his mouth.

"And what were you doing there?" asked Drevin, ignoring Teelan's outburst.

"That is none of your business," she retorted. "Oh wait, I see. I see where your grubby little mind is going with this. What did you think we were up in the hayloft, rutting like a pair of pig farmers on their first date? How dare you?" Teelan had the good grace to feel a blush blooming on his cheeks at her coarse language and imagery. Drevin, he could see, did not.

"I have heard of it happening in some circumstances." Drevin replied calmly.

"Well, not in this case. We were kindred spirits. There was no need to have physical contact to be intimate. We felt the same way, thought the same things, had the same dreams and ambitions. We would just lay next to each other and talk, that is all!"

"Why meet in a decrepit old barn, across the other side of the city then, and not just talk here in the castle?" Drevin pressed, leaning forward.

"Because if you haven't noticed, I am always surrounded by people here. Maids, servants, guards, sycophantic minor lordlings and common petitioners hound my movements. Not to mention that overwrought, overattentive, overpaid so-called steward. I don't get any privacy here and even when I am alone, there is always going to be someone with an ear to the door. So, I used to get my maid to cover for me, saying I was feeling unwell, then don a horrible old tatty cloak and sneak out."

"And what were these ambitions you and Ridozir shared?"

"My, aren't you a nosy one?" Her eyes narrowed in irritation, and Teelan was amazed at how much emotion she displayed with just her eyes.

Drevin just shrugged at her sharp tone. "The more I know about him the easier it will be to find out who killed him."

"Well, if you must know, we had a grand plan. When Ridozir became baron, we were going to be married and I would rule at his side as an equal partner, as Baroness Islia Sutter. We had great ideas for the future of the barony to grow and prosper, to become the greatest city in Eltor, equal to the capital, Torgor. After a few years of success, we were going to approach King Mabdoris and asked to be recognised as the Capital of the North." Islia said wistfully, her eyes shining. She took another drink from her glass.

"Ambitious indeed." whistled Drevin. "Did anyone else know about the two of you and your plans? What about your father? What would he have made of it?"

"Huh," Islia huffed. "My father probably wouldn't have even noticed. He has spent the last few years wallowing in self-pity and grief for my dearly departed mother. He has let his fat pig of a brother take over the running of the barony whilst he skulks around his dark, empty rooms. Who knows, the shock of Ridozir and I getting married might have been enough to make him actually speak to me again. As for who else knew about us, that would be no-one. After all, it is not the sort of thing that one advertises in advance."

Teelan watched Drevin mulling this over, his hand stroking his stubbled chin, chewing at his lip. "I take it you are not fond of Serzin, then?" He asked, changing the focus of the questioning.

"Hah," Islia barked a short laugh, "Dear uncle Serzin may be great at throwing a party or hosting guests, but ruling a castle, let alone a whole barony, is well beyond him. He is content to sit on his corpulent arse and let things carry on the way they always have."

Teelan was shocked by her manners and language and wriggled in his chair. It seemed that she was not the prim, noble lady that everyone made her out to be. As if reading his mind she turned to him.

"You, boy, are you mute? Do you find my manner offensive? Am I not behaving as a lady should? Well, I have found that being a lady only gets you so far and sometimes you just have to act like a man to get what you want." She said, taking another big gulp of her wine as if to demonstrate the point.

Teelan, startled at her attention, stammered, "No my lady, of course not my lady, erm no my lady?" trying to understand and answer all of her questions, without offending her. Islia just laughed at him, then turned back to Drevin.

"So what happened that day in the barn, Islia?" Drevin asked intensely.

Islia's face lost its forced humour instantly and instead pain and grief took its place. "We were up in the hayloft, talking as usual," she said, catching Drevin's eye meaningfully. "Then suddenly we heard a noise outside, people talking and then someone was trying to open the doors. Ridozir said he would go down and see off whoever was disturbing us. I begged him to stay with me, but he was stubborn and wanted to prove himself capable of defending me. By the time he got to the ground floor, the door burst open, and two men dashed in."

"What did they look like?"

"It was hard to tell. I was lying down and could only see through a gap in the wooden railings. They looked short and thin, with long, greasy hair. They were wearing grubby cloaks. One of them grabbed Ridozir by the arms before he could get to his dagger, and the other pulled a sword from his belt." Islia was breathing hard now, the words trembling.

"What kind of sword was it?" Drevin asked.

"I don't know. What does it matter?" She looked at Drevin, who just stared back at her. "It wasn't a proper sword like nobles have. It was much shorter and looked darker."

"That's good Islia. What happened next?" Teelan found himself edging forward in his seat, caught up in the tension of her retelling.

"The man holding his arms shouted, 'This is what you get for not paying your debts to the Hammer.' Then the other one.." she broke off with a sob and held her face in her hands, weeping.

After a few moments, Drevin spoke softly, "What happened next Islia?"

She looked up at him, tears streaming down her face, which had become a mess of wet tracks, revealing her natural pinkish flesh colour where the white powder had washed away. "The other one stabbed him in the stomach shouting 'For the Hammer'. Ridozir sagged in the first man's arms whilst the one with the sword stabbed him again and again. Then they swapped over, and the first man used his sword to stab him a few more times.

Eventually, they let Ridozir fall to the ground. Then one of them said that they had better get the cart and they both left." She paused for a moment, catching her breath. The words had spilled out of her quickly, tonelessly, as if she wanted to be rid of them.

"I ran down the ladder to him and knelt beside him. There was so much blood. I lifted his head and cried out his name, but his eyes were closed and he only gurgled in response. Then he sighed deeply and stopped breathing. I sat with him for a few minutes crying over his body, then I heard the noise of a cart pulling up outside. I panicked and ran out of the back door." Islia stopped talking and looked at Drevin as if daring him to doubt her story, the glass forgotten in her hand.

"Why didn't you go to the guards?" he asked quietly instead.

"As I said I was panicking. I knew Ridozir was dead, and I didn't want anyone to know that I had been with him there. I didn't want people to suspect me like you did. And they would have. So, I ran to the nearest market, bought a new cloak and disposed of my blood stained one, then returned to the castle."

"And you told no one about this?"

"No, of course not. What could I say to explain why I was there?"

"Didn't anyone notice you were upset?"

"Of course they did. My maids asked me what was wrong, but I just told them I had been to see my paramour in the Upper District, and he had rejected me and didn't want to see me anymore."

"I see," said Drevin, and Teelan could see he was considering her words.

"Now I am tired, and I have told you everything. Go find these men, Master Drevin, and make them pay." She said, slumping back on her sofa and draining the last of the wine. "Guards!" she called out suddenly.

Teelan jumped, thinking that she had changed her mind and meant to send them to the dungeons after all. His heart hammered in his chest.

The door opened and a standard issue guard entered, armour gleaming. "Yes, mistress?" he asked, bowing and not displaying any emotion at her mess of a face.

"Please escort these men out for me, would you? And tell everyone that I am not to be disturbed as I shall be resting."

"Of course, mistress," he replied. "This way gentlemen."

Teelan and Drevin both stood. "Thank you for your time, Mistress Islia," said Drevin with a deep bow.

"Yes, good day to you, mistress." Teelan squeaked. Hurrying out of the door after the departing guard and Drevin.

Once out in the long corridor, Drevin turned to Teelan and murmured, "Well that was very interesting, wasn't it?"

"Quite." said Teelan, not sure what to make of all that he had heard. He needed time to think it through and to discuss it properly with Drevin, but this was not the place for it. Drevin, for once, seemed to be of the same opinion and didn't speak again.

They reached the spacious dining hall with its long, dark tables, rows of chairs, and several cavernous fireplaces. Some of the higher-ranking staff were eating an early lunch off copper plates with breads and meats and bowls of fruits on the tables. As they passed through, they heard a voice coming from a side corridor.

"Master Drevin, please wait." From out of the corridor bustled the steward, Wilburton, carrying several sheets of parchments in his arms. His dark blue robe had stains of ink, and his chain of office weighed heavily on his thin neck. He hurried over to them. "Master Serzin would like to see you. This way please," he said, passing by a table and snatching up an apple. Drevin gave Teelan a quizzical look and they both followed the bustling steward, who was nibbling at the apple.

He soon led them into the west part of the castle and up to a heavy door with two guards standing outside it. He walked past the guards and opened the door calling in, "Masters Drevin and Teelan to see you my lord," with a deep bow. Then he stepped aside and ushered them into the room.

Teelan followed Drevin in and heard the door shut behind him. He looked around at a room not dissimilar in size to Islia's, but unlike it in every other way. Where her room had been full of pale silks, fluffiness and delicate femininity, Serzin's was a picture of manliness. Rich red and blue tapestries, heavy dark tables and chairs, a sturdy, cluttered desk, oversized candelabras shaped like exotic animals, and many paintings of hunting scenes clearly depicted this as a man's room.

The man himself was standing in front of a large chair, which had enough padded leather to outfit several soldiers. A fine white silk shirt stretched tight over his broad chest and broader stomach. Over that, he wore a long, cobalt blue velvet robe, which he belted at the waist with a strap of black leather featuring an ornate silver belt buckle. "Ah, welcome gentlemen," he gushed. "Please do take a seat." he waved to the chairs arranged opposite him.

Teelan waited until Serzin had sat heavily in his chair before he sat as proprietary demanded. Drevin, he noticed, did not and sat down with an uncultured groan. Once seated, Teelan noticed the round-faced young boy who he had seen before sitting on a large cushion rolling two marbles between his fingers and gazing at them intently.

"Would you like some wine?" Serzin asked, gesturing to the substantial table of drinks bottles and glasses of all shapes and sizes. A servant who stood statue-like next to it almost blended into the background with his innocuousness.

"Don't mind if I do," said Drevin eagerly. Serzin looked at Teelan questioningly.

"Uh, do you have any fresh milk please, my lord?" he asked quietly. He could feel Drevin's mirth without looking at him. Great, I am going to get ridiculed for this later.

"Of course. See to it please Milton." he said, waving to the servant. "Now, how are you finding everything? Do you have need of anything?"

"No, thank you my lord. We have what we need." Drevin replied graciously.

The servant glided over and handed Serzin a silver goblet engraved with a boar with enormous tusks on it. He then handed Drevin an elegant glass filled with a deep red wine and finally gave Teelan a small glass of milk. Teelan could feel Drevin's grin again.

"You may leave us now, Milton." Serzin said and the servant swiftly disappeared silently through one of the far doors.

"Now tell me how is your investigation going?" Serzin asked, taking a large swallow of his wine.

Drevin gave a pointed look at the young boy, then back to the baron's brother.

"Oh, don't worry about young Weslin there. He won't understand what we are saying. My son had an accident about three years ago and took a hefty blow to the head. He hasn't been the same since. He doesn't talk anymore and can only play with his old nursery toys for a while before he loses interest. Most of the time, he just stares at nothing in particular. The physicians say that something got knocked loose in his head and they don't know what is going on in there, but that is just the way he is now. However, he seems content enough and doesn't want for anything."

Teelan looked at the boy curiously. He had heard of people with head injuries losing their memories or being forgetful, or even acting differently before, but never in such a severe case as this. He would like to get inside that boy's head and examine his brain.

"I am sorry to hear that, my lord," Drevin replied, interrupting his thoughts. "As to our investigation it is progressing well. If I may ask, does the name 'The Hammer' mean anything to you?"

"Hmm, no I can't say that it does." Serzin said, taking another gulp, "Is it important?"

"Maybe," Drevin hedged, taking a sip of his wine. "Hmm, Adony Red. Very nice. Would you happen to know if Ridozir had any debts, my lord, maybe from gambling?"

"I wouldn't know about that. You see Esklin holds the keys to the treasury and keeps a track of everyone's finances. I am afraid that I am not very good with numbers."

Teelan could well believe that. Even though nobles received an education many found number work difficult and boring.

"Of course, no matter."

"Tell me," Serzin said leaning forward, looking eager to change the direction of the conversation, "How was Islia when you spoke to her?"

"Upset, as is to be expected. Were you aware of how close she was to her brother?" Drevin asked, taking another slug of wine.

No, Drevin don't elucidate. He surely doesn't need to know about that!

"Well, I knew they got on well. They used to spend a fair bit of time together. More so in the last few years as their father withdrew further. Why?"

Drevin was watching Serzin closely as he casually said, "Well, she was with Ridozir when he was attacked."

You had to go and tell him, didn't you? I hope he is a pragmatic man for our sake.

"What! What do you mean she was with him when he was attacked? Outside the castle? What were they doing together?"

"Making plans apparently." Drevin said casually.

Teelan wondered how much Drevin would reveal and felt sick inside as he realised that he already knew the answer to that. It occurred to him then that Drevin was enjoying this, having knowledge and power over those in charge.

"What sort of plans? Are you suggesting something inappropriate was going on?" Serzin's round face was colouring and not just from the wine. Teelan sipped his milk and tried to look unobtrusive.

"It depends on your interpretation of inappropriate, I suppose. They were planning to get married."

Serzin's reaction was immediate. He spluttered out the wine he was drinking, spattering it in fat red blobs on his tunic and proceeded to choke and cough for several seconds. When he regained control of himself, he rose and walked over to the drinks table, pouring himself more wine. "What! I did not know. Are you sure? You must let no one else know about this. They would mock us right across the kingdom." Serzin breathed, slumping back in his chair and taking a long swallow from his refilled goblet.

Teelan tried to hide in his chair, his face blushing from embarrassment at Drevin's bluntness with people who could order their demise at any second.

"Do you think anyone else knew about this? What about the baron?" Drevin asked, not responding to Serzin's reaction.

"No. Surely not. I mean, I don't think so."

"What would he make of it?"

"He wouldn't allow such a thing to happen. In fact, he would do anything he could to prevent it."

Teelan could definitely believe that. Baron Sutter was not a stable man to begin with. If he were to hear about this, Teelan wouldn't like to think about how it would affect him and what lengths he would go to in order to stop it.

"Hmm, why would Ridozir go along with this plan? Surely he could have had his pick of eligible noblewoman?" Drevin asked, again switching tact.

"Ridozir is…was a very headstrong young man and was not one to follow the rules. He was stubborn and had his own ideas about how things should work and how he wanted to run the barony. Ever since his mother died and my brother stopped being a father, he spent more and more time with Islia."

"So, I take it you didn't get on with him?" Drevin asked intently.

"Nobody got on with Ridozir, really. He was more tolerated and indulged than he was anyone's friend or confidante. His vanity and pettiness were legendary and he treated the servants harshly. He needed a firm hand to show him how to be a fair ruler. I tried my best, but he wouldn't listen to me. I think he resented me and my family for some reason."

"So, you won't be shedding any tears at his funeral, then?" Drevin said.

Teelan recoiled slightly at Drevin's words and the naked implication in them. That's it, you have gone and got us a residence in the dungeons now.

"I see what you are getting at Drevin." Serzin said, remarkably less angry but more warily. "Will I miss Ridozir? No. Do I think he would have made a good baron? Absolutely not. Did I want him dead? No! I still love my brother Drevin and losing his son as well as his wife has been devastating for him." Serzin sighed deeply and took another drink. "Do you know the story of how my brother's wife died?" he asked.

"No."

"It was at a time when Zandir was under pressure from the king in Eltor to send more funds to the capital. So Zandir, not thinking about the common people, raised the taxes across the barony to increase his income. However, as if often the way, the poorer people ended up worse off than those with money to spare.

"So, there were grumblings and complaints from the peasants and the occasional protest in the street. His wife Mielisa, being a kind-hearted soul, used to listen to the petitioners and do everything she could to make their lives better. She used to visit the markets and docks, speak to the people and find out what she could do to help. Well, it was on one such visit that a group of disgruntled workers approached her, protesting about the high taxes. Her guards tried to hold them back, but one young man squeezed through them and stabbed her with a dagger. The guards chased him and one of them eventually caught and slew him, but it was too late. The lady Mielisa died in the street.

"When Zandir was told, he cried all night and was inconsolable. She was the love and light of his life. One of the young guards gave him the black dagger that the killer used. But he still blamed all of them and had them thrown into the dungeons. That was the day his 'black moods' started. He then, ahem, questioned them for days afterwards, spending long hours in the dungeons. The young guard was the only one who survived.

"Zandir still carries the dagger that killed his wife to this day. I have tried to tell him to get rid of it, that it is not healthy to keep it, but he refuses, saying it is the last piece of his wife he has left. Since then, he withdrew and became lost in grief. At first, he ignored his children, then his duties. A few years ago, he asked me to take over the running of the barony, which I reluctantly agreed to do, thinking that if he didn't have any responsibilities to worry about for a while, he may snap out of it. Instead, he seems to have got worse.

"I do not enjoy ruling Drevin; it is a lot of bureaucracy, laws, regulations, customs and traditions. Endless hours of sitting still listening to people wittering on and then being asked to make a judgement or give advice, when most of the time I hadn't understood half of what has been said. Honestly, I much preferred just being the genial host for visiting worthies and throwing the odd banquet. I have my wife, my son and my two little girls and I was content with that." With that, he drained the last of his wine and sank further into his chair.

Teelan heard the passion in Serzin's voice and his grief and worry for his brother. Serzin, who was perhaps the most powerful man in the barony right now, just looked like a tired and sad middle-aged man. He noticed the lines on his forehead and grey hairs just peeping out on the sides of his head and he suspected they hadn't been there just a couple of years ago.

"Leave me now and go about your business. Milton!" he called out. The servant with the instantly forgettable face appeared through a door.

"Yes, my lord?"

"See these gentlemen out, would you?"

"Of course, my lord. This way gentlemen."

Teelan put his glass of mostly undrunk milk on a small table and stood. Drevin gulped down the last of his wine and followed suit.

"Oh, and Drevin," called Serzin, just as they were about to leave, "the baron needs no more complications right now. Just find out who actually killed Ridozir and either bring him here or deal with him yourself. My brother doesn't need to know all the gory details."

"I will do my best, my lord," said Drevin, bowing, then retreating from the room.

"Thank you, my lord," said Teelan, bowing, then hastening after Drevin.

He walked behind Drevin and the servant as they made their way back out of the castle. They both remained silent and Teelan thought he could hear Drevin's brain working as he looked like a picture of a man in contemplation. Teelan himself was also thinking through all that he had heard and trying to work out which aspects to focus on first. As usual, just as he was organising his mind and coming to some initial conclusions, Drevin interrupted him.

"Well, well, well, that was most interesting, I must say." He said as they were crossing the bridge over the north river, heading back into the city.

"Indeed," replied Teelan, his thoughts still awhirl.

"Where to start, eh?" Drevin said as if reading his mind. "Who would have thought that Islia was so ambitious for power that she would contemplate inter-family marriage?"

"I will say it again, Eeow." replied Teelan, scrunching up his nose. "What was she thinking? It was madness. What were they going to do when it was time to produce an heir? No, wait, don't answer that," he said, not wanting to know the answer.

"It happens, you know. Some families want to remain in power at all costs, and others do it to keep their bloodlines pure. Anyway, it tells us one important thing." Drevin paused and looked at Teelan as if waiting for him to ask what. He didn't oblige. "It means that she had nothing to do with his death."

"I hate to say this, but I agree with you," said Teelan, noting Drevin's surprised eyebrow. "What! As far as I can see, she had nothing to gain and everything to lose from his death."

"So, who benefits from his death?" asked Drevin.

They entered the north gates of the city under the watchful eyes of the guards.

"Serzin?" Teelan asked, checking that he was out of earshot of any guards.

"It's true that he will stay in charge for longer now until young Greffin comes of age in a few years' time. But he didn't seem to be enjoying it, did he? He sounded genuine about the burdens of responsibility, and it seems like it is ill suited to a man like him."

"Greffin then?" said Teelan. "With his big brother out of the way, he is next in succession to be baron." They had turned onto the wide outer road and were heading back towards the Upper District.

"Unlikely. By all accounts, Greffin is a quiet lad who spends most of his time with his head in a book and doing his studies. He mostly keeps to himself and doesn't like crowds or any attention. I can't see him murdering his brother."

"He sounds like a sensible lad."

"Right, let's take stock." Drevin said, all business now. "Ridozir was due to reach manhood at the end of Wilting, in just a few weeks time, then Zandir was going to appoint him as baron and officially step down. Maybe somebody didn't want that to happen. Islia is ambitious, but as you said, her best shot at power was with Ridozir.

"Serzin will now stay in charge but didn't seem too pleased by the situation. Greffin doesn't seem the type to kill his brother. The steward is anxious enough without plotting murder and the guard captain seems solid. Then again, it sounds like Ridozir was an A grade arsehole, so there would be no shortage of people with grudges against him, so maybe his ascension has nothing to do with it."

"How do you know so much about these people?" Teelan asked curiously. He was intrigued by how Drevin could learn and retain such information.

"How come you don't know this stuff?" Drevin retorted. "How long have you worked for the baron?"

"One year." Teelan muttered. They were walking through the Church District now with the churches of the five gods of the Union off to their right. The churches were all very different in appearance from the brown curved dome of Viterlea's, to the black stone of Necomthia's and the pure white marble inlaid with gems of Corpinious. Teelan noticed that the church to Sapious stood apart from the others and was much humbler than its counterparts. Priests of all the gods stood in the courtyard in their grey robes, trying to entice in anyone who looked in need of spiritual help, or who looked like they had a few coins in their purses.

"And you still know nothing about the people who run the city or what goes on in the castle? How is that possible?"

"Because, like young Greffin, I am a sensible lad," Teelan replied with a smirk.

Drevin gave him a look as if to say, very funny. "I know these things because I talk to people and listen to what they have to say. I keep my ear to the ground. The only thing that is bugging me is those men from Paska who are hanging around Islia. What are they after?"

"Oh, isn't it obvious, Drevin?" Teelan replied smugly. "They are here to arrange her marriage to the baron of Paska's eldest son. They are hoping that she will agree to the proposal this year in preparation for when the son turns eighteen next year."

"How do you know that?" Drevin asked, startled.

"Oh, you know me. I like to keep my ear to the ground." Teelan mocked, smiling. However, the effect was ruined when an inconsiderate merchant with a cart piled high with goods rolled down the street straight towards him, forcing him to quickly jump aside.

"Hmm, with that hair I am amazed that you can hear anything." Drevin replied grumpily, rejoining him as the cart trundled past. "Maybe it was those men who got rid of Ridozir." Drevin said, smiling at his choice of words. "Perhaps they heard about Islia's plans and decided to do away with the competition. Yes, that could be it."

"It's possible I suppose, but perilous on their part. Are you sure it isn't just you wanting to lay the blame on Paska's doorstep? What is your problem with them? I have noticed you trying to avoid their attention and the faces that you make when someone mentions them."

"It's nothing that concerns you." Drevin replied hastily. "Anyway, perhaps it was as Islia said and is about gambling debts, but that seems too simple for me."

Teelan refrained himself with difficulty from making a comment about simple plans and simple men. "Drevin, where exactly are we going?" Teelan asked as they continued heading south, towards the smoke and noise of the Foundry District.

"We are going to find 'The Hammer'. Which means that we are going to have to visit a number of shady taverns."

"Oh, great," said Teelan sarcastically.

"Don't worry," said Drevin, a slow smile creeping on his face. "I will try to find us taverns with some cows in their backyard for you."

Teelan sighed.

# CHAPTER 8

# A GAME OF CHANCE

The tavern smelled like every other tavern. The odours of cheap roasting meat, unwashed men, weak beer, stale piss, and the lingering, itchy smell of dry stone dust. Okay, so maybe that last one wasn't every tavern, but that is the price you pay for frequenting one of the lowest dives in the Stone District you can find. A fine and sometimes not so fine layer of grey dust covered every surface.

Cali looked around the table once more, at the men sitting around it, noting their expressions ranging from fear, hope, worry, and greed. They all had their eyes glued to the table, in particular at the two small, white bone cubes that sat there. The only other item of interest on the table was a not insignificant pile of copper bits.

Cali brushed back a long strand of her curly red hair behind her ear then leaned back nonchalantly, knowing that it would draw the eye of every man there to her chest, her green bodice laced tight over her white chemise, hoping to distract them from the remaining die in her left hand.

After a few seconds, she abruptly leant forward and threw the die onto the scarred, round tabletop. It bounced and rolled in a circular motion, seeming to dance around the table and ending up almost back in front of her. As it was about to come to a stop Cali twitched a finger at it, releasing some of her power. The die balanced on one corner for just a fraction of a second longer than natural, then tipped over to reveal six glorious circles facing up. It made for a beautiful sight, especially when matched with the other two dice that also displayed the same six coloured swirls.

Cali quickly moved to sweep the pile of coins from the middle of the table towards her with her right arm, while she hid her slightly trembling left hand under the table. "Sorry fellows," she said with a sly smile. "Looks like Lucianus is on my side tonight." She rarely liked to gamble in places close to home, so she knew she was sailing close to the wind, but there had been no work at the docks for days so she was scraping the bottom of the barrel. Also, she had been fleecing the patrons of the dockside taverns for a while now, so she thought it was time to give them a wide berth and try her luck elsewhere.

"I think that you have had too much luck," growled one man, a burly flat-faced fellow with a nose like a squashed parsnip. He placed his meaty arm on top of hers to prevent her from taking the pot of coins.

"Yeah," whined another one of the losers, his thin, sour face looking more sour than usual. "I think you have been cheating."

"Come off it," Cali laughed, "This was all above board. Just because you got beaten by a girl doesn't mean it wasn't fair. How could I possibly cheat at dice? You watched me roll them and I never touched them afterwards." Indeed, how could they know exactly how I cheated? Unless they were watching very carefully and knew something about Frags, that is.

"Maybe someone rigged the dice," said a third man with hair the colour and consistency of dry straw and a creased face. "I have heard that some people cut the dice in a certain way so that they always roll a six."

"Well, if that was the case you would have all rolled sixes as well, wouldn't you?" Cali challenged. "And you didn't, did you? Now stop being a bunch of stringy dick rats and give me my winnings."

The last man around the table had picked up the dice and was scrutinising them, turning them around in his long fingers. He had a nose to match his fingers and square, brown teeth that made him look like an old nag. "The dice look fine to me. Although I do agree with my robust companion that your luck has been…exceptionally lucky."

"Isn't that what luck is?" Cali asked testily, getting annoyed by these idiots and their attitudes. Some men just couldn't stand to lose to a woman, and it wouldn't matter to them even if she had played fair. This was going to be touch and go. She tried to remove her arm from underneath the grip of parsnip-nose, but he held it firm. "Let go of my arm," she spoke more calmly than she felt.

"No, I don't think I will," he replied in a slow voice. "In fact, I think we will divide up these coins between us lads and have another round of drinks, while you piss off!" he laughed.

"Now wait a minute." Cali said, feeling her anger rising and yanking her arm out from his grasp, albeit with no coins. “If you think I am just going to walk out of here without my money then you are more than three sheets to the wind.” She stood up and slung her bag over one shoulder and again reached for the coins, plucking a few from the pile.

“I didn’t say you would walk out. Stop her lads!” yelled the big man, standing up. His companions also got to their feet and started moving around the table towards her.

Cali panicked. Deepshit! What a foul up. She knew she shouldn’t have come here, especially in the middle of the day. There were not enough people in the tavern to prevent a mismatched bar fight. In fact, the few people she saw were watching with vague interest on their faces, as if they were looking for a bit of entertainment to brighten up their day.

Cali’s right hand strayed towards one of the daggers at her belt, but she restrained from drawing it yet. Don’t want things to get bloody. The four men closed on her and two of them grabbed her arms and started shaking her.

“Give those coins back.” Sour face said.

“Drop them or I drop you.” growled parsnip-nose.

“Ah, there you are!” a new gruff voice sounded directly behind her. “I have been looking for you everywhere. Your mother is waiting for you.” A thick arm with leather bracers wrapped itself around her shoulders and pulled her away from the angry men. Cali looked around at the owner of the arm and saw a middle-aged man in a rumpled leather jerkin and mail.

His short brown hair was scruffy and his bruised, stubbled face had a small scar running under his left eye and across his nose. A long sword poked up over his shoulder and a short sword and dagger hung at his belt. "Gentlemen, please forgive us. I am sure that there has just been a misunderstanding. My daughter here tends to forget her manners when out in public. Return the money to the nice men dear, then we can go home."

"Who, what? Screw that," Cali had no clue who this man was or what was going on.

"Now don't be stubborn," the man said again pointedly, eyeing the seething men behind her. "Give the money back."

Cali finally caught on that the man was trying to help get her out of this situation, which only served to make her even angrier. She did not need anyone's help, particularly a man's. However, she was now over a barrel, trapped between the five men and didn't see any easy way out. Unless…

"Fine," she grated. She slowly raised her hand holding the coins then threw them as hard as she could at parsnip-nose and straw-hair, who were off to her left. The coins hit them and they both cried out in pain, clutching their faces. Then she stamped her right foot down hard on the boot of the man behind her, hearing a satisfying yell from him as his arm released her shoulder.

Before the others could react, she grabbed hold of sour-face, and with a twist of her hips and an upward push of her arms, tossed him onto the table. His brief cry of alarm was almost drowned out by the thud of the impact and the clattering of the coins scattering across the table and tinkling onto the floor. Horse-face just stared at her in shock. Cali smiled at him, then turned and ran for the door.

She made it outside and took a few steps into the narrow alley before three of the men came tumbling out of the door after her. She turned and grinned cheekily at them, then prepared to sprint away, knowing that they would never catch her. Unfortunately, just as she started running, horse-face appeared at the other end of the alley, having left through the back door of the tavern and cutting through a side alley to block her off. Son of a bitch!

She ground to a halt. The distraction cost her as sour-face crashed into her, slamming her into the wall, her breath knocked out of her lungs. Gasping, she managed to bring her knee up into his balls and watched him sink to the floor groaning. That will give a few prostitutes some respite for a while.

As she was just getting her breathing back under control, straw-hair threw a punch into her stomach, starting the whole painful process again. She doubled over and almost threw up on his ragged brown boots. Parsnip-face then pushed her shoulder back against the wall, forcing her upright and crushing her against the wall. His hulking face filled her vision, his breath stinking of onions. Despite her situation, and it was bad, she was still pleased to see several small red welts on his face from where her coins had hit him.

"You made us look stupid. Maybe you should be nice to us now to make up for it hey?" he said, running one of his pudgy, dirty fingers down her cheek. Cali was trying to breathe normally but they were both pressing in close to her so she couldn't repeat her earlier trick.

"Hey! Leave her alone," a voice shouted from the door to the tavern. As one they all turned their heads. Cali saw the man who had pretended to be her father coming towards them, his scarred hands clenched into fists. Behind him a young, scared looking priest with long hair as white as his robe followed nervously.

"Stay out of this. It has nothing to do with you," yellow hair turned, releasing her and walking to face the newcomer.

"I'm afraid I can't do that," replied the fighter, as Cali could clearly see that he knew how to handle himself, judging by the way he walked and the fading bruises on his face. As the two men closed on each other with potential violence simmering in the air, the finger that had run down her face was now an entire hand running down her body and groping obscenely. Cali squirmed and decided enough was enough. She lifted her hand and released a small amount of her power. A blast of air shot from her outstretched hand and pushed the brute off her, far enough away that he stumbled into his friend, knocking them both off balance.

She watched for a moment as her saviour sprang forward and landed a heavy punch on the man with the crinkled face, which didn't improve its appearance. Then he ducked under the retort, which was a wild swing, and crunched his other fist into yellow-hair's stomach. The gambler went down on one knee, but his big companion crashed into her 'father' and bore them both to the opposite wall with a thud. Not wanting to hang around and see who came out on top, she turned and ran at the man approaching from the other end of the alleyway.

After being startled for a second, he ran towards her and threw a clumsy, predictable punch at her face. Cali easily ducked under it and twisted her body under his arm as she stepped behind him, delivering a sharp blow to his kidney as she passed. Once behind him she kicked him hard in the back of the knee, forcing him to kneel on the cobbles. She then aimed a two-fisted thump at his neck but he rolled away and jumped back to his feet, facing her quicker than she thought.

She glanced over his shoulder and saw the two gamblers both on their feet, now trying to take down the older man from either side. However, he was ready for them and rushed the bigger man, grabbing his arm and head-butting him, busting open his already squashed nose, then hurling him into his companion.

Horse-face then took up her attention as he came at her again, this time more cautiously. He feinted a punch to her head again but pulled back at the last second and jabbed it into her side. Cali grunted as the blow sent a shiver of pain through her. She kicked out at him, trying to connect with his vitals, but he raised his leg to block, and she only glanced a blow off his thigh.

He stepped forward, quickly aiming punches with both fists at her head and stomach simultaneously. Cali blocked the head shot with her arm and twisted her body nimbly to avoid most of the low blow, although it grazed her already bruised ribs. She dived forwards, sliding to her knees, feeling the skin scraping off them and launched three fast punches into his stomach, hoping to put him down. He gasped at the pain and bent over, but it wasn't enough.

He grabbed hold of her hair and savagely pulled her to her feet. Cali screamed at the pain shooting through her head. Instinctively, she bent down and grabbed his arm holding her hair with both her hands, one at his wrist and the other at his elbow, locking it tight. Then she jumped forward and twisted her body around fully in the air, doing a graceful spin and landing back on her feet. She felt an excruciating tug as some of her hair was ripped out, but she also heard a most satisfying loud crack, which echoed down the alleyway.

She screamed again at the pain from her head, but another high-pitched wailing scream overrode hers. The man in front of her was clutching his now useless arm, which hung limply and much lower from his dislocated shoulder. Halfway down his lower arm a glistening white bone covered in blood and sinews was visibly sticking up at an angle, a fat red rain dripping out of the opening. He staggered away from her in shock and stumbled off back the way he had come, crying for help.

Cali straightened up and rubbed at her sore head. She looked back up the alley to see the two men who had caught her were now both lying in the street, groaning, the cobbles red around them. The man who seemed desperate to help approached her, walking carefully, a fresh cut on his forehead dripping blood down his face. The young priest followed him, keeping his distance from her.

"We need to talk," said the man without preamble.

"Why? What do you want me to say? Thank you for saving me? You are my hero? How could I ever survive without you?" Cali replied sarcastically. She was still cross about the whole situation and having to need someone's help, but she was not sure if she was just mad at him or herself or both of them. Probably both. "I didn't need saving, thank you very much. I could have handled those bloody rats." She brushed the curly hair out of her face again.

"Yeah, it looked like it. Anyway, that is not what we need to talk about. I saw what you did in the tavern and out here."

Cali froze. Shit in a barrel! He couldn't have noticed her using her power, could he? She was so careful with it and only used small amounts so nobody would know. She knew what would happen to her if anyone important found out that she was a Frag. Attempting to conceal its shakiness, she clutched her still trembling arm to her side. "I don't know what you are talking about. If you mean my skill with dice and my fighting abilities then what of it?"

"I don't mean that. You know exactly what I mean. You are playing with fire. It is dangerous for someone like you to use your gifts like that."

"You are not making any sense," Bollocks! He knows! Time to cut and run. "Well, I need to shake a leg so I will be off now. Thank you for your assistance, kind sir," she said mockingly, then turned away from him.

Suddenly, he grabbed hold of her and pushed her against the wall, putting his weight on her. Not this again!

"Get off me!" she shouted, wriggling to get free. So much for a hero. Probably wants to claim his reward. Typical man!

"Drevin, what on earth are you doing? Have you gone mad?" the priest boy shouted from behind him in a shrieky voice.

"Stay out of this Teelan. You don't know what is going on. I am just trying to help you," this Drevin said, turning back to her.

"Looks like it. Do you want a feel as well, like him?" she said, nodding to the still groaning man with the busted face.

"What, no!" he exclaimed, sounding horrified.

Just then he swayed slightly and lost his balance, releasing his grip on her and holding his head. Cali took her chance and shoved him off making him stumble and made to run away. However, he recovered quickly and reached out a long arm, a meaty hand grabbing her wrist. Before she could twist away, his other arm seized her other wrist, and he held her fast at arm's length. She looked down at her trapped arms helplessly.

In the struggle, she noticed that the bracer on his right wrist had slid up his arm and his long shirt had become rucked up. On this exposed wrist she spotted a tattoo in black ink of two cupped hands with an eye in between them. An icy feeling of dread crept over her and her whole body went rigid. She could feel the blood draining from her usually rosy cheeks and her still aching stomach started churning. That is the symbol of the Gatherers. They have found me! How! Panic threatened to overwhelm her and the man holding her obviously knew something was wrong.

"What's wrong?" he said. Thought so.

"Y,Y,You're a Gatherer." it was all she could sputter out.

"What! No. Shit." he said in quick succession, glancing down at the betraying mark. "Wait, it's not what you think. I am an ex-Gatherer. I don't do that anymore. That's why I want to help you." he carried on talking but Cali stopped listening. Her thoughts were spiralling out of control, her worst fears realised, her hopes, dreams and ambitions of a normal life shattered. After what felt like a lifetime one word became the dominant one and quieted all others. Run, run, run!

Cali felt her hands lifting of their own accord, her wrists still in his bruising grip, her fingers spreading wide. She felt the power building in her, a swirling vortex in her mind gaining substance and momentum. This time she held nothing back, letting all of it coalesce before releasing it with a concussive blast of air.

The effect was instantaneous. One moment the man was standing at arm's length from her, the next he was lying in a crumpled heap, thirty yards away, half buried in a pile of broken rubbish. The loud crash and thump of his landing seemed to reach her ears a second later. Bits of broken crates, rotten food and scraps of rags slowly floated back down to the ground from where they had been disturbed. The man lay still, unmoving.

No, no, no, not again! She took one step forward towards him as the priest shouted out his name in worry. Then she heard a low groan, and the pile of refuse shifted slightly. Cali breathed a sigh of relief and stopped walking. She glanced at the wide eyed, pale priest who looked at her in horror and shock. She gave him a wink and turned away. Then she ran.

***

Sometime later she was back in her room at the brothel. Lisanne had noticed straight away that something had happened, but didn't press her when she said she didn't want to talk about it. After all, what could she say? I used my power to cheat at dice, then got into a fight and used it again to almost kill a man? Lisanne had been good to her, letting her stay here and not making her work with the other girls, but her charity would only extend so far. If she knew Cali was a Frag and valuable to those in power she wouldn't think twice about giving her up.

So now Cali sat on the thin, feather mattress on her bed thinking about what had happened, trying to still her shaking limbs. When she had first got back she had immediately started packing her things into her bag, ready to flee the city. Maybe she could try her luck in Paska, or head further south to Whitgard? But she had stopped halfway through, angry at herself for letting her emotions run away with her. And angry at the world and her situation. Why should others chase and hunt her just because she could do what they could not? Surely, others should treat her better and show her respect, shouldn't they?

But she was a realist and knew that was not how things worked. Those in charge, like the baron and his stuck-up family, used people like her. They would force her to work for them, keeping her locked up like a slave, even though they would pretend it was for her own good and give her fancy accommodation and nice clothes. She would have no freedom. No choice in what to do. She would have to follow orders and do their bidding. Like a soldier, only more dangerous. Ugh! She shuddered at the thought.

She wanted to live her own life in her own way. Until today she was relatively happy. She had a place to stay, a sometimes job at the dock to earn her a few coins and be able to spend some time with her friends. And her extra activities that made her more money, except when they went wrong like today. But you couldn't always have smooth sailing. That was part of life. Trying new things, being bold, brave and occasionally reckless.

The one thing she didn't enjoy was having to hide her gift from the world. Ever since she discovered her power a few years ago, she had tried to suppress it, to not use it, but it was getting harder. It seemed to want to be used and although she had more control of the power she expended now, after years of secret practice, it just seemed more natural to use it.

She was tired of hiding and running from the authorities and her brush with that Gatherer today had stirred up all her old fears. Except he said that he was an ex-Gatherer. Was that even possible? She had never heard of someone leaving that group of Frag hunters before. Maybe he was just saying that to throw her off so he could drag her to the baron. But for some unknown reason she believed him. He had an honest face and in a city like this that was very rare.

What if he could help her as he said? Lucianus knows I could do with someone to talk to, about my power if nothing else. But can I trust him? Not likely. He is a man, after all. But maybe he could still be useful. She needed to fathom him out. And discover why he was hanging out with a priest. She didn't mind priests. They had often given her food and shelter in the past, which she was grateful for. But why was one in a tavern with a warrior? I need to find some answers and I won't do that by sitting here. Her shaking had subsided now, and she felt a new determination welling up in her.

She stood up and pulled her long, green cloak off the chest, wrapping it around herself and tucking her unruly hair under the hood. Best not to be noticed so soon after my public display. Right, time to go ask around about a very strange couple.

# CHAPTER 9

# GETTING HAMMERED

"What in the name of all the supposed hells was that about?" Teelan demanded.

After the ruckus in the alleyway, Teelan had helped Drevin stand and patched up the cut on his forehead with a bandage he kept secreted in his robes. Then they had walked, unsteadily, a good distance away and deposited themselves in another, equally squalid tavern.

Teelan was still in a state of shock, and he could tell that Drevin was concerned too by the extra wrinkles on his battered face. So it was that they sat here now, Drevin nursing an ale and Teelan sipping at a particularly sour white wine. He had asked the barman for milk but as the stocky, bearded fellow just laughed in his face he assumed he didn't have any. Instead, he had asked for their finest white wine. Apparently, this was it.

"She's a Fragment, Teelan." Drevin finally replied, looking up from his beer.

"I gathered that! Considering she threw you down that alley like an old piece of meat. Why do you care?"

"Because it is dangerous to be a Fragment in a city like this. If the baron or his family found out they would hunt her down."

"Again, why do you care? Don't tell me you like her?" Teelan took another mouthful of wine from the crude clay mug. It tasted like a week-old lemon, left out in the sun to wither and die.

"Don't be disgusting," Drevin snorted. "She is young enough to be my daughter. She is more your age. Maybe she is more your type? Or let me guess do you prefer blondes?"

"I don't have a type. I find it ridiculous that people are only attracted to certain individuals based on insignificant details, such as the colour of their hair or their height." The wine, despite its hideous taste, was having an effect on him. His head was feeling slightly woolly.

"So, what do you look for, then?"

"If you must know, I am only drawn to people who intrigue me, regardless of their age, looks or gender." Teelan let that statement hang there, waiting for a narrow-minded comment from Drevin. Surprisingly, he just nodded. "Anyway, we are getting off topic. Why is it dangerous for her to have power like that?"

"Don't you know anything about Fragments Teelan?" Drevin asked, taking a gulp of his ale.

"Not really. I try to stay away from anything that isn't natural."

"You must know the history of the Minds?"

"Yes, yes, I know the story. Hundreds of years ago a comet fell from the sky and landed in the ocean. There was a Big Splash, flooding entire countries. Lots of simple-minded people believed it to be a God who had fallen to earth, like a clumsy jester, and they worshipped it and unimaginatively named it the Sunken God. Some time after this, some people developed certain powers which allowed them to do amazing things with their minds, such as lifting heavy weights, creating fire and redirecting the wind. These people, unsurprisingly, earned the name 'Minds' and gained respect and even reverence across the lands." Teelan finished with a flourish of his arm and took another long drink, grimacing at the taste.

"Very good. However, there is more to the 'story'. All was fine for a few hundred years. But as is always the case, those in charge wanted more power, more land, more Minds, more of pretty much everything, basically. So Dranbarl made war on Vangormia, with the Irians not wanting to miss out and also joining in. Even some of the Scorians came from their islands to get involved.

"After several years of fighting, it all came to a head on the west coast of Vangormia in a massive battle, now called the Final Battle. Stupid name really, as there have been plenty of battles since then and no doubt there will be plenty more. Anyway, it was during this battle that the second major flood occurred, sweeping most of both armies from the land. Some thought that the Minds had joined together to call the tidal wave, others believed it was the work of the Sunken God who was furious about the way his powers were being used.

"After that, people believe that the Sunken God left the world, and no more Minds were born. From then on, only a few people developed powers, and they could only utilise one Trait, hence they were called Fragments or Frags as they only had a slice of the overall power that a

Mind had. Initially, these Fragments were highly valued, but as time passed and fewer Frags emerged, those in power began seeking them more. Now, rulers in some countries hunt them down and treat them as little better than slaves, forcing them to work through threats or punishments." Drevin explained, beckoning for the young serving girl.

"Where do Gatherers come into the equation?" Teelan asked, finishing his wine. He had heard stories of Gatherers, but he suspected that most of those were fabricated.

"The creation of the Gatherers was prompted by the realisation that fewer people were developing Fragments and many of them might be going undiscovered in more remote locations. So local rulers established teams of trained soldiers to track down these Frags and bring them to the towns or cities, where they could train them to use their abilities and take care of them properly, and where their abilities could be utilised to assist a larger population."

"And you were one of these soldiers turned Gatherer?"

"Yes," Drevin said reluctantly. The serving girl came over with a fresh tankard of ale for Drevin and refilled Teelan's mug from a dirty bottle before he could stop her. Drevin flipped a coin to her, which she deftly caught, then whirled away.

"But you aren't a Gatherer anymore?" Teelan sipped the wine to see if the taste had improved. It hadn't.

"No, I didn't like the way things were going. We used to help Frags, give them a better life, teach them to understand and use their powers."

"In return for them helping your rulers, of course." Teelan pointed out snidely.

"Yes, but only for the benefit of everyone. Like helping to build houses or workshops, heating forges, moving rain clouds over parched crops. Things like that. But for some people that wasn't enough. They wanted Frags to enhance their power, to do their dirty work for them. They would send Frags with the Voice Trait to persuade those who opposed them to do what they wanted. Those with Ignite to burn rivals land and crops. When Frags refused, they forced them to comply. Threats of violence to them and their families usually worked. So I left." He took another swig of ale and leaned back against his bench. Teelan thought he looked old at that moment. Old and sad.

"Just like that?"

"No, not just like that. My employer and I had a difference of opinion." Teelan noticed his grimace.

"So, how did you manage to leave?"

"Let's just say that I convinced him in the end." Drevin said with a wry smile. "Anyway, why all the questions? I thought you didn't care about my life?"

"I didn't. But now you are getting interesting." Goodness me, why did I just say that? The wine must be having a greater effect on me than I thought.

"Well, don't start getting any ideas," Drevin said, smiling and winking at him suggestively.

"That is disgusting. And not what I meant at all." Teelan could feel the heat blooming in his cheeks like a furnace stoked to life. This is just one reason why he didn't drink. He always ended up saying something stupid.

"Anyway, the point is that the young girl is in danger." Drevin said, apparently done with his mocking. "Someone is bound to have noticed our little display earlier and alerted the baron to the fact that a rogue Frag is in his city. He will probably be sending out his Gatherers as we speak."

"Well, we can't worry about it for now. We have still got a killer to find, if you remember."

"Yes, I know. I have asked around and it looks like the Hammer is lying low, as nobody seems to know where he is at the moment. Come on, finish your drink and we will hit some more taverns. Someone must know something."

"Marvellous," said Teelan sarcastically, emptying his mug. "Eugh!".

****

In fact, it took four more taverns of decreasing reputability before they ended up in the one where they were told the Hammer was in residence. A burly barman, all hair and arms, begrudgingly informed them he was currently occupying one of his rooms, through the back and last door on the right. Drevin led the way down the short, dingy corridor, past closed doors where grotesque noises of people in either great pain or pleasure were audible.

When they reached the aforementioned door, Drevin, as uncouth as ever, didn't bother to knock. He swung the door open and quickly stepped inside. Teelan heard a loud clattering noise and shouts of surprise from within as he sneaked in behind Drevin, staying close to the entrance.

The room was small, musty and over inhabited. Three men had clearly occupied seats at a small round table, but their stools now lying on the floor revealed how quickly they had stood up and assumed their half-crouched positions. They were all hard looking men with thick arms and necks and greedy eyes. They already held a choice selection of bare steel and heavy clubs in their meaty hands. The fourth man stood from where he had been bent over a large chest, stuffing some belongings into a robust leather bag. He was as broad as the other men with a square, flat face, covered in old scars. A short black beard, cropped black hair and cold grey eyes completed his brutal features.

"You must be my ride," he said calmly in a gruff voice, waving an arm to his comrades to settle down. "About time. I need to get out of here."

"I'm afraid not," said Drevin with a false reluctance. "My name is Drevin, and I need to ask you some questions."

"Well Drevin, I have little time as I am leaving soon, so make it quick." Teelan noticed he looked calm and composed but his hands rested casually on the oversized iron headed hammer at his belt.

"Are you the Hammer?" Drevin asked

"Guilty as charged." The Hammer chuckled. "You're not going to arrest me, are you? Or have you come to kill me? Is that why you bought a priest, to read me my last rites?" Teelan shrank further back against the wall as the Hammer's gaze fell on him. The other men had not put away their weapons and were edging closer to Drevin from either side. Teelan felt his anxiety rise, as it often seemed to do in Drevin's company.

"Neither," Drevin replied, just as calmly. "I just want to talk is all. Tell me, did you get a job around six days ago to get rid of a young man who was in a barn in the Salt District?"

"Bollocks! I don't know what you're talking about. I have nothing to do with that sort of business. Buying and selling is my game." The Hammer exclaimed.

"Sure. And extortion, protection, robbery and murder, from what I have heard."

"Well, sometimes business doesn't always go so well and I have to ..adapt." The Hammer said, smiling at his own joke and patting the head of the hammer.

"Fine, if you don't want to talk, let me tell you what I think happened. Someone came to you and asked you to remove said young man. To dispose of him. And they paid you a lot of money to do so. You gladly took their coin and got two of your…employees who, shall we say, lack any moral compass, and paid them a fraction of the coin you got to do the job."

"Now, however, you have discovered that the man you were paid to eliminate is actually the baron's eldest son, and you do not want to be present when the baron and his knife find you. Hence why you are leaving the city in a hurry. How am I doing?" Drevin asked with a grim, smug smile on his face.

The Hammer's face lost its pretence of a pleasant smile, and the thugs moved in closer. Bloody Hell Drevin! Why do you have to be so confrontational with everyone? Especially when I am with you. You seem determined to get me beaten to a pulp or killed. Why did I agree to come with you? Teelan's recently mistreated stomach was unhappy again, fear and panic mixing together to make an unpleasant brew.

"That sounds like a damn fine story," replied the Hammer, frowning, "but it is just that, a story. Do you have any proof to back any of this up?"

"Not yet," said Drevin. "But if you haven't noticed, the baron doesn't seem too bothered about finding proof. If I went to him with my 'story', do you think he would let you leave the city unmolested? You see I don't think he would. I think he would drag you off to his dungeons and use his own unique brand of questioning on you to see if you would spill your guts before, well, before he spilled them for you." The Hammer's face had gone white at the mention of the baron, and even his thugs-in-arms had backed off slightly as they realised what Drevin was saying.

"Okay, okay, I get your point. And I suppose if you weren't able to leave this room to inform the baron, you already have someone else in place to pass the message along, right? Shitholes!" The Hammer was sweating now, clearly thinking about the punishment he might receive from his part in all this. "Look, I will tell you everything. Just don't drop my name to the baron. At least not until I am out of the city, which should be anytime now. Right?" Drevin remained silent, making no promises but not refusing the deal either. Apparently, the Hammer took that as consent.

"It was almost like you said. About six days ago a young boy came to find me and read out a note he had on a bit of paper. He said that there was a job for me to do if I wanted it. I asked what it was, and he read it out. He said 'you are to go to the old, falling down barn at the edge of the Salt District under the city wall at second bell today. There you will find a young man. You are to remove him, forcibly if necessary, and take him to a ship called 'The Endnote' at the main docks, where you are to hand him over to the captain. You will be paid in advance, but you must ensure that you remove the man from the city.' Then the lad handed me a fat pouch of silver." The Hammer paused for breath. Teelan was confused. What was this about a ship? That is not what happened at all.

"So you see, I was never going to kill him and I didn't know who he was, otherwise I wouldn't have taken the job." The Hammer grimaced, trying to placate Drevin.

"I take it you didn't do this job personally?" Drevin asked, "Who did you send?"

"Two of my lads who don't mind if things get rough. A couple of pricks who nobody else will work with."

"Picket and Sticket," Drevin guessed.

"Yeah, how did you know? Balls! I should have known those two arsewipes would cock this up. They're thick as shit and not very trustworthy, but I thought it was a simple enough job for them. I told them he owed me money and hadn't paid, so I was selling him into slavery. I didn't think that they were stupid enough to just murder him." Teelan smiled at that. How can anyone in a gang of criminals be considered trustworthy?

"Where can I find them?" Drevin asked intently.

"They've got a warehouse against the western wall, near the poor houses. If they are not there, they are usually in a tavern or at their favourite brothel, 'Cracks.'"

"What can you tell me about the boy who delivered the message?"

The Hammer shrugged his huge shoulders, "Not much, all kids look much the same don't they? Short, skinny little farts." Teelan didn't much care for his language, but essentially agreed with his description.

"Try," Drevin suggested pointedly.

"Fine. He was wearing a tatty old cloak, but his shoes were pretty clean, so I don't think he was a local. Boys 'round here either don't have shoes or they're caked in ash or rock dust."

"That's good. What else?"

"He didn't sound like a common street boy, he sounded more, what's the word..fancy, that's it. Also, when he left the bar the wind caught his cloak and it looked like he was wearing a blue tunic or tabard underneath, not like the brown or grey smocks most street boys wear."

"Very good. Now, what about the note he carried? Do you still have it?" Drevin asked forcefully.

"No, the boy took it away with him," the Hammer replied, but Teelan saw his eyes flick to the open chest.

Drevin obviously noticed that too. "You sure about that?" he asked.

"Course I'm sure! I'm not stupid enough to keep incrim.. incam.. proof against me," he said, stumbling over his words but puffing himself up. Easy Drevin. Don't push him too far. He might decide he would rather face the possibility of the baron's punishment rather than your impertinent questioning. A tense silence hung in the air and Teelan felt his pulse racing again. Just before the silence became unbearable, the door behind Teelan suddenly swung open, causing him to jump in alarm and let out an unmanly squeak.

"Someone else is here to see you now," said the hirsute barman, sticking his shaggy head in the room and then quickly departing.

"That must be my ticket out of here. Well, I must be going now." The Hammer said, bending down to continue stuffing clothes from his chest into his heavy bag. When Drevin didn't move he looked up again, his eyes narrowing. "Unless, of course you've changed your mind, you little prick, and think you can take me in?"

Teelan could see Drevin's hand twitch at the challenge. No, no, no, don't you dare. Teelan pressed himself against the wall, his hand on the door handle, ready to flee. Drevin at last had the decency to remember he was there and quickly glanced over his shoulder at him, then turned back to the Hammer.

"I will let you go on your way," he said reluctantly, much to Teelan's relief. "But if you want my advice, don't come back to the city anytime soon." He then turned and walked to the door. Teelan beat him to it and flung the door open and hastened back down the corridor.

As they entered the bar again a big man in a full-length brown leather coat with the hood up brushed past him as he headed the opposite way. Teelan led the way out of the bar and into the cool, dark evening, pleased to get some fresh air. Well, as fresh as dust tainted air can be, anyway. He looked up and saw the constellations of the stars twinkling coldly back at him like drops of ice on a basalt slab.

Drevin joined him and as usual, spoiled the solitude and beauty of the moment. "Well, where do you want to go next?" he asked.

Somewhere quiet where I can be alone with my thoughts. There was much to ponder, and he was feeling a bit overwhelmed by it all. Also, the wine he had drunk earlier was making him wistful and melancholy now. Another reason why he didn't drink.

"The warehouse or the whorehouse?" Drevin asked, chortling at his pathetic play on words. Teelan sighed. Oh well best to get this over with.

"I would like to go to the warehouse first to see if that is where they kept Ridozir. It may give us some more clues about why they killed him and what they are up to."

"Good idea. And they may be there." Drevin said, adjusting the sword on his belt. He looked keen to dispense his own brand of justice on those two men and headed off in what Teelan assumed was the right direction.

"So, did you believe him?" Teelan asked, catching up to him.

Drevin sighed before answering, "A man like that lives or dies by his reputation. He has to be hard, brutal sometimes, but also cunning and consistent. He has to weigh up the risks against the rewards of each job and earn enough coin to keep his operation going and to keep all his minions happy. Only someone crazy or desperate would have taken on this job, knowing who the target was, and he doesn't strike me as either. The fact that he is smart enough to leave his little criminal empire behind tells me he knows how much trouble he would be in once he was discovered. I don't think he would have undertaken this job had he known."

"You seem to know him well. Have you met him before?"

"Not him, but plenty like him in my time."

"What a colourful life you lead," Teelan said snippily. "So what, in your expert opinion, happened to the plan of getting him to the boat?"

"I'm not sure. It could be as he said, and those two scumheads he sent either didn't understand the message or just killed Ridozir for the fun of it. They were not exactly the most stable pair."

"And the messenger boy?"

"Well, he wasn't a street urchin." Drevin said, turning into a dimly lit street.

"Obviously." Teelan snorted, "But who sent him?"

"Think about it, Teelan. The boy was clean, well dressed and in disguise, educated and knew how to read. What does all that tell you?"

"He probably belonged to someone with money. A merchant maybe, or a minor noble."

"Possibly." said Drevin, skirting a group of men loitering outside a corner tavern. Teelan glanced over at them, and one of the younger men stared at him with interest. Teelan quickly looked away. "Although the boy could read, so his owners must be pretty rich or pretty indulgent."

"Why? Don't all children get taught their letters?"

"Ha, seriously!" Drevin laughed.

"Well, in Sempa all children from the age of six get lessons in reading and writing."

"In case you haven't noticed you are not in Vangormia now."

"Honestly, this backwards country disgusts me." Teelan was shocked once again at the barbarity of the people here. Their lack of culture and education was appalling. Once again, he questioned why he had come to this continent of Dranbarl. Then he remembered why and quickly shied away from those thoughts.

“You could always leave.” Drevin replied, smirking at him. “Anyway, that and the fact that he was likely wearing a blue tabard leads me to one conclusion.” Drevin looked at Teelan expectantly.

“He came from the castle,” Teelan said, following Drevin’s logic. “The serving boys wear blue tabards as it is the baron’s colour.”

“Exactly.” Teelan thought he heard a hint of respect in his voice, but maybe it was just his imagination and the effects of the wine.

“Drevin, don’t you think the baron will be upset that we let the Hammer get away? After all, he was the one who set the men on his son.”

Drevin frowned. “Maybe. But what did you want me to do about it, Teelan? I couldn’t take all of his men on in that room. Besides, even if they didn’t kill us and I somehow managed to subdue that mountain of a man, what then? Drag him all the way back to the castle? Through two districts filled with his and other gang members, who would happily slaughter us to free or kill him? I didn’t really have a choice.” Teelan saw him shake his head, clearly frustrated.

“We could get some guards to arrest him?” Teelan said hopefully. That would be the right thing to do, surely.

“Oh yeah, of course. I should have thought of that. Do you see any guards around here, Teelan?” Drevin asked as they carried on walking through the narrow, unfriendly looking streets. Teelan looked around. The streets were fairly quiet this late, but small groups of men stalked around, some talking loudly whilst others were more furtive. Most of them looked rough and ready, and all had weapons at their belts. The odd woman he saw was often in the company of several men, and some of them looked rougher than their companions. Of guards and any signs of authority, there were none.

Drevin obviously took his silence as accepting his point. "Besides, The Hammer didn't do the deed. If we give the baron Picket and Sticket, that will satisfy him. Ah, here we are."

Here was a narrow, curving road sitting in the shadow of the city wall. A row of bulky, uneven shapes nestled against the wall in various states of disrepair, dilapidation, and decrepitness. Some mean-looking houses were squashed together further down the street as the road veered off towards the south gate. Drevin approached one of the squat warehouses and Teelan, nervously glancing around, followed him.

"This is the one," Drevin said, stopping beside a wooden walled building. He then bent down to put his head to a gap in the planks and Teelan watched him squinting through. "All dark in there and I can't hear anything," he said, straightening up again.

They moved to the doors and Teelan saw a heavy padlock that looked sturdier than the rest of the building keeping the doors locked tight.

"Damn," Drevin swore. He pulled out his dagger from his belt and wedged it into the padlock, trying to twist it and lever the padlock open. A short squeal of metal followed and Drevin removed the blade, cursing. All he had achieved was to blunt the edge of his dagger and make a slight scrape on the lock. Drevin then picked up a heavy stone from the cobbled street and smashed it against the lock, making an awfully loud clanging noise, but having about as much effect as the dagger had.

"Stop, stop!" Teelan shouted with his hands over his ears. Drevin obliged. "Goodness, you are making enough noise to wake the dead," he said, anxiously looking around at the empty streets again. "Here, let me do it."

Drevin just looked at him sceptically, then stepped aside. Teelan pulled out two slim metal rods from one of his many pockets and bent down to put his head at the same level as the padlock. He inserted one rod into the top of the lock and applied a small amount of tension, then he put the other rod in the bottom of the lock and dragged it back and forth rapidly. After what felt like ages, but was actually only a few seconds, the top rod twisted right around, and the lock opened with a satisfying click.

Drevin looked at him with a raised eyebrow. "Wow, I'm impressed. I didn't take you as a lock picker."

Teelan felt both smug and embarrassed at the same time. "Well, it is just simple mechanics. And I do like to learn new things." He was not about to tell Drevin why he had learnt that particular skill, though.

"Shall we?" asked Drevin, swinging open the door.

They headed into an almost pitch black interior. The only light cast from the city wall above filtering through several small holes in the roof to make little circles of greyness to break up the black. Drevin found a lantern near the door and soon had it lit. Teelan almost wished he hadn't. There were piles of boxes and crates everywhere, most of them looking empty, but some contained spoiled food or broken tools. A black cart stood in one corner of the room, a loose tarpaulin in the back of it. A couple of rickety chairs and a small round table with three legs were the only proper furniture in the room. There were two straw pallets in one corner that looked like they had been used as beds.

“Let’s look around,” Drevin said, heading into the room and taking the lantern with him. Thanks a lot. Teelan found a stubby candle and got that lit then wandered in. The wooden floor was covered in a fine layer of rock dust and ash and as Teelan headed over to one corner of the room, he noticed that the floor looked cleaner there. He knelt down and saw a vague man-sized outline on the floor where the dust and ash stopped.

“It looks like a body was lying here, probably Ridozir’s.” He called over to Drevin. That would fit what he had found on Ridozir’s back.

Drevin looked up from where he was rummaging around in some crates. “I thought as much,” he said. “Check out the cart.”

Teelan went over to look at the cart. He pulled back the tarpaulin and smelt a familiar smell mixed with the stench of rancid vegetables. The back of the cart was mostly empty, with a few black carrots and soggy squashes scattered around. Teelan lifted his candle high and in the middle of the cart noticed a large, dark, irregular stain on the wooden slats. “This could be the cart they used to move the body. I can see dried blood on the bed of the cart.”

“Hmm, they have definitely been here recently,” Drevin called out from his squatting position next to the beds. “I found some half empty mugs of beer, a few coins under the straw and some of the red mushrooms that they seem to like. They wouldn’t leave those behind, so they must be planning on coming back.”

"What now?" Teelan hoped Drevin wouldn't suggest staying in this dismal place until they returned.

"We'll look around here for a bit, then try the brothel, see if they are there," Good. Wait, that's not much better.

They spent some time searching through the many crates and boxes but found nothing of interest. Eventually they headed back outside and Teelan replaced the slightly battered padlock, locking it up again. The night air felt cool on his skin and a slight breeze ruffled his long hair. It was welcoming after the mustiness inside. Drevin led the way to the brothel. Teelan wondered uncharitably whether he had needed the Hammer's directions to the place or whether he already knew where it was.

Upon their arrival at the two-storey tavern-come-brothel, Teelan sighed as his low expectations were unfortunately realised. The dark stone building was garishly painted with what he supposed were graphic pictures of naked men and women intertwined. However, the proportions were all wrong and he could tell immediately that whoever had painted them had no understanding of anatomy. Drevin, of course was grinning at it like a lustful teenage boy.

"This is the place." Drevin said.

"Really? What a surprise. And here I thought that this was a church of the Allmother."

Drevin just gave him a stare and entered. Teelan reluctantly followed him. Inside, lanterns were placed at strategic points, often close to fading red tapestries which covered much of the walls, to illuminate only certain areas. This arrangement cast a dim, eerie crimson glow throughout the entire room, which was no doubt intended to be enticing, but appeared more hellish to Teelan's eyes.

Lounging on padded benches and soft chairs, the emaciated girls, scantily clad in thin, cotton shifts with dead eyes, looked like they secretly agreed with him. An obese woman with long blonde hair and sharp blue eyes waddled over to them. She looked like she had eaten all the meals that the skinny girls had missed.

"Greetings, gentlemen," she said, in what Teelan supposed was meant to be a sultry voice. "Hello handsome," she continued, stroking Drevin's face. "What are you looking for tonight?"

Before Drevin could respond she turned to Teelan, "And you pretty boy, my girls would love to spend some time with you." She waved a flabby arm to some of the girls who rose and sauntered over to them.

Teelan felt his cheeks burning and panic rising. Two girls were approaching, a short girl with thick, long raven hair, a round face and dark brown eyes and a taller girl with short, curly blonde hair, a wide mouth and a slightly crooked nose. Both were thin and were wearing clothes that showed too much of their pale flesh.

Teelan didn't know where to look. He couldn't stand the sad look in their eyes and their fake practised smiles, so he looked elsewhere. But elsewhere were their youthful bodies in their almost see-through clothing. His face got even hotter. So Teelan looked in the only place he could. At Drevin.

"Just some information tonight, my lady." Drevin replied with a mock bow. Teelan noticed the disappointment on the fat woman's face. "However, I will pay you well for it." As if by magic, the disappointment vanished.

"Well then, ask away good sir," she said, all smiles again.

"We are looking for a couple of men who are known to visit your lovely establishment from time to time. They are short, weasley looking men with long greasy hair. Go by the names of Picket and Sticket."

Teelan had turned back to watch the faces of the woman and the two girls who were hovering uncertainly behind her. To her credit, the madam was all business and remained straight-faced, one eyebrow raised and hand extended, waiting for recompense before revealing anything. The girls, on the other hand, could not hide their emotions. And their wrinkled noses, lowered eyebrows and raised upper lips displayed their disgust and revulsion.

Drevin dutifully passed over a handful of coins, which the proprietor swiftly deposited into her cavernous cleavage. "Ah yes. Those two. I know them. Not the cleanest or the nicest I'll admit, and they can get rough with the girls, but they are usually so high on Reds that they are done quick."

"When did you last see them?"

"They was in earlier, sir," the curly blonde said. "Poor Elsina got them both tonight and she ain't come out of her room since, but I could hear her crying." Teelan felt sick. At that moment, he felt ashamed to be a man. He couldn't stop looking at their haunted faces.

"When did they leave?" Drevin asked. Teelan could hear the anger in his voice. Maybe they shared some things in common after all.

"About an hour or so ago, I think," she said, biting her lip.

"Thank you," said Drevin, tossing a coin to her and her friend. "We will be on our way."

"Are you sure you don't want to stay?" the madam said, gripping Drevin's arm, "I will give you a good discount and I have my best girls in tonight."

"No, thank you." Drevin replied. "Come on Teelan. And stop staring," he said, smirking at him.

Teelan jumped and tore his eyes away from the girls and their pitifulness, his cheeks flashing again. Once they were outside, Teelan rounded on Drevin. "I wasn't staring," he snapped.

"Really?"

"Well, maybe I was, but it is not in the way that you think. I felt sorry for them, that is all. They looked so neglected and hopeless." He started walking back down the darkened alleyways towards the Upper District.

"Woah, careful there kid, that almost sounds like empathy."

"Very funny. Actually, it is sympathy, not empathy," he said as they turned into a shadowy, crooked street.

"Same difference."

"No, you witless, feeble-minded, uneducated fool, they are not the same thing at all." Teelan said, annoyed both at Drevin and at himself. He really shouldn't drink wine. He stormed ahead of Drevin and headed for the side road that led back to the main street.

"And he's back," Drevin said dryly. "Hey Teelan, wait," he called from behind him. Teelan carried on walking, not wanting to hear anymore from him right now. "Teelan, I mean stop. Look over here."

Teelan stopped and turned back to see Drevin approaching a pile of refuse that was heaped against the alleyway, shrouded in shadow. What is he doing now? Looking for his next meal? Teelan sighed and trudged over to see what he was looking at. As he got closer, he saw that partially buried in the rubbish were two pairs of shoes. Then he noticed that there were two pairs of legs attached to these shoes. Drevin bent down and cleared away some of the larger pieces of ripped leather and food waste to expose the rest of their bodies.

"That's Picket and Sticket," he breathed.

In the dim light, Teelan could just about make out the bodies of two short men with long and no doubt greasy hair. He squatted down to get a closer look and immediately spotted the wide gashes across both of their throats, covered in blood. He put his hand to the wounds and touched the blood. It was still wet and only slightly tacky.

"Can you give me some light here?" he asked. Drevin quickly obliged by wrapping some of the loose cloth around a bent metal rod and setting it alight.

Teelan looked closely at the bodies, feeling their chests, lifting their arms and legs and pressing his fingers against their skin. "Their deaths occurred fairly recently. The bodies are still warm, their limbs are not stiff, and the blood hasn't dried yet. It probably only happened within the last couple of hours, I would say. You need to fetch my cart and bring it here." Teelan said, handing Drevin his key. He wanted to stay and examine the bodies further.

"Sure." said Drevin "I'll go get Harri. I guess it's time for Harri to carry."

Teelan didn't bother to reply to that.

***

Teelan heard the rumbling of the cart before he saw it and stood up from where he had been kneeling on the hard mud, trying unsuccessfully to brush the dirt from his robe.

"What have you found out?" Drevin asked as he stopped the cart on the wider side road and climbed down from the driving board.

"It looks like someone killed them further down the alley," said Teelan, pointing. "Then they dragged them up here and dumped them in this convenient refuse heap. There is a trail of blood leading from there to here. I found their short swords further down there too, so it looks like they tried to defend themselves. I am guessing even you could tell what the cause of death is." Teelan gestured at their slit throats. "Put them on the cart and we will take them back for further investigations."

Drevin gave a sigh, then bent to the grisly task. "You know, I find it a bit odd that not long after the Hammer tells us where these two are going to be that we find them dead. Do you think he ordered someone to kill them so that we couldn't question them? Maybe he hadn't been telling us the whole truth?" He grunted as he put one body on the cart and returned for the other one.

"What, a leader of a criminal gang not telling us the truth?" Teelan said in mock surprise. "Surely not!"

"I think we should stop back by the tavern he was hiding out in to see if he is still there and what he has to say about this," Drevin said, hefting the other body onto his shoulder.

"He will be long gone by now." Teelan snorted.

"Maybe, maybe not. It is worth a try and is on the way back anyway."

Teelan just shrugged his shoulders and climbed on the cart as Drevin dumped the other body in the back then took up the reins.

"Let's go Harri." he called, shaking the reins. Teelan sighed.

***

Drevin parked the cart outside, and they went back inside the hostile tavern. In a hushed tone, Drevin spoke to the bear of a barman, who angrily gestured towards the back door with his hairy arm. Drevin beckoned Teelan over, then headed through the door and down the corridor again, back towards the room the Hammer was in. Teelan followed cautiously, glad that the rooms on either side of them were at least quiet this time. Again Drevin showed no sense of propriety and swung the door open, quickly stepping inside. Teelan looked in from the corridor and couldn't contain his sharp gasp.

Four bodies were sprawled around the room in poses of twisted demise. Thick, red blood almost covered the entire floor of the small room, with deeper pools of it around the bodies. The Hammer lay in the centre of the room, his throat a raw, open mess, his discarded hammer at his feet now painted scarlet.

"Shit." Drevin gasped.

"Indeed." said Teelan, his eyes flicking everywhere to comprehend what had happened.

Drevin had squelched into the room and squatted down by the Hammer to check if he was still alive. Teelan was not sure why, as he was quite clearly dead. However, Drevin repeated the needless process with the other three thugs.

"They're all dead," he said. "What the hell is going on?"

Teelan entered, gingerly lifting his robe off the blood-stained floor, and looked at each of the men. All of them had the same deep gash in their throat. Scattered around the room were their weapons, all stained red.

Teelan pointed at a man lying on the left side of the room, near the sideboard. "They were surprised. This man was killed first."

"Horseshit," exclaimed Drevin, "How can you tell that?"

Indicating the sword still in its scabbard at his belt, he said, "Look, his weapon is still sheathed. The attacker approached him without alarming him then…whoosh!" Teelan lifted his right arm and, pretending he held a sword, swished it through the air in a horizontal swipe. "See the lines of blood on the wall? That is where his blood spurted out and as he fell it continued to spurt every time his heart beat until there was not enough blood left in him." Teelan gestured to the wall where thick, partially dried crimson lines ran in a descending arc down from around head height, almost to the ground.

"Then the killer proceeded to attack his seated companion here." Teelan walked over to the small table. A chair was lying on its side next to the fallen thug. "He just rose from his seat and drew his weapon before someone similarly slashed his throat. See the bloodstains here start lower down on that wall?" He pointed at the aforementioned stains, which were indeed lower than the first set, but otherwise almost identical.

"Bloody hell!" Drevin said, astonished. "Then what happened next?"

"It gets more difficult to tell after that. The last two men would have seen their friends brutally murdered and had time to draw their weapons and put up a fight. My best guess is that the two men fought with the attacker, mainly here in the centre of the room." Teelan continued, moving to the middle of the room, the plight of his robe forgotten as it soaked up the carmine liquid, still waving his imaginary sword around. "Blows would have been exchanged and landed here, spilling blood from several minor wounds. Then the attacker probably took out the club man next." Teelan pointed to the man lying on the right-hand side of the room with a metal club on the ground next to him. "Before turning to deal with the Hammer." Teelan finished, twirling around and slashing his arm through the air with a flourish. His face felt flushed again and he couldn't tell if it was from the excitement he felt, the exertion, or the wine. Possibly all three. Goodness. Sometimes, he loved his job.

"Shit!" Drevin said again.

"Well, don't just stand there gaping," Teelan snapped at him, "get them onto the cart so I can inspect them back at the mortuary."

"Teelan," Drevin said quietly, "I think you're gonna need a bigger shed."

# CHAPTER 10

# RED LETTER DAY

Drevin was back at the mortuary the next morning. The clouds were back today, obscuring the sun, and a fine mist hung in the still air, which clung to his face and hair. Last night he had carried the five dead men down into Teelan's basement and today his knees and back were making their feelings about this known. He had left Teelan and retired to his inn where he had enjoyed a warm meal, a tepid beer and a chilly night's sleep. In the morning, he had woken with a new extensive catalogue of hurts from his encounters yesterday that he wasn't keen to pursue.

As he entered the basement after a slow climb down those damn steps, he saw Teelan standing next to the slab with two small bodies on it. He noticed another stone slab filled with the bulky shape of the Hammer.

"Good morning Teelan." he said more brightly than he felt. He hoped Teelan was in a better mood than yesterday, although he had noticeably brightened up when he saw the carnage in that tavern room.

Teelan just glanced up at him and said nothing, concentrating on organising various bowls and tools around the slab. Apparently, his hopes were not to be fulfilled today then.

"So that was a fun evening, wasn't it?" Drevin tried again undeterred. "What a mess. What on earth is happening?"

"I haven't got a clue," Teelan replied sharply, "but I have got rather a lot of work to do, so if you don't mind." He looked pointedly at the stairs.

"I mean, first the Hammer gives up these two scumbags, then before we can question them they turn up dead." Drevin said, ignoring his comments. "And when we go back to see the Hammer, it is like a scene from an abattoir. It seems to me like someone is trying to get rid of any loose ends."

"Yes, and if I am going to find anything from these bodies I need to concentrate." Teelan snapped.

Drevin watched him pour some milk into a small metal bowl and use a metal rod to stir it into a white powder, forming a creamy paste. He then dipped his fingers into the paste and lifted them to his mouth, smearing the concoction over his gums.

"What the hell are you doing?" Drevin said, alarmed. "Is that what I think it is? I didn't take you for a Mushhead." Drevin couldn't believe that this intelligent, strait-laced kid would do drugs.

"I am not." Teelan retorted. "It is just some Whiteys. They help me focus."

"Sure," said Drevin sarcastically, "They focus your mind on one thing, to the exclusion of everything else. Take too much and you forget to eat or drink. Then you end up sitting in your own piss and shit, so intent on what you are doing, until you fall into a coma."

"And how exactly is that different from you getting intoxicated on alcohol? I have seen men in much the same state as you describe from drinking too much beer."

"It's not the same thing at all." Drevin said heatedly. Although now that Teelan had pointed it out it didn't sound too much different. But there was one big difference between them. "That muck is addictive, you know. Once you get started using it, you won't be able to stop. It won't do you any good in the long run you know."

"Really! And here I thought it was as pure as my mother's milk." Teelan sneered.

"Shit. And I thought you were supposed to be the smart one." Drevin shook his head.

"Haven't you learnt yet that intelligence and common sense very rarely make good bedfellows."

"Shit." Drevin was speechless. He was worried about the boy but knew that Teelan would never admit to needing help from him.

"There is that word again. What is it with you and faeces? You are obsessed, man."

"It's a good word." Drevin shrugged.

"Really?" Teelan's eyebrow was up again.

"Oh, I suppose you are too good to curse, is that it?" Drevin said, feeling his anger rise at the kid's judgement of him.

"Not at all. I just have a wider vocabulary than you, so see no need to use coarse and vulgar language. My mother always used to say, 'Be mindful of how you look and the words you use. The way someone dresses and speaks reflects their true character and intellect.'" Teelan said in an incredibly pompous tone.

"Well, she sounds like a right barrel of fun," Drevin said. He saw Teelan's face go hard as he stared at him. "No offence meant. It's just that you can't always judge people on such things, Teelan. People can be complicated and possess many sides to them. You have to get to know them to find out who they are and sometimes that takes a bit of effort."

"Yes, and with some people it takes a lot of effort." Teelan replied, fixing Drevin with his gaze. "Now please can you vacate my abode forthwith so that I can proceed with my dissection of the deceased with all celerity?"

Drevin just stared blankly at him. What the hell? Honestly, just because he got a fancy education didn't mean he was better than everyone else.

"That means go away quickly!" Teelan barked.

"Are you two always like this?"

Drevin spun around to face the owner of the female voice, his hand instinctively reaching for the sword at this belt. Standing at the entrance to the room was the young girl with the red hair that he had tried to help yesterday. The one with the Fragment. The one who had almost killed him! He kept his hand on his sword and edged backwards. He glanced at Teelan to see that he had nervously backed away and put the stone slab between himself and the newcomer.

"Who are you?" Drevin asked, lifting his other hand as if placating a skittish horse. "We were only trying to help you. We don't want to do you harm."

"My name is Cali. And I know that you ain't gonna harm me," the girl said, casually sauntering over to them. "In fact, I know all about you," she continued, sitting herself on the table against the wall and tucking her legs under her.

Drevin studied her. She was short, dressed in a white long-sleeved chemise under a tightly laced up yellow bodice. Black woollen stockings and a sturdy pair of black leather boots adorned her lower half. She had a cloak of pale green draped around her shoulders, fastened with an iron clasp in the shape of a ship.

Drevin noticed her deep green eyes when she looked back at him. She then spoke in a deliberately fake, practised voice. "You are Drevin Borlea, Borlea the Blade, Drevin the Drowner." Drevin grimaced as she said that title. "Sword master, sell-sword, blade tutor and occasional odd job man. The mercenary with the mysterious past. Arrived in Canor around nine months ago and started looking for work. Known as a reliable, trustworthy sort who will get jobs done. Definitely not a Gatherer, certainly not here anyway, and if you are working as one for someone else you are doing a piss-poor job of it. Usually does minor assignments for those who can afford to pay, such as teaching noble brats which end of a sword is which. Doesn't like too much attention so often takes on menial work, even though he is clearly capable of more. Which makes me wonder why you are working on your current job?"

"Desperate times." Drevin muttered uneasily. Damn! How did she know so much about me? We only met yesterday.

Cali suddenly shivered and wrapped her cloak tightly around herself. "By the deep. Why is it so cold in here?" she asked.

"Ice." said Drevin and Teelan at exactly the same time. Drevin looked at Teelan and his shocked expression must have matched his own.

"That's cute," laughed Cali. "you been practising that?"

"Anyway, what do you know about me?" Teelan asked haughtily.

"Ha, you Ghost Boy were even easier," she laughed.

Drevin chuckled at that. Ghost Boy! He would have to remember that one. From the spluttering noise Teelan was making he assumed he was none too keen on that moniker.

The girl continued talking, again in her voice mimicking a crier. "Teelan Esposito, coroner of Canor, also known as the Necromancer. Arrived around two years ago and worked in a small undertaker's business. Kept reporting suspicious deaths you noticed to the guards, who largely ignored you at first, until you uncovered the murder of a certain wealthy minor nobleman's son. Said nobleman put in a word with the baron and he made you understudy to his coroner. Some months later, when the old coroner died, they promoted you. You work for the baron, but rarely visit the castle, spending more time with the dead than the living. Highly educated, but snobby and stuck up, too good to mix with the common folk, except for when you need your special supplies…"

"How dare you!" Teelan shouted, outraged. Drevin could see Teelan's face turning as red as a tomato and his fists clenched at his sides. For his part, Drevin was trying his hardest not to laugh.

"You, you, you…" Teelan spluttered.

"What, lost for words Teelan? Where's that vast vocabulary of yours now?" Drevin said, unable to contain his mirth.

"Out, out, out. Get. Out. Now." Teelan spat.

"Come on Cali," said Drevin, "let's leave the lad to his work. Apparently, he needs to focus."

***

Drevin sat on the slightly damp wooden bench, adjusting the sword on his back so that it was more comfortable. Cali sat next to him, her hands twisting in her lap, drops of moisture glistening in her hair.

"What's got his rigging all in a twist?" Cali asked, looking up at Drevin.

"I'm not sure. You, maybe? I haven't quite worked him out yet. He clearly thinks he is better than everyone else and is often snappy and judgemental. But he is super smart though. Smarter than anyone I've ever known. I know he is from another land, another culture, but there is more to it than it. He is still young, and I am guessing he had childhood issues."

"Didn't we all?"

"Want to talk about it?" Drevin asked. No. Too soon.

"No." she said, scrunching up her freckled button nose. Thought so.

"What about your talents? Want to tell me about those? You know you are a Fragment don't you?"

"Yeh, I figured that. Not much to tell, really. What about you? Who did you used to work for?" She asked, pulling her cloak around her and wrapping her arms over her chest.

Drevin really didn't want to delve into his past, but he could tell that she didn't trust him yet, so he had to give her something. "I worked in Braka, first in Paska then in the capital Brakus."

"You worked for the king? Old Ironfinder himself?" Cali exclaimed, "Damn, you must have been good. Wait, why aren't you still there? King Gorak is a real hard arse from what I have heard."

Drevin looked around nervously to see if anyone had heard her raised voice. He noticed a couple of the city guards walking past on the main road who glanced over at them. He gave them a cheery wave and they nodded back and carried on walking. When he looked back at Cali, he noticed she had pulled her hood over her distinctive hair.

"Not so loud please," he said. "But yes, you heard right, and that is why I left." Drevin said wryly.

"Just like that?" Cali asked, unknowingly mimicking Teelan's expression when he had asked the same thing.

"Not you as well. No, not just like that. He wasn't happy about my decision to leave."

"Wait, that's why you're here, working as a mercenary. You're running from him, aren't you? Like a rat from a sinking ship. You're hiding, just like me," Cali said excitedly, leaning forward and jabbing him in the arm with her finger.

"Well, let's just say that I'm not too keen to let him know where I am. Now, your turn," Drevin said, looking at her pointedly.

Cali scrunched her legs up and put her head against her knees, looking at him sideways. She still seemed reluctant to talk.

"Ok, let me tell you what I think, then." Drevin said, "You grew up here in the city and have never left it. At least one of your parents, if not both abandoned you. You live or work around the docks, judging by your language and your ability to take care of yourself. But you are clean and your clothes are simple, but not dirty, so you are staying with someone: distant family or friends maybe. You discovered your Fragment a couple of years ago. Maybe you started getting the shakes, or just let your power out accidentally. Either way, it frightened you and you hide your power and use it only sparingly, like cheating at dice. How am I doing?" he said, raising an eyebrow at her questioningly.

"Wrong." she said spitefully, pushing some of her escaping hair back under her hood, "It was four years ago I found out about my power when I was fourteen. Other than that, not bad, I suppose, for a runaway old man."

"Thanks," Drevin said dryly. "So what happened?"

"Some guy at the south docks tried to have his dirty way with me and wouldn't take 'piss off' for an answer. I got angry and well, you can guess what happened next."

"Yes, I can," said Drevin, rubbing surreptitiously at his still throbbing back. He still couldn't quite believe how far she had thrown him down that alleyway.

"I was so scared about what I had done that I was shaking all over. You see the man was an official type and I would have been in big trouble for…hurting him," she said, looking guilty and glancing away.

"So, what did you do?"

"Well, my dad showed up just before, you know, but I hurt him as well, by accident. He told me to run away and not go back." Cali said, rubbing the iron ship brooch on her cloak. Drevin couldn't help but recognise the bitterness in her voice.

"Sounds like he was trying to help you."

"Yeh, that's what I thought too." Cali carried on quickly before Drevin could voice his question. "Anyway, after that I was too frightened to use my power again for ages. I kept my head down and found other work at the main docks, as I daren't return to the south dock and I didn't get into any more trouble. Well, not much anyway," she said, smiling slightly. "For the next couple of years it was all plain sailing. Then when I turned sixteen, I started to get twitches and my arms would shake real bad," she said, demonstrating by waving her arms around exaggeratedly.

"That is something Gatherers are trained to look for, as it is very common with Frags and part of their symptoms when their skills are developing."

"Well, luckily my symptoms weren't too bad, and I managed to keep them hidden. But I knew I was sailing close to the wind and could get found out at any time. So, I decided I needed to learn more about my power."

"It is called a Trait. There are six basic Traits that Fragments can develop, and they can manifest as either Minor Traits or Major ones. I would say that you have the Major Trait of Tempest."

"Tempest. Ha, that's neat! I like that. Well, whatever it's called, I started practising how to use it, in secret of course. I knew that I would have this power…Trait, for the long haul. Eventually, I learned how to just release small amounts of power rather than letting it all just blast out."

"And you thought to use this power to cheat at dice?" Drevin asked, his eyebrow raised again.

"Sure, why not? Thought I might as well make use of it. No point in being hard up if I didn't have to," she smiled. "But when I get angry or scared I can't control it and it all floods out."

"That is natural when Fragments are learning to use their Trait. But when that happens it is important to try to at least direct it away from people. Aim it at something solid, like a wall or out into an empty space. Think about your surroundings. That way you won't end up hurting people," he said, unconsciously rubbing at his bruised head. "But you can learn to control it, even when you are…emotional. The power comes from your mind, so if your mind is in a state of turmoil then so is your Trait and the way it resolves this is to let itself out. It is about stilling your mind. Being calm and centred. Then you can be in charge of your Trait rather than it being in charge of you." Drevin said, easily slipping back into his old mentor mode. He had forgotten just how much he had enjoyed teaching youngsters.

"Yeh and how do I do that exactly?"

"With time, practice and patience. I can teach you some techniques to help you, but you have to work at it."

"Great." Cali said sarcastically, "I guess there ain't no magic pill to keep me on an even keel then?"

"Afraid not. Listen. Try this for now. Close your eyes and breathe deeply, counting to ten. Then try not to think about anything. Listen to the sounds around you, smell the scents in the air, feel the clothes on your skin. Just be in the moment."

Cali looked at him as if he was crazy. "Really?" Drevin gave her a hard stare. "Okay, fine, I will give it a try."

For the next few minutes Drevin and Cali sat on the bench, legs crossed, looking at peace with the world. Drevin, however, could feel all his aches and pains, from his scraped head and bruised face right down to his pulsing back and stiff knees. He had never been very good at this and although age had helped in some ways it hindered in others.

Cali, he noticed, was also finding it difficult, judging from the fidgeting and wriggling she was doing next to him. She was also making loud sighing and huffing noises, which didn't sound like she was much enjoying his lesson. Pretty soon, his assumption was proven right.

"Crap! I can't do this," Cali said, frustrated. "You can't just ask someone to think of nothing. As soon as you say that you start thinking of things. It's impossible."

"No, it's not. But it takes a lot of practice." Drevin said calmly. "That's probably enough for now, anyway. But try to do it whenever you can."

"Fine", she huffed. Drevin had noticed already that she was very good at huffing.

"One more thing, Cali. You need to be careful of how often you use it. Frequent use can cause intense bouts of shaking, headaches and dizziness. Overuse it and you could even end up putting yourself in a coma for a few days."

"Damn! That's not exactly reassuring Dev." Cali said, shaking her head, her eyes wide in alarm.

"Don't worry. You are still young, so you shouldn't get such dangerous symptoms for many years yet."

"Something to look forward to then," she said, hunching her shoulders.

"Like I said, no need to worry about that now. Also, Dev?" he asked in surprise.

"Yeh, it's a nickname. All my friends have nicknames."

Drevin smiled at her. "Well, I guess I should be pleased then that I count as a friend."

Cali glanced at him and returned the smile.

"Well, I'm starving." Drevin said, standing up. "How about I buy you some lunch?"

"Sounds good." Cali replied, also rising.

Drevin set off walking towards the Central Compass market in search of something hot. A breeze had picked up and was blowing the moist air into his face as they walked in silence. The sun was still hiding behind the murky clouds and was doing little to warm his damp clothes. However, he realised he was content, happy even and glad to be in the girl's company. He was pleased that she had come to him, and he was looking forward to teaching her about her abilities.

It had been a long time since he had worked with a Frag and he was keen to get started, to be able to make a positive difference to someone's life again. He had missed that. Seeing what these people could do if given the opportunity and the right guidance. He wondered again at how different the world could be if everyone had such choices, at what significant accomplishments society could achieve if everyone worked together. Huh, now he sounded like his grandfather! He missed him, too.

He glanced over at Cali who was walking along next to him, her cloak tight around her. She also looked deep in thought, her eyes narrowed and eyebrows lowered. She kept her hands under her cloak and walked with a sure step, as if she knew every cobble of this city. Which she probably did, actually. Drevin remembered what it was like to be so young and so confident, yet also deeply insecure and vulnerable at the same time. He couldn't say that he particularly missed it.

As they entered the market from the north western spoke road the noise and smells suddenly hit them. Hundreds of people were crammed together into the great circle created by the ring of shops, taverns and houses that bordered the market. The circle brimmed with dozens of stalls, forming winding pathways between them. Many of them had long poles thrust into the ground next to them with strips of brightly coloured cloth or decorations made of metal, clay, wood, or bone tied to them to denote their trades.

Drevin noticed Cali's eyes light up at the amount of people here and the array of goods for sale. He suddenly hoped that she wasn't planning to steal anything! He led her through the press of bodies until they found a stall selling cooked, unidentified meat on a flatbread which then folded together. Drevin bought two and they carried on strolling, perusing the market whilst trying to eat the meaty bread without dropping it everywhere or burning their tongues.

As they finished their meal, Cali spied something of interest and ran over to a stall that was so colourful it hurt Drevin's eyes. She picked up a thin bright pink strip of silk from a table that was covered in garish coloured cottons, linens, and silks, and ran it through her fingers.

"I didn't think pink would be your colour." Drevin smiled.

“It’s not for me, it’s for a friend who is in the doldrums at the moment. She would love this to put in her hair. Anyway, I can’t afford it.” She said sadly, replacing it on the table and turning away.

Drevin picked it back up and looked at the shrewd eyed woman behind the stall. “How much is this?”

“A silver round,” she blurted.

Drevin almost choked on that price. “Bullshit!” he said. “I could rent a room for a month for that price. I’ll give you one copper bit.”

“What are you doing, Dev? I didn’t ask you to buy it for me.” Cali hissed at him.

“Ha,” the woman laughed scornfully. “If I sold it to you for that price my supplier would think I was stealing from him and chop my hand off. Eight bits.”

“Two bits,” replied Drevin, shushing Cali’s huff of indignation. There it is again.

“No,” replied the merchant. “You may as well use that to tie my hands together and rob me. It would amount to the same thing. That is pure silk all the way from Otori across the sea. Six bits.”

“I say again, bullshit. This silk is much coarser than Otori silk. It feels and looks more like wild silk from Satiria, which is much cheaper to buy. Three bits. Last offer.” Drevin said before she could protest further.

“Done.” she said quickly, holding her hand out for the coins. Drevin handed them over, then passed the silk tie to Cali. She snatched it off him ungratefully.

“I don’t need you pushing the boat out and buying things for me. I can manage on my own, you know. Have been for a long time now. I don’t want your charity,” Cali snapped at him.

Drevin was taken aback. Why was she so angry? He was only trying to do something nice for her. “I was just trying to be nice,” he said.

“Yeh, well don’t. People who do nice things for others always seem to want something in return. Something that you usually don’t want to give them,” she said bitterly.

“Well, I want nothing in return.” Drevin said irritably, “Except maybe a thank you.”

“Oh. I’m sorry.” Cali said, suddenly looking embarrassed. A red glow spread across her freckled cheeks. “I’m just not used to people being nice to me I guess. How do you know so much about silk anyway? I didn’t think that would be your sort of thing.”

“When I was just a lad I worked at a tailors for a while. It didn’t last long.”

“Why was that?”

“I hated it. I had to model clothes for the rich kids who couldn’t be bothered to stand still for long enough to be fitted. Essentially, I was just a dummy. It was so boring, standing still for hours, while the tailor pinned various garish, outlandish clothes to me. Then one day a particularly obnoxious brat was watching me having his new doublet fitted on me and the tailor said to me, ‘You might feel a little prick’ as he was jabbing needles into the material. The boy then said, ‘Well, that doesn’t matter as he already looks like a prick’, trying to be funny.”

“Very original.” Cali said. “What did you do?”

“I said ‘I may look like a prick, but at least I don’t look like an arsehole like you.’ Needless to say, the tailor wasn’t impressed and sent me packing.”

"Ha. I can imagine you saying that. Well, I for one am glad that you are not a tailor's dummy anymore. And thank you. This will cheer my friend up."

"You're welcome, Red." Drevin said, smiling at her. Her hood had fallen down and her curly crimson hair was blowing about in the breeze.

Cali looked at him with wide, wet eyes full of so many emotions that Drevin couldn't begin to separate them all.

"What?" he said jokingly, "Oh, am I not allowed to give you a nickname?"

"No, it's not that. It's just..nothing. It's fine. Honestly." Cali said, stumbling over her words, her head lowered, avoiding his gaze.

Well, that was awkward. Damn, he was out of practice dealing with emotional youngsters. He would have to be more careful with his approach.

"Come on," he said cheerfully. "Let's get a couple of those bowls of roasted nuts to warm us up, and then I will take you somewhere for some more practical training."

"Sounds good," said Cali, looking up at him and smiling weakly. "Where is this place?"

"Well, I just so happen to know of a certain warehouse in the Stone District that has just become vacant."

***

A short while later they were walking down increasingly narrow streets towards the old warehouse. Drevin's belly was still warm from the hot nuts he had eaten, and the sun had peeked out a bit from behind the clouds, but his clothes were still a tad damp. The breeze had picked up and was now rattling amongst the litter in the streets and making the odd shop signs sway and creak.

Cali had chatted away as they walked. She had pointed out places she knew or had been to. She mentioned some people she knew, what they did and who their friends and family were. As Drevin had suspected, she seemed very comfortable in the city and knew a lot of what went on there. However, she mostly talked about inconsequential things and steered away from talking about herself.

Drevin had wanted to ask her about her past, about who she was and who she wanted to be. But he didn't want to push her or scare her away, so he kept them to himself for now. She was obviously street smart and could take care of herself, but she was also temperamental and had her own issues to deal with. He hoped that in time she might share them with him.

Despite listening to Cali's chatter and ruminating on his thoughts, Drevin was still aware enough of his surroundings to suddenly get an uneasy feeling and a prickly sensation on the back of his neck. He glanced around casually and stretched his back as though it was aching, which, in fact it was. Shit! He knew something was up. They were being followed.

"Cali," he said quietly, "we are being followed."

"What!" she replied, turning around and looking behind them. "Who by?"

Drevin grabbed her shoulder and turned her back around swiftly, "Don't turn around." he hissed, "There is a man in a green cloak, behind us, off to the left. Portly and trying to look innocuous. Also, there is a woman in a red cloak with a sharp face and short black hair who is also tracking us off to the right. They look like Gatherers."

"Crap! How can you tell?"

"It's the way they walk. Casually but confidently, seeming to be just out for a stroll, but their eyes are constantly scanning everywhere, and they keep checking our position. It is something that they get taught, how to follow people without being noticed. Wait, how many Gatherers does the Baron have?"

Cali grimaced. "Three."

"Which means the third one is probably ahead of us, waiting for the right moment to cut us off. Damn! Do you know a safe place around here?"

"Yeh, I know safe places everywhere. Someone I know runs a little shop not far from here. We can hide out there. If we can make it."

"Lead the way," said Drevin.

Cali stepped up the pace and led him down several side streets and winding passageways. They sped up every time they got out of sight of their pursuers and were almost running at times, but Drevin could tell that they hadn't thrown them off. Just as they turned into a particularly narrow alley, a man appeared at the other end of it, blocking their exit. He looked young and was wearing a brown cloak with brown leather boots. Drevin stepped forward quickly intent on forcing his way past when he heard a voice from behind him that stopped him.

"Hey there," called a woman's high-pitched voice. "Stop a moment. We just want to talk to you."

Drevin pulled Cali behind him as he turned around. The owner of the voice was the woman he had seen tracking them. Her black hair framed her narrow face and ended in points below her chin on either side. Faded red burn marks streaked her cheeks, two on each side, running from her thin nose to her ears. Drevin also noted with growing dread that her cloak and stockings were bone dry. Bollocks. That is not good. We are in real trouble now. Next to her stood the sturdy man in the green cloak. He was bald at the front with long grey hair at the back and had a plain round, friendly looking face. But Drevin knew looks could be deceiving.

"Who are you and what do you want with us?" he said, trying not to let the panic building in him show in his voice.

"My name is Nylarian and I work for Baron Sutter. These are my companions Zortig," she said, nodding to the man on her right, "and Caderin." indicating the man at the other end of the alleyway. "We heard about a fight that happened near the Old Shovel tavern yesterday afternoon and about a young girl who did something extraordinary," she finished, looking at Cali hungrily. "The baron has generously offered employment for this girl and a place to stay in luxury and comfort."

"Yeh, in return for being his slave and doing his bidding." Cali retorted, poking her head out from behind Drevin.

"They will make good use of your skills and pay you handsomely for your services," Nylarian asked. "Surely that is better than scraping a living in the gutter?" Nylarian asked.

"Thank the baron for his kind offer, but I think her answer is no," Drevin said, a hard edge in his voice.

"Damn right," Cali echoed.

"Oh come now, mercenary. You know the baron doesn't take no for an answer. Release the girl to me or I will be forced to take her by…force," she said, smiling nastily. She raised her hands and cupped them together then a second later a small ball of fire appeared between them.

"Cali, run!" shouted Drevin, pushing her away from him as he advanced on the two Gatherers. The portly man reached into the pouch at his belt and pulled out a small metal ball, which he then casually tossed up into the air. Drevin watched it rise then suddenly it sped forward towards him. He instinctively flinched, but it whisked harmlessly past his shoulder. A second later he heard a thud and a cry of pain; glancing over his shoulder, he saw Cali rolling on the ground, clutching her leg, the ball lying next to her. Bastard! He ran at the man but a burst of fire from Nylarian's hands shot towards his head, and he had to quickly dive and roll out of the way. When he looked up again, he noticed a large black mark had charred the white stone wall, just where his head had been.

He heard a grunt of pain and a scuffle behind him and saw that Cali was grappling with the young man, both of them moving swiftly and landing blows on each other. He decided to change tactics. In a swift motion, he got to his feet and raced back to assist Cali. He figured if they could work together to take this Gatherer down then they might escape the trap. He almost made it to her. Just before he reached them a large, broken wooden sign that had been lying against a wall lifted into the air and slammed into him, sending him sprawling into the mud. Pain erupted from his ribs and back as he rolled on the ground, trying to avoid the heavy sign falling on him.

His eyes were watering at the pain and grit in them. But through the tears he saw Cali land a swift kick to her opponent's thigh, which sent him staggering away. Then she launched herself at him and landed a punch to his nose, blood splattering out and painting the wall he was leaning on red. He screamed in pain and fell against the wall, clutching his bleeding face. She glanced back to see Drevin lying on the floor, then back to the now empty end of the alleyway. Run, girl, run, Drevin implored her silently. She didn't run. Instead, she drew a dagger from her belt and raised her hands, walking towards him and the other Gatherers.

She threw the dagger in her right hand at the stocky man, but the woman blasted it out of the air with a tongue of fire. The blade darkened and clattered to the floor harmlessly in front of them, smoke rising lazily from it.

Drevin stood unsteadily, leaning on a wall for support, until Cali reached him.

"We don't want to hurt you, girl," called the woman, "but we will if you give us no choice. After all, a dead Frag is better than a rogue Frag."

Cali didn't answer. Her hands lifted and sent a blast of air at them, sending them staggering back a few steps. Drevin could tell however, that she was holding back as she hadn't sent them flying like she could have done. Fear still prevented her from using the full power of her Trait.

Drevin picked up the heavy wooden sign from the ground and held it in front of them, using it as a makeshift shield. "You need to get me close to them," he hissed to Cali.

"No," she said, her eyes wide and frightened as she caught on to his meaning. "What if I hurt you again?"

"If we don't take them down quickly we will both be dead. You can do this. Just breathe and focus. Remember?"

Cali nodded her head, but still looked uncertain.

"Good." said Drevin, hoisting the sign higher, bracing his shoulder behind it and ducking his head down. Just in time! A loud thud sounded as something small and heavy whacked into the shield, making his whole arm tremble at the impact. Splinters of wood flew off from the sign. "Now!" he shouted.

The next thing he knew, he was shooting along the alleyway, his feet barely touching the floor as he struggled to remain upright. The walls on either side flashed past him and he shut his eyes, trusting Cali to direct his movement. A brief flash of heat flicked over the side of the sign, singeing the hair on his arms and the side of his head. The hot wood burnt his fingers. He ducked his head lower. Then a heartbeat later, he crunched into something soft and heard satisfying shouts of pain and alarm. The makeshift shield broke apart in his hands at the collision: splinters of wood digging painfully into his hands. He fell and landed in an ungraceful heap, toppling the two Gatherers by his forceful arrival.

Drevin groggily raised his head to look around. Zortig was lying face up, his eyes closed, a small pool of blood collecting under his grey hair. One down. Drevin glanced at his chest. Still breathing. That's good. He didn't want to kill them. That would be a one-way ticket to the baron's dungeons. He heard a groan and saw that Nylarian, on the other hand was getting to her knees, her face covered in minor cuts, her cold blue eyes blazing with hate.

Drevin risked a glance behind him. Cali stood in the centre of the alley, looking smug. But Drevin saw that the third Gatherer had recovered and was racing up behind her, his speed unnatural. Before he could even shout a warning, Caderin had grabbed her, and they started their deadly dance again. Shit! As he looked back, he noticed the female Gatherer was on her feet, her hands reaching out to him. He rolled away from her and got to his feet, only slightly wobbly. He took a couple of steps forward and launched a fast punch into her stomach, forcing air from her lungs. She bent double, but kicked out and caught him in the shin, forcing him to step back painfully.

Drevin quickly drew his short sword and swiped it through the air, only intending to force her backwards. She sneered at him but stepped back, getting closer to one of the side walls. He noticed her steps were uneven and she swayed slightly. He swung his sword low, the blade vertical so that the flat side of it smacked into her knee, making it buckle. Then he quickly followed up by slamming his whole body into her and crushing her against the wall.

"Ha, ha," Nylarian laughed in his face. "Like it rough, do you? Come on then. But I think you might find I'm too hot for you to handle."

Drevin ignored her, trying to keep his body pressed tight to hers and her arms trapped between them so she couldn't use her Fragment. However, suddenly he started feeling a warmth spread across his chest and down his legs. At first, it was pleasant, soothing his aching muscles and drying out his damp clothes. But it kept getting hotter and hotter, the gentle warmth turning into a blistering heat and he started sweating as if it was the middle of summer. Dammit. She's using her Ignite power to heat her whole body. Her face had gone bright red, the scars on her cheeks now showing as thick white lines. The heat continued to build until it was painful to bear. Drevin could smell burning and see wisps of smoke rising from his clothes. He sprang away from her, patting desperately at his smouldering jerkin and trousers. The acrid stench of burnt hair filled the air.

"Ha, see what I mean." she laughed nastily, the glow fading from her face, returning to its natural paleness.

Just then, Drevin heard a wailing scream from down the alleyway. Cali! But it wasn't Cali. He glanced over and saw the young man now pinned to the wall, a dagger protruding from his wrist. Cali leaned in close and said something to him, but Drevin was too far away to hear her words. She then turned and looked at him grinning wildly, blood splattered over her face, looking like extra freckles. He hoped that wasn't her blood.

Then an arm clamped itself around his throat and Nylarian yanked him in front of her, her head leaning against his. Her other hand glowed red, and she raised it to his face, a finger hovering inches away from his eye. Shit! He had got distracted. Nylarian trapped his arms behind him, pressing them tight against her body, causing his sword to fall to the floor. He tried to wriggle free.

"Don't try anything bitch!" she shouted to Cali, "Or your friend here will soon be shopping for an eye patch."

Drevin froze. He could feel the heat from her hand and believed she was crazy enough to burn his eyes out. "Just let us go," he pleaded. "We will leave the city and won't cause anyone any harm."

"I can't do that. You know how the baron hates a failure." Nylarian sneered into his ear.

"Tell him you couldn't find her." Drevin suggested desperately.

"No, why should I? Why should she get to roam around free while the rest of us have to work for maniacs like

Sutter." She said venomously, spittle flying from her mouth. "Having to be cooped up in our 'comfortable' prisons. Forced to do their mad bidding, to make them richer and more powerful. No, I say. She needs to suffer like the rest of us."

"So much for luxury and comfort, huh," Drevin said, trying to buy time. He could feel her body shaking, whether from rage or the effects of using her power, he wasn't sure. Probably both.

Cali had stayed standing where she was in the alley, glancing between the two of them. The man pinned to the wall was sobbing quietly and seemed torn between ripping the dagger out or leaving it in. His free hand rising towards the dagger then dropping again to his side continuously. Drevin hoped for his sake and theirs that he left it in.

"Hey, Dev," Cali called suddenly, "remember how we met? How I greeted you in the tavern? Well, I think it's time for you to greet this lovely lady."

What? What was she talking about? Wait. Yes, I remember. The thoughts flashed across his mind and when he looked at Cali again she had whipped a dagger out from somewhere and tossed it into the air. With one hand extended she sent it flying towards them. Straight towards him!

Nylarian's finger jabbed towards his face, but he ducked his head to the side, then remembering Cali's words, stamped down hard on her foot. She released her grip on him and hopped backwards. Drevin ducked lower as the dagger flew directly at him, then panicked as he realised he wouldn't be able to avoid it. Cali had mis-thrown! It was still heading straight towards his face. He watched it as if in slow motion as it flew through the air, spinning end over end, the tip glistening in the damp air. It was less than an inch from his nose when it abruptly, unnaturally changed direction and veered off to his right. He breathed a heavy sigh of relief and heard a scream from Nylarian. He looked round to see her lying on the floor again, the dagger stuck in her left thigh.

He ran towards Cali and embraced her when they met. She laughed and held him tight for a moment, before seeming to remember herself, then she let go and stepped back.

"Let's go," he said.

"Wait!" shouted a shrill voice. "You are not going anywhere. Better dead than free, remember?"

They both looked back at Nylarian who was sitting in the mud, her hands rotating around a large ball of fire that was growing with every second. It looked like she intended to incinerate everything and everyone in the alleyway.

"Shit. Cali, we need to run now." Drevin said, tugging on her arm.

"We won't make it." Cali said, tears in her eyes. "I know what I have to do." She raised her arms, and Drevin could see her face scrunch up as she gathered all of her power.

"Cali, no, don't kill her," Drevin urged desperately. "There is another way. Use your surroundings, remember. Don't focus your power on her."

Cali glanced at him briefly and Drevin could not tell if the look in her eyes was one of hope or desperation. He felt the surge of force as an enormous blast erupted from her hands and poured along the alleyway. But instead of smashing into the prone Gatherer, the force picked up all the debris and litter in the alley, swirling it together into a ferocious whirlwind of refuse. Bits of old metal, shards of glass, broken pots, cast out chunks of wood, spoiled food and old rags whisked around and around, dust and mud spinning out of it as it gathered speed and headed towards the far end of the alley.

Cali and Drevin backed slowly away down the alleyway, Cali still focusing on her construction. The whirlwind now obscured their view, and they could no longer see Nylarian, but Drevin heard her gasp at what she was seeing. He imagined her trying to hobble away, hoping to escape, and smiled grimly. However, the next second a large ball of fire crashed into the maelstrom, causing a concussive blast of air along both sides of the alleyway.

Drevin pulled Cali into the side junction that they had just reached, and they both hunched down as flaming bits of debris flittered down around them for several seconds. When it had stopped, Drevin peeked his head out cautiously to look back. A fierce fire raged near the far end. A pile of burning rubbish sending flames five feet high, blocking off the entire alleyway. Of Nylarian, there was no sight.

"Well done," said Drevin, ducking back and clutching Cali's shoulder. He could feel her shaking. "Now let's get out of here. Go to your friend's shop and lie low. I will go a different way. You know where to find me."

Cali just nodded at him. She looked too tired to do anything else. Her face was pale and frightened. Then, once again, they ran.

# CHAPTER 11

# CAT AND MOUSE

Cali slammed the door shut behind her causing Teelan to wake with a start. She grinned mischievously at his startled expression. Then she looked more closely at him and noticed the dark circles under his eyes, his tangled hair and his crumpled robe and felt slightly guilty.

"Morning," Drevin said to Teelan, having entered the small room before her and slumped into a chair. "Gods, you look like shit."

Cali looked over at Drevin and thought he wasn't one to talk. His face was a mass of cuts and bruises, and his hair and stubble were singed down one side. He looked like he had been keel-hauled, then shoved head first onto a bonfire. Mind you, she supposed she probably looked little better herself.

After their ambush and then escape yesterday, Cali had spent the rest of the day moving from one safe place to the next, never staying for long in one location. When it got late, she had snuck back to her room and peeled off her dirty and ragged clothes. She had looked at herself in her small, polished brass mirror and grimaced. Her hair was stuck out in every direction, more wild than usual. Her face was too pale with red, blotchy patches and multiple minor scrapes and specks of blood covering it. And her arms were still trembling. She felt like she could sleep for two weeks. Once she had washed off most of the grime and blood, she collapsed onto her straw bed. She had slept deeply for a few hours, then had woken and had slept fitfully after that. Nightmares of raging fires and swirling winds plagued her.

When she had risen, just after first bell, she had felt more tired than before she had slept. After washing and dressing in clean clothes, she had scouted around her usual haunts, listening out for any news of the fight or for any signs of alarm. Satisfied that everything seemed as normal she had then headed to the place where Teelan worked and had met Drevin on her way in.

Teelan's voice interrupted her thoughts. "Look who's talking. What happened to you?" he snapped. "And what is she doing here?" Teelan flicked a glance at her.

Cali had been walking around the room, looking at the rows and rows of filled bookcases. "Hi Tee," she said, turning to him with a smile. "That's a shitload of books you've got here. Have you read them all?"

"Yes, of course I have," he said indignantly. Then "Tee!" he exclaimed, horrified, obviously just realising what she had said.

Cali's smile widened. That had woken him up! Damn, but it was so simple to provoke him. The boy was as sensitive as a seal's whiskers.

"Don't worry, it's a good sign. Means that you are her friend," Drevin said.

"Well, I am not sure if I want to be her friend. Especially if she keeps calling me that." Teelan said, glaring at her.

"Actually Dev, it's not just my friends I give nicknames to. I give everyone a nickname, even people I don't like," Cali said, staring back at Teelan. This was going to be fun. "For instance, there is this stupid boy who works at the docks with big puffy cheeks and wide lips, and I call him 'Carpface'. Then there is this really tall fellow…"

"Let me guess," Drevin interrupted, "you call him lofty, or maybe shorty?"

"No," she said, looking at Drevin as innocently as she could. "I call him Dirk, cos that's his name."

They both just looked at her incredulously. Gods, but they were easy to tease.

"What?" she said, defensively. "He's a big fella and I don't want to offend him."

"Anyway," Drevin said, shaking his head and turning back to Teelan, "as to what happened to us, the baron's delightful Gatherers set upon us yesterday. They wanted our young friend here to join their gang and didn't want to take no for an answer."

"Oh no," said Teelan, "you didn't kill them, did you? Drevin, are we about to be dragged off to the dungeons?"

"Don't worry kid," Drevin said casually. "They don't know who I am yet or who I'm working with. You are perfectly safe."

"I have heard that before." Teelan replied, getting to his feet quickly, then wobbling slightly and having to brace himself on the arm of the chair.

"Easy," said Drevin, quickly standing and supporting him with his arm. "Those mushrooms can leave you feeling weak for a while afterwards. How much sleep have you had?"

"What time is it?" Teelan asked, shaking off Drevin's arm.

"A couple of hours past first bell."

"A couple of hours then." Teelan said with a grimace.

"Shit Teelan. You need to look after yourself better than this," Drevin said, shaking his head at him. Cali wondered at their relationship. It was clear that they hadn't known each other long, but Drevin obviously cared for him. As for Teelan, she was not sure that he could care about anyone other than himself.

"I don't need your concern Drevin. I can look after myself. Anyway, I had all those bodies to examine, remember? Come on, let me show you what I found." Teelan walked out of the room and headed to the back of the building then down some steps to the basement. Cali followed behind Drevin. They arrived back in the room she had found them in before. Wooden shelves, tables, and benches lined the edges of the room, while the stone slabs dominated the middle. Both of which were filled with bodies with their guts open. The stench of rotting meat hit her like a slap, despite the freezing air.

"Eugh, that's gross." Cali declared, scrunching up her nose. Teelan just looked at her like it was her problem and not his.

Teelan led them back to the slabs with the grisly bodies on them. Cali tried to imagine them as oversized fish that someone had gutted, as she had seen plenty of those, but there were too many weird looking things in these bodies.

She suppressed a shudder and tried to focus on what Teelan was saying.

"Someone killed them quickly and efficiently. It looks like they tried to fight back but were disarmed with straight cuts to their sword arms here." Teelan said, lifting one of their right arms to display a long, deep cut running across the wrist. "Then a precise, neat slash across the throat finished them off," he continued, pointing to almost identical red lines across their throats.

Drevin leant closer to have a good look. "Shit. That is some neat blade work. Those are clean cuts, no rips or tears, no jagged lines. It is, as you say Teelan, likely done by a professional."

Cali saw Teelan's eyes go wide at Drevin's comments. He looked both shocked and offended at the same time. Maybe he doesn't like others agreeing with him?

Drevin had also obviously noticed his look. "What? Aren't I allowed to know stuff too? I have seen enough battle wounds to know a clean kill from a nasty gash that takes hours to finish you off."

Cali couldn't help but chuckle at that.

"May I continue?" Teelan asked, obviously still annoyed. He carried on talking without waiting for an answer, so Cali wasn't sure why he had asked in the first place. "I found similar wounds on the Hammer and his cronies. Some of them had more wounds than others, as they obviously put up more of a fight, but a single swipe across the throat killed all of them. The swipe was deep enough to sever the artery, causing them to bleed to death within seconds. I would say it was the work of the same one man as the wounds are almost impossibly identical.

Seems like the killer has a preferred method of dispatching his victims."

Cali took a closer look though she still had her nose wrinkled up at the nauseating smell. "Could've been some soldiers of the baron's, finally caught up to the bloody villains."

"Possibly," said Drevin, rubbing his chin, "but unlikely. They would all have had to be the same height, carrying identical blades and using the same strokes and force of swing. Right Teelan?"

"That is correct." Teelan said. Cali noticed Teelan's glance at Drevin and couldn't determine if he was still annoyed at Drevin's knowledge or if he was pleased to be asked if he was right or not.

Drevin spoke again, "So most likely it was the one man then. But he would have to be damn good to have killed all of them. Picket and Sticket would have been easy. But the Hammer and his thugs were seasoned hard men and would have known how to handle their weapons."

Cali chuckled again. She wondered if he knew what he was saying and was doing it on purpose or not. Probably not. Maybe her mind just worked that way because of where she had been brought up.

"Well," Teelan carried on, ignoring her outburst and turning back to Drevin, "another thing is that a heavy blade held horizontally made the wounds. There were no thrusts, stabs, or angled slashes, just perfectly horizontal cuts."

"What does that matter? Dead is dead right." Cali said. She glanced at Drevin's face and could tell that to him it mattered.

"Oh, shit!" Drevin said, his face draining of colour. "Shit, shit, shit."

"Yes, we know you love that word." Teelan snapped impatiently, "What is it?"

Cali saw Drevin pause before he said. "In Satiria, they practise a method of fighting known as 'Libratto' where the blade is always held horizontally, and all strikes are made in a straight line. There are only a few sword masters who teach their students to fight this way. It is incredibly difficult to learn, as you naturally want to rotate the blade to block or thrust. It is a purist's technique and is usually only employed in competitions, but some adapt it in their day-to-day life. Only those with great skill can learn this and as you can see, it can be incredibly effective."

"So what," Cali said. She hadn't been expecting a lesson this morning and had no interest in fancy sword techniques. She was getting fidgety and felt idle. When were they going to get to the point?

"So," Drevin continued, "I would say that it was an Irian that killed these men, and I know of a certain Irian mercenary who is currently here in the city. Goes by the name of Hascor Proxin. Wait. No. Dammit! Teelan, when we left the tavern after meeting the Hammer, did you see anyone there?"

"No, not really. I was too relieved to get out of that room alive." Teelan said, shaking his head, his long hair swinging, "Oh. Hold on. Yes, there was a rather large man who rudely rushed past me. What of it?"

"What did he look like, Teelan?" Drevin pressed.

"I am not sure. All of you big brutes look much the same to me," Teelan replied. Cali saw him smirk at

Drevin. Drevin, however, was not smiling back. "Fine. I couldn't really see his face as he had a hood on, but he was wearing a long brown leather coat and bizarrely, I thought I could hear a tinkling of metal coming from under the hood."

"That would be Hascor." Drevin said, nodding. "He wears a coat like that, and he has tiny metal sword decorations tied in his hair."

"I say again. So what? Why is this a problem?" Cali huffed. She was getting very impatient now and was feeling left out of the conversation.

"Because he's good. Very good." Drevin mused.

"Better than you?" Teelan asked him with a wry smile. How dare he ask that? Cali felt like punching him.

"Maybe," Drevin said thoughtfully, "Someone must have paid him to do the job, but even if we could find him, he wouldn't disclose who sent him. Professional discretion and all that. He is fair and dependable but is not too picky about who he works for. He has done some shady stuff before so he could be working for anyone. Did you find anything else?"

"Oh yes," said Teelan, nonchalantly. "I almost forgot. I found this clutched in the Hammer's fist." He pulled out a small, ragged, misshapen scrap of red paper out of a pocket of his robe and handed it to Drevin.

Drevin looked at it carefully, turning it over in his hand, "What is it?" Cali couldn't really see what it was from here and found herself annoyed that nobody had bothered to show it to her.

"It is a piece of paper that was ripped out of the Hammer's hand. The paper is thick and good quality and there are some words written on it but the blood stains covering it obscure most of them. I can just make out the words 'man' and 'city' at the bottom. I compared it to the paper correspondence I receive from the castle and guess what, it is identical!" Teelan finished smugly.

"And you couldn't have told us this to start with," Drevin said, clearly frustrated. Go on Drevin, hit him! Wipe that smugness off his face.

"Oh, you know me, I like to build to a big climax." Teelan grinned.

Cali burst out laughing. She couldn't help herself. Honestly, did they not think about what they were saying? She held her sides as she laughed heartily.

"What is it with you?" Teelan suddenly snapped at her.

"Sorry," she said, still unable to stop her laughter. "Too long living in a brothel I think." She thought of the girls she lived with and how they used similar language to what Drevin and Teelan were just using, but in completely different circumstances.

"Wait. What! You live in a brothel!" Teelan asked shocked, "Do you..I mean are you..?"

Here we go. Bring on the judgement, "Spit it out Tee." Cali said, anger replacing her mirth. "No, I don't, and I am not one of 'those' girls. I just live there, not work there. Not that there would be anything wrong if I were one of those girls. They work hard for their money. Harder than most people. And they don't do it because they want to, or they enjoy it. Most of them have no other choice." She could feel her face heating from her tirade, and she crossed her arms to hide her shaking. She wasn't sure if she was shaking from her anger or from the cold seeping through her. Either way, she didn't want them to see it.

She stared at the two of them. Drevin looked sheepish and remained quiet. Teelan was wild-eyed and looked from her to Drevin desperately as if he wanted someone to rescue him. Luckily for him, after a brief silence Drevin did just that.

"Well, that is very interesting," Drevin said, pretending that the previous conversation had not just happened. "This could be the remaining part of the note that the Hammer received, instructing him to remove Ridozir. And along with the fact that it was most likely delivered by a messenger boy in the baron's colours leads us back to one place."

"The castle." Teelan said gloomily.

"What!" Cali said. She was still mad with Teelan, and it took her a moment to realise what Drevin had just said. When she did, she couldn't believe what she had just heard. "Crap. You can't seriously be thinking of going to the castle after what we did to those Gatherers yesterday, Dev? They will arrest you on sight, just because." This was madness. He couldn't just walk in there and expect to see the baron's brother after almost killing the baron's Gatherers. Could he?

"I hate to agree with her, but I think for once she is right." Teelan said reluctantly. Cali stuck her tongue out at him because she knew it would annoy him. And right now, she didn't want his help.

"We have to." Drevin said, seriously, "Someone there has been behind this the whole time, and we need to find out who, for the baron's sake. Besides, I don't enjoy leaving a job half done. Teelan and I will go." Cali felt a bit of satisfaction at the look of panic on Teelan's face when he said that. "Cali, it is best if you stay hidden for a while. Don't worry, I will be back, and I won't tell them anything about you."

"You had better not." Cali replied fiercely, "And you had better come back, otherwise I will come and get you." Cali felt moisture build up in her eyes. What! Was she about to cry? She was a bit taken aback at how she felt. She barely knew Drevin, yet she already knew that she didn't want him to come to harm. He was the first genuine person she had met for a long time.

He had told her the truth and been honest with her from the start and hadn't asked for anything in return. There were not many people like him around. Bloody hell! Get a grip, girl.

"Well, I need to get some supplies anyway," she said, trying to sound casual and indifferent. "I'll come back here later and you had better be here!" she warned as she sauntered over to the stairs. Once she was halfway up and out of sight, she stopped to gather herself and heard Teelan's whining voice.

"Drevin, you can't possibly think that we can just walk into the castle after you had a public brawl with the Gatherers, can you?" Teelan pleaded.

"We have to Teelan. The captain is a reasonable man. If I explain to him they set upon us first I am sure he'll understand. Especially if we can tell him who was responsible for the death of Ridozir."

Cali didn't mean to eavesdrop, but she couldn't help herself. Besides, she was very good at it.

She heard Teelan speak again, “But we can’t tell him that yet, can we? As there is just the small matter that we don’t know who is responsible yet.”

“We’ll figure it out. Come on, might as well get it over with.” Drevin said, and she heard him walking towards the stairs. She hurried up to the top but could still hear them talking. “By the way, don’t you have a bedroom, rather than sleeping in that chair in your study?” she heard Drevin ask.

“I do. But I was too tired to climb the stairs to get to it,” she heard Teelan say wearily.

She couldn’t see them, but she could almost feel Drevin’s disapproval from here.

She quickly scampered out of the building and into the greyness of the morning, pulling up her hood. She had a bad feeling about what was going to happen next. Knowing she would need to be prepared; she headed towards the Iron Market to stock up on supplies of essentials. Food, drink, clothes, candles and lots of sharp iron.

***

“So, what is the plan, then?” Teelan asked nervously as they headed out of the north gate towards the bridge linking the castle to the city. A light drizzle was trickling out of the dense, iron grey clouds that hung low overhead. “We just march in there and accuse everyone with any authority until someone confesses?” He was still feeling washed out from the aftereffects of the drugs and lack of sleep. That, along with his uncomfortable confrontation with Cali and his growing anxiety was making him snippy. He didn’t know what it was about that girl that aggravated him so.

"Something like that," replied Drevin infuriatingly, then he saw the look on Teelan's face and continued, "Look, we know that the messenger and the letter both came from the castle. So, someone with enough power had to organise both of them. It also had to be someone who would gain from his disappearance, which given what an arsehole Ridozir was, could be anyone who just wanted a quieter life. We need to find out who has access to that kind of paper there and the money to hire a mercenary. Who sends you letters from the castle?"

"Some come from the priests, but most of them are regarding supplies and finances, and these come from Wilburton." They crossed the bridge, and Teelan kept his eyes averted from the watchful guards.

"So, we start with the steward. Show him the remnant of the letter. See if he shows any signs of guilt or if he knows who sent it."

"Actually, that might work," Teelan said hopefully. "Wilburton is the one who usually deals with all the correspondence going in and out. He might be able to help. Presuming we can get to him, of course. Do you think he could be behind it?" Teelan couldn't imagine the overanxious steward being capable of putting together such a plot, but you never knew.

"Relax, we'll get to him." Drevin was still too calm for Teelan's liking. "I am not sure if he would be up to this, but if he heard about Ridozir's and Islia's plans he might have acted to protect the baron and the barony. He is fiercely loyal to Zandir and has been in his household for many years." Drevin explained as they carried on up the winding path that led to the dark grey imposing castle on the hill looming above them. "Or the men from Paska might have arranged it to clear the way for Islia's marriage to their baron's eldest son. An alliance like that would be a significant achievement for a small barony like Paska, and they wouldn't want anything impeding it."

"You really dislike those men, don't you? Or is it just Paska you have a grudge against?" Teelan asked, keen to understand what his issue was. Every time they were mentioned, Drevin's behaviour became strange, and he avoided all contact with them. He was definitely hiding something.

"We've got to consider all possibilities," Drevin replied defensively, "such as the baron himself."

"What!" Teelan stopped in the middle of the road in shock. A few passing merchants looked over at them curiously, then carried on wheeling their carts back towards the city, "You are not serious. Why would Zandir kill his own son?"

"Remember, the intention was not to kill him," Drevin pointed out. "The plan was to send him away. Maybe Zandir thought he wasn't ready to run the barony and wanted to give him the chance to grow up a bit more and gain more experience before he took charge."

"Maybe. But surely Zandir could have just delayed his ascension and stayed in control for a few more years himself. That would have been much easier than all this."

"Yes, you're right. But who knows how the minds of these arrogant noble's work? Sometimes they complicate things just for the sake of it."

"What about Serzin, Zandir's brother? I still have doubts about him, too."

"Hmm, I'm not sure. He plainly didn't like Ridozir, but he seemed genuinely upset by how it had affected his brother. Once again though, we don't know how these people think. To them, other people are just pawns to be moved around and disposed of as befits their whims. I don't think we can rule anyone out yet."

Teelan found that offensive but wasn't about to tell Drevin that. Not all nobles were the same. Drevin obviously didn't much care for those in authority. He noticed Drevin was spinning the ring on his finger again, lost in thought.

They crossed the field outside the walls where several enterprising merchants had set up stalls. There were quite a few people in the field, talking, trading, or just waiting around. They approached the broad open gates, and the guards allowed them in once Drevin told them who they were and that they were there to see the steward.

As Drevin was once again relieved of all of his weapons by the bored-looking guard in the small reception room, Teelan paced around, his emotions a mix of fear, worry, nervousness and excitement. But mostly fear. After a brief wait, Wilburton appeared, looking the same as ever. His long blue robe had a small creamy stain down the front and his hands were doing their usual jittery dance. Although for once Teelan noticed his hands were empty of food. The black cat was back at his feet, jumping around, trying to catch the tail of his slightly swishing robe.

"Master Drevin, Master Teelan." he welcomed them. "What can I do for you today? Have you had any luck finding the killer of poor Ridozir?"

"We have made some progress, yes," said Drevin casually, "but we need to ask you a few questions if you can spare us the time. Is there anywhere more private we can go?" he asked, eycing the guard.

"Me!" exclaimed the steward. "I am not sure how I can help, but if that is what you want. Come this way."

They followed him as he headed deeper into the castle, past grand halls and less grand waiting rooms, kitchens and dining rooms. They crossed an inner courtyard, where young men were beating at each other with wooden swords, trying to prove just how manly they were. Teelan shook his head. Why do you have to be violent and aggressive to be seen as a proper man?

Eventually the steward ushered them into a sparse, modest sized room with a solid table and four chairs the only furniture in the room. The drizzle outside had turned into a solid rain and was beating a steady, pattering rhythm against the room's sole window.

"Please be seated, gentlemen." Wilburton said, indicating the chairs.

Teelan and Drevin sat on one side of the table and the steward sat down across from them. The cat had followed him all the way and now prowled under the table.

"How can I help you?" Wilburton asked.

Drevin leant forward, his arms leaning on the table. "We have found out who killed Ridozir," he said, watching the steward intensely.

"Well, that is excellent news," said Wilburton brightly, standing up. "Let's tell the baron immediately." The cat let out a yelp and dashed to the door.

"Wait a minute Esklin, sit down." Drevin waved him back to his seat.

The steward sat back down with a frown on his face. "What is it?"

"We have found out who killed him," Drevin repeated, "but not who wanted him dead."

Teelan could tell from the confused look on the steward's face that he didn't understand. The cat had noticed that Wilburton had sat down again and resumed its position under the table.

Drevin continued speaking. "A couple of lowlifes from the Stone District killed him. They were sent by a man called 'The Hammer'. Do you know that name at all?"

"No, I don't think so," Wilburton said, still looking confused. Teelan thought he looked genuinely puzzled and if he was lying, then he was very good at it.

"Well, someone dispatched a messenger boy to the Hammer with a note, requesting him to abduct Ridozir and informing him of the location and time to find him on that day."

"So?" Here it comes.

"The messenger boy came from here."

Teelan heard the steward's gasp of surprise. "Surely not. You must be mistaken. That can't be true." Wilburton was shaking his head in denial, his hands wringing like a washerwoman drying out her clothes.

"It is true. Who here has the authority to order messenger lads around?" Drevin pressed.

The steward grimaced at this question. From somewhere in his robe he pulled out a hard lump of cheese and started nibbling on it like a nervous mouse. Teelan thought it was more to stop his hands twitching than out of any hunger. "Well, the noble families obviously and all the senior staff, so I am afraid that it is quite a long list of people."

"What about visiting nobles?" Drevin asked. Teelan glanced at him. He would not let that one go, would he?

"Of course, if they needed something." The cat dashed out from under the table to sniff at some crumbs of cheese Wilburton had dropped before licking them up quickly.

"Hmm. Additionally, the paper used for the note appears to have come from the castle. Who would have access to this?"

"Again, it would be all the nobles, myself, Captain Korac and a few of the higher-ranking staff." Wilburton said, fidgeting in his seat as if he wasn't used to sitting still for too long. Either that or the questions were making him uncomfortable.

"And what about hiring mercenaries? Who would have the authority to do that?"

"Mercenaries. What!" the steward cried, half rising from his seat.

"Sit down and answer the question Esklin." Drevin said firmly.

"Well, anyone of the noble family could do it, or Korac or myself," he said, swallowing hard.

"So, you have access to all three things then?" Drevin asked curiously, one eyebrow raised.

"Well, yes," Wilburton said, puffing himself up, "as steward I deal with most of the administration, the running of the castle which involves sending messengers and …dealing with more delicate matters." He finished, deflating and blushing slightly, "Hold on. Wait a moment. What are you implying? You don't think that I had anything to do with this, do you?"

Teelan could see the sweat gathering on his bald head as he worked out the implications of what Drevin was asking him. The cheese was poised in his hand, forgotten. The cat looked up expectantly, waiting for more largesse to fall its way.

"You tell me?" Drevin asked smugly, leaning back in his chair.

"I, I, I would never do anything to harm the baron or his family. I have lived in this castle since I was a young boy. Baron Sutter's father took my parents and I in when they had a falling out with the King of Torgar's son. We fled the capital with only our clothes to our name but found refuge and a place of honour here. I used to play with Zandir when we were both boys and I was the closest thing he had to a best friend. When he became baron he kept all of us on his staff and then promoted me to be his steward." Wilburton was shaking now, his face red. Whether from fear or anger, Teelan couldn't tell.

"Fine." said Drevin, lifting his hands placatingly. "Who would want to harm his family then?"

"I couldn't tell you. Ridozir was not well liked, but I don't think anyone would go so far as to murder him." Wilburton said, shuddering. He munched on the cheese again, scattering more crumbs for the efficient cat to gobble up.

"What can you tell me about this?" Drevin asked, pushing the scrap of paper that Teelan had found in the Hammer's hand across the table.

"What is this? Is that blood?" Wilburton grimaced at the sight of it and his face went a shade paler. Teelan thought he might faint. Lightweight.

"Is this the paper you use here?" Drevin asked him, ignoring his reaction.

Wilburton reluctantly looked closer at it. “Yes, it looks like the paper we use, although it is not normally that colour.”

“What about the writing on it?” Teelan asked. “Can you tell who may have written it?” He knew that everyone’s handwriting was unique to them. He had briefly studied how to recognise different styles of handwriting and discern what sort of person had written it but had quickly grown bored with the monotony of the work.

The steward looked at Teelan incredulously before forcing his gaze back to the paper. “It’s very smudged and blurred, with that stain on it. I am not sure I can recognise it.”

“Look closely.” Drevin urged, pushing it closer to him. Teelan felt himself leaning across the table as well. This could be the breakthrough they need.

“I don’t know. Hold on. Hmm. Maybe.” Wilburton said as he squinted at it and took his time considering. Teelan noticed however, that he had not picked it up. “Yes. See the word that looks like ‘city’,” he said, pointing to, but not touching the paper, “The letter ‘i’ doesn’t appear to have a dot above it. It is a simplistic style of writing, and I know someone who writes like that.”

“Who?” Drevin breathed.

“Lord Serzin,” said Wilburton, sitting up straight again.

“Shit!” said Drevin.

“Oh no. Goodness me. No!” said Wilburton, his face turning even whiter than as he clearly remembered something else.

"What is it Esklin?"

"You mentioned something about a mercenary? Why?" he asked, not looking like he actually wanted to know the answer Teelan thought.

"Someone hired one to kill off the Hammer and his goons. Trying to cover their tracks, no doubt." Drevin replied, "Why?"

"A few days ago, Lord Serzin asked me for the name of a mercenary. He said he had a small matter to take care of. I gave him your name first of course, Master Drevin, but he said he wanted someone else. The only other mercenary I know currently in the city was the one who signed up to help search for Ridozir." Wilburton stammered out.

"Let me guess, Hascor Proxin?" Drevin asked.

"Yes, that is right. How did you know?"

"Never mind. Go on Esklin."

"Well, that is it really. I gave him the mercenary's name and he went away with it. I thought it was a bit strange as usually he would ask me to contact such people directly." Well, if Serzin wanted to murder a bunch of people, I am not surprised he didn't ask the fretful steward to arrange it.

"Anything else?" Drevin asked.

"No. Wait. Yes. A couple of nights ago this mercenary turned up here demanding to see Serzin. The guards wouldn't let him in as it was late, but I heard Serzin did go and meet with him. Oh no! That doesn't sound very good, does it?" Wilburton said, holding his head in his hands. He looked as white as a ghost now, fear plain to see in his wide eyes.

"No, it doesn't." Drevin said sadly, "Esklin, take us to see the baron's brother. It's time we had another chat with Serzin Sutter."

# CHAPTER 12

# A MOTIVE FOR MURDER

Teelan stood outside the door to Serzin's room, nervously shuffling from one foot to the other. They had been left outside, waiting whilst the steward went in. Drevin stood nearby, also pensive, twiddling the ring on his finger again. Teelan hoped he knew what he was doing. Wilburton finally opened the door and beckoned them in, then exited quickly, clearly not wanting to get caught up in this conversation. Drevin however, caught the steward's arm on his way past and whispered something urgently into his ear, too quiet for Teelan to hear. Wilburton's face quivered at his words, and he reluctantly nodded his head before hastening away.

They entered the same room that they had met Serzin in before, its overt manliness still very much on display. Serzin sat in his same chair, his same goblet of wine in hand. Teelan experienced a moment of déjà vu. Serzin's son, Weslin, was lying on a large leather cushion, staring into a polished copper disk at his wavy reflection.

On a padded chair to Serzin's right sat his wife, Myelandra. She was wearing a tightly laced pale blue dress, her long black hair falling over one eye. Her hands were busy sewing together the pieces of a child's green doublet and she only glanced up at them briefly.

"Sit down," Serzin said to them, waving a hand lazily at the chairs opposite him. "Can I get you anything? Wine? Milk?"

"No thank you," Drevin said quickly before Teelan could respond. They both sat in the same chairs as before, although Teelan noticed that this time Drevin sat on the edge of his seat much like him. It seemed that even he was aware of the precariousness of their situation and wary of how this conversation might go.

"What can I do for you now?" Serzin asked tersely, as if he sensed their tension and knew what they were about to say.

"Can we speak in private, my lord?" Drevin asked, looking over at Myelandra.

"My wife and I have no secrets. You can speak plainly." Teelan noticed her look up from her work for a moment to stare at them before continuing her sewing.

"Fine. We have found out who killed Ridozir," Drevin said, straight to the point.

"Excellent." Though Serzin didn't look as pleased as Teelan thought he should. "Who was it and where are they? I will inform the baron, and we will arrest them."

"I'm afraid it is not as simple as that," said Drevin solemnly.

"Oh," said Serzin, taking a drink from his goblet, his eyebrow raised.

"You see, a couple of street criminals who worked for someone called The Hammer killed Ridozir. But the problem is that they were just hired to do the job by someone else."

"I see. But does that matter? If they were responsible for killing him, then they will have to pay."

"Oh, don't worry, they have paid. We know someone from the castle hired them. Someone with money, power and authority."

"Who?" Here it comes! Teelan clenched all of his muscles in anticipation and held his breath.

"You, my lord." Drevin stated simply.

Serzin leaned back in his chair and roared with laughter. Well, that was not the reaction Teelan expected.

After a few moments, he managed to get himself under control and stopped laughing as he saw both of their concerned expressions. "Seriously. You think I did this?" he finally said.

"Yes, my lord." Drevin said, ignoring his reaction completely. "We know you sent a messenger boy to the Hammer telling him where and when Ridozir would be and to remove him. We also know that you then hired a mercenary and sent him after the Hammer so that he couldn't testify against you."

"Nonsense! Poppycock." snorted Serzin. "This is all fabrication or conjecture at best. You have no proof and no motive. You ought to be careful about throwing accusations like that around."

"What about this, then?" Drevin said, digging out the scrap of paper from his pouch and holding it in front of Serzin. "This is a piece of the letter you sent to the Hammer. We have reliable information that this is your handwriting." Drevin pulled the piece of paper away as

Serzin squinted at it and before he could snatch it out of his hand.

Teelan noticed Serzin had suddenly lost his humour, his face going dark and angry before he spoke again. “Well, as this Hammer and his cronies are all dead, there is no-one who can corroborate your story that this letter was sent to him. It could be an innocent letter I sent to anyone.”

“I never said that the Hammer was dead. How did you know that? We got to his body not long after his death and we have told no one yet.”

“I, I hear things.” Serzin growled. Teelan thought he detected a hint of worry in his voice.

“Well, we also have the messenger boy you sent and the mercenary and they will both inform the baron about the.. interesting tasks you gave them to do.” Drevin said, leaning forward. Wait! What! That is simply not true Drevin. We don’t have them at all. How can you lie so casually like that?

“Really?” Serzin said. “And the rest of that letter? I suppose you have that somewhere too?”

Teelan felt his eyebrows go up in surprise at that remark. They had thought that Serzin had the rest of the letter. If he didn’t have it, then who did and where was it? Fortunately, Drevin had more control of his expressions and kept a neutral look on his face.

“It’s in a safe place,” Drevin lied casually. Again, Teelan marvelled at his nonchalance when telling an untruth. Teelan’s nerves were completely frayed, but Drevin looked like he was just having a chat with an old friend.

"Well, it seems as if you know everything, then." Serzin sighed heavily, draining the last of his wine.

"Not quite everything," Drevin replied. "There are two things I still don't know. First, why did you organise the search in the city for Ridozir if you were behind his disappearance? And second, why? Why did you want him out of the way?"

"I had to do something," Serzin said unhappily, looking into his empty goblet. "Zandir became incensed when he heard his son was missing. He was going to let all his guards loose in the city to tear the place apart looking for him. It would have become a bloodbath, and within hours he would have filled his dungeons with innocent victims. I thought Ridozir would be long gone, so I didn't see the harm in it. Besides, I didn't think there would be anyone competent enough to actually find out what had happened to him," he said, looking hard at Drevin.

"As to the why. You have to understand Ridozir was a nasty piece of work. He was always jealous of what we had, a nice, happy, normal family. It was something he would never have. So, he threatened to throw me and my family out of the castle when he became baron, to leave us homeless and penniless. I had to do something to stop him.

"I tried reasoning with him, threatening to tell his father, even offering him land and money, but he wouldn't listen to anything. So, I came up with the plan to send him to my cousin in Adony. He has a large estate and vineyards, out in the countryside, where he could have kept Ridozir out of the way and in relative comfort. I hoped that spending some time there would help to mature him and curb his temperament."

"Of course. The Endnote!" Teelan exclaimed. "I should have caught on."

"What." Drevin said, turning to him. Teelan flushed as everyone stared at him, but it was too late to retract his outburst now.

"The name of the ship that Ridozir was meant to get on belonged to your cousin, didn't it?" Teelan continued quickly to Serzin. "The word 'endnote' is a terminology used in wine. It means the aftertaste. In other words, how long you can still taste the wine after you have swallowed it. The better the wine, the longer the endnote."

"That's right," Serzin said, sounding impressed. "My cousin does so love his wine."

"The Adony Red. Of course," said Drevin, finally catching on. "But what about your brother?" he said, turning back to Serzin. "It seems harsh to make his son disappear forever with no explanation. That is almost worse than having him killed."

"It would not be forever." Serzin sighed. "Once he arrived there my cousin was going to write to Zandir to let him know Ridozir was staying with him. He would explain that Ridozir fled there, as he didn't feel ready to rule and wanted to get some life experience. I had hoped that in time Ridozir would come to enjoy his time there and correspond with his father directly."

"A neat plan," said Drevin, rubbing his stubbled chin. "So what went wrong?"

"I honestly don't know Drevin, you have to believe me. If you have read the note as you claim, then you know that I never intended to kill Ridozir. I was just doing what

I felt I must to protect my family and for the greater good of the barony. I didn't want to see him dead." Serzin pleaded, leaning forward, hands clasped tightly around his goblet.

"No, but I did." For a second Teelan didn't know where the female voice had come from. Then he glanced over and saw Serzin's wife, stony faced, her needles gripped tight in her hands. She had been so quiet up to now he had forgotten she was in the room.

"What! What are you saying, Myelandra?" Serzin spluttered.

"He was a monster, Serzin. You knew that. I told you about him wanting us gone, but I didn't tell you everything." She put down her needle carefully in her lap before looking at her husband and continuing. "He came to my room one evening a couple of weeks ago when you were out entertaining those young men from Paska. Then he tried to seduce me, acting all charming, making me all kinds of promises, but I could see right through him. He just wanted to get me into bed. Another conquest for the young baron to be. No doubt he would have bragged about it to everyone as well." She pushed her hair back away from her face and lifted her head to gaze at them.

Teelan looked at her properly for the first time. She was an attractive woman. Her face was round and smooth skinned with just a few lines at the eyes and mouth, which was full-lipped. Her eyes were a deep brown and were currently smouldering with suppressed anger. The dress showed off her ample cleavage and curvy body shape so he could see why a lusty young man such as the baron's son would be interested in her.

"What happened?" breathed Serzin. Teelan thought he looked absolutely stunned.

"What do you think happened? I turned him down of course," she said dismissively, tossing her head and making her curls bounce. "Needless to say, he didn't take the rejection very well. Then he showed his true nature. He ranted about how he hated us and was envious of our family. In his opinion, it wasn't fair that we should be content and that we flaunted it in his face just because his family was such a mess. He thought we were laughing at him behind his back. That is when he told me he intended to throw us out when he was in charge, and I came and told you straight away Serz."

"Yes, that is why I made the plan to send him away." Serzin said, confused, "Look, I know Ridozir was a cruel, vindictive and selfish boy, but did he deserve to die?"

"Yes, he did." Myelandra said sternly, "He told me one more thing that night. He did it, Serz!" Teelan could see tears gathering in the corners of her eyes.

"Did what? What are you talking about?"

"He did this to our son," she shouted, waving her arm at Weslin, who had forgotten his shiny mirror and was now sitting up and staring at the wall.

"What!" Serzin shouted back, half rising from his chair.

"Ridozir boasted of it to hurt me as I had hurt him by turning him down," she said, tears escaping from her eyes and rolling down her face. "He said that on the day it happened he saw Wes playing at sword fighting with some of the other young squires, so he decided to show him what it meant to be a man. He took up a wooden sword and duelled with our little boy. Of course, he was much older and bigger than him, so he beat him easily.

"He laughed as he told me how simple it was for him to smack Weslin around. Then he knocked the sword out of Wes' hand and our son got angry and charged at him. He caught Ridozir off guard and punched him in the stomach. Ridozir didn't like that, so he whacked his sword so hard against the back of Wes' head that the wooden blade snapped in half. Wes collapsed to the floor and has been like this ever since," she said, pointing at the vacant-looking boy.

"Ridozir then threatened the other squires to keep quiet and made them tell everyone that Weslin had just fallen over and banged his head," she finished, lifting her hands to her face to wipe away the tears.

"By the Gods!" exclaimed Serzin, collapsing back into his chair. "Whyever didn't you tell me this?"

"Because I knew you would want to kill him, and I didn't want you to be responsible for hurting Ridozir. I know you still love your brother and wouldn't want to cause him pain like that, not after you watched his decline following his wife's death. But I couldn't let Ridozir just go off and live a life of luxury, unpunished."

"But how did you..?" Serzin asked. Teelan could see his puzzlement. At how she had arranged this and, perhaps more importantly, at how she had kept it from him.

Myelandra continued matter-of-factly, "I followed your messenger boy and when I saw who he spoke to, I waited until he called some of his men in. After they came out of the tavern, I approached them and inquired if they had been assigned to abduct a man from a barn. When they refused to answer, I gave them some coins and said there would be more if they cooperated.

"When I finally got the truth out of them, I told them to kill this man instead of taking him to the ship and to get rid of his body permanently and I would reward them well. I went back to their warehouse later that night to check that they had done the deed and to give them the rest of the money. They had Ridozir's body there.

"When I looked down at his corpse on the dirty floor, I thought I would feel relieved, satisfied, maybe even happy. But I didn't. Do you know what I felt? Anger. Anger at who he was. Anger that he had aimed his vindictiveness at us and our son. Anger at what he had forced me to do. At making me have to lie to you. And that anger hasn't gone away," she finished quietly. Her eyes were dry now and smouldering, like two hot coals. The tears were gone too, only a faint trace of them left on her cheeks.

"Wow. So much for no secrets between you two," Drevin said. Great, that's just what we need right now Drevin. Sarcasm. Teelan felt hollowed out by her confession, her emotions plain to see and hear. It was not a feeling he enjoyed.

"By the Gods!" Serzin repeated, "What have you done, Mya?"

"I have done what was necessary to keep us safe. To get justice for our son," she said fiercely.

Serzin turned back to Drevin, his hand wiping his face. He looked pale and drawn, as if he had just aged ten years in a few minutes. "Drevin, this must stay between us. My brother doesn't need to know. Surely you can see that we were only defending ourselves, acting in the interests of our family. The barony is better off without him anyway.

"I tell you what. I will send some guards to collect the bodies of 'those responsible', inform the baron that the deed is done, and give you a big fat reward. That way everyone's a winner. What do you say?" Serzin had returned to pleading, almost begging. Teelan squirmed uncomfortably on his chair. However, he thought that proposition sounded very reasonable actually and for the first time tonight he had hope that he might leave here in one piece.

"I understand what you did and why you did it. Both of you." Drevin said, looking sadly from Serzin to his wife. "I am sorry for what he did to your son and can sympathise with your actions and need for revenge." He shot Teelan a quick look when he said the word 'sympathise.'

"But you are going to tell my brother anyway, aren't you? I can see it in your eyes. Why?" Serzin said quietly.

What! No, no, no, Drevin. Don't be an idiot. He is offering us a way out of this. Please take it, for my sake if not for yours. Teelan's mind went into panic mode. His hopes of not getting tortured and executed seemingly short lived.

"Because it's the right thing to do," Drevin said calmly, as if talking about the weather and not just initiating their death sentence.

"Well, that is a shame. I thought we could come to a deal." Serzin shook his head slowly. "Never mind. In that case, let me tell you what else I have heard." Serzin said, smiling grimly. Teelan did not like that smile. "I heard that yesterday a rogue Fragment attacked our Gatherers, severely injuring them. That this girl was in the company of a mercenary matching your description. Did you know, I wonder, that an act of violence towards the baron's Gatherers counts as treason?"

This was it! Teelan was ready to bolt. His legs jiggled nervously together, his feet bouncing on the floor. Time's up.

"Guards!" Serzin shouted.

Teelan jumped as the doors at either end of the room opened and four muscled men clanged into the room, two from each side. They looked like normal men in chain mail and blue tabards, swords hanging at their belts, but to Teelan right now they might as well have been death itself stalking him.

Drevin stood and shook his head at Serzin sadly, "You don't have to do this my lord." he said.

"I am truly sorry Drevin, but you have left me no choice. My family comes first," he said to Drevin with what looked like genuine regret. "Guards, arrest these men for treason against the barony of Canor. Take them to the dungeons."

Teelan stood quickly and almost fainted. His heart was beating so fast he could barely hear the slow clomping of metal boots approaching them. Well done Drevin. You have finally gone and done it this time. What a splendid plan. Just walk in here and accuse the most powerful man in the barony of murdering his brother's son. Brilliant. Now we are both headed for the dungeons and a slow, no doubt excruciatingly painful death. Thanks a lot. Why did I ever get involved with you? I knew it was a bad idea to work with someone. I am better off being alone. Teelan's thoughts were spinning faster than a tornado, whirling out of control.

Drevin meekly walked towards the pair of guards nearest the door they came in and Teelan, lacking any better options, numbly followed him. I hope that you have got a way out of this. Please Drevin. Do something. Now!

Amazingly, Drevin did do something. He suddenly lunged forward shoving the closest guard against the wall with a thud. Then, quick as a flash, he slammed his elbow into his head. The guard, stunned, slid slowly down the wall, blood leaking from his face.

As he fell, Drevin reached out and grabbed hold of the sword at his belt. He pulled it free and in the same motion swung it over his shoulder, hilt first. It connected solidly with the temple of the guard who was just about to grab him from behind. Within the space of a few heartbeats, both guards were lying on the floor. Teelan was astonished. He had never seen Drevin move so fast. The other guards hadn't yet made it halfway across the room.

"Run Teelan!" Drevin shouted at him as he brandished the sword at the now cautiously approaching guards.

Teelan shook off his shock and forced his legs to move, dashing past Drevin and out into the corridor. He glanced back once to see Drevin racing after him, his sword still in his hand, then he focused on where he was going. Luckily, he had a good sense of direction and with nervous energy lending him strength he literally flew through the castle.

Halls, rooms, kitchens and corridors flashed past him, so fast he barely had time to register them. A maid shrieked and jumped out of his way as he hurtled past, her linen cascading to the floor in a heap. Shouts and cries of alarm echoed around them as they raced along, but Teelan ignored them all, intent only on getting outside.

He thought he could hear the pounding of many feet pursuing them, but he couldn't guarantee that it wasn't just the thumping of his heart. However, he was sure that he could hear Drevin's heavy breathing and cursing just behind him, which oddly comforted him. As he got nearer the entrance he glanced down a corridor and thought he saw the steward Wilburton arguing with Captain Korac, but he didn't slow down to check.

As he sprinted down the final corridor, Teelan heard the welcoming spattering of rain and could see grey light coming in through the open doors to the courtyard. We are going to make it! Just then a heavy bell began ringing, a rapid tolling which could only be a sign of alarm and his heart sunk. Or maybe not.

He burst past the startled guard who was just poking his head out of his little room by the door to see what the commotion was. A second later he heard a thump and a groan behind him, and he instinctively knew that Drevin had just slammed that door into the poor man's head.

They both erupted from the castle doors and spilled down the grand steps until they were standing in the cobbled courtyard, breathing hard, pausing for a moment.

"My….weapons," Drevin puffed, looking back longingly at the gatehouse.

"N,no time," gasped Teelan. "We need to get out of here."

Drevin reluctantly nodded, then they both turned towards the outer gate. Four guards were staring at them in shock, hands on the hilts of their weapons. Two other men were desperately trying to close the heavy wooden gates by winding levers around to make them sway inwards.

"Time to go," Drevin said, jogging towards the men by the gate, the sword gripped tightly in his fist.

The bell continued its noisy, rapid clanging above them, making it hard for Teelan to think. He could barely breathe either, a sharp pain having made itself known in his side due to his sudden and unexpected exertions. But he didn't want to be left behind so he quick-stepped behind Drevin, trying to keep up.

They made it halfway across the courtyard when the sound of metal shod boots thumping on stone alerted them to the presence of others behind them. Teelan looked back and saw guards pouring out of the castle, all armed and dangerous looking. There were at least a dozen of them. He looked ahead again and saw the four guards closing ranks, blocking the gateway, their long spears extended. Damnation! They were trapped! They both stopped where they were.

"Drevin!" Teelan shouted. "Behind us," he said, indicating the men coming out of the castle. Drevin turned and looked at him, then at the guards and grimaced. Great. That is not a good sign. I guess there is no plan then.

Just then they heard a high-pitched whinnying coming from the stables off to their right. They both looked over and saw a young groom shouting and slapping the rumps of several of the horses inside, forcing them to gallop out into the courtyard. They stampeded out in a herd, neighing loudly, hooves clomping on the hard cobbles, running between them and the guards behind them. Confusion and panic followed. The freed horses rushed around the guards, forcing them to back away and protect themselves from flashing hooves and tossing snouts.

Teelan noticed the boy in the stables look at Drevin and raise a hand, giving a quick wave, before he went back to instilling fear into his charges. Drevin waved back to the boy. Teelan could see he had a smile on his face.

"Come on," Drevin said, "almost there." He started jogging towards the gate again. The doors were almost closed as they neared the guards, only a thin sliver of pale light seeping through them. Teelan feared again that they wouldn't make it.

Just as that thought crossed his mind a sudden fierce wind blew through the gap in the gates. It stopped just inside the courtyard, swirled into a tight ball then blew backwards, forcing the gates wide open again in an instant with a loud thump. The levers that operated them were spinning wildly by themselves. The guards operating them cried out in pain as the sudden change in movement ripped and tore their hands.

The soldiers facing them turned as they heard the gates crash open and the next moment Teelan saw them bowled to the ground as another invisible wave swept over them. They literally got rolled away from the gate, shouting and cursing, their spears scattered to the floor. After a few moments they eventually stopped, some distance away, and didn't look like they would be getting up again in a hurry.

Teelan looked out the now wide open gates to see a small, red-haired figure in a brown jerkin standing there with a cheeky smile on her freckled face.

"What took you so long?" Cali said. "Well, shake a leg. Are you coming or not?"

Drevin raced out of the gates with Teelan hot on his heels. Drevin squeezed Cali's shoulder when he got to her, smiling from ear to ear. Teelan gave her a reluctant nod of gratitude.

"I think it's time for us to leave," said Drevin.

"I know somewhere we can go. We'll head out the West Gate and up into the hills," said Cali. "Just give me a minute."

Teelan looked back nervously. He wasn't sure that they had a minute to spare. In the wide courtyard the horses were still prancing around, but less agitated than before, some of them now under control.

A few of the soldiers were still lying on the ground or just getting up, but many more were organising themselves into a solid group and looking towards the three of them. Teelan then saw the captain rush out of the castle and head towards the knot of soldiers shouting urgently at them, but he was too far away to make out what he was saying. Teelan glanced at Cali. Whatever she was going to do, it was imperative she do it quickly.

Just then she raised her arms and Teelan felt the surrounding air intensify. A blast of wind gusted from her hands and the great wooden gates slammed shut with a resounding boom. Teelan turned to run, but it appeared she had more to do. She quickly rotated her arms in a circular motion. The wind swirled around the field outside the castle, picking up speed, rustling the grass, and lifting minor items off the merchant's carts into the air. The zephyr intensified and slowly dragged the large carts away from their owners, spinning them in a tight circle.

Shouts and cries rang out as people either ran for cover or chased after their now moving carts. A whirlwind formed in the middle of the field, comprising the carts and their contents, rapidly spinning round and round. Then, with a forceful shove of her arms, Cali sent the maelstrom hurtling towards the closed gates, a deafening smashing sound of splintering wood denoting the impact.

Teelan closed his eyes and covered his ears at the sound. When he looked again, he saw a makeshift barricade of shattered carts and ruined produce piled in an untidy heap against the centre of the gates.

"That should slow them down for a while," Cali said, grinning again, but Teelan could see the sweat on her face and the trembling in her arms. "Follow me," she said, racing off down the road.

Teelan rushed after her and Drevin as the wails of the poor merchants rose into the air, like lonely cats calling out in the night. The persistent rain suddenly became a deluge; heavy sheets of water obscured his vision and soaked right through his robe within minutes. As he came closer to the bridge, he saw the guards at this end looking in their direction, listening to the ringing bell that was muted but still audible.

Drevin and Cali spoke briefly, their words lost in the wind, then they both angled their runs so that they were each heading straight at a guardsman. Cali sent a powerful gust into the one on the right, sending him tumbling backwards over the bridge. Teelan couldn't hear the splash he must have made landing in the river below over the noise of the rain. He then watched as Drevin simply shoulder-barged his man into the low wall of the bridge, then shoved him over it whilst he was unsteadily trying to regain his balance. They carried on running.

Teelan held back as he saw the guards at the other end of the bridge come jogging towards them, having seen their comrades' plight. However, they clearly had learnt nothing from it as they were swiftly dealt with in exactly the same manner, leaving the road ahead clear.

Teelan was worried about how they would get through the north gate into the city, but apparently for once Drevin did have a plan. Drevin began shouting at the guards as soon as they came within sight, waving his arms behind him frantically.

"Help! Come quickly," he shouted to them. "There has been an attack at the castle."

Several guards were gathered there, having heard the alarm bell, and most of them now ran towards them, bare steel in their hands. I hope you know what you are doing, Drevin.

"What's going on?" shouted a bearded, dripping giant of a man.

"Someone has infiltrated the castle and tried to assassinate the baron." Drevin lied effortlessly. "You must go and help them. They think the attacker may have fled into the countryside around the castle. Hurry," he said, pointing back to the way they had come urgently.

That's your plan? What a pathetic story. Surely he is not going to believe that? Now we are going to be questioned then arrested.

"Come on, men," shouted the guard, turning to his squad, "Protect the baron. Find the assassin." Then they raced off down the road to the castle.

By the living! I don't believe it. That actually worked. Teelan was incredulous.

They entered the gateway as the remaining guards were just closing the double gates, the soldiers helpfully ushering them inside. Voices assailed them from all sides.

"What's going on?"

"What is it?"

"Who are you?"

Drevin quickly took control of the situation. "I am a mercenary working for the baron. I was just up at the castle on his business when the alarm sounded. It seems like someone attempted to kill the baron and fled when he was discovered making the attempt. The baron sent me here to get some help."

"Who was it?"

"Why would they want to kill him?"

"Where did he flee to?" The questions kept coming from the curious guards.

"Fellas, I'm afraid I don't have time to answer your questions right now. The baron charged me with the job of alerting the guards at the other gates. Stay sharp lads. And keep an eye out for anyone suspicious." Drevin said, patting a couple of them on the shoulders.

With that he nodded to Teelan and Cali and they jogged away, Cali leading the way towards the Upper District. Teelan hastened after them, still unable to believe quite how gullible they were. And how effectively Drevin could make falsehoods sound like the truth.

They jogged into the Upper District, Teelan's side still hurting and his heart still thumping away. As they neared the Church District they heard the huge bell above the merchant's guild in the Central Compass toll, echoing the bell from the castle. Wonderful! Now the entire city is on high alert.

They were close to Teelan's mortuary now and he paused for a second, looking longingly towards where he could see the dome of its roof. Drevin screeched to a halt just ahead of him and looked back.

"What is it?" Drevin called to him.

"My books," Teelan said forlornly.

"No time. Come on. We are not out of here yet."

Teelan pulled his gaze away and reluctantly headed after Drevin, who had trotted away. My books. It took me years and a lot of money to get that collection together. Not to mention all my tools and my robes. Teelan forced his mind away from everything that he was leaving behind, knowing that to dwell on it might leave him paralysed.

Cali led them towards the West Gate, but by the time they could see the tall towers flanking them it was too late. The gates had been closed. A small contingent of soldiers stood in front of them, warily scanning the area for any threats.

Drevin quickly pulled them into an alleyway, out of sight of the guards.

"Dammit!" he cursed. "It looks like we are too late."

"Can't we just try your spectacular ruse again?" Teelan panted, only half mockingly.

"I don't think it will work this time." Drevin said, risking a quick glance out of the alley. "They are now warned and alert, not in a state of panic like the first group were. Besides, it looks like there are a couple of veterans there who will want to ask too many questions."

"I could try to charm our way out," Cali said, throwing her head back, her soggy curls flicking water off in every direction. Some of it spattered onto Teelan's face.

"Hey!" he said, wiping his face, which had minimal effect due to the rain still hammering down onto him.

"Too risky," said Drevin, ignoring him. "They have probably got a description of you at least by now if not of the rest of us," Drevin said, grimacing again. Teelan decided he didn't much like his grimaces. "Let me think for a moment."

"We could try the South Gate." Cali said, ignoring his request. Teelan shot her a glare.

"There would be no point," Teelan snapped. "All the gates will be closed now that the city bell is hammering out its warning. Or can't you hear its dulcet tones?"

"Fine," she huffed, crossing her arms. "Then we disguise ourselves as merchants or priests and beg the guards to let us leave on emergency business."

"Oh, that is a marvellous plan. Why didn't I think of that?" Teelan said. "Of course, the guards will just open the gates for us then, won't they? They wouldn't question us at all or search us, would they?"

"I am only trying to help," Cali said defensively.

Teelan didn't respond. He leaned against the cold, wet wall, water dripping off his long hair, his clothes plastered to his skin, thoroughly miserable. How had it come to this? He glanced over at Cali, ready with another caustic response then stopped. She was leaning against the other wall, just as wet as him, her folded arms failing to contain the shivering in her body. He wondered if that was from the cold or from the use of her Fragment and decided it didn't really matter. She looked just as miserable as him, only shorter and redder. Like it or not, they were in this situation together.

Teelan looked at Drevin who remained lost in thought, glancing back and forth at the gate, the soldiers, the road and the passing traffic. Teelan hoped he would think of something soon before they all died of pneumonia. For want of anything better to do, he followed Drevin's gaze. Despite the horrible weather, the streets were still busy, people hurrying past, going about their business as usual, albeit perhaps in a more expeditious manner than normal. The clamouring of the bell throughout the city seemed to have little effect on the behaviour of the citizens.

Drevin suddenly turned to them with a look in his eye that Teelan hoped was a way out of here. "I've got an idea. Wait here. In a few minutes make your way casually to the gates. There is a smaller door set within the gates that is just big enough for one person at a time to go through. I bet the door is still unlocked. When the time is right, get through that door as fast as you can."

"What about you?" Cali asked, before Teelan could ask his more appropriate questions.

"I will be there and will hopefully be able to follow you." Drevin said reassuringly.

"What about the guards?" Teelan said quickly before Cali could protest. "And how will we know when it is the 'right time'?"

"I will deal with the guards and trust me you will know when to go. I will give you a sign."

Before either of them could say anything else, Drevin disappeared down the alley, back towards one of the main roads. Great. Marvellous. Now what? I suppose we just have to wait and see what harebrained scheme he has come up with this time.

As the minutes dragged by slowly Teelan became more and more anxious, pacing up and down their narrow alley. His thoughts turned to one of his favourite topics, self-preservation. Surely the baron wouldn't be interested in him. After all, it was Drevin and Cali who wounded the Gatherers. He had nothing to do with it. He was only guilty by association. And it wasn't his idea to be associated with them in the first place. Maybe he could just slip back to his mortuary and plead his ignorance and innocence. Just as he was contemplating slinking away a sudden commotion sounded from the main outer road, south of the gate.

Teelan risked a glance out and saw that a short way down the main road a large cart had tipped sideways and skewed across the cobbled road, blocking most of it. The contents of the cart, paraphernalia of all shapes and sizes made of wood and metal, were strewn across the width of the road. A small crowd had gathered around it. A few people tried to help, whilst most of them either shouted at the careless driver who was slowly rising to his feet or were kicking the merchant's products to the side of the road, trying to clear a path.

Another cart came up the road from the south and tried to squeeze past the blockage, its driver impatient. It made it only a short distance before one of its wheels hit a particularly large and solid object, which tipped the cart up at an alarming angle. Unable to right itself the momentum carried the cart into the wall of the building bordering the other side of the road. It leaned on the wall drunkenly; the horse pulling in its now trapped tethers, whinnying and kicking out. Teelan looked over at the guards by the gate and saw that all of them had turned towards the disturbance and taken a few steps down the road. I guess this is the right time then.

Cali and Teelan left the relative safety of the alleyway and walked with what he hoped looked like confidence out onto the road. They circled to the north of the gate in a wide, seemingly innocuous looking arc, but they firmly fixed their eyes on the massive gates.

Teelan looked back at the soldiers and saw an old man approaching them from the scene of the crash, limping along the road as fast as he could with his infirmity. He was wearing a ragged green cloak with the hood pulled low and carried a long wooden stick. He spoke urgently to the guards and gestured frantically back towards the scene of devastation. Teelan was too far away to hear his words, but it was obvious that he was imploring them for their help.

Teelan and Cali continued their measured approach towards the currently unwatched gate. He could see the small door set into the larger gate now and prayed that Drevin was right about it being unlocked. So far, nobody was paying them any attention, much to his relief.

They were within a few feet of sanctuary when Teelan glanced again at the guards and the merchant still pleading with them. He caught some of the words that the old man was saying.

"Please, you must help me, good sirs. My goods are all over the road back there, my cart is blocking the street. If you don't help me clear it, there will be more trouble. The crowd might get angry and start fighting. Thieves and bandits will steal all my merchandise. Please come and help me. It won't take long with a few strong men like you."

Teelan stopped for a moment, absolutely stunned. It wasn't the words that had shocked him or the wavering voice that they had come from. It was the stubbled, battered face that had spoken the words that had left him frozen. Drevin's face!

As Teelan stood there one of the older guards said something to their companions and several of them trotted off down the road, leaving just four behind. He heard Cali hiss at him from ahead and saw that she was standing against the city wall, in the tower's shadow, close to the door, beckoning to him. Teelan shook himself and continued his easy walk, making sure to stay well behind the guards. He couldn't help but watch, though.

He saw Drevin turn around to limp back to his 'supposed cart' when one of the younger guards called him back. Oh no!

"Good merchant," said the youngster in a deep voice, "Why don't you wait here a moment and rest your legs whilst my comrades go right your cart for you?"

"Why, that is awfully kind of you, young man," said Drevin the merchant, in a fake old man's voice. Well, 'older' man's voice. "My leg is playing me up something fierce today. You don't mind giving me a shoulder to lean on, do you? You look nice and strong."

"Sure," replied the guard.

What was Drevin playing at now? Teelan had made it to the wall and pressed himself into the corner, behind where the tower jutted out. Cali hunched up next to him, uncomfortably close and both of them peered out.

Drevin was leaning heavily on the young guard, looking the other way, but as if sensing his gaze he glanced over his shoulder at him. He nodded towards the door quickly, then turned back to watch the rescue efforts.

"Say, why don't you other fellows go and help them?" Drevin said.

Teelan knew he should move, make his way around the tower to the door, but fear had again frozen his legs. The guards were still too close. If any of them turned their heads this way once they left the shelter of the tower, they would be instantly spotted. He glanced at Cali and saw that she didn't seem inclined to move either, although Teelan suspected that might be for entirely different reasons. It seemed that she had quickly formed a bond with Drevin and didn't want to leave without him. Teelan was not sure what his feelings were about that. At the moment, he felt too scared to allow any other emotion to emerge.

"We have to guard the gate," said one of the older men.

"Aw, don't be such a stickler. Go on, I will stay here and keep a lookout. You know I have better eyes than you anyway," said the young guard that Drevin was leaning on.

"Yes, and a stronger back Pols." the older man replied. "Which is why you should go help and leave me here."

"I would, of course, but I am assisting our friend here as you can see," the guard called Pols said, nodding at Drevin, "Unless you want to take over from me of course."

"Bah, come on fellows," the veteran grumbled. "Leave the lad to his good deed. But we won't be long Pols, and we will have sight of that gate the whole time, you hear me?"

"Loud and clear," replied Pols, and Teelan could hear the smile in his voice.

Everyone watched them leave and when they were out of earshot Drevin stood up straight and turned to the young soldier.

"Thanks Pols!" he said, gripping the boy's shoulder tightly. "That's two I owe you."

"No problem," replied the guard.

"How did you know it was me?" Drevin asked.

"Oh, I have good eyes and an excellent memory, remember? Even your fake voice couldn't fool me. For some reason, when I heard those bells chiming your face popped into my head and I thought you might be in trouble."

"Yeh, you could say that," Drevin said wryly.

"I take it you didn't commit whatever it is you are accused of then?" Pols said, one eyebrow raised.

"Not exactly. Well, sort of. But that is not the point. Someone wants us out of the way for their own purposes and doesn't want us to tell the baron the truth." Drevin explained lamely.

"What truth? Wait, you said us?"

Drevin beckoned to Cali and Teelan. Teelan stayed where he was, unsure whether to trust this unknown guard. Cali, of course just rushed out and ran straight to Drevin. Teelan, now feeling foolish, shuffled after her.

"These are my friends Pols, and we need to get out of the city. Sorry I don't have time to explain further."

Drevin said, glancing anxiously down the road. Teelan followed his gaze.

Some guards were trying to right the cart leaning against the wall, but the horse was now panicking and kicking his front legs high in the air, forcing everyone away from him. Others had picked up most of the strange-looking objects and piled them alongside the other side of the road and were working out how to lift the merchant's cart whilst staying out of the reach of the wild horse. The rest of them were trying to hold back a crowd of angry people who either wanted to pass through or who just wanted to make their feelings known about the whole situation.

"Fine," said the guard. "Quickly use the postern gate. It's unlocked." Teelan scowled as Drevin smiled at him as he heard that. "I will tell the guards that you returned to your warehouse to fetch the rest of your staff to help."

"Thanks again Pols." said Drevin, patting him on the back as he headed to the door. "Stay safe."

Drevin opened the door and headed out onto the wide road, Cali close behind him. Teelan was just closing the door behind him when he heard the guard reply quietly, "You too."

# CHAPTER 13

# A GATHERING

Teelan's legs throbbed. They had kept up a steady jog since leaving the city, first heading west along the main road to Paska, then cutting north across farmland. He saw a few of the farmers raise their arms at them from a distance but couldn't tell if they were friendly waves or 'get off my land' gestures. The way his luck was going lately he had feared it was most likely the latter and that he would soon find himself accosted by an angry sheepherder.

However, they had eventually left the farmlands behind unscathed, and they were now traversing rough scrubland, heading towards the northern hills, their humps just visible in the distance. None of them had spoken since leaving the city and Teelan was unsure if it was because of their dire circumstances or just that they didn't have the breath to spare. He certainly knew which one applied to him. As they entered a particularly dense patch of wasteland, Teelan stumbled to a halt, his hands on his knees, wheezing.

"Stop..a.. moment please," he gasped to the others.

Drevin looked even more fatigued than him and Teelan saw relief fight with wariness on his drawn, ashen face. Cali's cheeks were bright red, but apart from that, she still seemed as sprightly as a lamb.

"Fine," Drevin said, as relief obviously won out. "We will rest for a bit, but not for long," he said, scanning the horizon behind them.

Teelan had already collapsed to the ground as soon as he heard the word 'fine'. He lay on the prickly grass, stretching his long legs out and trying to massage the hurt from them. His left side was burning from a persistent stitch and his heart obviously hadn't got the message that he had stopped now, as it was still dashing along at a merry rate. He let the rain fall on his face and opened his mouth to catch the salty drops.

Drevin eased himself slowly to the ground and sat with his knees bent. He had discarded his tatty cloak but still carried the hefty staff-come-walking stick and the purloined naked sword was thrust into his belt. Cali sat down lightly, crossing her legs and adjusting the hood of her cloak, which had been blowing in her face whilst running. The rain had eased a bit, but the wind had picked up, seeming to blow fiercely directly into their faces, no matter which way they turned.

"How did you know?" Teelan panted out after a few moments, levering himself up to a sitting position and looking at Drevin.

"Know what?" Drevin replied, equally short of breath.

"That the guards at the north gate would just do what you said. You have no authority or power over them, but they jumped to your orders."

Teelan saw Drevin smile slyly. “Soldiers are a simple lot. They are trained to take orders and not to think for themselves. They rarely react well to unexpected situations, so if anyone appears who seems to know what is going on and tells them what to do, they usually hop to it. It’s ingrained in them. As long as you deliver the orders with confidence, they will usually follow them.”

“And what about that distraction at the gate?” Teelan queried. He still wasn’t sure how that had worked.

“Yeh, that was real smart. Even if you did pinch my idea to disguise yourself as a merchant.” Cali said, smiling at Drevin but also sounding a bit peeved.

“An old trick.” Drevin said, “Make people look where you want them to and not where they are supposed to. It took a bit of coin to convince the merchant to deliberately tip his cart over, but he was up for a bit of mischief. Most of his goods would have survived, so he had little to lose.”

“Neat,” said Cali appreciatively. “Now is anyone going to tell me just what in the name of the Allmother happened back there? Why are we running and from who?” she asked, suddenly sounding much less respectful.

“Whom.” Teelan said, pointing out her grammatical ignorance. Cali just glared at him.

“Serzin,” Drevin said simply. “He was responsible for Ridozir’s abduction, but his wife interfered and ordered him to be killed instead. Apparently they didn’t get along.”

Well, that is putting it mildly. Teelan decided he needed to elaborate on Drevin’s rather terse and inadequate response. “Ridozir hated them and threatened to cast them out into the streets, bereft and penniless. He also tried to seduce Serzin's wife and was the one responsible for the debilitation of their son. All in all, he was a thoroughly despicable man. Hence why she plotted her revenge by having him murdered."

"Huh, sounds like he had it coming. Typical man, always wanting what he can't have. Trying to have his way with a woman who isn't interested in him." Cali said bitterly, adjusting the strap on her heavy looking bag so that it sat in her lap. "So, why are we on the run?"

"Because our virtuous friend here thinks that the almost equally despicable, and definitely unhinged baron, should be told of his brother's actions. And he rather bluntly, and foolishly in my opinion, made this known to said brother, who is currently in control of the barony." Teelan said caustically.

"Crap! Why did you do that, Dev? That's nuts. You got a death wish or something? That guy's as slippery as a barrel full of eels," Cali asked incredulously.

Drevin just looked at them and shrugged. "It was the right thing to do. I thought that once exposed he might do the decent thing and confess to his brother. I thought that he was different from other nobles. That he was an honourable man. Turns out I was wrong and they are all alike. Once they have money and power, they will do whatever it takes to hold on to it."

A grim silence fell for a moment as everyone considered those words. Teelan still felt that Drevin was being overly judgemental on everyone who held some level of authority, but he could partly understand why now. He has obviously had unpleasant experiences with such people.

"Where are we going anyway?" Teelan asked, deciding to change the subject. He looked around at the flat, windswept, bleak landscape. To the west was nothing but featureless plains whilst in the south the farmlands they had tramped through were still visible. The only features of note were to the north and east, where the small hills gradually transformed into jagged mountains far into the distance.

Cali glanced at him then looked as Drevin as she answered. "There are some caves in the hills to the north that I sometimes go to. Nobody goes there. The mines in those lower hills have all run dry so the miners head further north and east, towards the coast to dig up their iron ore."

"Sounds delightful." Teelan remarked sarcastically. Great. The three of us sharing a damp, cold, smelly cave for who knows how long. What could be better? Teelan's mood was sinking even further.

"Well, it sounds better than a dungeon to me," Drevin said, standing up again and scanning the horizons.

Huh. Barely. Teelan rummaged in his bag to see if there was anything to eat in there. His stomach had not stopped churning since this morning. He knew most of that was down to fear and stress, but now maybe hunger had added its voice to the mix. Disappointingly, he only found some slightly stale bread, one apple, and a handful of nuts.

"Shit!" said Drevin. Here he goes again. "We need to move now!" he shouted, looking to the south.

Cali had jumped up and was looking around in alarm. Teelan felt too worn out to be scared anymore and slowly prised himself from the ground, tracking Drevin's gaze.

Beyond the long grasses and patches of shrubs and weeds lay the farmers' fields. Beyond those, a thin, grey, straight line that denoted the road to Canor was just about distinguishable. But it was what was in the middle of all this that had caught Drevin's attention. Three horses! With people riding them who definitely did not look like farmers. A dozen or so other distinctly 'unfarmely' looking men were running ahead of the horses.

The worst thing of all was the fact that they were all heading straight towards them. Apparently Teelan wasn't too tired to be scared after all as the fear struck him again, causing tingling goosebumps on his neck and his mouth to dry out instantly. As one they turned and ran.

Teelan found some extra energy from somewhere and overtook the others, even though he had no idea where he was going, other than 'away'. He could hear the squelching of his companion's feet behind him in the soaked grasses and Drevin's laboured breathing. The wind buffeted him, making his hair whip wildly around his head and tears stream from his eyes.

They bolted away into the wild, uninhabited and uninhabitable region south of the still too distant hills. As they left the long grasses behind, the ground gradually turned firmer underfoot, revealing short wiry turf and stony soil that the rain had failed to muddy. After what felt like an age, but was probably only a few moments, Drevin shouted at them to stop.

Teelan obliged gratefully, only resisting the urge to sink to the ground by checking to see where their pursuers were. Too close, that's where. He settled for hanging his head, his breath coming out in rapid gasps. Drevin sounded worse than he did, his breathing resounding like the great bellows used in a forge, only being pumped at ten times their normal speed. Even Cali was breathing hard after their mad dash, but it seemed like it had all been to no avail.

The sound of the horses' hooves galloping along drifted up to them, carried in the rain stinging wind. The sound of many footsteps closely followed this, thumping hard and rhythmically, accompanied by a jangling of metal. Teelan looked at their pursuers and despair almost finished him off. There were too many of them!

The three riders in cloaks were in the lead now and, if as he suspected, they were the baron's Gatherers, in all honesty, they were probably capable enough to deal with them on their own. Except they weren't on their own! Thirteen men in mail jogged along steadily behind them, the symbol of the white compass of Canor standing out on their glistening, wet indigo blue tabards.

"We can't outrun them," Drevin eventually panted. "Their men are fresher than us and they have horses. We will have to make a stand here."

Teelan looked around grimly. 'Here' didn't exactly inspire hope. They were on an open, rocky plain that had a slight incline on its northern side where there was a small scattering of dark stones. The foothills were a bit further north, agonisingly close, and beyond them rose the Canorian Mountains. Their sheer dark sides and pointed peaks rose majestically directly ahead, whilst the ones further east towards the coast had their tips lost in the swollen, grey clouds. Around them, in every other direction, were more flat windswept plains, devoid of any notable features or places to hide.

"Teelan, get behind those rocks." Drevin said, pointing to the waist high rocks that were jutting out from the ground behind them. Teelan quickly obliged. He was too numb to do anything else. Even though he didn't see how a collection of unimpressive looking stones could save him. But he trudged over and knelt down behind the biggest one he could find, which wasn't particularly big. Even kneeling his head still showed above it. Still, at least he could watch their impending deaths he supposed. Cali removed several items from her bag, then came over and dumped the still bulging sack at his feet. "Watch this for me would you Tee?" she asked, winking at him then walking away before he could answer.

Drevin and Cali positioned themselves in front of him, a few paces apart. Drevin held the sturdy staff in both hands, like a longsword, rotating his shoulders and swinging it gently back and forth. Cali held a dagger loosely in each hand, glancing nervously between Drevin and the fast approaching soldiers.

Far too soon, the riders pulled up their horses, stopping about thirty paces away. Teelan studied them. The man on the right was young, wearing a long brown cloak and a nasty smile that marred what should have been a handsome face. A strip of linen stained red encased his wrist.

The man on the left was older, and sturdier. His rounded face looked like it could be friendly, but it certainly didn't look that way right now. A large irregular shaped purple bruise adorned his forehead.

Between them was a woman with hair as black as a raven's wings and cut to look like them too. Her face was narrow and pale, her expression twisted in a half smile, half sneer, which didn't bode well. Her crimson cloak draped over her horse's flanks and Teelan's professional eye noticed a bandage wrapped tight around her left thigh. So, these must be the Gatherers that Drevin and Cali ran into. Looks like they gave them a good showing, at least.

"Ah, we meet again," said the woman. "Only this time I have brought some friends along." She waved her arm to encompass the guards who were trotting up behind her. "You know the baron wants you back alive, but for some reason, his brother disagrees and would rather you just disappeared for good. For once, I agree with Serzin."

"Nylarian. You don't know what Serzin did. To his own brother. The baron needs to know the truth." Drevin shouted back.

Nylarian shook her head. "I don't care about the baron or the goings on between those two. As long as I still get paid, of course. What I don't need is someone like you stirring up trouble between them, so I'm afraid it is time for you to disappear. Besides, we have some unfinished business to resolve. Kill them all!" she suddenly shouted to the soldiers who had now reached her.

The soldiers looked nervously between themselves until eventually one soldier turned to Nylarian. "My lady, Captain Korac, was telling all his men not to kill them. That he wanted to talk to them first," he stammered out.

"Well, captain good-for-nothing isn't here, is he? I am in charge here and I say kill them. Unless you want me to tell the baron you disobeyed a direct order, of course?" Nylarian said, smiling wickedly.

"No, of course not, my lady," the soldier stuttered. "Come on men. Loose formation. Let's go."

With that, the soldiers all turned towards them and started a slow jog forward. Teelan didn't think that they looked particularly happy, but then he supposed that most reasonable soldiers about to go and do bloody murder, with the potential for them to end up on the receiving end, were not the most sanguine.

"Let's try not to kill them, eh!" he heard Drevin mutter to Cali. Cali looked across at Drevin and Teelan couldn't decipher what her expression meant.

Then Cali was in motion. When the soldiers were still twenty paces away she threw both of her daggers, one high, one low. A guard at the far left of the line let out a howl and fell to the ground, clutching his leg, which now had a new adornment in it. The one next to him took her other dagger in his upper arm, his sword dropping first, then his body following not long after. Teelan noticed she had aimed at parts of their bodies that their mail didn't cover and where the wounds would be non-fatal. Apparently, she did agree with Drevin then.

When he looked back at Cali, two more daggers had appeared in her hands and she started moving forwards, first at a jog, then a run. Drevin adjusted his stance, right foot in front of the left and crouched slightly, knees bent, standing on the balls of his feet, waiting.

Teelan watched as Cali ran at the soldiers. She headed straight towards two of them, then at the last moment dived forwards under their clumsy swipes. She rolled between them, then came to her knees behind them. Her arms whipped out and her daggers slashed deeply into the backs of both of their legs, hamstringing them. Before they had even finished toppling, she was up again and away, heading towards another small group of now wary guards.

Teelan switched his focus to Drevin as three soldiers approached him, steel held before them. Drevin waited as they circled him, spinning his staff lazily around his body, waiting for them to make the first move.

The soldier to his left darted in, jabbing at his side. Drevin did a half turn to his left and took a quick step backwards. His staff flicked out and cracked against the soldier's extended wrist as their lunge jabbed empty air, missing Drevin's stomach. His sword dropped to the floor from his numb hand. Drevin kicked him in the knee, then reversed his turn, knowing that the soldier on his other side would attempt to strike him behind.

He did. But Drevin was too fast. He swayed away from the thrust and jabbed his staff into his mailed stomach, hard, forcing him to stagger away. The third guard now came at him, sword raised high for an overhead chop. Drevin sidestepped, the blade whistling inches past his ear, then lashed out high with the staff, cracking the off-balance soldier across the head with a sickening thump. He fell bonelessly. The other two soldiers left standing backed away as others came running in.

Teelan heard a yell from Cali and looked her way. She was battling two more soldiers, but this pair seemed to know how to work together and they were holding her at bay with the reach of their longer swords. Cali yelled again in frustration as she tried to dart in close to one of them, but the other whipped his sword up to intercept her, just missing her arm by a fraction.

They closed on her, one on either side. Cali backed away slowly, her twin daggers raised. Then with a flick of her hand she sent out a powerful gust of air, shoving the soldier on her left into his partner, crashing them together. With a blur of motion, she leapt forward and struck with both daggers at once, pommels first, connecting solidly with their heads as they tried to untangle themselves. Both went down soundlessly.

Drevin had another two men around him, one of them a gigantic beast of a man. This brute swung a long, heavy blade straight down at Drevin's head, clearly intending to chop him in half. Teelan gasped as he couldn't see how Drevin could avoid the long blade as there was another soldier closing behind him. Teelan held his breath.

Drevin raised his staff in both hands, high in front of him, to block the blow. A resounding crack sounded as the enormous sword split his staff in two, splinters flying off. The blade, although deflected, continued its downward motion and sliced through Drevin's shirt from his elbow up to his wrist, where it continued on to score a deep gouge through his vambrace. Teelan could see blood blossom on his shirt instantly.

Drevin yelled, then threw the remnants of the stick into his opponent's face, forcing him back. He drew his sword as he ducked and spun around. The soldier behind him clearly wasn't expecting that and had rushed in, thinking to strike from behind. However, all he did was impale himself through the midriff on Drevin's outstretched sword.

Drevin continued his spin, his momentum only partially slowed by the man skewered on his blade. The huge soldier had recovered and promptly thrust his sword through his unfortunate comrade's head, believing that he was instead about to shove it through Drevin's back. His face held a look of panic and horror as he tried to free his oversized sword from his fellow guard's skull.

Drevin wrenched his sword out from the poor, twice-impaled man's stomach and slashed it high into the giant's face. The blade ripped open a wide gash from ear to chin, exposing white bones and stringy red sinews. The man fell gurgling, clutching at his ruined face. So much for no killing!

Teelan took a quick glance around the field. Seven soldiers were lying on the now stained grass, some moaning softly or shrieking loudly, rolling around clutching at limbs. Others were still and silent.

Six more stood, most with wounds, leaking fat crimson drops which spattered on the ground. They had retreated to the other end of the field and looked between the two fighters and the Gatherers warily. The Gatherers slowly walked forwards across the field, frustration and anger etched into their features. Clearly they were not happy with how things were going. They forced the soldiers ahead of them, urging them on.

Cali was halfway across the field, off to Teelan's left, her daggers still in her fists. Drevin stood near to his original position, closer to Teelan. His left arm was still oozing blood and he stood in the same pose as before, his sword held at an angled low guard, blade red along its length. The soldiers reluctantly came at them again, splitting into two groups.

Movement suddenly caught Teelan's eye from the Gatherer in the green cloak. He watched as the chubby man threw two small metal balls straight up into the air. The next second they shot forward, one heading straight at Drevin, the other at Cali. Teelan shouted at them to duck. Luckily, they heard him and for once didn't waste time arguing or questioning him.

Drevin nimbly twisted and jerked his head back, the ball whisking just past his scarred nose. Cali threw herself backwards spectacularly and the ball fizzed over her, skimming her ear. She landed heavily on her back, breath whooshing out of her. But even as she lay gasping for breath she extended an arm above her head and twitched her hand.

Suddenly a gust of wind forced the ball to cease its onward flight and then it reversed its direction, hurtling back the other way. It connected forcibly with the head of the soldier who was now standing over her, sword poised to strike. He deflated limply sideways. Cali sprang back up.

A sizzling noise caught Teelan's attention, and he saw a line of fire fizzing through the air towards Drevin. Fortunately, Cali had also noticed. She waved her arm, and the fire changed direction mid-flight, blasting into the chest of another soldier nearby. He yelled as his tabard caught alight and threw himself to the floor, rolling in the damp grass, trying to extinguish himself. Teelan caught the Gatherer's look of annoyance as they shouted at the remaining soldiers to attack. Which they duly did.

Drevin, obviously tired of waiting, rushed forward at his pair of opponents, sending them hastily stumbling back, caught off guard. He swung his sword low, but the soldier recovered in time to just about parry the blow. The metallic clang of steel on steel echoed around the field.

Drevin instantly reversed his swing, aiming at the other guard's head. This one also barely got his blade up in time, resulting in another loud clang. Teelan could see that

Drevin was breathing hard now, clearly tiring, but his steps still seemed light and sure.

He moved with a grace and fluidity that Teelan hadn't expected. Swift, economical movements that carried him from one stance to another effortlessly. His steps were simple but assured and effective, each move carefully planned, switching from defence to attack with no indication of what he was about to do next. Teelan suddenly realised why he was called a blade master.

Cali yelled indistinctly and Teelan tore his gaze away from Drevin's mesmerising manoeuvres. She was facing two soldiers who again were forcing her backwards. She jumped and twisted in the air, somersaulting to the side, trying to get around them.

However, this time she wasn't quick enough, and a blade scraped along her thigh as she leaped, causing her to yelp in pain. She landed unsteadily, favouring her right leg, one dagger dropping from her hand. Teelan noticed that her body was shaking, and her arms were trembling.

He looked around desperately for some way to help her. Then he spotted the metal ball that Drevin had avoided lying on the floor near him. He quickly dashed out and picked it up. It felt warm and heavy in the palm of his hand.

Looking up he took aim and threw it at the soldier pressing Cali on her left side with all his strength. In his mind he envisaged the ball flying fast and true, slamming into the man's head and knocking him senseless, and Cali giving him a nod of respect. However, as usual, grim reality soon set in. He never had been very good at physical activities and so it proved again.

The ball fluttered along weakly and eventually patted softly against the guard's shoulder, causing no harm at all, except to Teelan's ego. The man turned to look at him and sneered. Mortified, Teelan felt embarrassment and sudden fear churn up his long-suffering stomach.

Nonetheless, the slight distraction proved enough for Cali. She launched herself at the unaware guard, planting her right foot on his knee and flipping herself completely over his head as the other guard thrust at the thin air where she had been standing a moment ago.

She landed in a crouch behind the guard Teelan had hit, her left leg wobbling. Then her remaining dagger flashed, slicing him across the back of the thigh and continuing its sweep towards his onrushing comrade. Unfortunately for him, the other soldier was slightly shorter in stature, so her blade ripped through a very delicate part of his body. Teelan winced involuntarily. The man issued such a high-pitched scream that Teelan had to cover his ears. As Cali rose both men collapsed, one face forward, the other clutching at his bloody groin.

Teelan stared at Cali who looked up and quickly grinned at him before brushing some hair away from her face. For some reason, that look made his cheeks burn just as much as his earlier embarrassment had.

He shook his head and looked away. But his warmth instantly turned to ice as he noticed the brown cloaked Gatherer was staring straight at him. Teelan watched as he tossed another metal ball into the air, his eyes not leaving his own. He instinctively knew what was about to happen and forced his legs to move. He threw himself back behind his rock, cradling his head in his hands. A fraction of a second later he heard a sharp crack, and splinters of rock and stone dust showered his head.

He took several deep breaths, trying to calm his emotions, curled up into a ball. When he dared to look out again, he saw Drevin had dispatched his last two opponents, both of them lying on the ground at his feet bleeding heavily. Drevin was breathing hard, his sword dripping red gore onto the grass. The Gatherers approached them slowly.

"It doesn't have to be like this," Nylarian called out. "Give yourselves up now and we'll tell the baron you came peacefully."

Drevin and Cali just looked at each other and remained silent. Teelan wasn't sure if they had nothing to say to the Gatherer or were just taking a moment to catch their breath. Nylarian apparently took their silence as a refusal.

"Fine," she shouted. "Don't say I didn't give you a choice. Caderin!"

The young Gatherer raced forwards at blinding speed, heading directly for Cali. Teelan was astonished at the lightning pace at which he ran, his legs a blur beneath him. Cali however, was unfazed.

She quickly lifted her hands and released a short, powerful burst of air at him, low to the ground. Caderin's legs were suddenly and catastrophically blasted out from underneath him, and he was hewn to the ground, spinning and rolling, limbs flying, careening past her like an out-of-control windmill. He continued on for several seconds before eventually coming to a stop, sprawled in an untidy heap.

Teelan heard Nylarian curse. Then she extended her arm out and a ring of fire suddenly burst to life around

Cali. The fire surrounded her, the flickering flames leaping at least four feet into the air, rain sizzling against them. Teelan gasped in horror.

Cali tried to blast a gap through the flames, but the wind only forced the flames to bend outwards for a moment before they snapped back, then roared even higher, so much so that Teelan could no longer see Cali beyond them. Nylarian carried on walking a smug expression on her face.

Teelan couldn't watch so he looked towards Drevin in desperation. But he saw Drevin had his own problems. Zortig was stalking towards him. As he approached he glanced around the battlefield and one by one his metal balls lifted in the air and floated over towards him. Teelan saw Drevin cast around frantically, checking for cover. There was none.

He was too far away from Teelan's meagre rocks. When Zortig had gathered six balls to him, he spun them in a circular pattern in the air, then they chased each other around in a complex pattern. Damn. He is showing off!

Then suddenly he launched all of them at Drevin. They sped along in a vertical zigzag line so that they would smash into every part of his body from head to toe. Teelan held his breath. Even Drevin couldn't withstand such an onslaught. Luckily, Drevin also realised that.

He bent down and quickly grabbed the body of a felled soldier, holding it in front of him like a human shield. The balls smacked into the man's flesh with sickening squelches, sending out spurts of viscera and gore. If the soldier wasn't dead before, he certainly was now. Drevin then advanced on Zortig, still holding the limp body in front of him. Zortig pulled out a long dagger and went to meet him.

Just as they closed the body was ripped out of Drevin's hands, the balls torn out of the dead flesh with a horrible sucking sound. Zortig set the balls flying around his body, interweaving them in an ever-changing arrangement and using them as a floating shield.

Drevin attacked with a high slash, but several of the balls immediately rushed to the point of impact and locked together, deflecting the blow. Then they instantly separated and resumed their spinning and whirling. Zortig stabbed out from within his protective ring, but Drevin quickly stepped sideways dodging the strike.

Teelan tore his eyes away from the fascinating fight as he realised Nylarian was still walking across the field. And that she was heading straight towards him! She still had an arm extended behind her, controlling the inferno that encased Cali, but her other arm was now raised, the spread palm facing towards him. Teelan crouched down lower, trying to hide, even though he knew she had already spotted him. His hands scrabbled frantically in the loose, stony soil, as if he could dig himself a way out of this.

"Give yourself up, or I give your too pale friend here a rosy colour to his cheeks." Nylarian called out.

"Run Teelan!" he heard Drevin shout.

Teelan stood up, fists clenched, but that was as far as he got. As he saw the Gatherer close on him, complete and utter panic overtook him and his limbs froze. He saw the old burn scars on her face, her eyes blazing with hate and her raised hands, both of which glowed amber with an intense heat. He couldn't tear his eyes away from those hands. No, no, no. This is it. I am going to be burnt alive. Why me? What have I done to deserve this?

She was just three paces away from him, and he could feel the heat of her hands already. It was now or never. Teelan lifted his traitorously trembling arms and desperately flung the contents of his hands at her. Fortunately, at this distance, even he couldn't miss. The dirt and gravel he had clawed up from the ground flew straight into her face, pattering against her cheeks and stinging her eyes.

Nylarian yelped and instinctively brought her hands to her face. Her glowing, fiery hands! Then she screamed. A piercing, ululating wail of a scream that echoed around the field accompanied by the nauseating stink of burning flesh.

Teelan couldn't take his eyes off her as she wrenched her hands away from her face, strips of red, burnt skin peeling away, stuck to her fingers. One of her eyes had fused shut and the other was red veined, weeping a creamy liquid. Her face was a mass of welts and blisters. She continued to wail horribly.

Until a moment later, she suddenly quieted and fell to her knees then toppled face first to the floor. A dagger protruded from between her shoulder blades. Teelan eventually forced his gaze away and saw Cali kneeling in a circle of scorched earth. Her clothes were smoke blackened, and her head was hanging low, her soot darkened hair covering her face. She turned her head slightly and gave him a weak grin. She looked exhausted.

A clash of metal on metal whipped Teelan's head back the other way. Drevin was still trying to find a way through Zortig's ever shifting shield. Teelan took a step forward as if to go help him, then stopped himself. What could he do? He was no warrior and had no clue of how he could be useful to Drevin.

Instead, he went to see if he could help Cali. Maybe he could treat her wounds, then she could assist Drevin. She was now lying flat out on her back. He took a step towards her when suddenly a meaty arm just appeared around his shoulders and pulled him backwards.

Teelan jumped in surprise and flailed around frantically, trying to get free. Then a sword materialised directly in front of his face and pressed itself against his neck. He stopped struggling instantly.

"I'm taking at least one of you back with me," a rough voice growled in his ear. Teelan risked a furtive glance over his shoulder and saw that he was in the grip of the ogre whose face Drevin had carved open.

*Will this nightmare never end?* The soldier dragged him slowly backwards across the field. Back towards where the soldiers had caught up with them. Back towards the farmer's fields. Back towards the road. Back to the city. Then to the dungeons. Teelan's mind was speeding ahead of him, already envisioning the torture the baron would inflict on him. In reality, they had only walked a dozen paces. His heartbeat, which had just about reached a more sedate beat, increased its tempo again. *Maybe I will have a heart attack before he takes me back. Then I won't have to worry about anything anymore.*

Then he heard a wet thunk and a length of metal zinged past right next to his ear. It was so close that he could hear the steel vibrating faintly. He could see a few inches of a gore covered sword and noticed, almost dreamily, a couple of his long white hairs floating in the air, one of them sticking to the end of the blade.

Shocked, he turned his head to the side to see the sword that had sprouted from the soldier's open mouth, like a grotesque extra tongue, blood pouring out of it like red wine at a festival. Then the blade vanished with a revolting slurping sound, and the guard simply slumped to the floor.

Behind him stood a blood spattered but grinning Drevin, sword in hand. Thoughts and emotions flashed through Teelan's mind. I'm alive. Drevin saved me! He saved my life. Oh no. How can I repay that? Will I have to be nicer to him now? Great, now I am in his debt. What am I supposed to say now?

In the end, the only thing he could stammer out was, "M..my hair."

Drevin looked at him oddly, still grinning, but there was also something else in his eyes as he looked closely at him. Teelan wasn't altogether sure what it was and if he liked it or not.

"You're welcome," Drevin said genuinely.

"Wait. That Gatherer. Zortig. Where is he?" Teelan's brain was still hurtling along.

Drevin just nodded behind him and Teelan glanced over. A short way back, Zortig was lying face up on the ground, his brown cloak spread out around him like a shroud. One of his metal balls was impaled into the centre of his forehead like a third eye and was just as sightless as his other two open eyes. The rest of the balls were spread on the ground around him, like sacrificial offerings to some minor, unknown god.

"Wow," Teelan said.

"Yeah," said Drevin, shrugging. "I couldn't get through his damn shield, so I thought I would make his defence my attack. Use what he had against him. Seemed to work out well enough."

"I would say so," replied Teelan. "Come on, let's go and get C..."

Suddenly a scream ripped across the field and they both turned to look at its source. Cali! She was on her knees. Caderin stood behind her, the young Gatherer's face bleeding from multiple scrapes and gashes, his right arm hanging limp. However, his left arm was working fine and was currently holding a sword which was sticking right through Cali's right shoulder, the point protruding in front of her.

As they watched, Caderin wrenched the sword out and stepped back. Cali screamed again as she twisted and fell to the floor on her back, staring up at him helplessly. Her left hand was scrabbling around for a weapon, any weapon, but there was none within reach. She feebly pushed herself backwards with her legs, but didn't have the strength left to move very far.

Drevin shouted her name and ran towards her. He was thirty paces away. Caderin raised his sword with a satisfied smirk on his boyish face and pointed it at her heart. Drevin was never going to make it!

Teelan held his breath again. This can't be happening. I thought we had won.

"STOP!" shouted Drevin, pointing his arm at the Gatherer.

And he did!

The word pulsed and vibrated across the field, heavy with the weight of the command. Caderin looked up at

Drevin and the word seemed to hit him like a physical blow, instantly paralysing him. He froze mid-thrust, seemingly unable to move any part of body, even a tiny fraction. Teelan gasped at what he was seeing. How did he do that? What does this mean? Questions and implications flooded his mind. Teelan was as frozen as Caderin by his churning thoughts.

Cali however wasn't. She quickly rolled away and grasped a fallen sword that a moment ago had been just far enough away as to be totally irrelevant. In a blur of motion, she went to one knee and jabbed upward, skewering Caderin through the heart. Either not satisfied or not convinced that was enough to stop him, she drew back the sword and stabbed again and again and again.

Her movements were inhumanly fast. All of this happening in the space of a couple of heartbeats. Then Caderin simply folded to the floor, without a sound, blood pouring from his wounds. Cali sagged to her knees.

Teelan blinked rapidly and finally managed to start thinking coherently again. Is it over? He looked around at the carnage. The field was strewn with dead and wounded men and women. None of them looked willing or able to continue the fight. It was over. We need to get out of here now. He turned to Drevin to voice just that sentiment.

"Drevin, we need to g…" Teelan stopped. Drevin was on his knees, trembling violently. As Teelan watched, his eyes rolled up in his head and he collapsed face first, his whole body convulsing. "Drevin! Drevin! DREVIIIN!!"

# CHAPTER 14

# CONSEQUENCES

Cali hacked at a thorny branch on the spindly bush, breaking it off and dropping it onto the nearby pile. Her dagger was notched and blunted, which was making it hard work to collect enough dry firewood. She huffed and bent down to chop at another twisted limb. At least the wood was dry now, the rain having held off. It had persisted for the rest of the day and night after their encounter, but the following day had been bright. Today had started misty again but was now clear with a chilly wind blowing in gusts, whistling through the passes.

She was hungry, restless, and worried. Two days! Two days they had been stuck out here in the foothills, waiting and hoping for Drevin to recover. Drevin! She recalled seeing him shaking on the floor after the fight and shivered. She had staggered over to him and tried to wake him but couldn't get any reaction from him. Teelan was already by his side and was panicking over the state he was in.

She had still been dazed and exhausted from the battle and wasn't sure what had happened to him. She had of course, heard Drevin's shout and then seen that young prick of a Gatherer freeze like a stone statue, so she had taken her chance and stabbed him. Then she heard Teelan's shouts and, when she had looked back, Drevin was on the ground. He had obviously done something, but she wasn't sure what. Did he have a Fragment? A Trait that can command people to do things? Is what was happening to him now the consequence he was talking about?

Oh crap! Talking of consequences. She had killed someone. Again. Only this time she had meant it and had wanted to do it. And at the time, it had felt good. Now however, she felt sick thinking about it and hurried her thoughts along.

She remembered she had then snatched up her bag and a couple of her daggers, then helped Teelan pick Drevin up. He had stopped shaking by then, but he was still unconscious and was a dead weight. They had eventually managed to get him standing with one of them under each of his arms. They intended to get him onto one of the Gatherers' horses, but they had typically bolted from the noise, blood, and fire of the battle.

So, between them they had somehow half carried, half dragged him away, heading north into the hills. They had staggered on for a couple of miles before none of them could go any further. Cali had taken them into a deserted cave, and they had laid Drevin down and there he had lain ever since, without waking.

She had slumped in a corner and watched numbly as Teelan had cleaned his wounds and bandaged his arm. Drevin had not even stirred during this. His body was as limp as a drunk prostitutes when they were with a volatile customer. Teelan had said that he was in a coma, and they just had to wait and see if or when he came out of it. Cali didn't like the sound of the word 'if'.

Then Teelan had seen to her injuries, putting some smelly herbs on her shoulder before wrapping a clean linen strip around it and tying it tight. He had fumbled with the bandage, his face close to hers, his hands awkward and as cold as a dead fish. It had hurt bad when he was doing it. Not that he cared. He just kept telling her to keep still, even though she was only wriggling slightly when it pained her too much. She could tell that he wasn't used to working on living people.

To take her mind off it, she had looked closely at him while he was tending to her. He was actually quite handsome, she supposed, when he wasn't sneering or being all high and mighty. His high cheekbones stuck out from his pale face, his skin was smooth, and his light blue eyes were the same colour as the ocean shallows. His long white hair was soft as it brushed against her cheek, and its paleness fascinated her.

He had then treated her thigh wound in much the same way, although with more fumbling and blushing than before. Her shoulder still stung and ached when she moved it but felt better than before and her leg was almost healed.

She dropped the last stick on the pile, then sat down on the rough grass, pulled out a strip of dried meat from her pouch and chewed on it. Thinking about Teelan brought back memories of their first night in the cave. When he realised that she only had beer or wine in her flasks, he became annoyed. Like he had thought to bring anything to drink at all. Ungrateful prick.

Seemingly reluctantly, he had started on the wine. After a while, he became very talkative. Started whining and complaining about how he hated this country and how brutal and uncultured it was compared to his homeland. She suggested to him that he could go home anytime he wanted. Then he had gone all sad and started talking about how beautiful the buildings were back in his city. How could buildings be beautiful?

He had carried on drinking and was soon three sheets to the wind. He asked her about her private life and her parents. She hadn't wanted to tell him about that, so had just said that they weren't around anymore. Then he asked her how many men she had been intimate with! How dare he! She knew he hadn't got over the fact that she lived in a brothel.

So, she offhandedly replied that she had been with 'as many men as she wanted whenever she wanted'. Which wasn't strictly true, but she didn't feel like he deserved the truth for his rudeness. She then turned the tables and asked him about his sexual encounters, fully expecting him to refuse to answer. Unfortunately for both of them, he did.

He told her he had been with one woman once and found the whole experience 'rather awkward and messy'. Then, to make it worse, he said that her parents had pressured her into doing it to get on good terms with his parents. Apparently Teelan's parents were well regarded and rich, ranking among the high and mighty. No shit.

He also said that he had had a close male friend, which surprised her, but this friend had abandoned Teelan for 'becoming a freak'. Cali hadn't known what he meant by that. The laughable thing was when he handed her back the flask of wine she realised he had drunk less than a quarter of it. Damn. That boy really couldn't handle his liquor.

She smiled at that now. Even though he was probably a couple of years older than her, she thought he was still like a boy in some ways. He was smart certainly, in his own way, but also very naïve. She didn't think he would last more than a couple of days on the streets. Still, he had cared for their hurts and was looking after Drevin intently, so she was grateful for that.

The following day he had been quiet, clearly embarrassed and annoyed about what had happened the night before. Since then they had barely spoken and when they did, they either snapped at each other or argued about their course of action. Cali wanted to move on, hating being stuck in one place, feeling vulnerable out here. However, Teelan kept insisting that they shouldn't move Drevin.

So, Cali had stayed out of his way most of the time. She had scouted around the hills, keeping a wary lookout for any approaching soldiers, sure that they would be searching for them. She had found a small stream nearby to refill their flasks, which for once Teelan had actually been grateful for. The food that she had brought with her, dried meat, hard cheese and slightly soft fruit was almost all gone.

She had foraged for some berries and wildflowers that they could eat and attempted to catch some wild squirrels and rabbits. So far however, she had only brought down one small rabbit with a well aimed dagger. And she collected firewood to keep their small fire going. This was how she had spent the last two days.

Two days of growing more and more frustrated, impatient and concerned. What if Drevin never woke up? He had to, didn't he? She knew he was strong. He would wake up again. And soon, hopefully. She sighed and picked up her bundle of branches and headed off to the stream. Better go get some more water for his lordship Teelan.

****

Teelan peeled off the bandage from around Drevin's arm and looked at the wound. A long, dark pink line scarred his arm from just above his wrist right up to his elbow. The neat yellow catgut stitches crisscrossing it were doing their job of holding the skin together tightly. He was satisfied to see that the initial swelling around the cut was starting to go down and the redness was fading.

When he had first treated the wound, he had poured some of the foul tasting wine over it to clean it and then packed it with mint, sage and myrrh and wrapped a linen bandage around it. He examined it now and was pleased to see that it was healing well. There was no putrid smell from it, no discharges, and no other signs of infection. He removed some herbs from his pouch and placed them on a large flat stone, then used a fist sized rock to crush them.

Drevin still would not wake. At least he was no longer shaking or twitching now, nor was he showing any signs of a fever. Teelan was still concerned however, as he knew that his condition was not caused by a medical reason but by a magical one. Drevin was a Fragment! How had he not realised that?

Thinking back, he remembered on a couple of occasions noticing Drevin stumbling and seeming dizzy before. Now they made sense. His vertigo must be part of the long-term effects of using his Trait. But why hadn't Drevin told him? Did he not trust him or just not think enough of him? Teelan had just begun to consider Drevin as trustworthy and honest. Obviously, Drevin didn't feel the same way about him. It was clear that he had used his power to prevent that Gatherer from killing Cali. Now he was suffering the consequences.

Two days! For the last two days Teelan had forced him to drink, first the beer, then the water in small amounts by trickling it into his mouth. He had also mashed up some of the fruit and stuffed it in, then massaged his throat to make him unconsciously swallow. But that and treating his wounds was about all he could do for him.

He just had to hope that the side effects of using his Fragment subsided soon. He sighed as he tipped a bit of water onto the pulverised herbs and used a small, thin, smooth pebble to mix them into a paste. That was about the only thing they had in abundance at the moment, stones. This cold, rocky cave was full of them. He sighed again as he scraped up the last of his herb paste and used the pebble to spread it over Drevin's arm. Then he rolled a clean strip of cloth around it and tied it tight. He was almost out of bandages as well.

Thinking about that reminded him he would need to check Cali's shoulder again soon. He shuddered as he remembered that awkward experience. Having to get so close to her and touching her warm, soft skin had been disconcerting, making him clumsy and inept. She kept squirming under his ministrations and complaining, which hadn't helped him to concentrate. She also kept staring at him, which was very off-putting. He much preferred working with the cold, quiet, non-judgemental dead.

To take his mind off what he was doing, and the complicated emotions he was feeling, he had studied her clinically as he worked on her wounds. She was certainly not a classical beauty, like the paintings neatly lined up in his father's study. She did not possess creamy or pale skin, but rather had a more ruddy complexion with a gentle sprinkling of pale freckles. Her nose was wider and shorter than traditional and her mouth fuller. She had eyes that, despite being a jade green in colour, always seemed to have a spark of fire in them. Her hair was not braided or coiffured but hung in wild curls down below her shoulders, the colour of a field of poppies. She was more petite than most of the ladies he knew from his homeland, but not as lean and had a more natural body shape.

And she definitely wasn't a lady. She didn't have the manners and culture of a lady, being as coarse as a sailor. Her attitude was wild and mischievous instead of being docile and demure. But he had never particularly cared for the girls back home, as he had found them generally staid and insipid. There was definitely something about Cali that put him off balance.

For one thing, she seemed absolutely intent on irritating him with every word she spoke and making fun of him whenever she could to cause him embarrassment. Although he had done rather a good job of that himself the other night. He winced as he recalled their mortifying conversation from two nights ago. Why did I say those things? What possessed me? I guess it was a combination of being exhausted, anxious and scared, but also elated that we had survived. That heady mix of emotions had led him to overindulge, to relax, which instead resulted in his rudeness and loquaciousness. Never again will I drink wine, even if I must die of thirst instead.

They had spoken little since then. Teelan was constantly tired, hungry, thirsty, fretful and uncomfortable, which he knew made him irritable and snappy. Cali had kept badgering him to move on, to head for a village or town, but he didn't want to try moving Drevin just yet. It could trigger a shaking fit again, which might reopen his wounds. Much as he hated it, they were stuck here until Drevin woke.

So, he sat here in this dank, mouldy, craggy hole in the hills, his back to the damp wall, poking the meagre fire with a stick. Waiting for the man who had saved his life to wake up. He couldn't sort out his feelings for Drevin any easier than he could for those about Cali.

On the one hand, Drevin was a coarse, brutish, unlearned oaf who lacked any social graces. He had a disreputable career, working for anyone who would pay him, to do jobs of a dubious and often violent nature. He clearly despised the noble and ruling classes, generalising all of them as self-serving egotistical despots, without knowing all of them. And his belief in the gods was almost preposterous and very naïve.

But on the other hand, Drevin was kind and caring in his way and had his own code of honour and belief in what was right and wrong. He was fearless, often to the point of stupidity, but always put himself in danger before allowing harm to come to others. Teelan was beginning to understand that Drevin was right, and that people were indeed more complicated than he had thought.

Drevin had saved his life. He was obviously grateful for that, but wondered how he should behave around Drevin now. Would he expect me to be fawning and subservient now? To repay the debt somehow? Or do we just ignore it and continue as we are? Could we even do that?

Teelan's solitude and boredom left too much time for his mind to come up with unanswerable questions. He sighed again and then realised that he was doing that far too often lately. He tossed the last twiggy branch onto the dying fire to keep it alive. After all, that's what it is all about, isn't it? Staying alive.

# CHAPTER 15

# DARK PASTS

Drevin's eyes flickered once, twice, three times, then finally opened. He stared up at a rough, wet, stone wall curving above him. He felt as if a mountain had crushed his whole body, leaving him as weak as a newborn baby. In his attempt to speak, only a thin croaking sound came out of his mouth.

Teelan's face suddenly appeared above him, his long hair tickling his nose. "Drevin. Drevin, you're awake. Thank goodness. Here, drink some water," he said, then his face disappeared.

Drevin then felt a flask pressed against his lips and he spluttered as he tried to take a few sips of the cold liquid. After a couple of attempts, he managed to swallow some. It felt like ice going down his throat and helped to wake him further.

"How long?" Drevin finally wheezed, weakly pushing the flask away.

"Two days," Teelan replied, resting back on his knees.

Dammit. Not again! “Help me sit up,” Drevin said, slowly trying to bend from the middle. Teelan quickly grabbed hold of his shoulders and together they propped him up against the chill wall.

“Here you must be hungry,” Teelan said, holding out a strip of dried beef.

Drevin realised he was. In fact, he was starving. He took the meat and started chomping on it, swallowing large chunks in his haste.

“Easy,” said Teelan, “Don’t choke on it.”

Drevin ignored him and kept chewing, trying to fill the yawning emptiness he felt in his belly. By the gods he felt like shit. In fact, there was only one other time in his life that he had felt worse than this. He felt like his head was packed with wool and his surroundings still appeared to spin slightly. His mouth and throat were as rough and dry as sand, and he felt every muscle and bone in his body throbbing and pulsing with a deep ache. Even though he had apparently been asleep for two days, he was so weary that he could barely hold his head up. He looked around slowly, his vision blurry.

He was in a small cave. Teelan sat next to him, looking thinner, paler, and dirtier than usual. A pathetic excuse for a fire sat in the middle of the space, flickering faintly, looking like it was about to peter out. Two cloaks lay on the floor at opposite sides of the caves. Presumably where Teelan and Cali were sleeping. Drevin noticed they were about as far apart as they could get. The opening to the outside world was a jagged cut in the rock, just big enough to allow one person in or out at a time. It let in a fading light, which told of another day just about to succumb to the blackness of night.

"Where's Cali?" he asked.

"Out, gathering more firewood," said Teelan. Huh. That would explain the fire situation then.

"How is she?" Drevin asked. He hoped she was faring better than Teelan looked to be.

"She is fine. You know how she is." Teelan said. Drevin could hear something in Teelan's voice but was too tired to work out what. He hoped that something hadn't happened between them.

"Talk to me Teelan. Otherwise, I will fall asleep again and I have slept long enough." Drevin said, resting his head against the wall and closing his eyes. Gods, but he was tired.

"What about?" Teelan asked, confused.

"Anything."

"You are a Fragment aren't you?" Shit. Not this. Not now.

"I don't want to talk about that now," Drevin said grimly.

"You said anything," Teelan said indignantly.

"Anything but that. Listen, I will tell you about it later. For now, just talk to me Teelan. Don't interrogate me." Drevin sighed.

"Okay, fine." Teelan replied, glancing at the cave entrance. "Cali. Did you see what she did during the fight? She moved as fast as that Gatherer. She was like a blur."

"I saw. She has the Move Trait." Damn. Another problem.

"But what does that mean? How can she have two Traits?"

"She can't. It's not possible. Unless.." There was only one possibility.

"Unless she's a Mind." Teelan surmised. He was quick, give him that.

"But there hasn't been a full Mind born for almost four hundred years." It seemed incredible that Cali could be a full Mind. He couldn't quite comprehend it yet.

"As far as we know. Do you think she knows? What are we going to do about it?"

"No, I don't think she knows and we are not going to tell her yet." Drevin saw Teelan open his mouth to object and quickly cut him off. "Not yet Teelan. We are not in a fit state to do anything about it right now. Let's wait until we are all recovered a bit more. Then we can tell her and decide what to do." Drevin gave a great yawn. "Now can you stop asking me troublesome questions and just talk to me, please?" Drevin could feel his mind wasn't up to making any decisions at the moment. He needed to rest and not worry about future problems right now. "Is there anything else to eat and drink?" he croaked.

Teelan stood and walked over to where one cloak lay and rummaged around for a moment in Cali's bag. He returned with his hands cupped, a flask dangling from his fingers.

"Some berries, a brownish apple and some beer."

Drevin smiled at that. At last, some good news.

"Don't drink too much of the beer," Teelan warned, pulling a face at him.

Drevin ignored him and took a big swig. It was very bitter, but was deliciously cold, yet somehow still warmed his belly a little. He chomped on the apple while Teelan sat next to him again. He watched him from the corner of his eye.

Drevin could almost feel Teelan's mind working as he pondered over different topics of conversation to start then discarded them. Drevin could tell that Teelan was still bursting with questions that he wanted to ask him, and he knew what they would be about. For now though, Drevin didn't feel up to answering them. He didn't want to see the reproachful look that he knew would form on Teelan's face.

After a few moments of silence, Teelan actually complied with Drevin's request and reluctantly uttered two words. "A doctor."

"What?" Drevin asked, confused.

"You asked me some days ago what I was training for at the academy. Well, I was supposed to be training to become a doctor. My father was a renowned doctor and wanted me to follow in his footsteps."

"Yeah, so what happened?" Drevin asked, intrigued. Of all the things he thought Teelan might talk about, this was not one of them. He had been adamant that he didn't want to discuss it before.

"I didn't much like it," Teelan said, shrugging and putting a berry in his mouth. "Oh, I enjoyed the science of it and learning about how the body works, but I didn't enjoy having to deal with the patients. All that screaming, crying and wailing. It was very unsettling. All the emotions people went through, from the grief of the families for those we couldn't save to the jubilance of those we cured. It was frankly exhausting. It affected my concentration and made me feel... odd."

"That would be empathy, Teelan." Drevin said, smiling. He took the berries off him and started popping them in his mouth.

"Well, whatever it was, I didn't much care for it." Teelan paused for a moment before speaking again. "Then when I was fourteen, my sister got ill. Very ill. My father and I tried every remedy we knew. Herbs, poultices, leeches, burning certain types of woods and oils. We even hired a Fragment with the Revive Trait. But nothing worked.

"She lay in her bed, wasting away, day by day. And day by day I sat at her bedside watching her. I knew she was dying. After months of despair and weeping every day I couldn't bear any more. But I also couldn't bear to be apart from her. So it was that my mind fractured.

"My emotions separated themselves from reality, hiding away in a dark corner of my brain to protect me. The parts of my psyche that were left were now free of emotions, cold, clinical, and detached. The body on the bed was no longer my sister. It became a stranger. A study of disease and death. Of how the body decays; how the muscles wither and atrophy; how the skin pales before yellowing; how the blisters and sores grow and spread; how the heartbeat slows; how the breathing becomes shallower; the wheezing noises the lungs and throat make; the discharge of fluids from every orifice; until the last gasp of life leaves the body."

Drevin sat stunned as Teelan reeled this off in a monotone, lifeless voice, tears trickling slowly down his face. "Gods, I'm so sorry Teelan."

"Even after she died," Teelan continued, as if wanting to finish now that he had started, "I sat with her. Watching her eyes glaze over, her limbs stiffen then go flaccid again, feeling the warmth leave her body, smelling the contents of her stomach emptying. Eventually my parents forced me to leave her side, but since then I have been obsessed with death, as strange as it may seem."

"It's not strange at all, Teelan," Drevin said understandingly. "You went through a horribly traumatic experience when you were young. Things like that affect you and you have to find a way of dealing with it, otherwise it can drive you to a lifetime of grief and misery. This is just your way of handling it. There is nothing wrong with that."

"Ha, try telling that to my parents. My mother was aghast when I dropped out of the university to study 'stinking dead people' and my father was very disappointed in me." Teelan said bitterly.

"Well, that's fathers for you, always full of disappointment." Drevin said grimly.

"It wasn't just them. My friends also thought that I was weird and called me a freak. Almost everyone ostracised me. I had to continue my studies alone, learning what I could from books and any undertakers or disreputable physicians who would talk to me. Eventually, I found someone who shared my interest. A man who had also been studying the effects of death and trying to understand how people died. He took me in and together we made some significant discoveries." Teelan's voice grew wistful. Drevin hoped he hadn't been on the wine again.

Drevin waited in silence to see if he would say any more, but he seemed to have run out of words, lost in his own memories. Bloody shit. He was not expecting that! He knew the kid was unusual in his interests, but that was dark. That was a terrible thing for any family to go through, especially a young boy at that time in his life. No wonder he chose the profession he did.

Drevin still couldn't believe that he had told him all this. Maybe it was because of the state he was in, or because of what they had just been through, but Teelan's revelation still shocked him. He didn't know how to respond to that, but luckily Teelan didn't seem to require one, so they both sat in thoughtful stillness for a while.

Soon Drevin felt his eyes grow heavy and his head dropped to his chest. He found himself drifting again. No. Must stay awake. I owe the kid that much. His fingers found the ring on his left hand, and he spun it round, the metal cold to the touch. Well, I guess it's my turn now.

"My wife's," Drevin said obliquely.

"I beg your pardon?" Teelan asked, coming out of his reverie.

"This ring you asked me about before," Drevin explained, holding out his hand. "It belonged to my wife."

"I didn't know that you were married. Where is she now?" Teelan asked quietly.

"She's dead." Drevin stated flatly.

"Oh, I'm sorry. Do you want to tell me more?"

"She's very dead." Drevin said, attempting to lighten the moment whilst trying to keep his emotions in check. Damn. He couldn't believe he was going to do this. He took another swig of beer.

"Touché," Teelan smiled sadly. "I guess I deserved that. What happened to her?"

Drevin sighed before he spoke. "I used to work for King Vesgar Ironfinder in the capital of Braka as a captain in his guard at first, then his personal bodyguard. He kept me close and used my 'special talents' often. But he treated me well and asked nothing of me I was uncomfortable with. After a while I met Rylia there.

"She was a serving maid in the castle and she stole my heart. Her hair was the colour of the rising sun and her face as pretty as a field of spring flowers. Everyone said that she was beneath my station. That I should just bed her then move on to someone more befitting who would make a good match for me. But I couldn't forget her. We fell in love and got married soon after.

"She continued to work as a maid, even though she didn't have to. Said she enjoyed being busy and having a purpose. She was like that. Always wanting to help and look after others before thinking of herself. She was much better than me in that way." Drevin paused for a moment as he remembered the smell of her hair and her playful smile when he teased her for working too hard. Gods, but this was hard. But I have started now.

"Anyway, we were happy together there for seven years, the only sore point being that we were unable to have any children. Not for a want of trying mind," Drevin said, smiling. He watched Teelan squirm at that.

"What happened after seven years?" Teelan asked, obviously keen to move the story along.

Drevin wondered again at Teelan's innocence and aversion to physical contact. He shrugged as he continued. "Vesgar died and his son Gorak became king. Gorak was not like his father. He was hard and ruthless, always after more land and status. A typical power hungry, self-serving, arsehole of a king. Needless to say he didn't much like me either. However, I had many friends and supporters within the castle who regarded me well, so he couldn't dismiss me for no reason. So, he gave me a new role as a Gatherer.

"I undertook the role to the best of my ability and enjoyed it, even though it often meant spending long periods away from the castle, searching for Fragments. My team did some good work though. We discovered a number of Frags and helped them to understand their powers. They stayed in rooms in the castle and received good payment for the work they did for the kingdom. At first, we found many such Fragments and everything was well. But after a few years, it became harder and harder to find more. We had to go out further into the countryside and wilderness to search for them, which meant I spent even less time with Rylia.

"Gorak was unhappy with our meagre findings and became more aggressive in his pursuits, ordering us to capture anyone who could become a Fragment. He told us to gather up local children who were between twelve and fifteen. They kept them in the castle in a large room that they turned into a dormitory, keeping an eye on them day and night in case any of them developed a Trait. They were poorly treated. Confined to the castle, they lived in squalor and were given little food and drink. When I found out how they were being treated I protested of course."

Drevin heard Teelan snort a laugh as he said that. He took another big gulp of the cold beer, shivering as it chilled him. His throat still felt gritty.

"Anyway, Gorak ignored me," Drevin continued. "He went to greater and greater lengths to get Fragments, even torturing some of the poor children to see if it sparked any latent powers in them. I couldn't be a part of that, so I told him I was leaving. But he forbade me from going. Said that I was still in his service and only he could release me."

"Somehow I can't imagine you just accepting that." Teelan interjected.

"I didn't. I ignored Gorak, went back to my room, and started packing my things. Then I went to search for Rylia to tell her we were leaving. But I couldn't find her anywhere. I asked everyone I saw where she was, but nobody either knew or would tell me. I was getting worried.

"Eventually I found the guard captain who I had promoted when I left that role. He was still grateful to me and was a friend. So, he reluctantly informed me that Gorak's personal bodyguards had taken her and were keeping her in a heavily guarded room in his quarters. I was so angry I headed straight back to confront Gorak. He said that he was keeping my wife under guard to ensure my 'good behaviour and continued loyal service'. I almost killed him then. Only the thought of what would happen to Rylia stayed my hand."

"That's awful. So what did you do?"

"What could I do?" Drevin spat bitterly. "They allowed me to visit her, under supervision of course, and only at certain times. So, I spent months playing along with his sick game whilst all the while planning how to get us both out of there. As I said, I still had a lot of friends in the castle, but no-one was willing to openly cross Gorak. Besides, men loyal to him always watched her.

"Eventually, I came up with a plan and put it into motion. I won't bore you with the details of it but suffice to say that it didn't work out as planned. After that failed attempt they moved her to a more secure cell in the tower and any further chances of a rescue seemed impossible." Drevin took another drink, finishing the flask and wiping his mouth with his sleeve. He shook the flask sadly and looked at Teelan hopefully. Teelan sighed and reluctantly fetched him another one.

Drevin took the offered flask, but didn't drink yet. "But I didn't give up hope and kept plotting. I could still visit her occasionally and she was always happy to see me. But she worried about me. Of all things. She was the one locked up, deprived of freedom, comforts, adequate food and water, but she fretted over me. That was the kind of person she was.

"She said I looked tired and anxious all the time. That I was ageing in front of her eyes. She thought she was the cause of the state that I was in, and she hated that. I kept telling her I was fine, but she knew I wasn't. I said that I was just concerned for her, that it wasn't her fault and that I didn't blame her. Damn. Looking back, I wish I hadn't said that now.

"I knew it was all Gorak's doing. I had thought of a dozen ways to kill him, but each plan ended with my death too. That wouldn't have bothered me, but I knew Rylia would also be killed shortly after. You see, he was afraid of me and always kept at least four or five men around him so that I couldn't use my Trait on him. He knew I could force him to release us if I could get to him alone," he said, hardness in his voice.

Drevin saw Teelan shiver at his words, whether from his casual talk of murdering someone or of using his Fragment to force someone to do something, he wasn't sure which. He didn't quite know himself which one was worse.

"So how did she ...?" Teelan's words trailed off.

Drevin took a long swallow before speaking. "After several months, I went to visit her one day and found her cell empty. I asked the guards where she was, but they wouldn't tell me. I was frantic and questioned everyone I saw, but nobody would even look at me.

"Finally I found the captain again and he took me aside and gave me the news. He told me that Rylia had asked for a mirror and the guards had relented and given her a small glass disk. Apparently, she then smashed the glass and used the slivers to slice her own wrists. The guards rushed in and tried to stop the bleeding but couldn't save her. He said her last words were 'Now he can be free.' He then gave me her ring and said how sorry he was." Drevin laughed bitterly. He wasn't sorry enough to help me get her out the castle earlier though, was he?

Drevin paused as the emotions welled up in him as he recalled that catastrophic moment again. "You see Teelan, she chose to die rather than see me suffer living under the king's yoke. That was how selfless she was. She died for me. It was my fault. If I had not been so worried, or spent all my time plotting our escape, she might not have fretted for me. Or if I had not stirred up trouble with Gorak in the first place, she would still be alive."

"I'm sorry Drevin," Teelan said genuinely. Drevin almost thought that he could see moisture in his eyes. "But you can't blame yourself for having principles. You stood up to him because what he was doing was wrong. And you were concerned for your wife's safety and tried to get her out of captivity, which is only natural. So don't rebuke yourself for having some moral decency. After all, it is one of your only redeeming qualities." Teelan said, smiling softly at him. "So, what did you do then? How did you get away from Gorak Ironfinder?"

"I grabbed my meagre bag of belongings and stormed into the throne room to assault the king. Of course, he had his usual sycophants and guards around him, but I didn't care. I was so furious I was prepared to die if I could just get to him first. But his four guards closed in on me before I reached him. They were in full plate armour and had swords levelled at me. They were his best fighters, so I knew I couldn't fight them all and get to Gorak. So, I vented my frustration another way. I used my Voice Trait and commanded them to release me. All four of them at once."

"Goodness." Teelan exclaimed, shocked. "I know little about that Trait but isn't that supposed to be impossible?"

"Almost impossible, yes. The Voice is only meant to be used on one person at a time," Drevin replied, smiling sadly. "Using it on multiple people is very difficult and dangerous to do. Both for the Fragment and for their targets. But I was beyond reason at that point. And amazingly, it worked.

"The guards' eyes glazed over, and they instantly lowered their weapons and stepped back. I lunged straight for Gorak, sword raised to strike him down. But instead of cowering or preparing to defend himself, I saw he was quickly writing something down, so I stayed my hand. Then he handed me a signed parchment. It was my release papers. I hadn't realised that my Voice had worked on him too and he had obeyed my command as well."

"Wow, five people at once. That is incredible." Teelan sounded stunned.

Drevin drank again. He could feel the beer having an effect on him, weak as they both were. It wasn't helping his dizziness but was reliving some of his aches and pains. "Yes, but at the time I was too angry to recognise that fact. I was shocked by what I had done sure, but still intent on killing him for what he had done to me and Rylia. My sword swung again but stopped just short of his throat. I suddenly thought of her and what she would want. She wanted me to be free, and now I was.

"I knew the effect of my command would wear off shortly, but I had a legal document from the king that I was a free man. If I killed him in front of all those witnesses, I would be throwing that freedom away, along with my life. So, I made the hardest decision of my life and let him live. I fled from the castle like a thief in the night as fast as I could manage.

"You see, the effects of using my Voice on so many people was taking a toll on me already. I was trembling badly and so dizzy that I couldn't run in a straight line. Eventually, I staggered out of the city and to a waiting barge that belonged to a friend. I had previously asked him to take the both of us downriver when I had planned the earlier escape attempt. Now it was just me. He took one look at me and pushed off from the dock. Then I passed out.

"When I next woke up it was seven days later, and I was back in Lakeview in Paska. My home. I stayed for a few days to recover my strength and spend some time with what family I had left there. My mother was pleased to see me, my father less so, especially after I told them a brief account of what had happened. You see, you are not alone in having to bear the weight of a disgruntled parent, Teelan." he said, giving Teelan a quick smile.

"But soon I heard rumours that Ironfinder was hunting for someone. A man who he claimed was dangerous and manipulative and who had abandoned his duties. It didn't take a genius to work out it was me he was looking for. So, I did what I do best. I ran. And I guess that I have been running ever since. I wear Rylia's ring as a reminder of her and as a warning not to trust those in power."

Drevin sighed deeply, sadness washing over him again as he recalled the most traumatic event of his life. But he also felt oddly lighter at having spoken of it to someone. It was the first time he had told anyone the full tale and for some strange reason he was glad that it was Teelan he had told. This strange, complicated, clever, haughty, innocent boy had been through his own ordeals. But by sharing his, Drevin hoped he had helped him feel a bit less alone.

"Sounds to me like you had little choice," Teelan said matter-of-factly. "If you had killed the king or stayed in his castle you would be dead by now."

"Death can be a choice too, Teelan." Drevin said grimly.

"There is no glory in death, Drevin." Teelan said vehemently, "It is not glamorous or noble. The body shrivels up and emits foul odours, then rots and decays and withers until the skin sloughs off, leaving nothing but bones."

"But that is just the physical body, Teelan. The spirit surely lives on. To find lost loved ones and some peace and happiness at last."

"You really believe that?" Teelan asked sceptically.

"I have to." Drevin said. And it was true. He had to believe that he would one day see Rylia again, even if it was after his death. To believe that there was a reward for living a good life, for being a good person, for doing the right things. Otherwise, what was the point of it all? A heavy silence fell as both of them sat in deep thought, contemplating all that they had said and heard.

"Drevin! You're awake." Cali's excited voice came from the entrance to the cave, shattering the stillness.

Drevin looked over to see her compact frame highlighted in the opening, her hair aflame with the setting sun behind her. She instantly dropped the bundle of sticks she had been carrying with a loud clatter and rushed over to him. She threw herself at him and hugged him tightly. Too tightly.

"Ow, ouch," he complained as she crushed his wounded arm, "Easy Cali."

"Oh, I'm sorry," Cali said, pulling back from him a little. "Does your arm hurt?"

"A bit," Drevin lied. In fact, his arm felt like there were smouldering coals buried just beneath the skin.

"Oh, well in that case," Cali said, then she punched him hard in his good arm. Oww! "That is for making me worried about you. And for sleeping for days on end and leaving me all alone."

Drevin raised his eyebrows at that and glanced at Teelan, expecting him to come back with a snappy remark. Instead, to his surprise, Teelan just looked sheepish and hung his head. What had gone on between them?

"So, what happened to you?" Cali asked, sitting down cross-legged next to him. Drevin could see a bulge around her shoulder under her jerkin covering a bandage and she looked paler than usual, but otherwise she seemed fine. He was relieved about that.

Drevin shrugged before speaking, "I used my Trait to help you. This is the consequence."

"But I didn't even know that you were a Fragment. What Trait do you have? Why didn't you tell me?" Cali asked, speaking urgently. Drevin could tell that she needed to know, and he couldn't put her off. I guess it's time then.

"Is there any more of this piss weak beer?" he asked, shaking his now empty second flask.

Cali dashed to her bag and retrieved two flasks, handing one to Drevin and taking a gulp from the other one. Drevin noticed she didn't offer Teelan one. He shook his head slowly, then took another long swallow of the beer, waiting for it to slide down into his stomach.

"I have the Major Voice Trait. It means that I can sometimes use it to convince people to do what I say or to follow a certain course of action that they are unsure about. I can get people to tell me things and reveal truths they might want to keep hidden. Or I can issue a command to a person, and they will obey it instantly, without thought."

"Bloody hell!" Cali gasped, stunned. "So, you can make anyone do whatever you want, when you want? That is some goddamn power. So why aren't you king or something then? Or a rich merchant? Or a baron? Or, or, or.." she rattled out.

"It doesn't work like that, Cali," Drevin interrupted. "There are limits to what you can do. Usually, you cannot force people to do things that are far against their nature or that cause them or those that they care about harm. It is more subtle than that, more like swaying their opinion, convincing them to your way of thinking, giving them a little prod in the right direction. It is not just about using the Trait as a bludgeoning weapon."

"Did you use it on those guards in the city to make them obey you? Is that how we escaped?" Cali asked.

"No. I haven't used it for a long while, until the other day. As you can see, it is not good for my health." Drevin said, smiling sadly. "But," he continued before Cali could ask another question, "when they teach you to use the Voice, you learn a lot of different tricks and techniques to help you maximise its power and potential.

"They teach you how to read people. How to judge their moods, how to understand them, how to think like they do. You learn how to adapt your tone of voice and your body language to suit various situations and circumstances. To determine what approaches work best with different people in order to make them relax and trust you. To get what you want from them. More often than not, these skills are enough on their own.

"But if they still resist, then they are primed for a suggestion with a bit of the Voice power behind it. Even then, it doesn't always work. Some people are more resistant to it than others, and some principles and ideas are so set in people's heads that you will never change them."

"That's insidious." Teelan blurted out, then blushed guiltily as Drevin looked at him.

"But you could just command them to do something, couldn't you?" Cali pressed.

"Yes, but that only works for a very short while." Drevin replied, sighing. "Seconds or minutes maybe, not much longer than that. Then the command fades from their mind and they wonder why they did what you just told them to do. That's why I only ever used it when in extreme need. Like saving your life. Besides, the consequences are always worse when using it."

"Yes, I can see that," Cali said, hugging her knees to her chest.

Drevin glanced over at Teelan who still sat near him, his head leaning back against the stone wall. "You're awfully quiet, Teelan. Do you have nothing to say about this?"

"I thought you were too tired for questions," Teelan replied bitterly.

"I have woken up now. Come on, spit it out."

"Fine." Teelan replied, tossing his head. "Have you ever used your Trait on me? Made me do or say something I didn't want to? Is that why I am in this situation now, because you made me go along with you?" Teelan stared at him and Drevin could see the vulnerability in his eyes.

"No dammit. Of course not. Shit, I wouldn't do that Teelan." Drevin replied vehemently.

"Then why didn't you tell me about it?" Teelan said, sounding hurt.

Drevin took another drink. "For exactly that reason. As soon as people know about my Trait they become wary of me. Everyone thinks I am influencing them or manipulating them the whole time. That I can control their minds. People don't understand this power and they generally fear and despise those who have it. Everyone believes that these Fragments employ this sly, evil power to manipulate people's thoughts for their own purposes. Nobody wants to spend time alone with someone with that power." Drevin finished sadly.

"Well, I do," Cali said, "I don't care about what Fragment you have. You saved my life."

"Mine too." Teelan said. "Thank you."

"You're welcome. Both of you." Drevin smiled.

"Wait. As we are talking about Traits, there's one thing I don't understand." Teelan said, clearly remembering something. Drevin shot him a warning glance. No Teelan, now was not the time to bring up Cali's use of multiple Traits.

"Just the one thing?" Cali muttered.

"During the fight," Teelan continued, ignoring both Cali's comment and Drevin's warning. "The Gatherer who used fire seemed to be immune to its effects. Her hands glowed red hot and she held a ball of fire in them."

"So what?" Cali interrupted.

"So," Teelan continued snippily, "When I rather bravely threw that dirt at her, she put her hands on her face to wipe it off but ended up horribly burning her face. Why did that happen if she was immune?"

"Because she isn't immune," Drevin stated. "Fragments with the Ignite Trait can create and control fire. They can make it do all kinds of things, including warming and even setting alight their own bodies without harm if they want to. But as I told you before Cali, it is all about control.

"They must concentrate to make the fire do their bidding, to know where it is going and what they intend it to do. They can create a fire shield around their body to protect themselves from its effects, but they have to focus on it. When you 'bravely' threw mud in her eyes, Teelan, Nylarian instinctively pressed her hands to her face, but she had lost her focus and control and hadn't protected herself. She forgot about the fire in her hands and suffered the consequences."

They all sat in silence for a moment after that. Drevin remembered the stink of burning flesh and her piercing wailing scream that had echoed around the field.

"So, what do we do next?" Cali said, going to retrieve her discarded branches and piling them on the practically dead fire. "Head south. Try our luck in another city? Or maybe a smaller, quieter town. I for one will not miss looking over my shoulder for Gatherers to come and take me away to some greedy baron."

Drevin could feel his tiredness creeping back into him, making his arms and legs feel like dead weights. The fire sparked and popped briefly under Cali's attempts to get it going again and Drevin stared at the flames for a moment, preparing himself. He knew what he was about to say would not go down well.

"We have to go back," he said tiredly.

"What!" Teelan and Cali both said at the same time, with identical looks of horror on their faces.

"That's cute," he said, smiling.

"You can't be serious! Are you mad? Did you take a blow to the head when you collapsed, old man?" Teelan of course, was the first to complain.

"Dev, you are joking, right?" Now it was Cali's turn. "I mean you must be as crazy as a sand crab to want to go back there."

"I have to," Drevin said as firmly as he could manage. "It is not right that the baron doesn't know the truth about his brother and his wife. About what they did to his son. I know Zandir is not the most amicable or benevolent ruler, but he still warrants the truth. He deserves to know why his son died. I can empathise with that."

"Yes and look where your empathy has got you so far." Teelan spat disgustedly. "Surely you can see that it would be incredibly foolish to return to the castle, not to mention highly dangerous, practically suicidal in fact."

"I know that." Drevin sighed. "Doesn't change the facts though. I don't expect either of you to come with me. It is too risky. I will go on my own."

"The hell you will!" Cali shouted. "I'm not staying here in this mouldy cave any longer. And as I've got nowhere else to go I'm coming with you. Besides, you need me to watch your back."

"You're both lunatics you know." Teelan stated. "But I will not stay here by myself, so I guess that makes us all mad, doesn't it? So, what's the plan?" Teelan said reluctantly.

"First, we sleep. Then in the morning we head south, find a friendly farmer and eat as much of his food as he can spare." Drevin said, rubbing his grumbling belly. "Then we head back to the city and try to get in to see the baron without getting noticed."

"And how do you intend to do that?" Teelan said caustically.

"I will think of something. Agreed?"

"Agreed." Cali said enthusiastically.

Drevin looked at Teelan who seemed at a loss for words for once. He could tell he was desperate to reject his plan, to point out how ridiculous it was. How it was no plan at all. How they would all end up dead or imprisoned. And he was probably right. But he obviously had no other ideas of what to do or how to proceed. Teelan's mouth opened and closed several times, but no words came out. Eventually, when he spoke, it was the most unexpected thing Drevin had ever thought he would say.

"Shit!" Teelan said.

# CHAPTER 16

# DOING THE RIGHT THING?

The farmer turned out to be a 'she' not a 'he', but fortunately they did still have plenty of food. Cali helped herself to another slab of bread to mop up the dregs of the pottage in her wooden bowl. The thin stew with freshly picked vegetables had a nice crunchy texture, because of the addition of some thick grains. She glanced up, chewing her bread, and saw that Drevin had polished off his third bowl. Even Teelan had managed to eat his way through two of them.

She sighed inwardly as she looked at Drevin. She was really worried about him. Cali had heard most of his incredibly sad story from outside the cave when he was talking to Teelan. She hadn't meant to eavesdrop but couldn't help herself. When she had first heard his voice and knew that he was awake, she was about to rush in headlong, shouting for joy. But the tone of his voice had frozen her. It was so flat and lifeless, so unlike him. There was none of his dry humour or sarcasm in it, only bitterness.

So she had waited. And listened. His story about his wife almost broke her heart. To think that a person could love you so much to take their own life for yours was way beyond her comprehension. The only couples that she had known had got together either for physical pleasure, for convenience, or occasionally to share their meagre wealth so that they might both live more comfortably. Even those who did claim to be 'in love' seemed to spend most of their time arguing with each other or complaining about their partner to their friends.

So, she had decided that she needed to be the one who would buck him up, keep him happy and his thoughts away from such things. She would be the perfect positive, cheerful, chatty companion who lifted his spirits in the hopes that she never had to hear that tone of voice from him again. So it was that she had talked aimlessly to him all morning as they had left their makeshift, temporary home and headed back south.

They had come across Oylia's farm earlier this morning and the stout, brash woman had eventually agreed to feed them after Drevin had parted with some of his coins. Oylia grew an assortment of vegetables and grains on her farm and lived here with her young teenage son Yoslin. Cali didn't like the way the nervous boy kept ogling her, as if he had never seen a girl before. Actually, thinking about it maybe he hadn't. He had greasy, mousy hair which kept flopping in front of his ratty dark eyes. Oylia had told them that her husband had died a few years back and they managed the farm on their own now, hard as it was for them.

Drevin was now chatting amiably to the farmer who kept putting her hand on his arm, whilst Cali was doing her best to avoid her son's scrutiny. Teelan just sat quietly for once, staring into his empty bowl. He looked older than he had when she had first met him just a few days ago. His cheeks were hollower and his eyes had dark rings under them, which stood out in stark contrast to his freakishly pale skin. Mind you, she supposed she didn't exactly look at her best.

She had splashed some water from the rain barrel on her face and arms and scrubbed off what dirt and grime she could, but she still felt grubby. The colour of her chemise had changed from white to grey, her woollen stockings had multiple rips and tears, and a mixture of blood and smoke had stained her yellow jerkin.

Drevin's voice suddenly caught her attention and brought her out of her vain musings. "Have you heard anything from the city lately?" he asked Oylia. "We are heading there shortly, and I wondered if you had heard any news that might be important."

"Only what everyone else already knows. That it is the day of the baron's son's funeral today," she replied offhandedly.

What! The funeral of Ridozir was today? That might be a great opportunity for us to sneak back into the city.

"Yes, of course." Drevin lied casually, "Everyone knows that. And are you heading into the city to join in the mourning?"

"We're going. But not to mourn. Didn't know the brat and don't care about him or his dad. We're going to sell our produce and for the free grub that our lords and masters are dishing out. Apparently, the streets are going to be lined with tables of food, and everyone can help themselves to as much as they want." Oylia replied.

“Do you mind if we tag along with you?” Drevin asked. “We can help you with your cart or carrying anything you need to take with you.” Smart. Drevin was obviously thinking the same thing as her. Blend in with a local farmer's family visiting the city for the funeral.

“Sure. You can ride in the back of the cart and make sure that nothing falls out. We will leave as soon as you have finished eating,” Oylia said pointedly, looking at the sparseness of the table.

All of their bowls were now empty, and they had also munched their way through a selection of fruits, some nuts and most of the cheese and bread. Cali finally felt full again after days of not having enough to eat. At least she was more used to going without food than the others, having grown up poor and often having to scavenge or steal what she needed. She couldn’t imagine snooty ‘lord’ Teelan ever going without basic necessities, even though he was skinnier than she was. Drevin at least, unlike Teelan, hadn’t complained, but she knew he had needed this to recover his strength, and he was looking much more like his old self now.

“Maybe just a few more minutes,” said Drevin, smiling and reaching for another slice of cheese.

***

Drevin sat in the back of the cart as it bumped along the track, full crates and bulging sacks piled around him, threatening to swamp him at any moment. He questioned again whether he was doing the right thing by returning to the city. He was sure that the baron deserved to know about his brother’s involvement in his son’s death. But he was unsure if this was the best way to go about it.

He knew he was putting himself in extreme danger, which he accepted. But he wished he didn't have to subject Cali and Teelan to the same risks. Much as he was glad to have them for company, he almost wished that they had refused to go with him. At least that way they would be safer.

Drevin glanced over at them now. Cali sat with her knees drawn up to her chest, rocking slightly with the motion of the cart. She had pulled her hood up and rested her head on her knees. She still seemed her usual bright and optimistic self when he talked to her, but Drevin could tell that some of it was forced. It was evident that she was worried and concerned about something.

Teelan sat further back, leaning against the low board that separated the storage area from the driver's seats. Drevin was anxious about him. Since the battle and the recounting of his disturbing past, he had become withdrawn and solemn. He looked tired and wrung out, as if there were no more feelings left within him. Drevin pondered his story again. Damn! No wonder the kid was so strange, having to go through that at such an impressionable age.

He hadn't mentioned his parents much, so Drevin assumed they didn't get on well. His sister was probably the closest person to him, and her death obviously scarred him deeply. Poor sod. That explained a lot about why he was like he was. Why he seemed so aloof, uncaring, and uninterested in other people. He was probably afraid of getting too close to someone again, in case they were taken away from him as well. Drevin would have to tread carefully around him for a while.

The wagon jolted suddenly as it hit a large bump, and Drevin had to steady the teetering stack of crates next to him. A sharp pain lurched through his back and his arm felt like a row of hot needles had pierced it at the sudden movement. After a moment, and a few deep breaths, the pain subsided back to its former dull, throbbing, persistent pulsing.

"Sorry," Oylia called back to them, "There was a big dip to get back on the main road, but it should be a nice, smooth ride from here on." She gave him a wide smile.

Drevin looked at her and nodded. He had picked up on her over friendliness to him and he didn't think it was just because of the money he had given her. *Wrong time, wrong place.*

He switched his gaze to her son, who was sitting next to her on the wooden driver's plank. His head kept swivelling back to check on them and Drevin noticed his eyes lingered on Cali for far longer than they should have. Drevin glared at him until he finally noticed, then quickly faced forward again. *Not long now then until we get there.* Drevin closed his eyes and tried to still his troublesome thoughts. But he had little success.

*Getting into the city should be easy enough. We can pose as hired labourers to Oylia. There should be plenty of people coming and going for the funeral, so the guards probably won't have time to check everybody in and out carefully. Getting into the castle however, will be much trickier.*

Oylia had told him that the baron's brother was going to host a feast there tonight, but only for nobles, priests, and rich folk. *The guards will definitely be on high alert there and will scrutinise everyone closely who wants* entrance in order to keep out the riffraff. He sat silently for a while. Ideas and schemes sprung up in his head, each one analysed and swiftly picked apart before being discarded. The cart rumbled on.

The abrupt halt of the cart jolted Drevin out of his thoughts. He turned his head and saw that they had joined the long queue of commoners waiting to gain admittance to the city. Farmers, merchants, peddlers, peasants, travelling priests, and hired thugs lined the road, all jostling for position. He nodded to the others and they all reluctantly got out and stood behind the cart.

Oylia had given them all a grubby brown robe each to wear to mark them as labourers and which worked well as a disguise. Teelan had taken his robe in two fingers with a look of horror and Drevin had expected him to make some sarcastic or snappy comment and refuse to wear it. But in the end, he had just sighed heavily and accepted it. There was definitely something up with that boy.

Drevin adjusted his smelly robe, pulling it tight and tying up the cord around the middle to hide his chain mail vest. His pilfered sword was stashed in the back of the cart, under a pile of heavy sacks in case they were searched. He watched the people in the queue as they waited their turn. There were people of all ages: from greybeards who could barely stand, to whole families with little children scampering around between the wagons and babes cradled in arms. Drevin highly doubted that they were all here to pay their respects to young Ridozir. He shook his head. It was amazing what the promise of free food, drink and festivities could do.

He tensed as they neared the gate and saw the guards outside ushering people in. He glanced at Cali and Teelan and saw them stiffen too. Teelan pulled his hood lower over his face to hide his distinctive hair. Cali, unconsciously, did the same. They all grabbed some sacks loaded with vegetables from the cart and hefted them over their shoulders, trying to look like average farm hands. If he wasn't so nervous, Drevin would have laughed as he saw Teelan struggle under the weight of his bag. They were definitely the oddest looking hired help he had ever seen!

Luckily, it was as he expected, and the frantic and harassed guards only took a cursory look at them and the contents of the cart before waving them through quickly. There was still a long queue behind them that wanted to get in before the third bell rung and their free lunch was served.

Drevin breathed a sigh of relief as they made it through and into the city. Past the first obstacle. Oylia steered her cart south a little way, then pulled it into a side street. Drevin and the others deposited their bags back in the cart and Drevin retrieved his sword, hiding it under his cloak.

"Many thanks, Oylia," he said, handing her a few more coins.

"You're welcome, Drevin," she said, a wide smile on her equally wide face. "And if you ever need anything, or just get lonely, you come and see me anytime. But next time maybe come on your own, if you know what I mean." She winked at him and patted his chest, then climbed back up on the board and retrieved the horse's reins.

Yoslin stood staring at Cali, squirming on the spot "B.b..bye Cali." he eventually stammered, blushing and flicking his hair back. Oylia called down to him and he scrambled up to sit next to her. With a flick of her wrists, the horse plodded off into the heavy stream of traffic, heading towards the nearest market.

"Disgusting. Both of you. Leading those poor people on like that. It's shameless" It was practically the first words that Teelan had spoken all morning. At least that sounded more like him.

"Leading him on!" Cali spat. "It weren't exactly my choice to have him ogling me like a hundred pound codfish that'd just landed at his feet."

Drevin chuckled to himself.

"And what about you?" Teelan rounded on him, "Flirting with that poor lonely farm lady who had lost her husband. Honestly, it's like travelling with a group of camp followers."

"What's the matter Tee? Jealous that nobody was interested in you?" Cali teased.

Drevin could see Teelan's cheeks turn crimson as he puffed himself up ready to retort and decided enough was enough, "All right, that's enough you two." Teelan glared at him clearly feeling hard done by. "Come on," Drevin continued quickly. "We need to move or people will wonder what we are doing. Let's wander round some markets, look like we are here doing some trading. Then we can join in the feasting and bide our time until this evening when we will have to try to find a way back into the castle."

He set off north towards the Upper District and could feel the heat of Teelan's glare on his back as they followed him. At least he seems to have got some of his fire back. They browsed around the Upper Market for a while, then walked through the decorative gardens, always on the lookout for any guards who might recognise them. When third bell rang, they headed to the northwest spoke road leading out from the Central Market and to one of the many long rows of tables that had been set out throughout the city.

They sat on some mismatched stools that had clearly been brought out of people's homes and nearby taverns. Soon the table was filled with a selection of simple fare. Large pots of simmering stews sat next to huge steaming pies and piles of raw and cooked vegetables. Thin metal platters held dozens of types of fish, some fried or roasted with butter and garlic, while others had been boiled in ale and water and flavoured with mint and parsley. Loaves of bread sat next to enormous rounds of cheese and slabs of butter. Overflowing, oversized jugs and giant pitchers of beer and wine were carried carefully to the table, their contents sloshing about.

Drevin helped himself to a wooden mug and filled it with a dark beer before tucking into the bountiful food. He ate for a long while, talking occasionally to Cali who sat on his right and an earnest merchant who sat on his left. Teelan sat beyond Cali and had retreated back to his sullen silence again.

Eventually, when Drevin thought his stomach was just about to burst, the tables were rearranged to clear a space and a group of travelling troubadours appeared. They carried a selection of instruments, many of which Drevin did not recognise, but which seemed well kept.

They played several tunes ranging from poignant vignettes to more raucous, bawdy tavern songs, with seemingly no structure. Their female singer was a young woman with piercing blue eyes who had a strong, melodious voice. She was backed by a younger boy whose voice was surprisingly very accomplished, although he was obviously shy as he kept sidling behind the woman.

For a while Drevin just sat and enjoyed the spectacle, trying to imagine that today was just another ordinary day. For a while, it worked, and he felt at peace. But as the musicians finished up, to the generous applause and welcomed tossing of coins from the crowd, his thoughts inevitably turned to their problems again.

How to get into the castle unnoticed? Even if we can get in, then how do we get to speak to the baron without Serzin finding out or catching us first? Maybe the funeral feast will give us an opportunity. Zandir will surely be at the feast for his son. Perhaps we can find him there, then try to isolate him somehow?

But he will surely be surrounded by many guards, his family and a host of 'condolence givers'. Perhaps we can get someone to help us? Wilburton, maybe? He at least knows the situation. But would he have the courage to aid us in the face of Serzin? And we would still need to get in and find him and no doubt he will be doubly busy and stressed with the feast going on. There seemed to be no simple solution to the problem and his thoughts were going round and round in circles.

"Dev. Dev!" Cali was calling him. He shook his head to clear his mind and looked at her.

"Sorry, what is it?" he asked.

"I think it's time we moved on. Most people have left now, and I think the owners of these stools want them back," she said quietly, nodding to a group of women who were loitering nearby.

Drevin looked around. Cali was right. The street was emptying, the crowd having faded away unnoticed. The women were ostensibly just chatting, but they were casting meaningful looks their way every so often. They would be the owners of the stools then.

"Come on then let's go," he said, rising slowly. He really had eaten too much, his mail pressing tight against his swollen stomach. "Thank you, good ladies, for the use of your wonderful seats and for the hospitality," he said in his most charming voice to the women. They nodded politely at him and one of the older ones actually blushed. Damn. Better go before Teelan notices and accuses me of something again.

Drevin led them off at a slow walk, as that was all that he could manage at the moment. They wandered through the Church District where there were crowds of people outside the churches listening to the priests of the Union giving sermons and partaking of their charity.

"I've got an idea," Cali suddenly said brightly, "Wait here for me, would you?"

Before Drevin could answer, she had dashed away into the crowds, heading towards the throng. What is she up to now? I hope whatever she's doing she doesn't get caught. The last thing we need right now is unwanted attention.

"Drevin," Teelan said, suddenly closing next to him. "We are near to my mortuary. Do you think we could head there? I would love to see if my books are still there and I could really do with a clean robe," he said, tugging the sleeve of his grubby white robe which protruded from underneath the brown one.

"No, it's too risky." Drevin said instantly, shaking his head. "Serzin is a sly one. He will know by now that we escaped the city and that the Gatherers didn't capture us. No doubt he will probably have men watching the place in case we are stupid enough to come back." Which, of course we were. But not quite stupid enough to go back to our old haunts.

Drevin wondered about his room in the inn. It was still officially his for a few more days, but he was concerned that the landlady may have rented it out to someone else, as he hadn't been back there for so long. All of his meagre personal possessions were still in there, along with his secret stash of coins. He would love to go back and retrieve them, but was afraid that Serzin might have found out where he was staying and would be monitoring the inn as well.

"You think so? Well, I suppose I will just have to remain looking like a vagabond. And smelling like one too." Teelan said, sniffing under his arms, before swiftly recoiling, nose scrunched up.

"Don't worry. You get used to the smell after a while," Drevin said smiling.

They moved closer to the crowds around the churches, and Drevin could see the various priests on their wooden platforms. Despite all wearing grey robes with the symbol of the Union on their right breast, they all looked very different. The priest of Corpinious was a grossly fat man with at least three chins, whilst Necomthia's priest was an old lady with long grey hair who was as thin as a twig.

The representative of Lucianous was an attractive young lady with a glint in her eye and the Allmother's priest was a middle-aged, kindly looking woman. Erebonia's priest was a stout older man whose greying black hair and beard were so long that they seemed to merge into one mass. Well, it was good to see that the stereotypes were still working for them.

Drevin stood and listened for a while. Whilst all the sermons were different and tailored to their specific audience, they all ran along on pretty much the same themes. Being a good person. Looking out for others, but also taking care of yourself. Realising that everyone is an individual and is just a part of a larger world. Respecting others. Doing the right thing. Drevin wondered again at his choice of actions. He sent a quick prayer to the Allmother to watch over them. And one to Lucianous as well, because they were going to need all the luck that they could get.

"Right, let's get going," Cali said, emerging from out of the crowd and hustling over.

"What have you been up to?" he asked her suspiciously.

"Bagged us these," she said, opening a corner of her stuffed bag surreptitiously. Drevin squinted through the narrow gap she had opened. There was a lot of material in her bag. Grey material. And he could just make out part of an emblem on the one on top, which looked a bit like a triangle.

"Cali, is that what I think it is?" Drevin asked, shocked.

"I don't know, as I can't tell what you are thinking, can I?" she replied innocently.

Drevin saw Teelan smile at that. At least that cheered him up.

"I think that looks like a priest's robe in your bag," he hissed quietly, steering them away from the supplicants.

"Well then, you are wrong," Cali huffed indignantly. "It's actually three priest's robes. Thought they might come in handy later to get us into the castle."

"Wonderful," said Teelan sarcastically, having leant in to also take a peek inside the bag. "First, I have to dress as a common farm hand, now a priest." The smile had disappeared from his face now.

"Come on, let's get further away from here before anyone notices they are missing." Drevin said, heading towards the centre of the city.

They wandered around for a while, blending in with the crowds of people drinking, talking and preparing for the evening's festivities. In preparation for the evening's entertainment, most of the stalls in the Central Market were empty, although the surrounding shops and inns were, of course, open and doing a roaring trade. Eventually they heard the fourth bell, and Drevin knew it was time to head to the castle. All the 'good and the great' or in other words the 'rich and the entitled' would make their way there now for the evening feast. This was going to be their best chance to get in. Worries and doubt crowded his mind again. It was make or break time. He just hoped that he wasn't about to get them all killed.

***

Teelan hated his life right now. Which was probably just as well, as he didn't think he had much of it left anyway. Not for the first time, he hoped Drevin knew what he was doing and wasn't about to get him killed.

They huddled together in a narrow street, close to the north gates, getting ready to attempt their reckless and probably fatal mission.

"Here you go, Dev," Cali said, delving into her bag and handing him a grey priest's robe with the symbol of the Union on the right breast. On the left breast was an image of an obese man's face and shoulders and his two hands which each held a gold coin. Teelan snorted.

"You're a priest of Corpinius," she told Drevin, "The Golden One. God of merchants and riches."

"Fitting," said Drevin, discarding his brown worker's cloak and shrugging the robe on.

Cali pulled out another grey robe. "Ah, this is my one," she said, pulling off her cloak and whisking the garment over her head. Teelan noticed this one had an image of a young woman on the front with long wavy hair who seemed to be winking. "I am a priest of Lucianus, the Sly One. God of luck and good fortune."

"Of course you are," Teelan said impatiently. "What about me?"

"Here's yours, Tee," Cali said, withdrawing the final gown from her sack.

Teelan held it up to have a look at it. This one had a depiction of a robust middle-aged woman on it with a baby in her arms.

"What is this?" Teelan said, aghast.

"You are a priest of Viterlea, the Allmother. God of health, vitality and fertility." Cali said, smirking at him.

Teelan glared at her. "You have got to be joking."

"What!" she replied innocently. "I couldn't get into Necomthia's church. It was packed full. It seems that Death's Accomplice is in high demand today."

"And what am I supposed to do if anyone asks me about this 'Allmother'. I know nothing of your religion and your practices." Teelan snapped. Honestly, this was too much.

"Relax Tee," Cali said infuriatingly, grinning widely at him, "Just talk about loving everybody and having relationships and encourage everyone to have like, a hundred babies. And you can go into graphic detail if you like. In fact, it's practically expected of you."

Teelan was both horrified and mortified at the same time. He couldn't tell how much of this she was concocting, or if any of it was true, but he was not happy about it. "You are enjoying this aren't you?" he said scathingly.

"Damn right I am," she said laughing.

"All right enough, you two," Drevin said. "Teelan just put the robe on. And let me do the talking. Let's go before they close the gates."

Teelan threw off his ragged cloak and hurriedly pulled on the robe. It was made of heavy cotton and smelled of lavender. He followed Drevin and Cali as they left the street and headed towards the gate. There was a queue of people waiting to go through and they joined the line near the back. Teelan felt his muscles tense as they waited, slowly edging closer to the gate and the polished, burly guards who were checking everyone over. He self-consciously pulled his hood lower and noticed that the others also had their hoods up.

When they reached the overworked guards, Drevin spoke to them. He used another fake voice, this one sounding like a pompous man who was used to being respected and obeyed. He said that they were travelling priests from a nearby town, here to pay their respects to the baron. The guard just grunted and let them pass. And just like that, they were on the road to the castle.

Teelan was slightly stunned at the ease of their passage but knew that the next challenge would be at the castle gates. They joined the throng making their way over the bridge and up the hill to the stone edifice, squatting menacingly above them. Most of the other people with them looked like local minor nobles from their richly coloured robes and dresses.

There were also several merchants with flamboyantly garish clothes, denoting their great wealth but poor fashion sense. Teelan also spotted several high-ranking city officials, marked by their chains of office, on the road as well as a number of 'other' priests. Teelan avoided making eye contact with them in case they wanted to start a theological debate and expose his ignorance.

Just before they reached the castle gates, Cali squeezed in between him and Drevin and hissed at them. "We may need something extra to persuade them to let us in, so take one of these," she said, handing each of them a small silver cross. Teelan examined his one. It felt cold but solid in his hand and was inlaid with multiple tiny green jade gemstones around its edges.

"Damn it Cali," he heard Drevin curse. "This must be worth at least a year's wages for a soldier."

Teelan glanced over and saw that the cross in Drevin's hand was glinting with small chunks of gold in it. He looked at Cali and in her hands was a cross that had dark rubies in it which reflected the colour of the setting sun.

"Well, we have to bring an offering to a funeral. It's traditional," she protested. "Besides, the church can afford it. Corpinius' church, Drevin, is practically made entirely out of precious stones."

"It's blasphemy," he heard Drevin mutter.

But it was too late now. There were only a few people left in front of them, being admitted one at a time. Teelan suddenly had a horrible thought. He hoped that none of the guards on duty were the same ones that they had run into during their escape. His legs were trembling by the time they reached the pack of weary looking guards.

"Names and occupations," one of them called out boredly.

Names! Nobody mentioned that they would ask for our names. Teelan panicked, his mind going blank. Suddenly, he couldn't think of a single name. Luckily, Drevin spoke for all of them.

"Brother Erngid, Priest of Corpinius," Drevin said solemnly, indicating himself. "This is Sister Jaydi, priest of Lucianus and Brother Rocha, priest of Viterlea." he pointed to Cali and Teelan in turn. "We were travelling in the area when we heard the sad news and came here at once. We bring offerings to the baron and have come to pay our respects to his dear departed son," he continued, holding out his cross and indicating to the others to do the same.

Teelan saw the guard's eyes widen at the sight of the riches in their hands and he seemed momentarily lost for words.

"Hhmmp," he coughed, "Yes, well, that all seems to be in order," he said, snatching the crosses out of their hands and stuffing them into a large pouch on his belt. "Very good. In you go. I am sure your generosity will delight the baron, and he will be happy to have you with him at this time." Huh. Teelan highly doubted that the baron would ever be made aware of their generosity, as he suspected those crosses would never make it to him. He also hoped that the baron remained completely unaware of their presence, at least until they were ready to make themselves known.

Still, he supposed he should be grateful. It seemed like a combination of blasphemy and bribery seemed to have done the job of getting them inside. He followed Drevin up the steps that they had so recently fled down. Goosebumps prickled up his arms as he recalled that mad flight. He shook himself to dispel the memories and they followed the crowd into one of the smaller side halls.

Long tables were laid out, filling much of the space with benches or wooden chairs placed alongside them. Many diners had already taken their seats and were enjoying the appetisers of boiled and poached eggs, smoked salmon, shrimps, and dark breads.

They found a place at the end of a bench and partook of the food. Teelan groaned inwardly. He was still full from earlier and he felt sick from a combination of overeating and nervous anxiety. He grudgingly selected a few small morsels and placed them on the patterned ceramic plate in front of him, just to look the part. A serving girl came round with ornate flasks full of wine and offered him some. He declined politely and asked for some lemon and honey water instead, which she duly brought out.

Teelan looked down the table and saw Drevin eagerly attacking any food that was within his reach and piling it up. It seemed like it would take more than a few nerves to stop him from eating. He did notice however, that he was being more conservative with his wine intake, which was good to see considering what they still had to do tonight. Cali, sitting on the other side of Drevin, was as lethal with her eating knife as she was with daggers, gleefully stabbing the food and dragging it onto her plate. That girl was always hungry and had the table manners of a chimpanzee.

Teelan slowly nibbled his way through a ridiculously ostentatious number of courses, lost in contemplation, barely registering what was going on around him. Despite his concerns for their current situation and the potential of being discovered at any moment and thrown in the dungeons, something else was also preying on his mind. He couldn't stop thinking about his conversations with Drevin in that dreadful cave.

What had possessed him to tell Drevin about his sister? He had never spoken to anyone about that before because of the emotions it stirred up within him. Sadness, guilt, pain and embarrassment being the key ones amongst them. Now Drevin would think of him as a freak, an aberration, like everyone else did. A strange, eccentric boy whose only close companion and relationship was with death itself. An unfeeling, uncaring boy who couldn't even cry at his own sister's funeral. Who avoided the living to spend time alone with the dead.

Except that Drevin hadn't rejected him yet. He hadn't run away or abandoned him. He had said that he understood. But did he truly? Was he just saying that to be kind? Could anyone ever really understand him? He couldn't see how they could, as he didn't truly understand himself yet. Teelan didn't know the answers to any of these questions and that was what he was struggling with.

To distract himself from those thoughts he recalled Drevin's story again. He had sat in a kind of shocked stupor when Drevin had told his tale. At first, he wasn't sure if he believed him. If he was just making it up so as to have something relatable to him. But he soon realised that it was true from the tone of Drevin's voice.

Teelan knew he wasn't great at discerning other people's emotions, but even he couldn't miss the pain and sadness in Drevin's voice, it being so raw. He wondered again at the life that Drevin had led and how he had ended up here. His own life certainly hadn't been easy, but he could really comprehend now that others also suffered hardships and traumatic experiences.

Since their revelations he had felt closer to Drevin, but he still fretted over how he looked at him now. He could see that Drevin was concerned for him, but he didn't want his pity or his sympathy. However, he was learning that showing compassion and thinking about others' feelings was part of being a good friend and he felt that now perhaps Drevin could become a friend.

He just hoped that his confession hadn't led to Drevin's disgust and to him turning his back on him, like so many others in his life before him. Of course, Teelan would not tell him any of this. And none of this meant that Teelan was going to go easy on the man now.

Drevin still had plenty of character flaws and irritating habits and needed someone to remind him of them from time to time. Just as this thought crossed his mind, Drevin sat back in his chair and belched loudly. That is exactly the kind of thing I was referring to.

Finally, the servers took away the dishes of rich meats, pies, fish, and vegetables and laid out small, delicate fruit tarts and sweet pastries. Some tables at the far wall got cleared and a lady with a harp positioned herself against the wall, her long fingers decorated with heavy rings. She played with great skill, the sombre music echoing around the crowded space, silencing most of the revellers.

After she had finished to a resounding applause came a weasley looking jester, tumbling and juggling, to lift everyone's volume and spirits. Everyone except Teelan that is. He hated jesters. Imbeciles in motley, that's all they were. And inevitably he would end up being singled out to be at the pinnacle of one of their desperately unfunny acts. When he departed, much to Teelan's relief, and a group of musicians entered, Drevin stood up and waved to the others to follow him.

"Come on," he said, patting his belly. "Let's take a peek in the grand hall, see if the baron is still there."

Teelan followed him as they wended their way through the throngs of people and approached the Great Hall. He kept his head lowered and his hood up, wary of encountering anyone that might recognise him. As they neared the open doors to the hall, a wave of sound rolled over Teelan like the surf of the ocean. Dozens of loud voices laughing, shouting, shrieking, cursing, sobbing and arguing all mingled together, along with music from at least three separate sources, into a deafening cacophony. Teelan had to resist the urge to put his hands over his ears.

He had just entered when a booming laugh reverberated around the room that chilled his spine. That was Serzin's laugh! He glanced furtively up at the top table at the far end of the room. There he sat, like a bloated shark. In rich blue silk robes decorated with gold, a heavy silver tankard in his hand. He was looking at one of the young nobles from Paska and still chuckling to himself whilst the target of his mirth blushed a delightful cherry colour. Teelan quickly sidled away from the doors, edging his way around the walls of the room into a less populated area.

The room was practically brimming with people. Many were still seated at their dark tables, which seemed to stretch on forever, while others were dancing in one of the cleared spaces near the three bands of minstrels. Some few were just loitering against the walls or around one of the many pillars, chatting in small groups or just observing everything like themselves.

Teelan spotted Wilburton over in the far corner, hovering near the side doors, a pastry in his hand. His eyes darted everywhere, and he looked more fretful and agitated than ever. There was no chance of getting his attention. He looked back to the top table and saw the baron seated next to his raucous brother. The two men were so different in appearance and demeanour that Teelan wondered how they could be brothers.

Zandir sat morosely, a slender golden chalice held loosely in one hand. A silver plate piled high with food in front of him looked like it had been barely touched. It seemed like Teelan was not the only one who had little appetite tonight.

They lingered for a short while, mingling with the crowd, but staying close to the walls. A young lady noticed the symbol on his robe and approached him, walking with the exaggerated care of the truly inebriated.

Her eyes had a glazed look, and her artful hair was ruffled as it escaped from its silver chains. Her silken dress made a swishing noise as she unsteadily sashayed over, and her expensive looking necklace sparkled in the many lights of the candle.

"Do you truly believe in Viterlea's desire that everyone should procreate?" She slurred brazenly to him. "And if that is the case, would you like to put it into practice right now?" she continued, gripping his arm.

Teelan blushed furiously and ungracefully yanked his arm away, almost causing her to topple over. "I am sorry, my lady," he said, not actually in the least bit sorry at all. "But I am in mourning tonight for the baron's son. I suggest you find yourself some other willing 'participant'. And may I also suggest that you take more water with your wine?" She glared curiously at him at that. "Uh, for the benefit of your health, or course," he blurted.

The lady took a final long look at him then staggered away a few steps before latching onto the arm of a merchant dressed like an egotistical peacock.

"May the Allmother watch over you." Teelan called out belatedly. Well, someone certainly should be watching out for her anyway.

He heard Cali's laughter even over all the other noise in the room and saw her doubled over in merriment at his expense. Thanks a lot!

Teelan retreated further and huddled against the wall. Soon after, he noticed the baron stand up and whisper something in Serzin's ear. His brother just nodded, not even deigning to look at him. Then the baron turned and walked to a door at the back of the hall. Several guards peeled themselves away from the wall and formed up around him as he left the hall.

"Looks like the baron has had his fill for tonight," Drevin said. "Let's see if we can get close to him."

With that he headed off in the general direction the baron had gone, steering a circuitous path through the milling horde. This is it then. The final showdown. Teelan suddenly had an overpowering urge to urinate. His last thought before they left the hall was that he wished he had visited the garderobe first!

# CHAPTER 17

# KEEPING IT IN THE FAMILY

"Hey, you in there! What are you doing here?" Teelan froze as he heard the guard's shout from the corridor outside. Oh no!

They had surreptitiously trailed the baron, staying a discrete distance behind his armed escort and blending in with the guests, for some time. He had appeared to be heading for his private chambers in the west wing of the castle, no doubt getting ready to retire for the night. But the closer they had got to his wing, the harder it had become to remain inconspicuous. Fewer revellers were present here, and more soldiers, so when the baron entered the final heavily guarded corridor, they had to stop and rethink. No one was allowed any further without express permission.

So, they had sequestered themselves in this small reception room within sight of the corridor and tried to come up with a plan. Drevin had suggested causing a distraction, but they couldn't decide what form that might take and had discarded several potential ideas already.

Cali, of course, just wanted to blast her way in and confront the baron and all his soldiers head on. Teelan had objected strongly to that suggestion. And so it had continued, each putting forward a proposition which the others swiftly dismissed. Except now they had tallied too long and had eventually been spotted.

The guard entered the room, closely followed by four of his equally imposing and menacing colleagues. Teelan's heart first skipped a beat, then doubled its pace as he looked more closely at him. His broad, blunt face was clean shaven, his nose wide and eyes narrow. Teelan didn't recall his features. But it was the bruise in the rough shape of Drevin's elbow that was changing colour from a dark purple to a sickly green on his forehead that had caught his attention. Oh, wonderful! It was the guard from Serzin's room. He was bound to recognise them.

The soldier took one look at Teelan and his eyes widened. I knew it! He then swung his gaze to Drevin and his face coalesced into a sneering mask of hatred.

"You!" he shouted, whipping out his sword with a hiss of steel and pointing it at Drevin.

The other guards quickly followed suit and soon a ring of shining, sharp metal surrounded them. Teelan saw Drevin's hand go to his concealed sword under his robe. Don't be an idiot, Drevin. If you draw that blade we are all dead. Fortunately, he seemed to have come to the same conclusion as his hand remained motionless.

"You are under arrest, all of you!" The guard bawled. "I'm taking you straight to the dungeons."

"No, you are not," Drevin said calmly, raising his hands in a show of peace. "We are here to see the baron on personal business. We have vital information for him about his son's killers."

"Ha. Nice try, but you ain't fooling me with that shit." The man sneered, waving his sword dangerously close to Drevin. "The only business you got with the baron is at the end of his dagger when he comes to pay you a visit in the dungeon," the guard spat.

"You're wrong. And if the baron doesn't get this information, soldier, he will not be pleased with you. Send for Captain Korac or Steward Wilburton. They know what is going on," Drevin said.

"I ain't sending for no-one you little prick. You can't order me about. Now move. Otherwise, we might have to give you a little poking to help you along," he replied nastily, pushing the point of his sword against Drevin's stomach.

Teelan's fear rose in him again. His back started sweating and his mouth felt as dry as dust. He watched Drevin desperately for any signs of a plan, a way out, no matter how crazy or ill-thought out. But he seemed to have nothing. Instead, it was Cali who made a move. Her arms snapped up and out at full stretch. A powerful blast of wind shot out from both her hands, sending the five guards flying backwards, crashing heavily into the walls of the room with loud thumps.

"Cali, no!" Drevin shouted.

She either didn't hear him or just ignored him as she remained in her current stance. However, the swirling wind seemed to ease slightly. But the soldiers remained pressed tight against the walls, unable to prise themselves away. They let out gasps of shock and stifled cries of outrage as they tried to recover their breaths.

"Now listen to me," Drevin said calmly, walking over to the guard with the bruised head. He was struggling fiercely to free himself, to no avail, his face turning red with the effort.

"You are going to send one of your men to fetch Captain Korac here. He is to do so whilst alerting no one else or raising any alarms. This castle is full of people tonight, soldier. Important, wealthy people. People who have noble and influential friends and family who are not here tonight. So, tell me, what do you think will happen if I let her off the leash, huh?"

Blimey! Teelan couldn't believe that Drevin could sound so calm yet so menacing at the same time. His threat sounded so genuinely sincere and terrifying that it convinced even him. And he also rather liked the imagery of having Cali on a leash. No, wait, not like that!

The guard obviously believed Drevin too, as his eyes went as round as the plates that they had been eating off earlier. "Fine," he said, nodding his head. Well, he couldn't move much else of his body right now. "Eikna, go get Korac." He looked at the young guard nearest the door.

"Remember, if we hear the slightest sound of alarm the consequences will be on your head." Drevin reminded his victim. The guard just nodded again. "Cail, release him."

Cali flicked her hand at the one called Eikna and the wind buffeting him dissipated instantly. He staggered away from the wall and sagged forwards for a moment. Then he straightened, took a quick look at his companions who were still stuck tight and bolted out of the door. Then they waited.

Teelan could see sweat forming on Cali's head and her arms trembled. Drevin walked over and rested a hand on her shoulder. It was a tense few moments. The guards remained quiet, having given up their futile straining to escape. Drevin muttered a few quiet words of encouragement to the tiring Cali. Otherwise, all was silent. Just when Teelan thought he could bear it no longer, they heard footsteps approaching. Drevin stuck his head out the door and sighed, his shoulders relaxing. Teelan breathed again.

Captain Korac entered the room and took a shocked look around. "What is going on here? Release my men at once. Drevin? What are you doing here?"

"Tell your men to stand down Korac, then we can talk." Drevin replied.

Teelan saw Korac's eyes narrow as he obviously didn't like being told what to do in front of his men. "You have killed two of the baron's Gatherers and many of our soldiers. So, tell me why I don't just raise the alarm and have my men set to on you." Korac grated.

Wait, only two of the Gatherers died? That means that one survived? How was that possible? And who was it?

"We didn't want to kill them, Korac. We were just defending ourselves. The Gatherer Nylarian came at us, told the soldiers to kill us all. She said it was an order from Serzin himself."

"That is not the way she tells it. Anyway, why would Serzin order you dead?" Korac quizzed.

Nylarian! She survived. Teelan felt his stomach clench and he shuddered as he remembered her glowing hands reaching out for him.

"Didn't Wilburton talk to you? Didn't he explain what we discovered?" Drevin asked.

"Yes, well, kind of. But he made little sense. He was in a right state, practically beside himself."

"Drevin, hurry," Cali grated from clenched teeth. Teelan could see her whole body shaking now. Drevin raised an eyebrow at Korac imploringly.

"Alright. Hang on. Men, put your weapons away and leave us." The captain called to his men.

Drevin nodded to Cali and she dropped her arms, sighing in relief. The wind ceased immediately, and the guards stumbled on their feet, a couple of them sliding to the floor. Those that remained standing glared at the three of them but put their weapons away, much to Teelan's relief.

"But captain," the bruised head man said. "These are dangerous fugitives. Traitors. I can't leave you alone with them."

"I will be fine. Wait outside, please." Korac said firmly.

"But Serzin has ordered…"

"I said. Wait. Outside. Or did you lose your hearing along with your common sense when you got that bang on the head?" Korac snapped.

The guard gave a final venomous stare at Drevin, then shuffled out of the room, followed by his companions. They stopped literally just outside the door, watching them all like hawks. The captain walked over and firmly shut the door in their faces, then returned and sat down at the table, indicating that they did the same.

Korac gave a heavy sigh when they were all seated. "The steward came to me with a wild story about Serzin being involved with Ridozir's disappearance. Said that you had a theory that he was the one who sent some thugs to kill Zandir's son and then hired a mercenary to get rid of the thugs. It all sounded rather implausible to me."

"It's true Korac," Drevin said sadly. "Although it was Serzin's wife who ordered him killed. Look, I don't want to go through it all again now, but I really need to talk to the baron. Tell him the whole truth."

"Do you have any actual proof of this?"

"Some," Drevin said, but Teelan spotted his grimace. "But he confessed it to us, Korac. Both of them did. That's why they chased us out of the castle and sent the Gatherers and her men to hunt us down like animals."

"It is true, captain." Teelan added. "I was in the room when they blatantly confessed. They asked us not to tell the baron. Said something about it being for the 'greater good'."

"What about you, girl?" Korac asked, looking at Cali. "Were you there too? The Gatherers have been looking for you for days, you know."

"No, I wasn't," Cali said, sounding tired and leaning back in her chair. "But I believe Drevin. And that fire throwing hag can eat my dagger. Again. She attacked us. Twice. And she clearly wanted to kill us both times. As for 'lord' Serzin. He is a lying snake, saying one thing to your face and another behind your back."

"Hmm, well I ordered all my men not to kill you. I said that I wanted to speak to you first, get the truth out of you. But Nylarian and her cronies always did have their admirers though. Some soldiers who wanted to be part of their gang. They were not our finest recruits, I have to say," the captain said wryly.

"You can say that again," Cali scoffed.

"Come on Korac." Drevin pleaded. "You know me. I saved you and your men once. Remember. Drevin the Drowner."

"I remember," Korac said thoughtfully.

Wait! What was this? Teelan had heard Cali call him that name before but hadn't had a chance to question what it meant at the time. He wasn't about to miss another opportunity.

"What is this?" Teelan enquired, leaning forward his arms on the table.

"Hasn't he told you that story yet?" the captain said, looking at Teelan. Teelan just shook his head. He looked at Cali and could tell that she was equally in the dark about this, despite having heard the moniker before. Despite the precarious nature of their predicament, he found himself intrigued.

"Well, about four or five months ago we had a rogue Fragment with the Ignite Trait haunting the docksides. He used to rob the businesses and houses in the area, but the problem was that he wasn't a very good thief. So, when someone inevitably saw him, he would intentionally set fire to the place to ensure his escape. But of course, many of those buildings are made of wood, so the fires would spread and cause a lot of damage to the surrounding properties. He was looting and lighting up half of the city. What was it that the commoners called him again?" he asked Drevin.

"The Red-Handed Rogue." Drevin said with a twist of his lips.

"Yes, that was it. Well, they sent out the Gatherers to catch him, but they couldn't find him. I increased the patrols around the docks but equally had no luck, so eventually we put a bounty out on him. Within two days, Drevin here unearthed him. He chased him throughout the south docks, forcing him away from the tightly packed houses and right up to the waterfront. I was on patrol with some of my men nearby and heard the commotion. We eventually cornered him on the boardwalk, near a jetty.

"The Rogue panicked then seeing no way out and started focussing his power. The next minute, he suddenly burst into flames. They were flickering off his entire body like a human torch. But he didn't stop there. We could sense him preparing to do something terrible. He gathered an enormous ball of fire in his hands and was getting ready to unleash it on us in a devastating inferno that would incinerate the entire district and everyone in it. Me and my men sensibly backed away from him. Your friend here did not.

"You know what this crazy idiot did? He put his head down and charged straight at him! It took everyone by surprise. Including the Rogue fortunately, as he lost control and his ball of fire flickered out. However, he was still burning fiercely. But Drevin didn't stop, and he crashed into the fiery Fragment, lifted him up onto his shoulder and raced down the jetty.

"By the time he got to the end of it they were both aflame and smoke was rising from them. Then he jumped straight into the ocean. Well, that put them out soon enough. They struggled in the water for a while, then Drevin thrashed his way back to a nearby boat that was moored there and hauled himself overboard. We never saw the Rogue again, so assumed that he drowned. Hence Drevin the Drowner."

"Wow, Dev, that is some story. But it sounds just like the kind of bonkers thing that you would do." Cali said, sounding impressed.

However, Teelan was not impressed. In fact, he was horrified at the brutality of it. "My goodness," Teelan said, as he looked at Drevin in shock.

"What. Don't give me that look," Drevin retorted. "I never meant to drown him. Just wanted to cool him off. Stop him from burning up half the city. But he wouldn't give in and kept fighting me. I guess I must have hit him too hard and knocked him out. I tried to grab him and drag him back to shore, but the tide swiftly took him away and I....couldn't go after him," he finished lamely.

"Wait. I thought you didn't like the water." Teelan said, remembering Drevin's aversion. He still didn't know where his fear of water had come from. Maybe this was it?

"I don't."

"So, why did you jump into the ocean?" Teelan pressed.

"It was instinctive. I didn't think about what I was doing. When I realised where I was, I panicked. I floundered around and desperately tried to get out as soon as I could. But he kept holding onto me and dragging me back from the shore. That is why I hit him too hard to get away. And that is why I couldn't swim out and save him." Drevin finished sadly. "Anyway Korac, as I said you owe me. Take us to the baron with no fuss, and I will consider the debt repaid."

Korac leaned back in his chair and stroked the scar on his left cheek with a finger, clearly considering. "Do you know how I got these scars Drevin?" he asked, pointing to the faded white lines on each cheek. Teelan saw Drevin shake his head. "I was on the patrol designated to protect Zandir's wife when she was attacked and killed in the city."

Teelan gasped involuntarily. Serzin had told him the story of course but from a distant, second-hand perspective. He had a bad feeling that he was about to get a more up close and personal account of the tale now.

Korac laced his fingers together on the table before he began speaking. "I was a trainee guard back then, just a kid really. Full of optimism, confidence and self-assurance, like most lads. Full of an unfounded belief that people were essentially good and lived fulfilled and contented lives. Well, that all went to shit that day.

"When we saw the protesters, I felt sorry for them at first, thinking that they just wanted to be heard. Most of the other soldiers felt the same way too. We were too lax with them. When that protester darted between us and stabbed the baron's wife, I was shocked. We all were. But I shook it off and chased after him. We hurtled through the streets, faces flashing by. I didn't know where I was or where we were going. I just ran, keeping him in my sights. Eventually, he ran down a narrow alley and noticed that the other end of it was blocked by a vast pile of garbage. I can still remember the stench coming off that rotten heap.

"He had no choice except to finally stop running. When he turned around, he saw I was on my own. I had outrun my colleagues. His eyes were wide with desperation and sweat had plastered his mousy hair to his head. I noticed then that he was just as young as I was. He raised his dagger and simply charged at me, frantically trying to escape. So, not knowing what else to do, other than that I had to stop him, I ran at him, sword levelled."

Korac chuckled sadly before continuing. "There was no skill of arms or fancy sword work involved, Drevin. In that instant, I completely forgot all my training. I was just lucky that when we clashed I had the longer blade.

"After the impact, I was astonished that I was still alive and uninjured. Even more so when I realised I had run that young man through as he slumped to the ground. His blood gushed over my hand and arm, soaking my sleeve right up the elbow. I remember it felt pleasant at first, warm and thick, like heated honey, until I realised what it was, of course. I wrenched my sword out of him in disgust and promptly added to his indignity by losing my breakfast over his corpse. It was the first time I had ever killed anyone."

"The first time is never easy." Drevin said consolingly.

Teelan glanced at Drevin and saw the pain of remembrance on his face. Thinking of their recent battle he then looked at Cali. She had gone almost as pale as him and was hugging her knees to her chest again, her eyes wide and moist. She had slain people during that fight but hadn't seemed too perturbed by it. Had she killed before?

"Anyway," Korac continued, dragging Teelan's mind back to his story. "Once I had recovered a bit, I took the black dagger off his body and went to find my unit. When we returned to the castle with Mielisa's body, Zandir was naturally devastated. I gave him the cursed dagger, hoping it might comfort him to know that her death was avenged. He lost it then. Went into a rage and threw us all into the dungeon. For several days, I sat in a tiny, dark cell on my own. The baron would walk past every day, clutching that damn blade, and then I would hear the screams and wails of my tormented companions.

"One day, he finally came into my cell. I feared it was my turn now. Two guards stood me up and pinned my arms whilst Zandir raised the dagger and carefully cut these two scars into my face. He said that it was my punishment and would serve as a constant reminder of my failure to protect his wife. Then he stated that the only reason I was still alive was because I had sought justice for her. He warned me never to fail him again. And I haven't.

"Since that day, I have served him as best as I can and been a loyal and dedicated soldier. I try to instil the same attitude on all the guards, to keep everyone safe and the baron content. To his credit Zandir has not held this against me. Many years later, he recognised my commitment and made me captain of the castle guards." Korac finished his story and sighed deeply.

Teelan felt numb. It was an even more disturbing account than he had anticipated. Why were there such violent, unpredictable men in this world? And why did they always seem to be the ones who ended up in power? No. Stop. Now he was starting to think like Drevin. He did question again though why they were risking everything for a man like that.

"Gods, I'm so sorry," Drevin breathed. "So, what does this mean? You're not going to help us? What exactly are you saying Korac?"

"What I am saying," Korac replied, leaning forward again, his hands clasped and staring intently at Drevin. "Is that you had better bloody well be right, Drevin.

Otherwise, we are all going to end up a sight worse off than just having a couple of scratches on our faces." He sighed again and stood up abruptly. "Come on, I'll take you to see Zandir."

***

Teelan waited nervously outside the baron's ornate door. The captain had entered some time ago and was yet to emerge. He hoped the baron was listening to him as a reasonable man would. But he knew Zandir was not a reasonable man. He couldn't shake the ghastly image from his mind of Korac's body being held down on the floor while the baron carved open his chest, all the while demanding answers to his nonsensical questions.

He jumped as the door suddenly swung open and Korac peered out, thankfully still whole and hearty.

"He will see you and will listen to you. But don't expect much sympathy from him. He has just buried his son today, so tread lightly." Korac cautioned quietly, opening the door wider.

"Thank you, captain," Drevin said sincerely. "Can you do me one more favour? Fetch Wilburton and bring him here."

"I'm not going anywhere. The baron has insisted that I stay. I will send one of my men though." Korac said, motioning to a guard hovering nearby.

"Run and fetch the steward will you Prixsa," Korac said to the guard. "Tell him to come to the baron's private study with all haste. Say that it is an emergency."

The guard nodded and made to leave.

"Wait!" Drevin called out to him. "Can you ask him to bring the things that I asked him for before, when we were here a few days ago, please?"

The guard looked to his captain who nodded his assent, then he hurried away down the corridor. What exactly was that about? What was Drevin up to now? There was no time to ponder it as they were heading into the room. Teelan reluctantly followed, his nerves jangling.

The baron's room looked much as it had before, only it seemed darker and more foreboding now. Only a handful of the expensive wall sconces held lit candles, and they cast a faint, ominous glow over the proceedings. Shadows shrouded much of the room, and Teelan could vaguely make out the shapes of inert guards against the walls.

Baron Zandir sat in his usual thickly cushioned chair, seeming lost in its patterned depths. His rich, deep blue silk robe draped around him and looked big enough to swathe at least two men of his diminutive size. When he looked up at them, his blue eyes were as cold as a frozen lake and as devoid of life.

"My captain tells me you have some very important news that I must hear at once. I hope for all of your sakes that he is right." Zandir said, his voice as icy as his gaze. "You already stand accused of treason and killing my Gatherers and soldiers. It is only because I respect Korac's judgement that you are even still alive. But you are going to have to work very hard to remain that way."

Teelan felt as if he had just stepped into that frozen lake depicted in Zandir's eyes as a biting chill shivered through him, goosebumps springing up all over his body in fear. It hadn't escaped his attention that they hadn't been invited to sit, so they remained standing in front of him like supplicants. Which he supposed in a way they were.

"My lord," Drevin began with a shallow bow, using his courtly voice. "Thank you for agreeing to hear us out. I am deeply saddened to bring you the news that it was your brother, Lord Serzin, and his wife who were behind your son's demise."

Good old Drevin. Straight to the point as usual. And as blunt as a hammer. He may be able to sound courteous, but he lacks finesse.

"Pah, what nonsense!" Zandir scoffed. "What are you dribbling on about? Korac, I hope you haven't wasted my time," he said, glaring at the captain. He turned back to Drevin. "I already have the bodies of the thugs who killed Ridozir. They were common criminals who made an example of him for not paying his gambling debts."

"That is only partially true, my lord. Those men killed your son, but they were hired to do it. Serzin recruited the gang leader to abduct Ridozir and spirit him away, but his wife intervened and changed the order to ensure his death." Drevin insisted.

"Poppycock. Why on earth would they do that?"

"Because they said that your son was going to cast them out into the street after his ascension. Apparently, he had some private feud with them. Then Serzin's wife also found out that Ridozir had caused the injury to their son Weslin, making him responsible for his current 'condition' and she wanted revenge."

"This all sounds like a fairytale man. Do you have any proof?" Zandir demanded. Teelan noticed the baron's cheeks flushing and his eyes narrowing. His hand had strayed to the hilt of the black-bladed dagger at his belt and was stroking its hilt. That is not a good sign!

"They both confessed to the crime to me. Teelan was with me at the time." Drevin said, nodding towards him. Great. Thanks for that Drevin. Make him notice me, why don't you?

The baron glanced briefly at him before turning back to Drevin. Teelan breathed an inaudible sigh of relief.

"Anything else?" Zandir asked sceptically. "After all, at the moment it is just your word against his. And I know who I would prefer to believe."

"Yes, my lord. We found this note on the gang leader." Drevin said, fishing out the small scrap of stained paper from a pouch and handing it over. "It is part of the message Serzin sent to order the kidnap. That is his writing I believe?"

Zandir squinted at the note in the dim light for a moment. "Yes, it looks like his scribbling. My brother never bothered to learn the proper forms. But this note could be about anything. Do you have the rest of the letter?"

Drevin grimaced. Teelan still didn't like that look on him. "No, I am afraid not, my lord. But," he carried on quickly, "Your steward admitted Serzin asked him to contact a mercenary and that he spoke to him twice, in private. We believe he hired him to kill the gang members to cover up his involvement."

"Well, you would be right," said a new, slightly accented voice from the doorway.

The sound startled Teelan, causing him to spin around in shock. He hadn't even heard the door open. Outlined in the entrance's frame stood a hulking shape that almost filled the whole doorway. His long black hair, tied in a ponytail, had small metal objects that glittered from the candlelit corridor. A full-length brown leather coat reached down to his ankles and was open, displaying a red jerkin over his immense mail covered chest.

It was the mercenary Teelan had seen in the tavern where they had met The Hammer. Behind him, Teelan could just make out the sweating bald head of the steward, trying to peek over his shoulder. His strained voice drifted into the room. "Apologies, my lord, but he wouldn't wait outside."

"Who the devil are you?" Zandir asked angrily. The previously motionless guards stationed around the walls suddenly burst into life, stepping forwards, hands on their swords. Teelan tensed.

"My name is Hascor Proxin, my lord," the man stated calmly, despite being surrounded by twitchy guards. "I am the mercenary that your brother hired to murder those imbeciles who were foolish enough to take on his contract. Oh, by the way, are you looking for this?" he asked, smiling smugly and pulling out a sheet of paper from within his cloak. Teelan noticed that the bottom corner of it had been torn away.

Drevin took the letter off him with a big smile on his face. "Nice to see you again, Hascor. I have to say that your timing, as ever, is impeccable." The huge mercenary grinned back at him and gave him a mock bow.

"Here is the rest of that order, my lord, in Serzin's own hand," Drevin said, returning and handing it to the Baron.

Zandir waved for his guards to stand down, then sat in silence for a moment as he scanned the words. Teelan braced himself, thinking that he would explode in fury at this betrayal and still decide to have them all killed for their impudence. Instead, he gave a long, deep sigh and shrivelled further back into his chair.

"There is more, my lord," said Wilburton, nervously entering the room and pushing a young lad in front of him. The boy was about ten years old with short blonde hair and was wearing a blue tabard. "Go on. Tell the baron what you told me," the steward urged him.

"M,m,my lord," the boy stammered. "About ten or so days ago, Lord Serzin sent me to deliver a message to a man in the Stone District called The Hammer."

Zandir leaned forwards and held the note in front of the boy's face. "Is this the message that he sent you to deliver?" he asked quietly.

"Yes, my lord," the boy replied, having quickly glanced at it. Zandir sighed again and sank back into his chair. "May I be excused, my lord?" he stuttered. Zandir waved a lazy hand at him and the boy scurried back behind Wilburton's long legs.

So that was what Drevin was up to with the steward. Well played! He may have just saved our skin. But the baron is unpredictable, so who knows what he would do next. Teelan shuffled on his feet anxiously as a nervous silence fell over the room. Eventually, the baron spoke again. "Korac, send someone to fetch my brother. I would like to hear what he has to say about all of this."

"Yes, my lord at once," Korac replied smartly, then he left the room.

"I am truly sorry to bring you this news, my lord. Especially on today of all days." Drevin said.

"So why did you?" Zandir asked, sounding genuinely puzzled. "Why did you risk your life coming back here to tell me this? I mean it is clear that you don't even like me.

No, don't deny it," the baron said quickly as Drevin tried to object. "I know I am not well loved. And I know why. I have not been a good baron or even a good man at times.

"Since my wife died I have been lost and alone, even when surrounded by family. And I get these black moods that descend on me, filling me with rage and frustration. It's no wonder Ridozir turned out like he did. I knew he was cruel and spiteful and petty. But it was partly my fault. I was a terrible father to him. I practically abandoned him." Zandir shook his head as if trying to wake up from a bad dream. "So, I ask again, why are you telling me this?"

Drevin looked sadly at the baron and said simply, "Because I had to. Because it was the right thing to do. Because everyone deserves to know the truth of how and why their loved ones died, no matter who they are."

Teelan saw Zandir look at Drevin and thought that his eyes actually held a modicum of respect for him. For his part, Teelan was just glad that they were not heading for the dungeons. But thinking about what Drevin had chosen to do, putting his life at risk for his sense of duty and honour, he found his emotion surprisingly matched that of the baron's. Even if he wished he hadn't had to risk his own life as well.

"Zandir, what have you summoned me for?" Serzin's booming voice echoed through the open door, shattering the contemplative silence. "I was just telling Lord Feldur that story about young Master Dilgana, his maid and his prize pig when…." His words trailed off as he entered the room and saw the motley assortment of its inhabitants.

His eyes flickered around the room. He spotted the three of them standing before the baron first; then the steward with the messenger boy huddled against the wall; before glancing at the mercenary who had sat uninvited, his leg draped over an arm of a chair; then at the captain, who lingered near the door.

His eyes seemed to go wider with every person he saw, and he licked his lips nervously. "Brother," he said, more quietly this time. "What is going on here? Why are these traitors not already in the dungeons or, better yet, in the ground? Captain, arrest these three immediately," he ordered. Korac, to his credit, didn't move a muscle.

"Serzin," the baron said equally quietly but firmly, "You forget that I am in charge here. These people bring me the disturbing news that you and your wife were responsible for my son's murder."

"Zand. Brother." Serzin said in a conciliatory tone. "Surely you can't believe a word these people say. They are mercenaries, a rogue Fragment and an impressionable boy. They are fugitives, traitors who will do or say anything to get into your good graces," he said, pointing them out one by one.

Teelan disliked him even more now that he indicated him when he said the words 'impressionable boy'. Clearly, he was desperate now to find some way out of this. He just hoped that the baron could see that too.

"And what about my messenger boy, my steward, and my captain? Are they all liars and traitors too? What about this note that you penned, which you asked the boy to deliver to a gang leader?" Zandir retorted angrily, waving the message at him. "Don't lie to me, Serzin. You know I can always tell when you are lying."

Serzin Sutter, the second most powerful man in the barony, looked like a hunted man at that moment. His eyes were wide in panic, darting everywhere as if trying to work out a way to escape his fate. He puffed up his chest and clenched his thick hands into fists. Sweat started beading on his cheeks as sobriety instantly returned to him.

For an alarming moment, Teelan feared Serzin might rush at one of them, try to overpower them and use them as a hostage to flee. Knowing his luck, Teelan had no doubt that he would be the victim of such a scenario. But in the next moment, Serzin suddenly deflated. His shoulders slumped in defeat, his fists unclenched, and he walked over and flopped heavily into a chair. Teelan breathed a little easier.

"Brother, I didn't mean for it to end like this. I swear to you. I only wanted him out of the way for a while," Serzin pleaded. "He was going to oust my family and I from the castle, discredit us, leave us bereft. I had to do something to protect my family. I told Myelandra my plan, but I didn't know that she would have him murdered! Not that I would necessarily have stopped her mind had I known the truth of what he had done. He was a monster, Zand. He hated and resented us and wouldn't have stopped trying to do us harm."

"Why didn't you tell me?" the baron said sadly.

"I wanted to. But you were always so distant. Always eaten up by grief and despair or consumed by rage and anger. I didn't want to bother you with it. I wasn't sure how you would react. If you would even notice or care. You haven't taken any interest in much of anything these last few years. It's just one of the reasons why things have gone to shit," Serzin said bitterly.

"That's enough Serzin! I know I haven't been there for you lately. For anyone, really. But you go too far." Zandir spat. He turned to the captain who stood by the door. "Korac, escort Serzin back to his rooms and make sure that he and his family stay there until I decide what to do with them."

Korac waved to the guards outside and two of them entered and took Serzin by the arms, leading him away.

"Brother. You can't do this to me. After everything I have done for you. Please," Serzin's voice echoed down the corridor as they manhandled him out of the room. Teelan felt a moment of satisfaction at hearing the begging tone in his voice.

"Now, what to do with the rest of you?" The baron said thoughtfully, stroking his chin.

Teelan's smugness faded instantly. What! We have just exposed your son's murderer. I should think a big thank you, recognition and a reward should be on your mind. Maybe a medal even. Teelan almost said as much, but clamped his mouth shut in time. They were not free yet.

"You." Zandir said, looking at Cali suddenly as if noticing her for the first time. "You are the rogue Fragment I have been hearing about, I assume."

"My name is Cali." she replied huffily, hands on her hips. Oh, no. Don't start with an attitude, Cali. He thought she had been unusually quiet for a while and was hoping that no-one would notice her. So much for hopes.

"Well Cali. I don't suppose that you will reconsider your stance and come and work for me, would you? It seems like I am a couple of Fragments short now," he replied, a twist to his lips which could have been a smile or a sneer. Teelan wasn't sure which.

"Ha! Thank you for the generous and most welcoming offer, but no thank you," Cali said in a sweet voice, heavily laced with sarcasm. "My lord," she added belatedly.

"Well, you can't keep running free around my barony, that's for sure." Zandir replied.

Teelan could see Cali tense up. Her hands twitched and her arms lifted a little. No, no, no. Don't even think about it.

"You, boy," Zandir said, turning his attention to him. Teelan stiffened. "I understand from the captain that you identified the killers from the wounds on my son's body and from the attackers' weapons. I would like to thank you for your unique skills and service in finding the actual killers."

"You are most welcome, my lord," Teelan stammered, completely caught off guard.

Zandir turned back to face Drevin. "Drevin, you have proven to be an honest and honourable man, putting others' needs above your own, even at significant risk to yourself. I can always use men like you in my service. But," Zandir said, raising a hand to still Drevin's response. "I haven't decided what to do with my brother yet. I don't think I can have him killed and he has many friends in the castle and the city. It is my belief that it would not be safe for you to be here. Besides which, you have another problem.

"Those ambassadors from Paska recognised your name and sent a bird to King Ironfinder in Braka. I received a message back from him several days ago. He says that he has dispatched some of his men on their way here to fetch you and that I am to hold you here until they arrive."

Teelan heard Cali gasp and noticed that now it was Drevin's turn to tense up, his hands clenching into fists. Zandir obviously noticed it too.

"I assume you do not wish to go back to Braka then?" he asked, mildly.

"No, my lord. I would rather not." Drevin said through clenched teeth.

Time seemed to stop as Zandir pondered that, the room as tense as a drawn bowstring. Oh no. We were so close to getting out of here.

Eventually, Zandir spoke again. "Hmm. Well then. Damn Ironfinder I say. What has he ever done for me, anyway? I'll tell him you escaped and fled north into the mountains. That should keep his men busy for a while," he chuckled softly.

Teelan exhaled his held breath, and it felt like everyone else in the room did the same.

"Thank you, my lord." Drevin said gratefully.

"But all three of you must leave the barony as soon as possible. Tomorrow would be best. Wilburton!" Zandir called out to the steward who was trying to look inconspicuous.

"Yes, my lord?" he stuttered, hands wringing.

"Arrange accommodation for our guests for tonight and in the morning make sure that they have any supplies and equipment that they need. Oh, and give Master Drevin here a pouch of fifty silver rounds for his exemplary service."

"Yes, my lord. Of course. Come this way if you please." Wilburton fawned.

Teelan felt faint with relief, the blood rushing to his head in a wave making him feel woozy. He couldn't quite take in all that had happened and all that he heard. His brain was just focussing on the fact that he was still alive, that they were all still alive and free. He followed numbly after the others as they trailed the steward out of the door.

"Oh, and Drevin," the baron's voice called out as they were about to leave. "I do thank you for your bravery in telling me the truth. Despite the fact that it has caused me more pain and left me with some tough decisions to make. You are right. Everyone should know the truth. Oh, and one more thing. Don't let me ever see you again," he finished and smiled. And this time it was an actual, genuine smile.

Teelan couldn't believe it. It had all worked out. They were all still whole and unfettered. And the baron seemed satisfied. In a kind of sad, resigned way. But still. He could sleep tonight in the castle, then go back to his mortuary in the morning and back to his life and work and forget….Wait a minute. Had he said 'all three of you must leave'?

# CHAPTER 18

# A BEGINNING

Drevin pulled the last leather-bound, heavy book off the shelf and glanced at the cover. 'Pathogens and Pustules by Zeliranski Van Protoriuos'. Damn, that boy sure had some strange reading habits. He placed it in the full crate along with the others and lifted it with a groan. Staggering outside with the load, he hefted it onto the waiting cart gratefully. He gave a nod to the stable boy, who was minding the horses for them.

At least the baron had actually lived up to his word. He had provided them with a large, covered wagon, two horses to pull it, and enough food and drink to last them for a month, along with the promised coin. Drevin had retrieved his weapons from the castle, and they were granted unrestricted access to the armoury, which Cali had been delighted with.

He had just selected a new knife whilst she was now loaded up with plenty of sharp daggers and had even added a thin-bladed short sword to her belt. Drevin wasn't sure that she even knew how to use that and thought that he might end up having to show her. Another thing for me to teach her then!

After they had rolled out of the castle gates, Drevin had stopped first at his inn and retrieved his bag of belongings, including his official release papers, and his money pouch. He now had a couple of fat purses at his belt, which was more money than he had owned in a long time.

Cali had disappeared off to her room at the brothel to gather her things whilst Teelan and Drevin had come to the mortuary to collect Teelan's possessions. And he had a lot of them. The cart was now stacked with boxes, crates, bags and sacks of his books, clothes and tools.

Cali had returned well before they had finished loading up here with just a couple of large bags and was now 'helping' Teelan to pack his clothes. Those two still argued like brother and sister, but it seemed they had forgotten the earlier animosity between them from their time in the cave.

Drevin leaned against the wagon and wiped the sweat from his forehead, despite the chill morning, and considered what they should do next and where they should go. Clearly, he had to help Cali learn about her powers and test out her abilities.

If she was a full Mind, as he believed she must be, then she needed to know how to use all the Traits, in case one of them materialised unexpectedly in a moment of high emotion. Knowing Cali, that could happen anytime. The last thing he wanted was her getting angry with someone and accidentally setting their hair on fire!

They would need somewhere quiet and remote to practise and test out her skills, but also be in or around a town or city so that he and Teelan could work. After all, the money from the baron would only last so long. He hoped they could find somewhere suitable for all of them. He was also concerned that Ironfinder was on his tail again and would be happy to put some distance between him and his men.

He headed back into the glaringly white building which was reflecting the morning sun and stood for a moment, letting his eyes adjust to the dim interior. He took a few deep breaths, enjoying the peace and solitude of the moment.

“I told you they wouldn’t fit like that. You have to roll them up first before shoving them in the bag.” Cali’s heated voice broke the stillness, drifting down the stairs.

“Well, I would rather have fewer clothes than crumpled ones, if that is the case. And I wasn’t shoving them in, I was placing them carefully and neatly. Something that you seem completely incapable of doing.” Teelan’s indignant voice chased her down the steps.

“Why do you have so many robes, anyway?” Cali asked, appearing in the room with a bulging leather bag over her shoulder, clothes protruding from it. “And for that matter, why robes? It makes you look like a priest.”

“Not this again,” Teelan said, entering behind her carrying a full crate and giving Drevin a meaningful stare. Drevin kept quiet and watched on bemused.

“What do you mean ‘again’ I haven’t mentioned it before?” Cali said, confused.

“No. but others have, and I still take it as an insult,” Teelan said, glaring at Drevin.

“Wow, sensitive much.”

“Besides, as you well know, your priests wear grey robes, not white. Only the High Priests wear white robes.”

"Fine, so you look like a High Priest then." Cali smirked.

"That is even more insulting," Teelan sneered.

"So why do you wear a white robe if you don't want to look like a priest?"

"Because it brings out the colour in my hair." Teelan said, flicking the pale strands of his long hair.

"But your hair is white." Cali said, looking even more confused.

"Exactly." Teelan said smugly.

Drevin smiled and watched as they headed out the door to deposit their loads in the cart. That must be the last of it now, surely. He went back into Teelan's study to double check that there was nothing left.

"Anyway, some priests are actually very nice Tee, so don't be such a hardarse on them. Just because you have never had to rely on their charity doesn't mean that they aren't kind and generous." Drevin heard Cali say as they came back in.

"And foolish, misguided, disingenuous, and misleading. Convincing the poor and weak and gullible to believe in their gods in order to control them. Not to mention…" Teelan stopped abruptly as they both entered the study and saw Drevin standing there, arms crossed. Drevin noticed with satisfaction that Teelan actually looked embarrassed and guilty for once. He knew Drevin believed in the gods, but he still couldn't stop deriding them and those who followed them.

"Are you two quite done?" Drevin asked them.

"Hmph, well, yes I think that is everything now." Teelan stammered, making a show of looking around at the empty bookcases.

"Good. Before we leave, there is something that we need to tell you, Cali." Drevin said earnestly, looking at the girl. "You might want to have a seat." Now was as good a time as any.

"Ut ho. That doesn't sound good." Cali said, sitting nervously in a chair. "If it's about those crosses that I stole, I will not apologise for that. The churches..."

"No Cali, it's not about that." Drevin interrupted. Teelan had sat in the chair opposite her, so Drevin perched himself on the arm of that chair so he could face Cali. "It's about the fight with the Gatherers."

"What about it? Wait. I never meant to kill anyone, Dev. I tried not to, just like you asked, but it got desperate, and I lost control. But you killed people too and…" Cali said in a rush.

"It's not about killing anyone, Cali. I know you tried your best not to. But during the fight, both Teelan and I noticed you moved with incredible speed." Drevin said, stopping her flow of words.

"So," Cali said, shrugging her shoulders, "I have always been fast. I can outrun everyone I know. It's just because you two are as slow as starfish that makes me seem faster."

"No, it was more than just being fast. You were unnaturally quick. As swift as that Gatherer you faced. You actually blurred, Cali." Drevin said. He hoped she got the point that he was trying to make.

"What are you saying, Dev?" Cali asked, wide eyed. Apparently she didn't. How could he put it gently to her?

"What he is trying to say in his convoluted and excruciating slow way is that you used the Move Trait,"

Teelan interjected impatiently. Great. Thanks Teelan. And you say I'm too blunt.

"But I can't have done," Cali said bewildered. "You said I had the Tempest Trait Dev."

"You do." Drevin said simply. He waited for her to work it out for herself.

"But I can't have two Traits, can I? The only people who ever had more than one Trait were…"

"Minds." Drevin said. Here we go.

"WHAT!" Cali shouted, leaping out of her chair. "Crap on a cockle! How can I be a Mind? There aren't any Minds anymore. Hasn't been for ages. Everyone knows that."

"I don't know Cali." Drevin said, raising his hands. "But we need to find out more. Think. Have you ever displayed any of the other Traits? Have you ever accidentally set fire to something, healed a wound, moved an object without using wind or persuaded someone to do what you want?" Drevin pressed.

"No! I mean. I don't think so. Wait a minute," she said, sinking back into her chair. "Well, I certainly haven't set fire to anything. I would remember that. Nor have I healed anyone. But. Well, sometimes I may have moved small items without noticing the usual gust of air. Usually when I don't want someone to notice that their belongings are heading in my direction," she said, smiling cheekily. "And I guess I have always been good at talking my way out of trouble and talking others into it. But I thought that was just down to my natural charm," she finished flicking her hair.

Drevin heard Teelan choke as she said that. "Shit! It definitely sounds like you could have been using the

Displace and Voice Traits without knowing it. I think you are indeed a full Mind Cali." Drevin said, awestruck. He was completely stunned. If Cali was a full Mind then she might be the first one born for hundreds of years. But why her? And why now? Shit. This was big. Really big. And really dangerous.

"Bloody hell! So, what does that mean?" Cali asked, wild-eyed.

"Damned if I know. But I will do everything I can to find out," he said reassuringly. "However, it means that we need to be even more careful now. If anyone found out about this you would be the most wanted person in the world. For breeding stock, if nothing else."

This time he heard Teelan chuckle softly. That's not helping!

"Eeww, that's both disgusting and disturbing, Drevin." Cali said, scrunching up her nose.

"Yes, but unfortunately, it's true. If people discovered you are a true Mind, they would believe that any children you have could also have the potential to become one too. You would be considered the mother of the Minds, the second coming, so to speak.

"Ha, 'gods' help us all in that case," Teelan said sarcastically.

"Well, it's still gross," Cali said, ignoring Teelan. "And not what I want at all. I think it's time we left this so-called civilisation behind us if that's how they want to treat me."

"So, what do we do?" Teelan asked.

Drevin sighed. "We leave here. Try to find someplace safe so that I can teach Cali how to control and use her powers and to test out if she does indeed have all six Traits. If she is a full Mind, we need to know for sure."

"We could go to Vangormia," Teelan said. "Minds are revered and given places of status and honour there. You wouldn't be hunted like you are here but welcomed and treated like royalty. Well, semi-royalty maybe," he finished, looking her up and down.

"I like the sound of that. I could be Queen Cali and make everyone bow down to me and do whatever I wanted," she said, smiling.

"No." Drevin said instantly. "The whole idea is to keep this secret, not announce it to the world. Besides, it wouldn't be long before your emperor heard about her and no matter how benevolent you believe him to be, he would want to use her, just like the kings and barons here would. Also, it would be very expensive for all of us to buy passage on a ship with all of our gear." Drevin stared at Teelan as he said the word 'our'. "I have just got a full purse and don't want to deplete it just yet."

"Are you sure it is not just that you don't want to travel on the ocean?" Teelan replied knowingly.

"Anyway," Drevin said, ignoring Teelan's comment, even though it was partly true. "If we are talking about going to another country, we could head north to Satiria. Take the wagon up the causeway before the floods come and find a place to settle. There's a lot of wild, sparsely inhabited land up there where it would be safe to test out her skills."

"And what would we do for money?" Teelan retorted. "You just said yourself that our funds are not limitless. Become cattle herders? Or woodcutters? No, thank you!

The people up there are more barbaric and uncivilised than those in this country. And that is saying something."

"We go south," Cali said quietly.

They both turned and looked at her. She had drawn her legs up to the chest and rested her chin on her knees, studying them. Drevin thought she looked very young and scared right then.

"It's our only real option, isn't it?" she said sadly.

"South then," Drevin agreed, looking at Teelan.

"South it is then." Teelan said reluctantly, "But can we try to find someplace that needs the services of a skilled coroner?"

"Or an unskilled priest." Cali said, smirking.

Teelan glared at her. "Or we could go somewhere with no laws so that missy here can steal everything we need. On the other hand, if we go to a place with tight security, then we would pretty quickly only have to worry about providing for the two of us," Teelan said sarcastically.

"Come on, let's go. Before the baron changes his mind." Drevin said, once again ignoring their bickering. He had a feeling he was going to have to get used to doing that. He stood up and walked back out into the morning brightness and went to see the stable lad, Ostin. "Thanks again for watching the wagon for us. And for your help the other day, when we had to leave the castle in a bit of a hurry."

"No problem," said the boy, squinting up at him. "Even though I'm still stuck on mucking out duties for doing that. Probably will be for ever and ever now. Still, it was worth it. That was a right laugh."

"Well, we appreciate it," Drevin said, handing him several copper bits. "And if you fancy a change of employment, go see old Firdinamo at his stables on Cobbler Street by the west gate. He is a friend of mine and could no doubt use a smart young lad to help him out."

"Thanks. I'll go see him now," Ostin said, dashing off.

"Tell him Drevin sent you!" Drevin called out after him. The boy raised his hand as he ran off.

Drevin climbed on the driver's board along with Cali and Teelan and took up the reins. He got the horses plodding along the street, heading towards the south gate. He noticed Cali taking a good look around, no doubt remembering all of her time spent in the city. All the places she had been and the people she had met. It was probably going to be hard for her to adapt to leaving the only home she had ever known. But she was still young, and they adjusted well to change. Unlike us older folk!

Soon they were at the gate, and Drevin spotted a familiar figure. "Pols," he said, hailing the young guard. "Good to see you again."

"You too, Drevin," Pols replied in his too manly voice. "I didn't think that you would be back so soon. And now you are leaving again? For a long time, I am guessing, judging by the amount of stuff you are carrying in that wagon."

"Yes, going for good this time," Drevin replied. "Wait a minute. Pols, you can't see into the back of the wagon. How do you know we have a lot of gear in there?"

"I could tell by the sound the wagon made as it came down the road. Your cart rumbled and crunched the pebbles and gravel beneath the wheels, leaving deep indents where the stones have worn away, which means that it is heavy. An empty wagon bumps and bounces off the cobbles and jostles and shakes around more."

"Damn, you have sharp ears as well as sharp eyes, Pols. You will go far." Drevin said, amazed at the boy's talents, "Thanks again for your help a few days ago. It was greatly needed," he continued, carefully eyeing the other guards around him.

"Don't mention it. I can usually tell good and bad people apart and you are a good person, Drevin."

"Thanks. Well, we had best be off. Take care Pols." Drevin said.

"You too," the guard said, waving at them as they rolled out of the gates.

The road stretched ahead of them, long and straight, covered in a sparkling fine frost. Winter was on its way and change was in the air.

"Why do you have an aversion to water anyway, Drevin?" Teelan asked suddenly, "I mean, didn't you say that you grew up in Lakeview? I guess that means that there is a lake there?"

"There is," Drevin sighed. "A big one too. It's a long and sad story, Teelan."

"Well, we have a long road ahead of us," Teelan replied, obviously not wanting to let him off the hook.

"Maybe later," Drevin said. He didn't want to drag up any more of the past right now. Instead, he wanted to look to the future.

They sat in silence for a while, each lost in their own thoughts. Drevin flicked the reins to send the horses into a steady trot. He was keen to get away from the city and the past, which seemed to be catching up to him. He still had many concerns and worries, about Cali, about Ironfinder, hell even about Teelan. But for some unknown reason, he thought everything would work out fine. He felt content for the first time in a long while. As the city dwindled behind them, Drevin noticed with satisfaction that none of them looked back.

"Hey Teelan," Drevin said suddenly. "I've just had a thought. We're going to need to name our new horses."

"Oh no. Don't start this again." Teelan warned. But Drevin could tell he only said it half-heartedly, though.

"What about Darri and Jarri?" Drevin said, grinning like a child.

"Seriously? Damn, you are so immature. If you think I am going to........"

# ABOUT THE AUTHOR

Paul Smith was born in Cambridge and currently works in a library where he tries to pry people away from the computers to look at the lovely books instead. He was introduced to the role-playing game Dungeons and Dragons at an early age and has been obsessed with fantasy worlds ever since. Having written many roleplaying campaigns and read 'almost every fantasy book' he thought that he should get on with it and write his own fantasy novel.

His somewhat morbid fascination with crime dramas has led him to blend these passions together to create a 'forensic/fantasy' genre. When not working or writing he spends time with his family or 'makes things out of leather', which he gives as ‘lovely gifts’ or wears them to emulate his favourite characters at Comic Cons.

'A Noble Murder' is his first novel in the Fragmented series.

Printed in Great Britain
by Amazon

59053636R00205